# WITH NO TIME

"We'll come up whe. ____, said Rick. But do yourself a favour. Don't head farther down the road."

Derek shifted in his seat, and without turning his head, his gaze followed where Rick was looking.

There was a shadow. He couldn't see it clearly, but it was enough to make Rick more than a little jumpy. Derek looked closer at him and finally recognized what he was seeing on the man's face.

Fear.

Derek took a breath, not dropping the smile, but the quick double blink in Rick's direction hopefully told the other man that he understood the message Rick was trying to tell him. Whoever was behind that building was trouble.

*On our doorsteps already*, thought Derek. *Goddammit.*

## PRAISE FOR ASHES IN WINTER

"… like all good books it leaves you wanting more."

—Karen's Book Buzz

# MORE PRAISE FOR
## ASHES IN WINTER

"… the descriptions of scenery were superb. I've never been to Canada, but I can probably navigate Sudbury…"
—Common Book Sense

"Beautifully written."
—TDC Book reviews

"… no trouble getting into the story…"
—Paperback Darling

"Strongly written book… strong characters."
—Amy Shannon Book Reviews

# ASHES IN WINTER

K.M. CANNON

*Ashes in Winter* is a work of fiction. Names, characters, places, and incidents either are the product of the author's imagination or are used fictitiously. Any resemblance to actual persons, living or dead, events or locales, is entirely coincidental.

Published in Canada by Studio 465.

Anime North Pre-Release Edition May 2014 – Independently Published as *After Oil*
First Edition July 2014 – KCEditions as *After Oil*
Second Edition May 2021 – Northern Wolf Books (Complete Rewrite)
Third Edition May 2023 – Studio 465

www.studio465.ca
www.kmcannon.com

Library and Archives Canada Cataloguing in Publication
Cannon, K.M., 1980-, author
Pending

**Other books by K.M Cannon**

The Rangers of Walden Series
*Ashes in Winter*
*A Season of Wolves* (forthcoming)

The Karasa Trilogy
*The Starless Throne* (Forthcoming)

**As Eve Morrison**

The Dana McIntyre Series
*Lilies for the Reaper* (forthcoming)

*For Grampa—*
*Thank you for pushing me to follow my dreams.*

# ASHES IN WINTER

### K.M. CANNON

*Sudden endings are a myth.*

*But change is hard.*

*We often ignore warning signs in favour of the comfort of routine. We ignore the gigantic flashing signs which warn, 'Either reverse your course now or fall over that edge!'*

*Until, of course, change strikes like a thunderclap and sweeps our comfort zone out from under us. By then it's too late to change our course. Our skiff was too far into the rapids, and the waterfall now loomed in wait.*

*All we could do was hang on and hope to survive.*

*I know this from experience—until that one fateful winter, my life was as normal as the next. I had what I needed to live and perhaps more…*

*… And then it all vanished.*

—From the diary of the First Regent of Walden

# CHAPTER ONE

"Have you found a station yet?"

Marissa looked up from the middle console in the green SUV. "Obviously not."

"I didn't hit anything that hard to knock the aerial loose," Derek pointed out. "We should be picking up one of the stations by now. Or even on the sat."

"There's nothing," said Marissa again.

Derek Moss yawned as he rubbed his eyes with one hand. When they had started out, the sky had been gray but still bright enough to need his sunglasses. Between McKerrow and Sudbury the sky had darkened. Not only—had he been standing outside—would he have had trouble seeing the hand in front of him, but the road had vanished underneath a blanket of white.

Not that it worried him.

*Drove through far worse than this*, he thought. *Will probably do so again before it's time to hang up my keys for good.*

The aging Jeep Cherokee was showing hints of rust popping up on the hood again. He had a feeling it would be the last winter he drove it but wasn't sure if he would trade it in or pass it down to someone else in the family. That depended on what the dealership offered him.

*Not the Jeep's fault.* He looked over at his wife again as she watched the electronic scan in the radio flip around and start over again. *We should have been home long before this. The weather's just not cooperating…*

The clouds had shrouded the sinking of the sun hours ago. The only sign of afternoon becoming dusk, and then night, had been the progressive difficulty in seeing anything at all.

There were no other lights on the road or along the road. Derek hadn't seen another car or truck in hours—not since McKerrow and the Espanola turnoff.

He blew out a breath and squinted through the windshield.

He rubbed his eyes again, straining to see through the murk. Flicking his eyes right, and then left, he could just see the dip on either side of the highway where the ditches were. He tilted his head as he leaned forward. Marissa looked up from the radio.

Three large trucks blocked the road in the middle of the road at the lights in Denlou. He briefly glanced at Marissa, but only got a shrug in return.

Once they were close enough to see them, he knew the drivers could see him, but the three trucks didn't move. He didn't slow down—if he went any slower, the SUV wouldn't be in motion at all—but he did cautiously go around them until he found a cleared spot and stopped the SUV.

Three soldiers stared at his SUV, and it amused Derek as one looked through the gap between two of the trucks back down the highway.

His jaw dropped a little, but he motioned for Derek to drive into the actual blockade queue, even if it was the opposite direction and other lane. Once he had done so, they motioned for him to get out of the SUV.

Derek looked at Marissa as he unclipped his seatbelt. "That's odd."

She nodded in agreement. "Do you think they need both of us out?"

"I don't think so," answered Derek.

He opened the door, and the soldier said, "Can you kill your engine, sir?"

Derek blinked, but took a moment to turn the vehicle off. "It'll be a bit chilly for my wife in a minute."

"Can you both exit the vehicle then?"

Derek felt his eyebrows raising. "What?"

Thankfully, Marissa had already moved to exit and was putting her coat back on, her breath fogging the air in front of her as she wrapped her scarf over and under the top of her coat and put her gloves on.

"Sir, where did you and your wife come from?" asked the soldier.

"Blind River," he answered. "The wife and I have family there and… what are you doing?"

The soldiers were looking into the back of the Jeep, and one had even started the engine to check their fuel level. "Half a tank," she said. "Sounds right for that distance, if they started at full."

The first soldier looked at Derek, and Derek looked from each one and then to his wife again. "Look, we're just trying to get to our goddaughters' home close to here. The weather was clear and fine when we left—didn't hit the blizzard until McKerrow. Can I ask what the problem is?"

"You should have hit a roadblock back in McKerrow," said the first soldier. "Our orders tell us the highway was closed hours ago."

Derek shook his head. "Not a sign of anyone."

The three looked at each other, and one shifted his weight from side to side. The first one shrugged and looked at Derek. "How long ago was that?"

"Well, considering I had to take it slow here, it may have been as long as two, maybe two-and-a-half hours ago. We stopped a few times because I couldn't see past the hood.

"That would make sense," said one other. "They wouldn't have set up by then, especially if there wasn't weather to worry about."

The first soldier nodded, "Good point." He looked back up at Derek. "You said you weren't going far?"

Derek pointed to the south east. "Over there. I could almost walk, if not for the weather."

"Well, I guess that'd be okay," said the first soldier. "Just don't go further than that. There's a live fire exercise in Sudbury."

"Duly noted," said Derek, as he and Marissa returned to the Jeep.

Once their SUV headed down the road, and then onto the four lanes before turning off into Whitefish, Marissa finally asked, "A live fire exercise in Sudbury?"

"I never heard anything either," said Derek. "But now we know why the radio doesn't work."

Marissa slapped his arm. "You just didn't want to have to buy a new Jeep."

"What's wrong with this one?"

From Denlou, the drive took perhaps ten minutes to Sheridan's house. Leading up to the house, and into the garage, was not only a set of tire tracks but a path where a low-riding car had dragged the undercarriage through the snow. The tracks were narrow, and the path low. The snow was still stainless—the car hadn't been damaged as it pushed through the loose fluff.

"She didn't," said Marissa, shaking her head.

"If she needed groceries, she probably did," answered Derek, pulling the SUV up in front of the open garage. "I see one very dirty Smart Car."

Marissa groaned and lifted a hand to her forehead. She pushed the door open and walked into the garage, leaving Derek to catch up with her.

"Hello, the house!" she called, stopping mid step.

Derek squinted into the dark. Spots of light moved around in the garage, but the lights weren't even on.

"Why is it so dark in here?" asked Derek, stopping just beside her.

"The power's out," answered Terrence.

"Naturally," muttered Derek.

He then dug around in his coat, and he grinned as his hand fell on the cold metal of his penlight. Pulling it out and turning the barrel to turn it on, he shone the tiny flashlight's beam on the floor as he walked further into the garage. Sure enough, his goddaughters Sheridan and Shiloh Wither—and Sheridan's husband Terrance Scapael—stood just beside the slush-encrusted Smart Car.

"Hello, Sheri, I see you got some shopping done…" Derek flashed the light into her car. "Good grief, did you buy enough?"

Sheridan's car reminded him of the game "Tetris". Her car was packed solid with only the driver's seat left clear. Even the passenger seat had been crammed full up to the dashboard.

"Do you want to eat over the holidays?" asked Sheridan.

\* \* \* \* \*

*Green grass when you go to bed*, mused Gina as she leaned on the shovel near to the front window of her home, shaking her head at the sight of a neighbour across the road holding his shattered shovel in his hands and scowling at his driveway. *And then so much snowfall the next morning your shovel breaks…*

*… And someone always assumes those cheap plastic rigs from the local discount store are enough*, Gina smirked at her neighbour as she continued to shift the snow in the driveway from the asphalt to where she suspected her yard was. *Apparently, he just found out otherwise.*

She leaned on the shovel again, gazing out into the yard and stared at thick white blanket covering everything. She eyed her snowblower. It meant running into town to get gas. Gina compressed her lips into a thin line. *I'm gonna have to, anyway… Once I do this chore.*

Vincent opened the window and ducked his head out. "Gina, what the hell are you doing?"

"Gotta get the truck out somehow and someone's gotta do it. Since it's my shift, it's gonna have to be me," she yelled to him. He shook his head and then ducked back inside the house, shaking the snow out of his pullover.

Gina heaved a large, and obvious, sigh and then resumed cleaning the snow from their driveway. The issue wasn't the snow. It was that Gina needed the red SUV out of the driveway for work. She, unlike her friend and roommate, didn't have the leisure of claiming a snow day.

*Typical that it's my day to be on call*, she thought with a frown. *From the look of it, it's going to busy too...*

The SUV was on loan from the fire department and meant to get her back and forth from the fire station. Gina was a firefighter—something she never complained or begrudged. It was the life she had chosen for herself.

She had to go out for her shift, snow, or no snow. Snow wasn't new to Gina, having grown up around Mt. Kosciuszko in the Snowy Mountains but that was nothing compared to what she had experienced since participating in an exchange programme planned between Australia and Canada. She knew how to fight fires in Australia, her people had been doing it for 60,000 years or thereabouts, but she was curious how other countries fought fires. Australia's climate was so different to Canada's that even the bitter cold and snow were a refreshing change.

Finally, Gina dug her truck free, and she planted the shovel blade first into the snow and leaned on the handle.

Their driveway was at least now mostly bare enough that a small car could climb their hill with no trouble. There wasn't even a track to mar the snow that filled the road. *Where the hell is that snow plow? Should have been here hours ago. Made me cut through a snowbank harder than the hobs of hell…*

*I'd hear about it all day*, she thought.

Digging through a hardened snowbank left by a plow was almost a rite of passage in Northern Ontario. Vince was fond of telling her how Sudbury had certainly never been any different.

Had Gina had to cut through it, she knew he would tell their colleagues about it. Although, once she came back home, she would use it as an excuse for Vince to make her his specialty hot cocoas—a drink that had more than just mere cocoa in it for added 'warmth'. Honestly, if it were like this for the rest of the day, Gina would deserve the respite. Sitting with her feet up, under a fuzzy blanket, cocoa in one hand and Vince's hair in the other…

Gina sighed as she pulled herself from that train of thought.

Gina crinkled her brow, staring back up at the house before looking over the bypass close to where they lived. It was on days like this that she wished she hadn't taken part in the programme, but it was too late. She'd signed the papers and made the decision. And that was something she did—stuck by her decisions.

She stared at the snow covered highway. There hadn't been a single hint of a plow out there, and that was odd. *Did something happen to the crew?* she wondered.

Even if something had, there should have been another to cover for the first.

Chewing on her lip, she picked up the shovel and walked back to the house and to Vince.

# CHAPTER TWO

Daniel Wither rubbed his hands together and shivered as he stepped out of the elevator. While there was heat, the small room never quite warmed up with the constant flow of people in and out of the parking garage.

*It's going to be a cold one tonight*, he thought, pulling his gloves on before pushing and holding the door open for the tall woman just behind him.

"You are going home sometime today, aren't you?" asked Victoria Piacentini.

She paused as a shiver ran through her tall frame before striding forward.

Daniel lifted a brow as he had to push himself to keep up. While in the building, she had limited herself to a shorter stride so that others keep a reasonable pace with her. Now that she was outside, her normal stride became apparent. Despite the two-inch-high heels on her boots—even if those heels were on the chunkier side and not stilettos—Victoria had a few inches of height on him.

There were not too many people who didn't. Daniel Wither was on the shorter side of average, and the nearly five-foot-eleven Victoria was at least a few inches taller than he was.

Her heels made the difference that much more pronounced.

"Home, no, but to my daughter's and son-in-law's, yes," answered Daniel, shaking his head as he had to almost jog to keep up with her. "My daughter has a huge holiday week planned for her friends and family. I think she'd have plenty for dinner or to drink if you went out to see her."

"Thanks for the invite, and I'd love to see Sheri again, but I have plans as well—so long as I can get there first," she answered as she dropped her purse on the hood of her car and shoved a hand to the bottom.

He forced a cough as he covered his mouth with one hand. Miscellaneous items clattered as they were shoved around by her questing hand, and her brows knit together. She blew out a breath and said, "Blasted keys. Why are they always at the bottom of my purse?"

Daniel tilted his head as he leaned against the heavy cement column.

"Merry Christmas, Dan!" shouted one of the local police officers. "Looks like more snow. Might want to get out of here while you still can. You too, Madam Mayor."

Victoria waved in reply. Daniel gave a half wave as the other police officer drove by them.

When the cruiser was out of sight, Daniel turned back to Victoria as she continued to search her purse for her keys.

"Maybe if you had a smaller purse, you'd find them faster," he suggested. "Maybe something that doesn't quite resemble an overnight bag?"

Victoria's eyebrows rose and Daniel smirked as he met her glare. "Are you trying to tell me my purse is too big?"

"I'd never presume to—" he trailed off, staring past her.

Victoria lifted a brow, and half-turned around to see what had caught his attention before she turned back to Daniel. He smirked as she looked up at the ceiling and breathed out a near silent, "Dammit."

"Call of duty?" asked Daniel, ignoring her glare seconds later.

"Oh no, I am officially on holidays," began Victoria. "Nicholas, this can wait until after…"

The assistant stopped, bending over to catch his breath before he stood back up. "I'm sorry, Ms. Piacentini, but there's this Colonel from the Armed Forces insisting on talking to you. He said it was important."

"Always is," mused Victoria. She sighed and gave up her search for her keys. "Knowing my luck, I left my car keys up in my office."

Daniel snorted and lifted a brow. "You wouldn't be the only person alive to leave their keys on their desk."

"I didn't see them," offered her assistant.

"All right, since I have to go back upstairs anyway, you way as well arrange for him to meet me in my office. Have him wait in—" began Victoria.

"He's already waiting in your office," answered her assistant. "I'm really sorry, ma'am, but he barged in."

Victoria sighed heavily as she brought a hand up to pinch her nose. "Dan, I know you're on your way out too, but I would really appreciate it if you could be there with me for this."

"Why do you need me?" asked Daniel. "You're more than able to tear a strip off of someone on your own."

"Yes, that's my point," she answered. "I think I'll need you to keep me from tearing too much of a strip off a pompous arse who thinks he can throw his weight around."

"It's not too late to run... I do have a car," Daniel pointed out.

"Don't tempt me," she said, crinkling her nose.

He followed her back through the underground garage below City Hall to the entrance. The plain white tile floor, while clean, was scuffed and worn by the thousands of footsteps that walked through here every single day for the nearly thirty years since the three towers comprising the square were built.

"What do you think he wants?" asked Daniel as he stepped inside the elevator.

Victoria was right beside him as she leaned on the wooden rail and stared out the glass as the elevator ascended to the Fourth Floor.

"I have no idea what he wants," she answered with a shrug, staring down through the glass of the elevator and the wall of windows. She pointed to the snow-filled square just outside of these windows. "I'll deal with it. I hope whatever it is can be handled quickly so I can just grab my keys and go before we're socked in with snow and can't."

She paused and Daniel said, "Sheridan's house is in Whitefish."

"Like I said, don't tempt me. I don't get to see her often enough," answered Victoria and she grinned. "She still as horse crazy as I remember her being since grade eight?"

"Yep, more so now that she actually has horses," he chuckled as the lift opened and they stepped out onto the carpeted floor. "I'll stay here.

I'm sure you can resist the urge to murder someone. If not, well, I guess I'll have to arrest you."

She stuck her tongue out at him as she walked through the maze of desks to her office, motioning to her assistant to open the door.

"May as well get this over with," Daniel overheard her say from across the large open room as the door opened. "I'm sorry, didn't catch your name…"

What else she could have said or what the other man said in response was lost as the door closed. Daniel leaned against the rail of the balcony that overlooked the main lobby four floors. As he stared down at the brown hexagonal tiles of the mezzanine, he saw a small group of uniformed soldiers milled near the security desk.

*A group of armed soldiers—with their rifles in hand*, he noted. The first inkling of worry slid into his veins.

*This isn't a normal meeting*, he thought. *What the hell is going on?*

He walked down the stairs, the carpeted steps silencing his steps. Daniel slipped around by the elevator behind the security desk, which hid him from their sight.

Daniel sighed heavily.

While he had meant to see Victoria out, and remind her that one of her friends from high school was having a party over the holidays, there was one other he needed to meet before she headed out to her parents.

Daniel took out his BlackBerry and, keeping the camera lens aimed through a gap between his fingers but the rest of the phone hidden, he took a few pictures. He was not familiar with their patches—but he knew someone who was. *Failing all else, Terrence or Derek will know what this is all about. Then again, so would Fitz.*

* * * * *

Garrett watched as a set of headlights, barely visible through the driving snow, disappeared down the old highway heading into Whitefish. Garrett blinked and squinted as he looked in his mirror, but the green SUV vanished into the grey murk.

*Looks almost like Derek's Jeep...* thought Garrett, but this train of thought disappeared as Garrett pulled up to the military vehicles blocking the road right where the four lanes ended.

The lights were dark.

Garrett crinkled his brows. *Strange, normally when lights stop working, they flash...*

But these were off. Dark. With the blizzard making visibility murky, he would have never known they were even there.

Or the other trucks in the middle of the road.

He slowed the truck, noticing as one young man pointed at him, but didn't stop. Looking back in his rear view, he could see others milling about.

They didn't do anything to chase after him, though.

The snow fell in large flakes, and his headlights did little to dispel the predawn murk. Even as the sun rose, the thick clouds above blocked the warmth from reaching them.

*The back roads are going to be lonelier than this*, he thought, waving at the younger man as he drove by, and he was pleased when the younger man waved back.

The headlights on the truck were less than useless.

It wasn't as if they didn't work—the problem was Garrett couldn't see the road, let alone past the hood of the truck. He had already felt the tires slide over one icy patch despite their deep tread.

*No getting up there tonight*, he realized. *And barely a single soul in between.*

Getting stuck in between High Falls and the highway had not been in his plans, but there it was.

Plans or no, it had happened anyway.

Garrett pulled the truck over. Not that he could go extremely far off the road—and not that it mattered much. He highly doubted that there would be anyone this way before morning, and he wasn't sure if he were already off the side of the road. The road was so clogged of snow, the only reference he had was the clearing between trees with enough room for two vehicles to pass each other if they met each other.

He opened the door and sank to just under his knees.

"Jesus Christ," he murmured.

A foot and a half of snow, if loose and fresh, had fallen on the road. His truck had left a distinctive track. Not only had his tires left tracks, but the snow was deep enough that the drag of the truck's body over the road had also left tracks. His truck had modified suspension—lifts, as off-road enthusiasts liked to call them—and the tires had deep, aggressive treads. Seeing a path dragged through the snow by the bottom of the truck meant the snow was deeper than the clearance under it.

Garrett blew out a breath.

And it was still snowing—hard enough he could barely see his hand in front of him if he stretched it out.

*Like driving through milk*, he thought. *No going back, and no going forward.*

He eyed the back of the truck. Even if he tried to stay in the truck, it would eventually run out of gas and truly leave him stranded. Also, the heat within relied on the engine kept at a certain RPM, not just idle. There would be some heat, but not a whole lot. Garrett had no desire to freeze to death, and he didn't feel like walking.

He wasn't prepared to go camping, but every work truck had at least the basics of survival—including for winter. The roads between mines were sometimes only dirt paths. A breakdown here, with no traffic to flag down, meant contacting the office by satellite phone, and waiting for help to arrive. *Not the first time I've had to camp out on the side of the road, he thought. But I like to plan that sort of trip beforehand…*

He took in a breath and slogged around to the other side of the truck.

He had to grab the side of the truck as he felt his foot slide and he gasped. Had he moved any further over, he would have put the truck into the ditch. The worst part was that he couldn't even tell there was a ditch. The snow had filled it in.

"Son of a…" he murmured, and then chuckled, his shoulders relaxing only marginally. "I've had some close calls, but this one was damn close."

He wouldn't risk breaking an ankle, or soaked feet, if the ditch had water instead of solid ice. The area here was marshy and jagged cliffs where it wasn't.

Garrett took out a long steel rod from the back of the truck.

It wasn't meant as a ground prod, but it was better than nothing.

He poked the ground in the ditch and was rewarded with a solid thunk instead of the crumple of ice breaking.

The bottom was hard, unyielding.

It was solid—the water that may have been there earlier now froze like cement. The sides of the ditch felt like concrete, but given the mud was probably as frozen, he shrugged—a small sigh escaping his lips. He continued to poke the ground as he moved off the road and towards the bush, noting that the ground rose, and trees grew here.

Usually, trees meant dry land. It was unlikely that any serious growth, and these trees looked mature with trunks thick enough that his hands couldn't encircle around them, would grow in truly marshy land. They also couldn't get purchase in rocky land to grow without eventually falling over.

*Some days, even I get lucky on that front*, he mused. *If I had to be stuck on the side of the road, at least I have some place decent to make camp and stay warm.*

Garrett went back to the truck and retrieved the camping and survival gear from the truck. It took four trips, leaving him tired but not exhausted—even a bit exhilarated—to get what he needed from the truck to his camp spot.

He grinned.

Camping had always been a favourite pastime in his family. It had been something his father had passed to his sons, and then his sons to their sons and daughters. Garrett had always taken his son and daughter out camping. His son had taken to it more than his daughter, but she liked it well enough.

She ended up liking horses and boating more, but he didn't complain.

The outdoors was the outdoors—no matter how they chose to enjoy it.

A log windbreak and a roaring fire chased the darkness and the cold away, and Garrett finished it off by using some saplings as bracing to create pine and cedar insulation over the tent, using the shovel to create a snowbank where the wind was the harshest.

With a sigh, he crawled into the tent and onto the ground cover and insulation he had gathered before wrapping himself up in the sleeping bag. The warmth was no illusion, and the steam from his sweat soaked socks—left to dry in front of the fire—proved it.

Had it not been a life-or-death situation, Garrett would have enjoyed it more.

*If I'm stuck like this, there will be others*, he thought. *On the actual highway in between towns. I'm prepared. I know what I'm doing.*

*They won't.*

Garrett rolled over onto his side, facing away from the fire so that the light didn't sear into his eyeballs. He needed sleep. If he were stuck like this tomorrow, he would need every ounce of energy to get himself out.

Or he was walking on snowshoes the rest of the way.

*Yeah, and I really want to do that…* he blew out a breath as he closed his eyes.

The only sound to break the silence was the crackle of the fire.

# CHAPTER THREE

Derek's breath caught as the shock of the sub-zero air caught in his lungs and fogged in the air when he finally exhaled as he walked outside. Ice and frost crusted the bottoms of windows as the panes of glass failed to keep out the cold.

While Sheridan had not specifically asked him to head out and look for her neighbours, it certainly beat the alternative of sitting on his behind as he waited for news.

Jeremy walked around the corner in his heavy winter clothing. He nodded to Derek as he walked by and joined them.

"All right—we'll be heading across the bridge and to the south first. There's a small enclave of cabins and houses not too far from here," said Derek.

"What's past that?" asked Jeremy.

Derek shook his head. "A campground and marina. It's normally closed this time of year. I mean, the owner could still be there, but it's easily ten k's down and at the very end of the road."

"No chance they would have wintered there?" asked another.

Derek thought for a moment and then shook his head. "I doubt it. Even before all this, the drive down that way was nasty. You needed a four by four to make it, and half the time the plow never went that far. I think they shut it down at the first hint of snow—maybe after hunting season ends at the latest—and check on it from time to time, but after winter sets in its abandoned. Anyone still down there is more than able to handle this by themselves."

"So, we're not risking it," finished Jeremy for him. "I'm guessing we're going as far as the camps and homes that are probably occupied, and then we head back."

Derek led them out into the driveway. One very bored Terrence had kept the driveway clear of snow despite no traffic on the road, let alone in the driveway. Fuel was simply too difficult to get and too precious to squander unless they absolutely had to.

Derek's breath frosted in the air and he rubbed his hands together to keep them warm. "Damn, it's cold out here."

Jeremy was hopping up and down and shifting from side to side in same effort. "Oh my God, I think a certain part of my anatomy just shattered."

Derek snorted and shook his head. He walked over to his SUV and slid into the driver's seat. Jeremy moved over to the front passenger side and got in.

When Derek pulled out and headed down the south road, he came to two conclusions.

*One, I was crazy to drive here.*

And, moments later, *Two, I still have no idea how Sheridan's drove that little Smart Car from Lively to Panache Lake Road and then down to the farm in at least a foot of snow, even if it had still been loose and fluffy.*

The first conclusion... well... if he had not made it here, the point would be moot. With the power out and the general infrastructure collapsed, he was actually quite happy with where he was. He would have never made it home in Garson. Instead, they would have been still in Blind River. Outside of a few friends who were likely gone for the holidays anyway, they would have been alone and separated from the family that had practically adopted the both of them.

*And I'm definitely not going to complain about the relative comfort of Sheridan's home.*

He hoped others would be as lucky.

If they were not, then he had an ugly feeling that they wouldn't find very many survivors. *Assuming we find any survivors at all…*

As the little SUV pulled into the closest subdivision full of year-round cabins and small houses, the first thing they all noticed was the smoke rising from the chimneys of most of the homes. And that was a good sign, although the other two houses were cold and seemed deserted.

When he stopped, a few people came out of their houses. One man walked right up to the driver's side window and Derek rolled down the window. "How are you doing out here?" Derek asked.

"Could be better… but definitely could also be worse," he answered. His eyes grew wide as he noticed who it was. "Derek! Seeing you just made my day."

"How much in supplies do you have?" asked Derek, racking his memory for the man's name.

"Not a lot," he answered. "Why?"

"I've a bad feeling this might last awhile. Why don't you take what you need and what we can share and come up to our place?" Derek looked around. "We can send a sleigh… and forgive me, I can't seem to remember your name."

"You never do. It's Rick. Give me the night and we'll pack it up. Come back out early tomorrow," Rick answered. "If you had Terrence with you, he'd have told you that."

"He did," answered Derek, and Rick rolled his eyes. "We'll come out tomorrow. Stay safe... wish I could stay and talk, but we have other places to check out."

"No other houses that way but that camp, and they locked it up before heading south for the winter. We're at the end of the road here. The others who were farther that way—" Rick pointed down the side road that branched off. "—came up here to stay with us."

"You sure there's no one else?" asked Jeremy.

"All accounted for," he answered.

Derek's eyes thinned. Rick owned the marina, and he was definitely not 'south' like he claimed to be. That he was standing there in front of him and lying through his teeth, and seemed more nervous than he should have been. But Derek nodded and then turned to Jeremy. "Let's head back to your farm and we'll draw up a plan to come get them for tomorrow. I don't want to use too much of my gas. With the way things were in town, I don't have the foggiest when we'll be able to get more."

"We'll come up when we can," said Rick. "But do yourself a favour. Don't head farther down the road."

Derek shifted in his seat, and without turning his head, following where Rick was looking.

There was a shadow. He couldn't see it clearly, but it was enough to make Rick more than a little jumpy. Derek looked closer at him and finally recognized what he was seeing on the man's face.

Fear.

Derek took a breath, not dropping the smile, but the quick double blink in Rick's direction hopefully told the other man that he understood the message Rick was trying to tell him. Whoever was behind that building was trouble.

*On our doorsteps already*, thought Derek. *Goddammit*.

"All right then," said Derek. "We will see you tomorrow, then. I'm pretty sure Terrence will want to check up on you himself."

*Help is coming. Read between the lines, Rick*, thought Derek.

Rick visibly relaxed. "Great, fantastic."

Derek rolled up the window, and while he hated to leave the others without help, he knew there was absolutely no way to help them with only Jeremy and nothing but their bare hands and an old Jeep.

He reversed and turned around.

As he drove back up the road, he kept one eye on the road and the other in his rear-view mirror.

A blonde woman walked out and straight to Rick. Judging by the others with her, she wasn't there to just chat.

He lost sight of them after we went around the corner.

He blew out a breath.

"Okay, what the hell was that?" asked Jeremy.

"Trouble," answered Derek as he stopped the Jeep. "Real trouble—the kind that crops up when there's no one to stop it."

\* \* \* \* \*

Daniel leaned on the desk, tapping keys on his BlackBerry to encourage the tiny dragon on the screen to move through the level when the screen went black. Moments later, the screen lit up again but a message on it said, *We're sorry, we're experiencing an issue with your connection. Please try again later*.

He tapped on the app again.

His brow crinkled as the same message popped up. Daniel closed the app and slid his phone into his jacket pocket, looking around with a sigh.

One janitor had left a bucket on the floor with some caution tape and orange cones to warn people away from a slippery patch on the floor from a leak in the skylight above. Each drop of water dripping from four stories to the floor into the bucket echoed off the spartan cement and brick walls.

A blizzard howled outside City Hall. The snow piled into drifts, changing and shifting as the wind drove the snow into dunes. If not for how cold it was outside, and that the drifts were pure white or black dark of frozen ground, it could be mistaken for a desert just past the floor to ceiling windows.

The first pop, more like an abrupt crack from above, thundered through the open lobby. Daniel stiffened, the sense of icy fingers on his spine having nothing to do with the weather outside.

*That couldn't be...* ran through his mind first.

And then it repeated.

It was.

*Gun fire*, his eyes widened. *Repeating, semi-automatic...*

"What are you—" Daniel recognized the shocked cry of Victoria's assistant before the man cut off in a scream as more gunfire met his question.

Daniel flattened his palms on the counter of the security station and, using his arms to give himself momentum, vaulted over to stand behind the counter.

He peered into the computer screens, flicking his gaze from one camera feed to another.

The soldiers were sweeping each floor, each room, and... to his horror as it played out on different screens... shooting everyone they encountered. Police, office worker, one hapless city councillor in their office. It didn't matter.

*My God, why?*

Daniel couldn't answer his own question, but there was a clatter of footsteps to his right.

Pressing himself into the space between counters and underneath where the cabinets had this tiny space just out of sight, Daniel struggled to calm his panicked breathing. He knew, if he looked into a mirror, the whites around his irises would be obvious.

Daniel pushed himself to draw slow, even breaths.

Forced himself to work through the facts.

The first one was that he was alone. He was off duty, so didn't even have his side arm. He was only one person against a large squad of trained soldiers.

Secondly, he had no idea who they were. Who sent them? Were they even who they had claimed to be to get access to Tom Davies Square? His gut told him, No, they can't be.

No Canadian soldier, if legitimate, would fire on their own people for no reason. They had no reason—even if they had orders to, they would question the legitimacy of shooting unarmed Canadians especially those representing duly elected official positions.

That meant they weren't who they claimed to be.

And if they weren't who they claimed to be, then he had nothing to predict their next move.

Also, since he had come to that conclusion, as an officer of the peace sworn to protect the citizens of the city and enforce the laws, he had a duty to fight them.

*And die in the process, without making a dent on their numbers*, he thought. *Small consolation there.*

*The best idea would be to lay low, gather intel, and then make a plan.*

He silently blew out a breath.

His priority was to find Victoria Piacentini. If she still lived, as Mayor of Sudbury, she was the last and highest ranked duly elected official in the city unless he found one of the members of parliament. He had no idea where to look, or if anyone still lived, so that meant Victoria had to be protected. As far as he knew, she still lived. He had not heard her scream—and he would have since her office was close to the ledge on the fourth floor—nor had he heard any other gunfire since those soldiers moved off the fourth floor.

That meant she was alive… for now.

He crinkled his brow. *Why would they leave her alive and not others? She's the Mayor.*

Daniel let his head fall back gently to the back of the cabinet.

*Rescue the Mayor from lunatics with guns*, he thought. *Not how I thought I would spend my Christmas at all.*

# CHAPTER FOUR

Vince brought Gina a coffee and sat down beside her. The dining room and table in their house had a large picture window overlooking the lake. The view was often spectacular, especially in the autumn, when the leaves changed to fiery reds and oranges and reflected off the lake.

"Are the emergency channels all still down?" asked Vince, and Gina nodded. "That's not good."

"No, you're right there. Makes me wonder what's happened. I've got a gut feeling winter is going to be far worse than we're used to and that this is only the start of our problems." A shiver started at the base of her spine before running up her back like electric fire. "I've got a really bad feeling something is going to happen this winter."

"What type of thing?"

"I really don't know. The land feels wrong, it feels like it's in pain. Oh, I can't describe it," she put a palm on the window overlooking Middle Lake.

Vince's eyes never left her. "Well, I hope it gets feeling better."

"So do I." She took a sip of coffee and pushed away from the window. "The emergency network really worries me, though. It's supposed to survive cold weather. I've tried ringing the station captain, but the station phones are down and the radio's just not picking up anything. I can't get in touch with even the Lieutenant through his mobile. I— Oh, I don't know what's happened. I'm sure we'll find out soon."

*Can't help but wonder if some of my neighbours are safe, wherever they are*, she thought. She liked them, if she had to be honest. From a distance—but she still cared enough to be concerned over their welfare.

"So… circling back to the emergency lines still being down," said Vincent, and Gina fought to keep herself from rolling her eyes. "How long has it been?"

"Too long. But I can't get in touch with anyone to find out what's going on. I really don't think smoke signals or mirrors are going to work," she added, earning a light-hearted snigger from Vince.

Both fell into silence after that.

"What the hell? There are people on the lake," said Vincent.

Gina crinkled her brow. "People?" She looked up, widening her eyesight to take in the lake before her.

Vincent pointed across the lake. Gina blew out a breath as she saw the two snow machines heading from the other subdivision on the other side of Middle Lake and across the lake to them.

"Is it me or does something feel wrong about this?" asked Vincent, and he shrugged. "Correct me if I'm just jumpy as hell, though."

"No, you're not wrong. I've got the same feeling," she replied as she put the got up from the table.

Gina checked her weapon and headed down the now-cleared driveway as the first person stepped foot on land. The first snow machine stopped, and the man waved, and she blew out a breath in relief. "Relax, Vincent, it's just Paul," said Gina as she removed her hand from the holster on her hip as she waved back at him. "I'll go check out what he's come to see us about. Maybe he knows something that we don't."

By the time Gina walked down the length of the driveway and to the road, Paul had ridden across another neighbour's yard and to the road to meet her. "Gina, it's good to see you," he said as he held his hand out to her.

"You as well," answered Gina she shook his hand.

"I'm trying to reserve my gas for important trips," he answered, climbing off the snow machine, and he hopped up and down to keep warm. "No offense, but it's colder than hell out here. Could we talk somewhere warmer?"

"Yeah, come inside and have a cuppa with us," she nodded and swung around behind him on the snow machine as they rode up the hill to the house.

As she climbed off, rubbing her face to get the blood circulating as even the quick trip had whipped the freezing cold air against her face, he killed the engine. She led the two men from their snow machines into the house, and Paul removed his helmet.

"Much nicer in here," he said.

With a snort, Gina nodded over at Vincent. As Vincent made a fresh round of coffee, the two men stripped off their sledding gear and hung it so that any snow would melt off but not leave it soaking by the time they had to get back into it. Gina handed them both a set of slippers, and they joined her in her dining room.

"Thanks for the hospitality, Gina, Vince. This is Noah," Paul introduced his companion as he accepted the coffee from Vince.

"Have you heard anything?" asked Noah.

Gina shook her head. "Not a word."

The two men looked at each other. "Nothing?" asked Paul, his eyebrows rising. "Not anything?"

"Not even static, Paul," answered Gina.

Paul blew out a breath and leaned back in his chair. "That shouldn't even be possible."

"I know. I've tried everything I can think of. I've radioed the station, I've radioed the water bombers' base, I've even tried calling my lieutenant on his mobile. I get nothing from the radios and a message saying the mobile service is out of service and they hope to bring it back online soon." She turned even more serious. "And our power is limited. I don't know how long it will continue for without degrading either further."

"Yeah, we noticed the same thing with the power. So, now what?" he asked.

Gina shook her head. "The best I can figure is that we just survive. Maybe it comes back. Maybe it doesn't. But I'm not about to roll over and just give up because my radio died and my heater stopped working. That's why we've got a fire."

"She has a point," mentioned Noah, as he also sighed. "And those of us with fires can house those who don't. Keep everyone warm."

They stood up. *No point in worrying about it now.* Gina blew out a breath. *Better to look forward and survive it — me and everyone here — so, if we're about done talking about it let's just get it done*, she thought before she said, "I'll get Vince to continue monitoring the channels. If it comes back on, he can tell me. In the meantime, I think we should turn our focus onto just how we are going to survive the winter."

Paul's eyebrows rose again.

"Okay," he said. "We'll follow your lead on this. What's our next step, then?"

"First, we're going to be working together—a lot—on this," she pointed out, and she pointed towards the lake that they could see through the window beside her entry door. "We need a way back and forth across the lake that isn't relying on gas burning snow machines or vehicles. The easiest way would be to use one run of gas right now to clear off and pack down what we can in the way of a path between the two sides of the lake."

"I think I see where you're going with this." Paul nodded. "Okay."

"What about what the others may think?" asked Vincent. "I know we're not panicking, that we have a focus. What about others? Won't they ask why?"

"If they can clear a skate path on Lake Ramsey every year for funsies then we can do it here and say it's for the same reason," said Gina. "And why the hell not? Skating on the lake and getting the ice huts back on it will give us all a sense of normalcy we'd be lacking if we didn't."

"Not to mention the fish we might catch from the lake may be our only, and best source of food, for a while," said Paul.

"Nah, we'd fish it out too fast, assuming we caught enough in the first place," Gina answered, but she pointed her thumb behind her. "However, there's another lake close to here that can be reached easily enough. Might even find a few other survivors capable of helping us out while we do the same for them. Bigger lake, more likely to have fish."

"We can't survive on fish all winter," said the other man. "We'll fish out both lakes."

"There's small game," said Vincent. "May be a little gamey, but we've always had rabbits and jackrabbits in the area. There's lots of bush tea as well to avoid scurvy. It won't be easy, but we can survive."

"Might be worthwhile taking a chance at Walmart, too," said Gina, but then she sighed. "Not that I want to. If things are falling apart in the city like I suspect they could be, that is the first place anyone is going to head. Assuming it hasn't already been looted."

Paul took in a deep breath before releasing it. "You really think that's happened?"

"I have no idea," answered Gina. "But I've also never lost my radio and server connection for so long before. Maybe once we're over that hill things will be all normal and all—and I hope so—and this is just an exercise in emergency preparedness."

"We could check it out," suggested Paul, and Gina felt her eyebrows raise. "From a distance. If it looks normal, then we know we're just jumping at shadows. If things look off, we know what we're up against."

Gina nodded. "That's a good idea."

Paul nodded to his friend. "Okay, Gina, get suited up. You can ride with me across the lake and then we can each take one of my machines up the hill to see what's going on."

Paul and the other man went outside, and Vincent grabbed Gina's arm as she was getting into her snow gear. "What do you really think? Are we just overreacting?"

Gina shook her head. "I hope so. But I don't know. Can't hurt to hope."

"Never hurts to hope," agreed Vincent.

\* \* \* \* \*

Garrett yawned and pushed open the flap to the tent, one hand scratching the back of his head and his other holding back a second yawn.

He grinned.

The sky was a shade darker than periwinkle, and the east was a fading purple and pink. Not a true red sky in the morning—and that boded well. With how clear it was, it meant no more snow for at least a few days.

The problem was how cold it likely would be.

More like frozen—enough to break even toughened plastic like brittle glass.

He blew into the ashes of the fire and fed it a few bits and pieces of branches and wood chips until it returned to a cheery fire.

*No use wasting a good fire… may as well make some proper tea*, he thought. *Or to warm up a bit with while packing everything up again.*

Tea and breakfast consumed, Garrett fed the fire more wood and stoked it to an aggressive, and good size, fire. He wouldn't have done this while breaking down camp in the summer. There wouldn't have been a need for it, and the chances of it jumping from fire pit to bush were too great. However, in the winter, everything was soaked and frozen. He would need the fire to keep himself warm and to dry off again. Perhaps even cook food.

He returned to the truck and swore.

Four by four or not, there was no using it. It started fine, but now the snow was too deep to gain any purchase. With no sign of any traffic, or even tracks in the snow at all, that meant no chance of rescue.

*Snowed enough to erase even my tracks.* Garrett sighed again and reached into the truck to try the satellite again. *The blizzard was too heavy for a signal. It's like that at camp with the damn TV, too.*

Garrett turned the phone on and waited for the acknowledgment of the signal. While it turned on, and the screen showed he had a connection to a satellite, there was no connection from the satellite to the other side. It was like the service provider had vanished. Garrett blinked, and looked up, and he forced himself to remain calm.

He knew enough.

No service… on a satellite phone.

The network was down on a network that never went down.

It was impossible.

But yet, there it was.

"Well, I guess that leaves it up to me to get myself out of this mess," he said aloud, and then he sighed. "So, what have we got?"

Garrett opened the back of the truck and rooted around in the back and then laughed. Half of it was nervous tension—but the rest was relief.

Snowshoes.

"Where the hell were you last night when I could have used you, eh?" he grumbled. "Would have saved me the soakers."

He leaned against the truck, and strapped the titanium framed heavy duty snowshoes to his boots, testing them on the snow. Now that he wasn't sinking to mid-thigh—it had snowed that much between last night and this morning—he was drier, warmer, and using less energy to just get around.

He took the travel and survival pack out of the truck and packed it full of every bit he would need, including some personal items. He tromped back around to the remains of his camp, dousing the fire, and strapping some kindling onto his back. There were a few saplings around the camp, and he found one that was promising. He tested the six-foot sapling the width of three of his fingers in his hand, and with a nod—after chopping it down—used it as a walking pole to keep himself steady.

With one last look at the camp, he returned to the truck and made sure there was nothing else he would need from it. He half considered leaving the useless satellite phone and charger, but grabbed it anyway. *It may be too much to hope for the service to come back, he thought. But I will hope for it, anyway.*

Garrett paused, his thumb on the lock button of the key fob of the truck.

He breathed in, and then let his breath out again, pressing it. A lonely beep, beep told him the truck was locked.

The trees and bush pushing in on either side of the road eventually thinned as Garrett walked down the hill. In the middle of the snow-covered field in the valley was a stone bridge—all that remained of old Worthington. A long time ago, back when mining in the area was new and during the copper and nickel rush, the mine beneath Worthington gave way. Within minutes, most of the town sank into the sinkhole created by the collapsing mine.

The only reason no one had died was because of a mine supervisor noticing some unusual shifting in the rock within the mine—and ordering an immediate evacuation.

All that remained now was a water filled crevice in the resulting crater… and the lonely bridge as a reminder.

The road skirted the edge of this swamp, built into the side of the rock where the builders could at least count on solid ground for the semis, smaller trucks, and cars to travel between Fairbanks Lake and the major highway.

Close to here was a newer part of the town, although it was not really a town. Not anymore.

A small clumping of houses and farmland— that was all that remained of Worthington.

It was a small subdivision, and it only had as many houses as he had fingers on his hands. He liked it up here for much the same reason these few bought their homes here.

It was quiet.

Garrett stopped, breathing hard after climbing up from the valley, sweat rolling down his back despite the freezing temperatures.

*I've overexerted myself*, he thought. Shouldn't have pushed. *Could have set up camp on the other side of that valley…*

He looked from house to house. There was a sense like someone had fingers on the back of his neck but each time he looked at a house no one was in any of the windows, but the curtains fluttered.

*I'm being watched*, he realized.

Garrett stopped and glared at one window. "Fine," he muttered, knocking on the door.

"Go away!" came the answer.

"Look, I'm tired, cold…"

"Just go away!"

Garrett sighed, but slogged on to the next house, but saw the curtains pulled shut seconds before he turned into the driveway. He blinked. *Jeez, you'd think I'd done something wrong here.*

He had never stopped in the small clump of houses on his way through from High Falls and back, but as far as he could remember, they had never been this afraid of strangers. He remembered seeing children playing outside in the yards and people going about their business. Some had even waved as he drove through.

*This is odd*, he thought. *What the hell is going on here?*

Garrett stopped in the middle of the subdivision—right in the middle of the road, his brows knitting. *I have no idea what the hell is going on here, but I'm not leaving until I find out.*

His legs shook, and his knees ached. The bag on his back felt heavier now that it had been when he started out in the morning. Looking up, even though there were bits of blue between the clouds, they were swiftly turning violet as the pale grey of the clouds turned to slate. Now that he had stopped pushing himself, the sweat was feeling icy as well.

I find shelter now or I won't need it, he thought, pressing his lips into a thin line.

There was one last house, and he trudged through the snow toward it.

A low rumble in the distance and a thin whistle pierced the silence. Garrett looked up and toward the sound, trying to place it. The rumble faded, and all that remained was the faint snapping crackle of frozen tree limbs rubbing against each other in the bush.

Garrett lifted a hand to knock on the door.

It was a long shot. The house appeared abandoned without even a rustle of curtain from inside. He tried the door, but it was locked tight.

The temptation to break in gnawed at him, but that would cause a draft he wouldn't be able to repair.

He sighed heavily, turning back to the road. Scanning the horizon, looking for a decent place to set up camp. He would never make it to High Falls now, and if he didn't warm up and rest, he would never make it there at all—he would die from hypothermia first.

The rumble sounded again, and this time it sounded closer, and with a mechanical whine.

*Like an engine labouring*, he thought, his brow crinkling. *Big engine… like a…*

The door opened so fast that Garrett stared at the old man in confusion, not even sure he was real.

"Get inside!" the man said. "Now! Before it's too late…"

Garrett blinked again, but released the snaps holding his feet to the snowshoes and entered the house. The man pulled him all the way in and then slammed the door shut, moving a chair in front of the door.

The man picked up the snowshoes and then turned to face him.

Garrett opened his mouth, but the old man motioned to a young woman who pulled him into a back room, pulling Garrett into a closet before hiding behind him in the same closet. She pressed herself right into the deepest part of the closet, using the clothes and other clutter to hide herself before sliding down the wall, trembling.

"What's going on?" he asked.

"Shhh!" she whispered. "They'll hear you."

He opened his mouth, but she grasped his hand and said, "Don't let them hear you."

# CHAPTER FIVE

Gina looked up, noticing that the shadows were getting longer. Her garage was already in shadows, and the first hint of pink was staining the sky to the west. She blew out a breath as the air fogging in front of her as she walked to the snow machines with her own helmet in her hand.

Paul looked up and nodded. "Good, you're prepared…"

He pivoted his entire body as her gaze shifted to the highway behind him.

A lonely vehicle—a small SUV by the look of it—slowly picked its way from around the corner heading towards the Long Lake overpass. It had come from the west. The only thing that way was Lively, and the four lanes beyond. Gina blinked in confusion as she tried to think of a reason anyone would take a chance on the obviously closed highway.

"Jesus!" exclaimed the other man with Paul.

Gina took a step as her jaw dropped slightly.

The SUV, she couldn't tell what kind it was from here, slid sideways. The driver attempted to straighten it out, but it had the opposite effect. It slid out of control, spinning twice before it went off the side of the road. A cloud of loose snow erupted into a cloud around it as it stopped, nose first, in the ditch. Taillights shone bright red and then faded slightly.

"He hit the brakes," said Paul, shaking his head. "Rookie mistake."

Gina ran over to the Noah's snow machine. "Can I borrow this?"

He nodded and dismounted, allowing her to take the machine.

"Paul, you're with me," said Gina. "He's probably going to need help."

They put their helmets on, securing the straps under their chins as they did so. She led him up and then across the rocky hill towards the highway. There was no point in heading down to the road— the machines, despite newer and powerful— wouldn't be able to climb the steep incline up to the highway.

Gina could hear the roar of the snow machine behind her, knowing that Paul had followed her without question.

It took only moments to get to the highway, and then over to the SUV.

Gina got off the machine, shutting the engine down as she did. Paul moved his machine around the other side of the SUV, but still within sight of her.

She crinkled her nose under the helmet. The door was open, and the driver wasn't in sight. A muffled, but still recognizable shout from Paul made her look up, and she followed where she was pointing.

There were footprints across the highway towards their subdivision—and right where the highway dropped off sharply and down to the end of her road well below.

Gina cursed and then shook her head.

*No good can come of that*, she thought. *Those rocks are not forgiving. If that driver fell there, we might be burying someone—not rescuing them.*

She pointed at Paul and then showed where she wanted him to head. She closed the SUV's door before running back to her snow machine. Once on it, she led him to the drop to her street.

The tracks from the SUV led straight to it.

Cautiously, she slid off the snow machine and moved to the edge.

There was no sign of a body at the bottom, but she could see the deep holes in the snow where someone had dropped a few times on their way down. Fresh, crimson-stained, and still steaming, on the surface of the snow. She followed the now less than steady tracks up the road.

She moved back to the snow machine and shook her head. Paul visibly slouched, and she realized she gave him the wrong impression. She lifted the visor of her helmet, and when he did, she said, "Couldn't see anyone down there, but there's blood."

"He fell then, but if he's still moving that means he's still breathing," said Paul.

"For now."

He nodded. "Let's track our lost sheep down, then."

Gina led the two to the edge of the man-made escarpment, and down a narrow gap. She held her breath as she did.

This was a risky move. There was a small gap— only a ditch—between the man-made part and the natural cliff. It was not a gentle incline, but it was not a sharp drop-off. It was also extremely narrow, with plenty of sharp rocks poking out from under the snow.

Or normally would poke out under the snow. There was too much snow to see any of this right now.

However, it was the only way down without backtracking.

*And he could be dead by the time we find him if we do*, she thought.

Gina gave the snow machine a bit of throttle and then took the chute.

She winced as a piece of rock scraped one side of the machine, and she moved up and put her the leg on that side on the seat, leaning one way on the machine so the track and skis took the worst of it. The man-made side was easier to react to as they had made it to be a slope.

The machine settled onto the flat of the road, and this jarred her through her arms as it landed on both skis. She goosed the throttle to get herself out of the way as Paul followed her path down.

With a thumbs up when he joined her at the bottom, she led him on the trail of the SUV driver.

He was easy enough to follow, having left obvious tracks in the otherwise undisturbed snow. He didn't appear to still be bleeding, which was a blessing, but the erratic path concerned her.

The tracks led from one house, and then another. *He's looking for help… or shelter*, she realized and scanned the horizon. With a blink, she saw the figure climbing her driveway, but he fell as he reached it.

She pointed, and Paul's gaze followed. The machines roared to life as they hit full throttle. She found this exhilarating on a normal day, but right now she was counting seconds that the man stayed down.

Once by him, she killed the motor and leapt from the machine, rolling the man over. His sleeve was torn and clumsily bandaged, but he didn't appear injured anywhere else. Gina felt down one leg, and then the other, before moving to his arms, head, chest and back. With a sigh of relief, as the only answering groan came from touching that arm, she took off her helmet and told Paul, "He hurt his arm, but other than that he looks okay. We need to get him inside, though."

"I'll go up and get some help. We won't be able to take him on the machines," said Paul, and he rode up the hill to the house before running inside.

Seconds later, Vincent and Noah slid—if a controlled slide on their feet—down the hill.

Between the four of them, they moved him inside the house.

Paul and Noah, once they had settled the injured man on the couch in Gina's living room, pulled her aside. "You'll need a few more supplies. We're going to head back across the lake and see if we can find anything that can help."

"All right, thanks," said Gina, and then she grinned sheepishly. "Tell Noah I'm sorry about that scratch from hell."

He waved it off. "Nothing he hasn't done before himself."

# CHAPTER SIX

Garrett lifted a brow but stayed silent as he leaned back into the closet, carefully avoiding the young woman sharing the space with him.

*Something spooked them*, he thought. *And whatever it is, if it's better to hide, then fine*.

The whine he had heard before then split up into four distinct howls, and he finally recognized them for what they were.

Snow machines.

Through the walls of the house and the closet, he could hear yelling and shouting from outside as the four machines rode through town. Bunch of yahoos, he thought, his brows knitting together as a lip curled.

He forced his fists to unclench, breathing as quietly as he could.

He looked over at the young woman. Even if he couldn't see her, he suspected he now knew why she had hidden.

The howl of the snow machines came to a stop, and he was about to leave the closet, but he felt a small hand grab and squeeze his. The meaning was clear—she didn't want him to leave just yet. Garrett blinked and settled back into the closet again.

"Open the door, old man," shouted a man from outside. "We both know you're in there."

"We haven't got anything else for you to take!" cried the old man who had taken him in.

"The others we took mentioned a granddaughter," said the same man. "Where are you hiding her?"

"They're lying!"

There was a crash, and Garrett cringed from the cold air that seeped into the closet. Muffled voices and shouting became clear. *They're inside now,* thought Garrett. *Wonder what brought them in?*

"I don't have all day," said the same man, and the clarity of his voice gave away that he stood in the house. "Where's the girl? I may not even take her from you, but you know how I don't like people lying to me."

"I swear to you, Mr. Kovach, there's no one else here!" said the old man.

"Eric, a neighbour of his said a stranger came through town on snowshoes. We didn't see any tracks from the other direction, so he had to find shelter in town somewhere…" said another voice.

"Got another guest, do we?" asked Kovach, and there was a large breath. "Don't make me search the house."

The hand on Garrett's arm trembled, and Garrett took a breath. He didn't even try to unclench his fist this time. *They're in here because of me… dammit.*

"Look, snowshoes and a pack!" said another voice.

There was a silence, and then a slap of a hand on someone's body. The old man cried out. Garrett heard only the sound of wood snapping, and that was enough for him.

He shoved the doors open and strode out into the living room.

A single man—one about the same age as his own son—stood over the old man who was sprawled over the remains of his coffee table, clutching at his face.

The man, Kovach he assumed, looked up, his eyes widening.

That was the only warning Garrett gave him.

Garrett's fist connected with Kovach's jaw and he whirled, landing heavily in a heap on the floor. Garrett glared at the others, and his voice was low, "Anyone else got a bright idea? Pick him up. Get out of town. If I see any one of you again outside of nicely coming into town for honest trade, I'll make you regret it. Now, get out of here."

The other two men picked up Kovach and dragged him outside. Two others stared in shock as Garrett followed them out. He pointed at the other two. "Those had better not be what I think they are on those wrists."

They looked at him, and then at their half-conscious boss.

Dropping the ropes and zip ties, they jumped onto the snow machines, throwing helmets on. A few minutes later, the whine of the snow machines was in the distance.

Garrett blew out a sigh, staring at the broken front door of the house that had sheltered him.

"Well, damn," he said. "What have I walked into now?"

\* \* \* \* \*

Gina had just settled into the comfort of the armchair when a groan from the settee part of her couch told her their guest was waking up. She moved over to the couch just as the man rolled over and opened his eyes. He stared at her, and she met his stare right back. "'Lexis?" he asked.

She shook her head. "Sorry, 'fraid not. I'm Gina."

"Russell." She smoothed the blanket over him again, helping him sit up slightly at the same time. "Where am I?"

"D'you remember anything?"

"The rental leaving the road. Hitting gravel, and then the ditch," he answered. "I knew I couldn't stay there, and I figured a house had to have someone in them to help me. Even if I could get a phone call—my iPhone didn't have any signal to call a tow—and warm up. But the two houses I tried were shut tight. Then I saw a cruiser… wait… I just totally intruded on your home, didn't I?"

Gina nodded. "Yeah, but that's okay. Oh, and it's not a cop car. I'm a firefighter. But if you were looking for emergency services, then you've come to the right house."

"I'm not complaining. My father was a fire chief a long time ago. Not anywhere close to the same size of town as Sudbury, though," answered Russell as he rubbed his temples. "I'd hate to complain, but I have a hell of a headache."

She snorted. "I'm not surprised. I don't think you have a concussion or anything, but from the impressive lump on your head, I'd say you hit the steering wheel."

"Yeah, I'm surprised the air bags didn't go off."

He fell silent as he compressed his lips into a thin line and stared at the fire burning away in the fireplace. Gina didn't push. She stood up and moved into the kitchen. *Hot cocoa always makes me feel better. Don't see a reason for it not to help here*, she thought as she made three cups.

She walked back over to Russell and handed him a cup and he murmured, "Thank you," before falling silent again.

Vincent accepted the third cup and then joined them in the living room. "I'm guessing the reason I'm here and not the ER is that there's no way to get there and I'm not the only one with no signal."

Gina nodded. "Yep. Not a sound from anyone for a few days, now."

"Days?" asked Russell. "How long have I been out?"

Gina pushed him back down. "It's okay, relax. You've been out for just on thirty hours. Vincent and I have done what we could to keep you hydrated, warm, and dry. Don't go stuffing it all up by running around before you're ready. You also cut your arm up pretty bad, so I've stitched that up for you as well."

"You don't understand—I was going to check on my Aunt and Uncle. They live close to here… I think. I know they live close to Long Lake," he said. "I promised my mother I would check on them before I left Whitefish."

"You did know the phones were out, didn't you?" asked Gina, and when Russell sighed heavily, she nodded. "Yeah, I thought so. Figured that little Ford Escape would be enough and got yourself in over your head."

"I know how to drive a four by four."

"Look," Gina held up his wallet and when his eyes widened, she handed it back to him. "Haven't

K.M. Cannon

touched a thing. And, with no internet or signal, couldn't exactly run up your credit cards either. I know where you're from. Don't get me wrong, I'm not great in the snow either—I'm from Australia, mate—but the one thing I know is that the snow up here is nothing like it is in Toronto."

"I live there now," he pointed out. "But I didn't always. I was born here in Sudbury, for your information. I graduated from Lockerby—and my first year of college was at Canadore. Most of my family is here… in Whitefish, except for my Uncle and Aunt on Long Lake. I know how to handle a four by four."

Her eyebrows rose. "Yeah, I could tell that from here."

"No one's perfect," he groused.

She looked over at Vincent, who only shrugged. "He has a point."

"On the top of his head," she grumbled, and she finally threw up her hands. "All right, look, tell us where to find your Aunt and Uncle, and I'll see if we can take a few snow machines to check up on them… if we can spare the fuel and the time. But, if they're all the way down at Long Lake, they're probably better off than we are right now."

"All right, fine," conceded Russell. "You have a deal."

Gina could hear the unspoken, *For now*, from where she sat. She didn't need him to say it. But if he was too stubborn to stay put after he was healthy enough to leave, then she couldn't keep him here. She only hoped that once he realized how dire the situation was, he wouldn't be that reckless. He didn't strike her as the reckless type. Concerned for his family, definitely, but not foolhardy.

"Good," she patted his leg. "Now, what I want you to do is rest up. You'll need your strength for whatever we're facing."

Russell leaned back in the cushions. "I think that's the best I can do right now. Even if you told me to leave now, I don't think I could."

"Might have something to do with the knock to your head, and the blood loss from that arm wound we stitched up. Hypothermia didn't help either," said Vincent. "You got yourself into a fine mess."

"Don't rub it in," said Russell, as he sipped the cocoa and looked around.

The house had once been a mid-century modern home. Vincent had spent a small fortune renovating it to bring the mid-century charm up to modern standards and finishing, even adding a massive steel beam the entire length of the house to support the room for the fully open concept living room, dining room, and kitchen and full-length glass windows overlooking both Middle Lake and the woodlands and rolling mountains to the east.

"Nice house," said Russell. "I think I've looked up at this house as I drove by here, but never saw it up close."

Vincent grinned. "Thanks. I like it."

"If I have to recover anywhere, I am definitely not complaining about the view," said Russell.

"When all this blows over, remind me to pay you rent for a hell of a few days."

"I'll send you the Airbnb bill," said Vincent, and he pointed over to Gina. "She thinks it could be permanent, though."

Gina turned to look over at Russell, whose head had whipped around to stare at her. "Why?"

"We've had no communication with anyone except our neighbours across the lake, and that was only face to face. There's no mobile network, no radio, no TV, nothing. Not even the emergency channels are working," she pointed out, quietly. "I've been trying to contact someone—actually anyone—for days and haven't been able to get through. Not even on the sat phone. I've never had this happen before and it doesn't happen—not for any reason."

Russell leaned back—his eyes wide. "You may be right."

Her eyebrows rose.

He continued, "I work in IT in Toronto. Well, I did until I retired. This kind of thing isn't something that happens. There should be something."

"Yeah, well, now you know why we're this cautious with everyone."

"I think I just joined you," said Russell.

# CHAPTER SEVEN

Daniel crept from his hiding place, and over to one of the vending machines. Warily, he eyed the floors above until he was well under the closest overhang and out of view. He brought out a knife—no delicate penknife, but a weighty jackknife his daughter had given him for his birthday. One end of the multi-tool was a glass breaker. It had amused him once. As a police officer, he had access to far better and more effective tools than from Amazon, but somehow—without access to his cruiser—her present was no longer amusing.

*Who thought that would happen?* Daniel mused as he tapped the edge of the glass.

Cracks appeared, and he held his breath. If the glass landed on the tile, the sound of it breaking would alert anyone listening that someone still moved… someone they hadn't killed yet.

It didn't.

He flicked open the flat head screwdriver bit and pried the glass, breathing a sigh of relief as the glass peeled open instead of shattering. It was plexiglass and coated in anti-shatter coating. Like a windshield, it meant he could peel it back almost like a candy wrapper.

Daniel snorted.

A candy wrapper was exactly what he had in mind. It wasn't the greatest way to survive, but the calories were better than nothing.

With the glass out of the vending machine, he eased it out and then slid it behind the machine. That way anyone looking would assume that the glass was just really, really clean instead of broken at first glance. *If I'm lucky, by the time anyone comes by here I'll be long gone*, he thought.

He looked at the machine and grinned. All they were left with was an empty vending machine and no idea what happened or who had emptied it.

A fabric bag, taken from behind the security desk and emblazoned with the city's logo, was perfect for looting the vending machine of every remaining snack from it. He eyed the other vending machine dispensing drinks, but there was no way to open it with no one immediately noticing someone had tampered with it from a distance.

Water was at least easy to get in the building, anyway. Not only were there quite a few water fountains, but a kitchen and a few bathrooms. Sinks were easy enough to find.

He looked up as he heard voices above him and moved as silently as he could down one of the side hallways.

One of these rooms had a sink, if memory served him correctly. When there were meetings, it was used to serve coffee and other drinks to entertain dignitaries and guests of the city. He remembered attending meetings in here when the city occasionally had to hear from community groups.

He crept in and closed the door behind him, turning around to look out the windows as he did.

A long, awkward moment ensued when he and one mercenary stared at each other.

*Well, shit*, he thought.

Daniel dropped the bag of candy bars from the vending machine. Instinct told him to go for his gun, but his hand went for the extendible baton that had replaced the 'billy'.

The soldier dropped his cup, and it fell silent on the carpet, spilling whatever had been in it. Water, from the look of it, but Daniel didn't pay any attention to that.

The baton came down on the soldier's hand just as he brought his gun up. Instead of the sharp retort of a gun, the soldier gasped. There was a sickening crunch. Bones—the soldier's hand.

Daniel had to give the man credit for not screaming.

Unfortunately, for the soldier, screaming would have saved his life and ended Daniel's.

With a punch up and into the man's nose, the soldier was dead before he hit the ground.

Daniel sucked in a breath. He almost dropped the baton from his hand.

Never in his fifteen years of being a cop had he ever had the misfortune of having to choose between his life and someone else's. Or a perp's life and an innocent. He had always prided himself on finding the peaceful way, or reasonably peaceful way, of making an arrest. He was more of a community connection—always one of the first to volunteer to go into schools and talk to kids and their parents.

*What have I done?* Daniel thought.

The soldier wasn't young—but he was younger. Only a few grey hairs peppered his hair.

Daniel dragged him into the closet. It wouldn't do for one of his buddies to happen by and see him. Well, not too soon anyway. Daniel steeled himself and reminded himself that this man, whoever he was, was party to killing unarmed civilians. He had been going for his gun when Daniel surprised him. A few more seconds the other way and Daniel would have been dead, and if there was any resistance in the building, they would have been one less person standing up for the duly elected official who hadn't given in yet.

*Score one for duty*, he mused. *A shitty way to go about it, but… what choice did I have?*

Daniel went back to his bag of junk food and picked it up. He stared at his stash and then back at the closet.

Opening the door again, he picked the soldier clean of anything useful. The gun and ammunition would help, even if it wasn't the same type of ammunition he used. As luck would have it, it was at least compatible with his own sidearm. The extra gun was welcome as well. If he found another civilian and they were able, that gave him someone he might deputize if he had to… and if he felt they could handle it.

Some could. Some couldn't.

He'd have to see.

Of course, finding Fitz in this mess would be useful. She probably wouldn't have a gun. Giving her one would definitely even the odds in his favour.

He grinned when he saw what law enforcement and other military organization affectionately nicknamed the 'earwig', which was nothing more than a tiny earpiece that fit subtly and almost invisibly into an ear. Most of the time, they appeared to be nothing more than hearing aids or a small ear pod for an iPhone.

After he cleaned it off, he slid it into his ear and the immediate reward of chatter and status updates from different mercenaries greeted him.

A sense of renewed purpose filled him, and for the first time since the entire mess had started, he felt like he had control again.

Their leader sounded familiar, and Daniel crinkled his brows. Through the earwig, the sound quality wasn't great, and it wasn't perfectly clear. It was more than a bit warbled… but something was familiar. He was sure he'd heard Harnet's voice before, but where?

He shoved this new puzzle off. It wasn't important right now.

What was important was that Victoria Piacentini still lived, and she wasn't giving them an inch. Even more important was the annoyed response to the fact that the police tower remained out of Harnet's control. Someone still lived over there, and they weren't buying what Harnet was selling.

Daniel grinned.

*That means allies*, he thought. *And allies means the odds just evened up*.

His grin faded as he drank the water he had come for and knelt to rummage through a cupboard for something to hold more water in that wouldn't spill like a cup. *Travel mug, empty pop bottle… or a full one—not going to complain about more calories I can use, something I can screw a lid on…* he sighed as he stood up again, opened the cupboards above the sink. *That wasn't used to hold cleaning solution…*

No amount of rinsing was worth that risk.

He paused. *Allies or no, how am I getting over there?*

Daniel couldn't walk there. The only hallway was long, narrow, and had no where to hide. Going outside through the promenade was worse. Not only was the weather freezing, but the whole reason City Hall had the wall of windows was for people to see that outdoor space.

*That leaves the parking garage*, he sighed, leaning his head against the cupboard.

He tilted his head as something across the room caught his eye.

*But first*, he thought, the grin returning to his face as he picked up the thermos. *I need water and a new hiding spot…*

\* \* \* \* \*

Marissa winced as she stepped into the living room and the din hit her. *Good heavens*, she thought, shuffling sideways to push through the crowd. Helen and Tyrell, who had joined them from up the road, were only the first ones to arrive on the farm. Sheridan's home was rapidly filling up with neighbours who were using her living room as a town meeting hall and its grand fireplace to warm up.

*Sheridan is going to have a real problem on her hands*, Marissa thought. *And really soon*.

The noise was enough to cause the two cats to vanish into the nether regions of the massive house—cold or no cold—and they had taken their two dogs to the barn.

*So familiar, yet so not*. Marissa watched Sheridan sitting on the couch in the living room, left alone despite in the middle of it all.

Sheridan and Terrence had met at an SCA event—a community of hobbyists who studied medieval history and then took it one step further by also living that history.

*Can't see how getting beaten by sticks, even if they're wrapped in foam, would be fun, but to each their own, I suppose*, she thought. *Especially while wearing full metal armour during the hottest times of the year. Her brain must be half-baked*.

Having so many people in her home had to remind her of that, but yet… it was entirely different.

Terrence was trying to get an accurate head count. With a shrug, he finally gave up. Sheridan sighed, pushed herself off the couch, and walked through the hallway into the foyer and up the stairs to the breezeway.

"How many?" asked Sheridan as she joined them.

"Well, I can tell you it's anyone that didn't rely on electricity—unless they were already off grid—for heat that's here," Terrence sighed and ran a hand over his face. "Unfortunately, there are quite a few people who didn't make it. We've confirmed at least ten households that are dead. Froze to death in their sleep last night."

"We're barely past our first week," pointed out Sheridan. "There are hundreds of homes past us and further down the road. Hundreds unaccounted for—they can't all be dead."

"Has anyone heard from Derek?" asked Terrence.

Marissa shook her head. "No, not yet. I'm a little worried. I didn't think he's stay out overnight."

Terrence frowned, running his fingers along the railing. "I still have a bad feeling about this. At least he took Jeremy with him, and his Jeep should be able to handle anything he gets himself into."

"But what would he get into?" asked Sheridan.

Marissa and Terrence looked at each other.

"That's the question, isn't it," said Marissa. "What *could* he get into? What, outside your neighbours, is there down that road?"

"My aunt on the Reserve, and there's Rick at the Marina," answered Sheridan. "Either would have put him and Jeremy up for the night. Maybe they're using it as a remote point to get further down the road?"

Terrence inclined his head, and sighed.

"Where does that leave us?" mused Terrence. "I mean, what can we even do? It's not like we can take in every single person in the entire area."

"Anything we can," answered Sheridan. "Everything we can. They're our neighbours... there are seniors and families."

Marissa sighed. Once Sheridan decided to help people, she knew there was no way of dissuading her. It was because she could not sit by and watch other people in her community suffer.

*This will make her particularly stubborn.*

Sheridan saw herself as part of her community and being a doctor only made that sense of responsibility all the stronger. "We could get a few teams of horses together and sleighs, but we've only two actual sleighs capable of carrying any amount of people."

"What about the carriages?" asked Sheridan.

"In three, four feet of snow?" Marissa lifted a brow. "Sheri, I know this is hard—"

"What if we sent teams with a few horses as pack animals and the people with snow shoes?" asked Terrence. "We could use the horses for the infirm and very young. The adults could walk, or even ski…"

"That would be better than nothing." Sheridan sighed and leaned on the railing. "In the meantime, we have more than enough scared people in our home that need an answer of what's coming next right now."

Marissa chewed her lip. Sheridan, would insist on finding aid for everyone, even if it meant stretching their already thin resources to the very limit.

*Uh oh*, Marissa thought.

Moments later, Sheridan turned to the both of them and said, "I have an idea."

"Christ," breathed Marissa. "Here we go, Terrence."

He groaned and leaned his head on the railing.

# CHAPTER EIGHT

"You can't be serious."

Derek looked over at Jeremy, and then in his rear-view mirror again. "I'm dead serious," said Derek, and he pointed back down the road with his thumb. "If that was you back there, what would you be hoping right now? And what kind of people would that make us if we didn't figure out a way to help? Especially after planting that false hope?"

Jeremy blew out a breath, tapping his fingers on the dash of the Derek's Jeep.

"It would make us shitty people," admitted Jeremy, and then he sighed. "Do you even have a plan?"

Derek shook his head. "Not at this point. Not beyond verbally challenging whoever cast that shadow behind Rick."

"You're counting on them to still have scruples with no sign of cops around," pointed out Jeremy. "Now, while normally that's a brilliant solution because usually we have 911 to fall back on… this is a very different situation because we don't have that."

"No, we have Terrence."

Jeremy's eyebrows rose, and Derek could almost hear Jeremy's: And what good will that do? "Think, Jeremy, what is Terrence well known for… almost infamous for?"

"Beyond being a pain in the ass?" asked Jeremy, and Derek lifted a single eyebrow. "The SCA, I guess. Ex-military, and not very, but… oh. He's a crotchety son of a bitch that everyone knows would turn tyrant if not for the long arm of the law holding him back. But all he has is that collection of swords. If whoever is back there has guns—well, you don't bring a sword to a gunfight. Even he knows that."

"And if they don't? What if all they have is intimidation?"

"Well, admittedly, the chance to see Terry go medieval on someone's ass is almost too good to pass up or seeing the threat of it be effective…"

Jeremy sighed. "I hope you know what you're doing."

*I won't say I'm hoping for the same thing*. Derek drove up the road slightly before finding a spot that was flat, and had plenty of room for him to turn the SUV around.

He only drove far enough to be within easy retreat to the Jeep before he turned it around again, this time facing back toward the Manor just in case they had to make a quick break for it. He got out of the Jeep and motioned to Jeremy. "Slide over here and take the wheel. If this goes south, I want to be able to just jump in and take off."

Jeremy walked around to the driver's side and got in. Derek watched him eye him all the way back around the corner. Once he was out of sight, he moved into the bush for cover.

Derek was a hunter.

He had always enjoyed spending time in the bush and in the peace that came with each camping trip. He hunted—but didn't like souvenirs. Hunting and fishing was for food, and he only ever took what would sustain him and those with him. Nothing more, nothing less.

However, a hunter and fisher who couldn't blend in and disappear when he had to was one that would starve.

Once into the cover the trees afforded him, Derek vanished.

He was confident that he wouldn't be found even if they knew to look for him. He stuck close to where the snow and ice could support his weight, or borrowed tracks and holes, so that he didn't leave his own tracks. Except for the whisper of wind through a gap in his jacket that he couldn't do anything about right now, he moved without a sound.

He wished he had enough time to get the rest of his hunting gear—the camo jacket would have been fantastic, and the hood and the white and black grease paint for his face. All he had was that the others he hunted weren't expecting him and would hopefully not look in his direction.

Derek took a breath.

If this went wrong, he was dead in five minutes. Instead of the shock and awe, they would shoot him. If they paused, he could use that to his advantage.

*If you don't see me coming, who else is with me?*

He hoped the bluff was enough.

He waited and then moved across by the house.

Still, no one spotted him.

Now, at least, he was close enough to hear what was said. His French wasn't the greatest, but he had a feeling the blonde woman was the one giving the orders. He didn't recognize her—but he knew a person more accustomed to the city and its comforts when he saw one.

Derek stepped out into the open.

He inwardly grinned as they looked up the road, and back at him, and then all around. He knew he hadn't left any tracks anywhere, so now they had a puzzle. With no idea how or where he had come from, was someone else with him?

Even Rick looked shocked.

"Where the hell did you come from?" demanded one man.

*Perfect, it's shock and awe*, Derek thought. *I can work with this.*

"Trade secret," Derek answered, finally grinning. "Where did you all come from? I know I didn't see you come down Panache Lake Road… so that means you came from somewhere else. I wonder where, though?"

"*Qui est-ce?*" demanded the woman.

Derek blew out a breath, and answered her demand to know who he was, "*Mon nom est Derek, qui êtes-vous?*"

"*Ce ne sont pas vos affaires! Je vous ai demandé en premier.*"

Derek sighed. *I think I told you, but anyway.*

The woman paced around and once her people came back and he heard them tell her there wasn't a trace. It was as if he had just popped up out of nowhere.

"*Oui, mais où venez-vous?*" she finally asked.

*Up the road, lady*, thought Derek. "*Le ranch sur la route. Je suis venu voir Rick, et maintenant je vous ai rencontré. Mais je ne te connais pas. Devrais-je?*"

The sudden chill in the air had absolutely nothing to do with the weather. Her eyes thinned, and she took a step toward him. "*Vous voulez dire que le Manor?*"

*Funny how she'd clarify if I meant the Manor or not*, realized Derek. That meant she knew of it. And judging by her reaction, she didn't like the idea he came from there. "*Oui.*"

"*Vous savez Terrence Scapael*," she finally said.

That wasn't a question. It was a statement. She knew who Terrence was, and she wasn't afraid of him in the least. Her previous—if dramatic—anger from before had become a chilly calm. *Oh crap*, realized Derek. *What have I done now?*

"And as you know him, then there's no point in continuing this in French. We both know he never learned a word of French outside of swearing in it," said Derek.

"An amusing fact about him, yes," she answered. "Not even the army could drill French into his stubborn head."

Derek breathed in deeply, forcing himself to remain calm. If she so much as got a hint of fear from him, he, Rick, and everyone else would be dead… and then she would be up the road and tearing Jeremy from Derek's Jeep.

Derek chuckled. "Stubborn. Yeah, that would fit him to a tee."

Her eyebrows rose, and a vaguely amused smile appeared. Some tension in the air dissipated. "So, Derek, who is from the Manor, how do you fit in? Did he send you?"

"Only to check on Rick, and see if he needed help," answered Derek. "Or anyone else."

"I am not interested in his help, nor his pretty little wife's help," snarled the woman. "Let us be frank with each other—Terrence would not send people to help anyone. He cares only for his own and no one else. But, Miss Perfect… her bleeding heart would care enough."

She waved this all off. "I am bored with this. State your wishes and begone."

Derek lifted a brow. "Get off Rick's land."

Her eyebrows rose at his tone. There was no question, no request. Derek's sharp bark was more of an order than anything else.

"Why the hell should I?" she demanded.

"Because it's not yours to take," answered Derek, and he leaned against the wall, crossing his arms as he did. "And, since we both know Terrence, I could get him to make you."

The woman took a step toward Derek, but he didn't move. His eyes narrowed slightly.

"You're bluffing. I don't hear any horses. No vehicles. You are alone." She took a step back and motioned toward him with her hand. "Kill them all."

Derek's eyes widened as he saw the first gun raise.

He dove behind a woodpile, and bits of wood and bark rained down over him as the gun fired. He heard more gunshots and poked his head out behind the woodpile. Rick was lying on the ground, the snow-stained red underneath him.

Derek closed his eyes and shook his head. *I'm so sorry*, he thought. *I honestly didn't think they would…*

He picked up a steel poker. A man, one of hers, came around the woodpile with his shotgun aimed just above Derek's head. A whoosh and a grunt were the only sounds Derek heard as he swept his feet out from under him. The ice cracked beneath him and the shotgun fired into the air.

Derek swallowed.

With his other hand, he swung a block of wood as hard as he could into the side of the man's head. Red stained the snow and ice. When the other man didn't get up, and Derek took the shotgun from him and what shells he could see. He loaded the shotgun as he pressed his back against one house, ducking back out as he fired at the woman as they retreated behind cover.

They still outnumbered Derek.

He took the momentary lull to disappear behind another woodpile, and from there into the bush. Finding a thick tree, he hid behind it as he willed his heart to slow down and his breathing to stop sounding so loud.

"*Où diable est-il allé?*" he heard her shout.

Another man answered, "*Je ne sais pas!*"

"*Cherchez des pistes!*"

"*Mais, Cecelie, il n'y en a pas à trouver! Il a disparu! Comme de la fumée…*"

Derek felt his heart slow down. He hadn't even left tracks for them to follow and had disappeared as completely as he had turned up. They couldn't find him.

He heard her wordless, frustrated shout and then nothing.

Derek looked around the tree and got his bearings.

As he had crept in, he snuck back out and back up to the Jeep.

Or where the Jeep should have been.

There were only tracks leading back up the road. Jeremy must have taken off when he heard the first of the gunshots, he thought, and he couldn't blame him, although his flighty nature had picked a bad time to leave Derek stranded.

At least the tracks were fresh.

Derek followed them until he saw taillights further up the road. Jeremy hadn't retreated far—just put a little distance between the fight and him. Derek pulled the passenger door open and jumped in, checking the back seat, and he looked at Jeremy.

Jeremy stared at him with wide eyes.

"What the hell happened back there?" he asked.

Derek shook his head and pointed towards the river. "Get us back to the ranch, Jeremy. I have something I need to tell Terrence."

# CHAPTER NINE

The darkened corner within the meeting room entry hid him from view. Daniel glanced down the wide hallway toward the Provincial Tower and then back to the rest of City Hall. The hallway was still deserted. He crept from one side to the glassed-in business centre, taking up a significant part of the main floor. He flattened himself against the wall, looking through the small windows that separated the business centre from the lobby of City Hall.

*Not out of the woods*, he thought. *Could still have a patrol in here…*

He ducked into a cubicle and crawled between the desks. Beads of sweat rolled down his neck and his legs ached from the strain. Poking his head around a last corner, he moved from the cubicles into the lobby of the business centre that led outside into the courtyard.

Sucking in a breath, he flattened himself on the floor, rolling to hide himself behind the low cupboards as a patrol walked outside. He held his breath, fully expecting the mercenaries to see him, but they kept walking. He relaxed on the floor, letting his head rest on the carpet. Entirely too close… he rolled over again, heading straight to the back of the business centre.

The door led from the business centre to a hallway separating the business centre from the cafeteria and another meeting room often used for Rental Tribunals, which also had a stairwell to the basement. Daniel tried the doorknob and almost groaned when the click softly echoed. The door didn't open. *Locked tight*, he thought. *Dammit. Now what?*

Daniel looked at the glass doors he had abandoned in favour of this path. *There are trees, and that stairwell down to the garage should be…*

Not twenty feet from the glass entry doors into the business centre was the stairwell down to the parking garage. It wasn't the stairwell he was looking for, but it would have to do. Daniel crawled to the doors and tested them.

They swung open with no hint of a problem, and he breathed out in relief. *Finally*, he thought. *Something goes my way.*

Daniel sucked in a breath as the freezing cold hit him. He stood up, keeping his body pressed against the building so that any observers looking out a window wouldn't immediately see an odd body suddenly end up out of place in the courtyard. Checking the area, he waited until the little hairs on the back of his neck settled before darting to the stairwell and — trying to not break his neck on the icy stairs in the process — he descended them until he stood in the parking garage.

Somewhere here was his own car, but it was his personal car — not his cruiser.

*Would have been nice — evened the odds a bit, but if I make it over to the police tower, I might get a bit of help there.*

He ducked between cars, hearing the echo of a set of footsteps. He peeked his head out, watching the soldiers as they walked towards the provincial tower parking garage.

Daniel resisted blowing out a sigh of relief.

Sound echoed too much down here. Moving around here was a risk — a large one.

The open space meant that the tiniest sound would travel from one end and back again. Thankfully, his boots were softer — quieter, with a thick tread meant for negotiating snow.

This made them far less likely to make noise—unlike the combat style boots the soldiers wore that clattered.

He waited until they started moving again.

The echo of their boots hid his own, and he matched their rhythm step for step.

For an hour, he ducked between cars, travelling in a zig-zag pattern from one end of the garage to the other while avoiding the circling patrol. Finally, he found himself at the entrance to the fenced off area for the city police, and waved at the camera, showing his badge as he did.

The gate creaked open, and Daniel winced.

The echo of footsteps changed.

Where before they were slow, almost relaxed, they were now quicker and moving his way. The gate opened enough for him to squeeze through just as the two soldiers came around the corner and spotted him.

Daniel couldn't resist.

He lifted one hand, his middle finger up, and then he ducked behind one cruiser as the soldiers opened fire. The gate creaked closed again just as one soldier reached it.

The rattle of the chain-link fence was telling.

"You son of a bitch," shouted the soldier. "Where the hell were you hiding?"

"Did I surprise you?" snapped Daniel. "You haven't beaten us yet. We're trapped now, but we won't always be."

Sparks flew from the metal fence and off the cars and cement dust as they peppered the wall behind him.

"You're wasting your ammo!" he shouted. "Best save it for later."

"Come out and say that!" shouted the other one.

"Okay, yeah, sure, there's this great coffee shop across the street," Daniel threw a patch where they could see it.

Their reflexes caused them to spray more bullets at the motion until one recognized it. "You... where did you get that?" he demanded.

"May want to check your numbers," said Daniel. "I'm just getting warmed up!"

"Report," came a voice in the earwig.

He heard the one soldier's response in both the earwig, and from the other side of the gate, "One man. Cop, I think. No idea where he came from, but he got into the police compound. He has one of our patches."

"Have everyone report in."

"Yes sir," said the soldier.

One by one, the mercenaries reported in.

All but one.

They called for him three times. The two soldiers turned silent. "Sir, Nigel isn't reporting in," said the one soldier.

"I can hear that," said their commander. "Nigel was where?"

"In Tom Davies," answered the soldier.

"Radio silence," came the order. "Return. Assume he has one of our radios."

"Good guess," said Daniel, loud enough for the two to hear him. "Best follow orders. Sorry about Nigel."

"You bastard," snarled the second soldier.

"I'm the bastard?" Daniel's voice rose. "I'm not the one who murdered unarmed citizens. That makes you murderers. *Criminals*. You know what my people do to criminals with guns?"

"Big talk for one man hiding behind a car."

"Run back to your Colonel, soldier boy," said Daniel. "And start praying."

"He's just trying to get a rise out of us," said the first one, calmer than he had been. "Worked for a bit. Won't for long."

Daniel waited until the footsteps were a long way away from him before taking a chance to even peek out from behind the cruiser. The door from the garage to the police door opened a crack, and Daniel took his chance to get through it before it slammed shut behind him, leaving him in complete darkness.

"That was the smartest thing I've ever heard, or the dumbest," said someone else. "Not sure on which." A flashlight lit up the darkness, and Daniel blinked in the sudden brightness. Holding the flashlight was a uniformed Greater City of Sudbury Police officer. "Now, who the hell are you?"

Daniel blinked again. "Constable Daniel Wither, Ontario Provincial Police."

"Sergeant Henri Lescelle," answered the other man, and they shook hands. "Did you really take down one of them?"

"Bare handed—not that I had much choice," said Daniel, as he followed Lescelle back up to the main floor of the tower. "I have never been so happy to see daylight without having to hide as I have been now."

"Where's your cruiser?"

"At home—with my uniform and sidearm," answered Daniel. "I was off duty. Came to see a friend and ran into another one. Got swept up in everything."

"So, that gun came from one of them?"

"Had little choice—we surprised each other. I wasn't about to make it easy, but with surprise on my side, it didn't take much to take him down. The baton came from one of the security guards. That poor bastard never even saw them coming," answered Daniel, shaking his head. "I... hid. I couldn't do anything."

"Sounds like you started right when you needed to," said Lescelle, with a shrug. "What could you do? With no vest and no side arm, or weapons at all, you did what you had to—you lived where others fell. That's one up for us, and a loss on their end. And then, to top it all off, you took one down."

Daniel blew out a breath. Lescelle was right.

"Listen, I think the Mayor is still alive," said Daniel.

"She's probably not even here," said Lescelle, his eyebrows rising. "I mean, why should she be? Probably at her cushy house wondering where the power is, like we all are… but… they are probably on their way there already."

"No, she's here," said Daniel, grabbing Lescelle's arm. "The friend I ran into was her. We were just about to part ways in the parking garage when her assistant came running downstairs and called us back upstairs."

Lescelle stared at Daniel. "You're serious?"

"Dead serious," said Daniel. "Listen, have you seen another woman? Around my height, light brown hair. Cuts it super short, prefers to wear northern Ontario formal wear…"

Lescelle squinted. "A woman with really short hair and I'm guessing blue jeans and a flannel coat."

"That'd be Fitz."

"I'm not even going to ask," said Lescelle. "I think I may have seen someone matching that description in the courtyard, but when things went haywire, she vanished. We have seen no one fitting that description since. Why?"

"If you want another person to help even the odds, Lance Corporal Moss, or Fitz, would be a significant addition to the team. Retired Navy SEAL. Never met up with her like we planned to, and I'm willing to bet she had to go to ground too."

"Shit, someone like that would be handy," admitted Lescelle. "I'll pass the word around. If she turns up, we'll make contact and bring her in."

He motioned to the room and over to the coffee machine. "For now, though, grab a coffee and warm up."

Daniel grinned and opened the bag of the junk food he had liberated from the vending machine. "Well, for that I think I can share this too."

Lescelle laughed. "Oh, I think you'll fit in fine here, being resourceful like that. Go, get yourself a coffee. I'm going to check on the others."

Daniel sighed and walked over to the window overlooking the old arena. Years ago, the arena had been the home of the local hockey team. Technically, it still should have been but, out of necessity, the team had moved out and now held their games at another local rink.

The city had never decided regarding the plan surrounding the arena. Some had always been in favour of moving the entire thing to another area of the city where there was more parking, while still others wanted to adopt a Toronto style of thought and just work with the area they had. After all, it was downtown—where everyone usually ended up.

Eventually, they left it downtown and use the parking across the street and in the City Hall garage. It wasn't as if they used the parking on the weekends or in the evenings.

Once they had made up their minds—and with a significant injection of funds from the owner of the team—they had gutted the arena. They propped up the front half of the building that held all the heritage with temporary steel beams.

Right now, all that remained of it was a snowy pit full of steel beams and concrete as midway through the builder pointed out that, like City Hall, there was more than enough space under the arena to dig out the parking with exits to Brady and the parking lot between City Hall and the arena.

Joining the steel girders and digging at the arena was that vacant area as plans for a parking garage and a new condo took form.

*It was nice while it lasted*, thought Daniel.

He had liked this idea. Condos were often great for an area, even if they added to the population load. Homeowners versus renters meant permanence and that the residents were slightly more invested in their home.

*Not that most renters aren't*, thought Daniel, as he knew this from experience. He still didn't own his own home and rented a small apartment close to here. *It's just that, by necessity, we often can't be.*

Lescelle came back, a few others with him. "So, if the Mayor is over in TDS, that means we have something we need to do."

Daniel put down his now empty coffee mug.

"We'll need a plan first," said one officer.

Daniel agreed with him, and Lescelle nodded. "All right, so here's my idea…"

\* \* \* \* \*

Garrett crossed his arms, standing in the middle of the road as he watched the snow machines leave. He squinted, noting that they headed in the same general direction as High Falls. He blew out a breath. Then again, the back road to Nairn is the same direction, he thought. They could have just as easily came from there.

There was a crunch—boots on hardened snow—as someone walked up behind him. He turned to look and saw that it was not either the old man or the young woman who had given him shelter.

He looked past the older woman to the others who were coming out of their homes.

Garrett looked from one face to the other.

There was no one younger than fifty in the entire group. Garrett remembered what Kovach had said about the old man 'holding back' and his stomach felt like it had sunk into his boots.

There were too few to fill all the houses in the subdivision, but there were enough cars in the driveways to suggest there once had been—and recently.

"What the hell happened here?" asked Garrett, his voice flat, looking from one person to the next. "And where are the cops? Why didn't any of you call them?"

The older woman closest to him blinked as she tilted her head up at him.

"You mean you had no idea?" she asked.

"About what?"

The others looked at each other before the old man who had sheltered him called from his doorway. "I kind of figured you didn't know."

His granddaughter helped him out of the house and over to Garrett. When he stumbled over a chunk of ice, Garrett reached out to help steady him. "You took a hell of a hit," said Garrett. "Not sure if it's wise to be up and around yet."

"And remind people that they nearly let you die out here?" asked the old man, waving off his concern. "Of which the lot of you should be ashamed. Even I could tell he wasn't one of 'em. Came from the wrong direction and alone."

"It could have been a trick," said the older woman who had first approached Garrett. "See if they could catch us out."

"They've already caught us out," answered the old man. "No point sending another one in."

"Who are they?" asked Garrett, throwing up his hands. "I'm no closer to an answer than I was when you first started talking."

"Slavers," answered the young woman.

Garrett's eyes widened, and for the half-dozenth time today he felt his eyebrows rising. "They're what?"

"They started coming here a few weeks ago," said the old man. "At first, didn't seem too bad.

Came asking for a cup of sugar, even exchanged stuff. But that didn't last long. Once they knew we were out here alone, the threats started."

"They killed some others," said the young woman. "Those who tried to stand up for themselves or others. Anyone else under fifty they started taking… just a few at first."

"I take it only what they could take on those snow machines?" asked Garrett, and she shook her head. "Then what?"

"That whistle you heard?" asked the old woman, and when he nodded. "Train. Came through here and bundled them off in boxcars and headed back west with them. It doesn't come all the way now. No point. We're all too old. But someone clearly tipped off Kovach about Mira."

Garrett looked at the young woman who the older woman was pointing at, the same one who had hidden in the closet with him. "Well, now I at least know your name," he groused, and she blushed. "Not that I told you what mine is."

"Well, you know Mira now, and I'm Roch." Garrett nodded, and Roch continued. "She's Josephine, but we usually just call her Jo."

Garrett looked around at the others. "Garrett."

"Pleased to meet you, especially after what you've done for Mira and me," said Roch. "It was certainly a pleasure watching that bastard get his for once. Never saw anyone actually put the run on them."

Josephine sighed from behind him. "It won't last long. Kovach will not suffer that insult. They'll be back, in force, and there will be hell to pay. You've bought Mira time, but that's all."

"Maybe he could get Mira out of here," said one other, and Garrett lifted his brow. "Go back in the direction you came from—get out of range."

"What about us?" asked another.

Roch put two fingers in his mouth and whistled, silencing them. "Hold on a minute. Maybe we should ask Garrett what he wants."

Garrett blew out a breath.

There was no way to evacuate the entire town. The tracks they would leave in the snow would leave the slavers straight to them. Could hide in the mountains and the bush, he thought. Not going to get a snow machine—or a train—up there.

He looked at what they left of the people living in the town.

They were all older, except for Mira. No one would get into the mountains easily. Garrett ran a hand down his face before putting his hands on his hips.

"Well, I'm not leaving you like this," he said finally. "I pissed of that Kovach fellow, so he'll be back looking for me. I won't disappoint him—but if he thinks I'm going to be easy to push over, he's got another surprise coming."

Roch stared at him. "I don't know what to say…"

"Say nothing," said Garrett. "You're the one that sheltered me."

# CHAPTER TEN

"If I could have your attention, please," shouted Sheridan.

The din below her didn't quite fall silent, but it was a start. Marissa compressed her lips into a thin line. As the murmur of voices quietened, they turned to look up at Sheridan where she stood flanked by Marissa and Terrence.

"I promise you everyone here will survive the winter," began Sheridan.

Marissa fought with her eyebrows to keep them from rising. That would take an actual miracle, but she could see some faces in the crowd lose the fear they had held. It wasn't quite hope, but they were listening.

Sheridan continued, "But I need something from you."

"What?" asked someone from within the crowd.

Another asked, "And how the hell are we going to survive all winter?"

Loud voices travelled back and forth as doubts filled the air.

Sheridan held up her hands, and the shouting that had risen once more fell back to scattered murmurs before the room silenced. She explained, "We are going to have to work together on this, but we can do it. First things first. We need to find all survivors in an area we can reach while on foot in half a day—half a day there... and then half a day back."

She let that sink in. Marissa looked at the crowd as a few shifted their weight from foot to foot, looking at each other. A pall had descended over the room. "These are our neighbours and friends. Some are even family. We can't leave anyone without what they need to survive through the winter if we can help it. And—I promise you—we can."

Marissa knew what they were thinking, but she wouldn't voice it. She didn't have to wait long for someone else to do it.

"How do you propose to do that?"

"Shared between all of us are enough resources, and this is the key point. We need to share evenly so that we all survive. Of course, we will accommodate those with special needs."

"And how will you know that?" came another voice.

This time Marissa didn't stay silent. "Sheridan is a doctor."

The answering silence was almost deafening. It was as though the din had been a wall she was leaning against and the wall had abruptly given way. And then the noise erupted again.

"Medical?"

"Or are you a vet?"

Terrence whistled through the din and everyone fell silent again.

"Medical," she answered. "A surgeon, to be more specific. There is a vet—my cousin Shiloh is one. We both have a thing for horses if you couldn't tell."

There were a few chortles at this, and some tension eased. Marissa looked over the crowd again. Lines of worry in many faces had faded. People were relaxing bit by bit. *Point out there's a doctor in the house and suddenly we all feel confident again,* thought Marissa.

"Now that we have that out of the way, let's get into the nitty gritty of just how we are going to survive," Terrence said as he leaned on the rail, letting Sheridan take a moment. "I'm Terrence, some of you know me. Those of you who don't soon will. This is going to be the hardest winter we've had in living memory. It's not just the weather—it's what we're facing. As my wife said, we can survive it. First—as she said—we're going to need to share resources. Food, water, blankets, tools, and building supplies. Everything and anything. People, we live in an area where there are more than enough resources under our noses to build what we need. The second part, however, will not be so pleasant. There are going to be those who didn't make it—and they also have resources. We're going to have to scavenge the rest... from them."

"You're kidding," said someone. "But... what about our neighbours?"

"The dead don't need it and the living do," said Terrence.

"What if someone doesn't want help, but also doesn't want to share?"

Terrence took a breath, but Sheridan stepped up and put a hand on his shoulder. Marissa swallowed her chuckle. She knew Terrence well enough to know what his answer would have been. "Leave them be," she answered. "We won't steal what's theirs, nor will we shove what's ours down their throats. If they change their minds later, so be it."

Terrence lifted a brow as he looked at his wife and she stared right back. Finally, he shrugged. Marissa had a sneaking suspicion he wouldn't leave that alone, but it was a fight for later. Right now, Sheridan had the right of it.

Aggression won't gain us allies at this stage of the game, and that's what we need right now, Marissa thought.

"How are we getting around?" came another voice in the crowd.

"We have horses," pointed out Terrence. "Mind you, this is also where teamwork comes into play. We need to clear the roads we need ourselves, but only enough for basic foot and horse traffic. It won't have to be perfect as we'll end up packing down most of it."

"We also can't all stay in the Manor, much as I'd like you to," said Sheridan. "We don't have the space for us all long term. Short term, it's fine—no one panic, you're all staying where you are for now. However, eventually, we will need to build a town around the Manor so we're all closer to each other. If your home is already close by, all the better."

Terrence and Sheridan looked at each other, and Marissa poked Terrence in the arm. "What about the wall Derek had thought about?"

"What wall?" asked someone close enough to hear.

Soon, the room was calling for another set of answers. Sheridan chuckled. "I guess the cat is out of the bag," she breathed, and then cleared her throat so that the entire room could hear her. "I'll let Terrence explain this one."

Terrence sighed. "Anyone north of the escarpment that's just up the road needs to move south of it. We will build an ice wall for the winter. I don't think we'll need it, but I'd rather be safe than sorry. We may not be aggressive about taking resources, but it doesn't mean someone else won't want what we have and be willing to just take it. In the summer, it will become a timber wall."

The murmuring and doubt had risen again, and Sheridan slapped her hand on the rail. "Listen to me! I know it will be hard. We weren't prepared. The best we can do is whatever we can with what we have… and we have quite a bit. If it's a waste of time, then fantastic. We lost nothing and kept our hands busy while waiting this out," she took a breath and continued. "But if it is necessary, then two ounces of prevention will beat the pound of cure we will need if it comes to it. I would sleep better at night knowing we took the precaution rather than not, and I know you all would, too."

"We'll need volunteers," said Terrence. "I won't lie and say this will be easy either, but many hands make quick work."

A good three quarters of the room raised their hands, and Marissa saw Terrence's eyebrows rise. "Fantastic," he exclaimed. "Great—we'll take your names later. With this many volunteers, it will be quick work."

Sheridan nodded. "We all know what we have to do. We'll reconvene as we need to."

The crowd dissipated in her living room, and Sheridan allowed herself to lean on the railing. "What have we done?" she asked quietly.

Marissa laid a hand on her shoulder. "The only thing we can do."

"There's still no word from either Derek or Jeremy," said Terrence, and he sighed. "I mean, keeping busy is great and all, but I'm getting worried."

\* \* \* \* \*

A small furrow formed just between Gina's eyes as she stared out at her driveway. The blizzard had buried everything in a sea of drifting snow. She sighed. *All of that hard work*, she thought, rolling her eyes. *And gone like I never did a damned thing*.

Beyond the driveway was a snow filled valley and frozen lake. Before, the highway would have been busy with traffic. But now it, too, had vanished beneath the drifting snow.

Now it was empty. Lonely.

Still.

She was alone except for Vincent, and now Russell.

She didn't know what she would have done if not for Vincent.

While dunes were not unfamiliar, she was used to sand and heat. And, compared to this, a little snow.

Growing up in the Kosciuszko area, she was used to snow, but until coming to Canada had never experienced even a small amount of it. To see snow turn into dune-like drifts that shifted and changed the same way as sand was... surreal.

She tapped the window ledge of the darkened house at the bottom of the hill.

The glass had frosted over. With no heat, everything froze solid quickly. She knew the house would be full of broken and burst pipes as the water froze and expanded in them.

The water damage would speed up the rate of decay in these houses.

Gina sighed as she pushed herself off from where she leaned against the wall as Paul rode up to her. "I don't have much fuel left," he said. "I'll be resorting to skis and snowshoes soon, unless..."

She followed his gaze.

"It'd be a huge risk going into Sudbury," she pointed out.

"We could find out for sure!" he said. "It'd be two birds with one stone. We could see what we could find for supplies and see what's going on — maybe things are fine in town and they just haven't gotten out here yet."

"You heard the explosions! What do you think they meant?" she asked. "I didn't hear any sirens from emergency services, did you?"

As if the former was bad enough, what the lack of the second meant was clear to Gina, even if Paul continued to hope. But she had to admit he had a point. "We're running out of food, Gina," said Paul. "This lake is too small to sustain us. We either get food or we're all going to starve to death."

"All right," she admitted.

Paul blew out a breath and then sighed. "Well, good then. Now what?"

Gina's eyebrows rose. "What, you didn't plan for this? Even though you kept at me about it?"

He shook his head. "I honestly thought you'd fight more, and I was busy planning arguments to convince you, and then I thought you'd figure it out," he admitted, and when she blinked slowly, he continued. "You've had an answer for everything so far."

Gina looked over the lake, and then around her subdivision where houses stood like silent sentinels, some half buried in snow. "We could start here," she pointed out, tapping the wall of the house she leaned against. "See if anyone has a way to open a door without destroying anything too badly. I don't want to empty a house only to have a bear move in, or animals, to further destroy it. Just in case this is only a blip."

Paul nodded. "All right."

She pointed her thumb at the house she had been leaning against, and Paul shook his head as he laughed. "Point taken," he said. "You want me to go get some gear?"

"Would be handy," she answered. "I have a few things in the car, but not much that would help here."

"Well, we can start this tomorrow," said Paul. "I'd like to get some fishing in while we have a good chance of catching something and the others are still out hunting."

"Good idea," said Gina. "Save your fuel— we'll probably need it when we take that chance and check out the city."

He nodded and waved as he turned his snowmobile around before riding back across the lake. Gina waited until he disappeared around the wooded point and to the bay where he lived, before she turned and trudged back up the hill to her house. Vincent brought her a cup of hot tea, and as she sipped at it, he said, "Russell was asking what your plan was."

"How's he doing?" she asked.

"Much better," answered Vincent. "He's not as dizzy, and his colour and energy are both far better than yesterday."

"Both good signs," she murmured, and then sighed as she looked at her roommate. "Paul wants to head into town and see what's going on and to see if he can get fuel. He's running low."

Vincent's eyebrows rose. "I don't think that's a good idea."

"Same here," admitted Gina. "But he had a point. We're running low on food and supplies. We need to get what we can—presuming there's something there to get, anyway."

"There's the rub, right?" asked Vincent. "May not be at this point. May have already been wiped clean."

"I think he just wants to check it out for himself," said Gina, sipping the tea again.

She allowed it to warm her from the insides out. It didn't seem to matter how many layers she put on before going out. The cold just seeped in. Her joints stiffened, and she had to force them to move. How Vincent, or Paul, or any of the others, ran around, fished, and even hunted in this was mind-boggling. Not for the first time, Gina wished for summer.

*I can wish for summer all I want. It won't get here any faster*, she thought. *It's getting colder. If what they tell me is true, January and February are worse than this. Jeez Louise, I hope this is just a blip...*

Gina sighed as she finished her tea, moving closer to the fireplace as she did. She stripped off the outer layers until she was to the dry, and warm, layer. She flopped onto the couch and put her feet up.

Vincent watched her. "Are you going to take him into town?" he asked, as if there had been any doubt that if Paul went who would lead the expedition.

She opened her eyes and sighed again. "Yeah, probably," she answered, throwing her hands up in the air before letting them fall again. "I mean, who else is there, am I right?"

Vincent lifted a single brow. "Who else indeed."

"What the hell happened? How did I end up leading everyone?" she wondered. "I'm from Australia—I don't have the required experience! Australia doesn't have this much snow, so this isn't exactly my natural habitat. Every single time I go outside I feel like I'm walking into a giant freezer determined to turn me into a meat Popsicle."

"It's because you took charge and gave people a sense of direction," said Russell as he walked into the living room, rubbing his eyes as he did so. "I'd like to see if I can find my Aunt and Uncle. They aren't far from here, as the crow flies, and if you're going into town anyway..."

"Look, much as I'd love to go looking for more survivors," started Gina.

"—They're right behind the Walmart," said Russell. "By a snow machine trail, two minutes. If that. My Uncle is an avid outdoorsman. Hunting, fishing, you name it. I know he's an old man, but his experience—and what he has for gear—would be invaluable to us if the world has gone up in smoke. You'd lose nothing to go look and possibly gain quite a bit in looking. If they're dead, I can tell you where they hide their key. Take his gear at least. At least I'll know."

Gina looked at Vincent, who only shrugged. "If they're as close as he says they are, they aren't out of the way at all. And if his Uncle has what he says he has, we have too much to lose by not at least looking."

"What if your uncle refuses to leave?" asked Gina.

"Oh, I *know* he will refuse," admitted Russell. "No 'if' there. However, give him a good reason to leave and get him to let you move his gear and we've got another person who can get us through the winter and then even the summer."

"All right," said Gina, holding up her hand. "You've convinced me. If Paul and I even go, I'll go look in on your Uncle."

"Thank you…"

"Don't thank me yet. Right now, you only have a gut feeling he's still alive," she said, and she pointed at him. "I might bring back bad news… and his stuff… instead of good news."

# CHAPTER ELEVEN

Even though the snow had stopped, it didn't mean that it had gone away. It now gathered in drifts enough to bury cars or valleys down to the pavement.

The latter was handy for Daniel.

The former, not so much.

He followed Lescelle between the tallest of the drifts, using them as camouflage and spots to hide until they had gone around the building to the entry to the front public entry just off Brady street. Here, the glass doors were next to the council chambers. A ramp and a set of stairs climbed to these doors directly from the sidewalk, close to the crosswalk and a set of lights.

Concrete planter boxes with evergreen shrubs planted in them blocked wind and snow from clogging the entry. *Not the most attractive choice they could have made to put into those boxes*, he thought. *But I imagine they're easier to keep tidy.*

Daniel hid behind one.

Lescelle moved to one side of the doors, behind one planter box, and Daniel took the other side. The team they had taken with them fell into place further down the steps.

Daniel looked up and pointed. Lescelle's gaze followed.

Directly above them was the corner office—the largest in the building—and it belonged to the Mayor. Lights moved around. Daniel sucked in a breath.

*If anyone looked out that window, we'd be sitting ducks*, he realized.

Lescelle motioned for them all to move a little closer to the building, hiding between the planter boxes. Once they had, they were well hidden—now that they were under the ledge. They designed the building entry like a cut-out box. The doors below were below the second floor as it jutted out above the stairs and ramp leading up to them. It served as a shelter from the weather below, and extra real estate above.

For them, it meant they were out of sight of anyone on the second floor and hidden from the street.

*Now we wait*, thought Daniel.

This was the hardest part. There were three other teams—one coming from the garage, one from the hallway connecting City Hall and the Police Tower, and a third that would serve as a decoy in the courtyard. Daniel and Lescelle had made it to where they needed to be a few minutes ahead of when the decoy team would start 'getting seen and heard'.

*I hope they're on time, too*. Daniel looked at the others, signing where he wanted them to be. *Even if they aren't, once we move in, they can catch up with us.*

Gunfire erupted, echoing over and around the buildings. Some of it wasn't gunfire, but liberated firecrackers from an evidence locker. Its entire purpose was a distraction, and once lit close to the Larch entrance of the courtyard—closer to the provincial building, it signalled it was time to go.

That had been the timed part. No one was there—it was just to draw attention to that side and hopefully split Harnet's forces.

He could hear swearing, and it wasn't anyone he recognized.

"That a southern accent?" asked one of the other city cops, and Daniel could hear what he was talking about.

Someone was giving orders, and the accent was clearly not Canadian. "I think you're right—these aren't our people at all," said Lescelle, his lips compressing into a thin line as he looked over at Daniel. "Well, shit… I thought we were on better terms than this with the US."

"I don't think they're actually US Army," said Daniel. "Private militia maybe. The patches I saw weren't government… or at least any I know."

"Opportunistic bastards," muttered Lescelle, but he motioned to the others to move up. "If they're up here, I don't even want to know what's going on south of the border."

One of the two that had hung back ran forward, a device in their hands. Daniel grinned, knowing what it was. It had a few nicknames, but his favourite was the Door Knocker—a powered siege battering ram meant for taking down doors. It was overkill on glass, but it was fast.

Both doors into Tom Davies Square fell off their hinges, and their team moved in, pressing themselves into corners for cover.

The unfortunate part about this entrance was there wasn't that much cover to be had. Glass walls, meant to give the floor an open sense, were the only barrier between them and death.

All they could do was stay low, and dart from hiding spot to hiding spot.

This didn't matter.

The distraction, one by Larch and the one coming from the courtyard itself, had taken all the mercenaries' attention. The team from the parking garage below came up, a few minutes late but still present, behind Harnet's people by the elevators and created an opening.

Minutes later, the fourth and final team flooded in from the hallway and swept in from the other side.

Gunfire from above rained down, but by then most of them hid below. Daniel motioned to the council chambers. "If memory serves, there's a direct elevator or set of stairs from there up to the fourth floor. I think Victoria told me it's been handy a few times."

"That's news to me," said Lescelle.

"It's new—they built it in a few years ago," said Daniel.

Lescelle motioned to the two teams from the hallway and the garage to hold where they were and to take the upper floors if they could. Lescelle looked over at Daniel, "Let's go."

Daniel led the way to the council chambers and down into the rotunda. There was a curtained off area behind the mayor's desk.

A fire door greeted them, and the paint on the wall and on the frame was significantly newer than the wall they set it into. "I'll be a monkey's uncle," breathed Lescelle.

They went through the door and followed the underground hallway until it met a set of stairs, and another door marked Exit. "Private fire exit," said Lescelle, and then he pointed at the other set of stairs. "Where do those go?"

"Victoria never said," answered Daniel, shrugging. "If I had to guess, panic exit in case of something like today."

Lescelle grunted, and they led the team up the stairs.

It was oddly quiet, but then again no one but the Mayor and her personal security was supposed to know this part existed.

*Yet*, thought Daniel. *A glowing exit sign is a little obvious to not get noticed for too long.*

He held up a hand, as he could hear voices on the other side of the door. One of them was Harnet, and the other was—ever defiant—Victoria. Lescelle looked over at Daniel, his eyebrows raised, as if to say, *Is she always like that?*

Daniel snorted and shrugged.

Gunfire on the same floor erupted, orders started getting shouted. Daniel held up his hand, three fingers held up.

A body hit the floor, and the sound of a chair behind a desk scraping the floor as it was pulled out. He hoped that meant Victoria had taken cover. He curled one finger so only two were up.

Harnet shouting more. Return fire. Their people yelling back and for the unknown militia to drop their weapons.

Daniel curled one more finger.

Harnet yelled again, but no one had fired a gun.

*Stalemate*, thought Daniel, and he nodded to Lescelle. *Time to change that.*

He dropped his hand and made a cutting motion at the door. The two cops with the Door Knocker took the last two steps up and the device slammed the door open.

"Drop your weapons!" shouted Lescelle. "You have nowhere to go!"

Daniel had a single moment of satisfaction at the shock and surprise on the mercenaries' faces before they recovered and sprayed bullets in their direction. Daniel fell back, dropped a few stairs as bullets embedded in the cement wall above him. Concrete chips and dust rained down on him.

Lescelle wasn't so lucky.

*Dammit*, Daniel swore, seeing the older man fall.

He knew Lescelle was dead. That much automatic fire tore through him like paper. Daniel looked through the door through the iron railings and saw Victoria looking back at him, staring from behind her desk.

He motioned for her to stay put. There was no way she could make a break for it and not get hit, and her desk was heavy enough to absorb the gunfire. He wasn't sure for how much longer, but they had at least stopped firing in their direction.

There was a blur of motion, and they wrenched the Mayor from her hiding spot. Daniel slapped the wall beside him.

If they had got her out, the mercenaries would not have had any leverage.

It would have ended one of two ways—either they would have had to surrender or… and Daniel didn't really like this option much… he and the other officers would have cleared them out forcibly.

"I think this is who you came for," said Harnet. "As you can see, this whole exercise will be pointless if she doesn't walk out of this."

"I'm not important," she yelled. "Do what you have to!"

"I think she's quite wrong on that," chuckled Harnet. "We both know she's the only one who can make sense of this situation we're all in. Without her, whatever civilization we have right now disappears."

"Kill her and your coup is illegal," said Daniel. "And we'll have full legal right to put you down."

"Not spoken like a cop, there," said Harnet.

Daniel still couldn't see him. All he could see was one of Victoria's high heeled feet and part of a leg. Now that he could hear him clearly, there was something familiar about the voice. "Wasn't always a cop," said Daniel, and he motioned to the other officer who probably could see them.

The woman shook her head.

*Not even a clear shot. Dammit*, thought Daniel.

With a few more motions, he clarified that the minute she had a clear shot to take it. She nodded, keeping her gun ready.

"Tell you what," said Harnet. "I will call this stalemate for what it is. I will give you back your Mayor, unharmed, but I expect the same courtesy. We can continue this another day."

Daniel crinkled his brow, and he looked at the others. "If he keeps his end of the deal, we get another crack at this," whispered one.

"If he does," whispered another.

"If he doesn't, shoot him… and clear out the others," whispered Daniel, and he motioned to the cop at the top of the stairs, and she nodded in understanding.

"Fine, but you send the Mayor over to the door. When she's clear, the others clear out," agreed Daniel, and he raised his voice. "Is that clear?"

"Crystal!" came a muffled answer from the other team.

Harnet allowed the Mayor to stand on her two feet. "Clear a path," said Daniel.

While the other officers disappeared into the various corners, Harnet and the others ran. Victoria ran down the six steps to the same landing as he stood on, and stripped off a vest, throwing it back into the office. "Get me out of here!" she shouted. "Everyone out!"

Daniel's eyes widened.

"That double-crossing bastard!" exclaimed the officer at the top of the stairs. "*Bomb!*"

Daniel had never descended an emergency exit so fast in his life. Just as they ran through the bottom door in the basement and slammed the fire door shut, a low rumble shook the building. Concrete and dust rained out on them. "Head count?" asked Daniel. "Everyone still breathing?"

"Yeah, we're still breathing."

"Back to the police tower, expect resistance," said Daniel, hiding the Mayor behind him. "Shoot any of them that poke their heads out."

He turned to face her. "I'm fine," she said. "Thank you for coming for me. I'm glad you didn't leave after all."

"Well, I didn't have to arrest you at least," said Daniel, and she rewarded him with one of her glares. "Come on, let's get you back to safety and we can work on getting the rest of this place back."

\* \* \* \* \*

Garrett shifted in the bed, stretching his legs as he found himself in an almost bone cracking yawn. He opened one eye a sliver and groaned as he rolled over and pulled the blanket over his shoulders. It was still dark out, but that meant little. It could have been noon and just as dark.

With a grunt, he flopped on his back and stared at the ceiling.

*I'm awake now,* though, he thought. Dammit.

He threw the blankets off, winced, and then pulled them back over his body while shivering. He was most definitely awake now—the crispness of the air hitting his bare legs had much to do with that.

Garrett pushed himself up and looked around the room.

The previous few days had not been a dream.

*I'd almost hoped.* He blew out another breath. *I'd almost hoped this was my bed and the whole thing was a bad dream.*

He grunted as he stood, hunting for his clothing.

A short while later, he was running his hand down the hallway wall as he made his way into the kitchen. His stomach protested a distinct lack of sustenance—and the tantalizing aromas of bacon and eggs were making those protests more insistent by the second. While he had never liked coffee, he did like the smell.

"I smell breakfast," he said as he walked into the kitchen.

Mira looked up, grinning as she flipped the eggs in the pan. "Grampa said you would probably want something to eat this morning." She frowned, staring at the pans. "I wish it wasn't the last, though."

Garrett crinkled his brow. "I don't follow."

She stared at him and then shook her head. "I keep forgetting you're from the city. You couldn't have known."

"Known what?" he asked.

Roch came around the corner from the living room. "Let it be, Mira, it was bound to run out sooner than later. Better it get eaten than go off."

"What the hell is going on out here?" asked Garrett. "First those yahoos come through here, and it's not the first time, and now you're telling me you couldn't just go to the grocery store?"

"Are you telling me there weren't any shortages?" asked Roch.

Garrett blew out a breath. But Roch had a point. For months, the shelves had sat mostly empty and there had been purchase limits on something as simple as flour and sugar. But this had only been for the major stores—the ones supplied by the chains and from out of town. The local farmers and food producers had been able to almost, but not quite, fill in the gaps.

"No, there was," admitted Garrett. "Sure, it was tight, but the local farmers could still supply at least the very basics."

"At what cost to supply a city?" asked Roch, leaning against the counter. "There was not enough to supply everyone. Sacrifices had to be made."

Garrett leaned against the doorjamb for support. "Wait, no, they couldn't have…" he breathed.

"They did." Mira's voice was quiet. "To supply the city, they starved the rural areas."

"But couldn't you just come to town?" asked Garrett, and then he sucked in a breath.

"Was there no one at those lights in Denlou to stop you?" asked Roch.

That military checkpoint.

Garrett had questioned it—but the dawning horror of its actual purpose came all too clear.

Roch nodded. "They weren't to keep you. But they will be now that you know."

"Who the hell is Kovach, then?" asked Garrett. "I didn't see a uniform on him."

Roch shrugged. "I don't think he is really connected to them. I don't know that for sure, but..."

"He seems to be just taking advantage of an opening," finished Mira, as she turned the little camp stove off.

Garrett looked at the food on his plate and nodded to her. Normally, he would have eaten was in front of him and not paid attention to what was sitting on the plate, but now he took his time with it. Once he finished, he sighed as he took his plate to the sink.

"There's a meeting at our community centre later," pointed out Roch. "I was hoping you'd come."

"All right," said Garrett. "I'll be there."

# CHAPTER TWELVE

Derek was silent the entire ride back to the Manor. He could see, in the reflection on the window, how many times Jeremy glanced in his direction. There was nothing he could say. Nothing he could have done.

Wasn't there?

Derek had been so sure that all he had to do was point out that just up the road was law and order—people who cared about others—and that this Cecelie wouldn't…

… *Wouldn't order the deaths of everyone.*

Derek blinked.

*Kill them all.*

Three simple words.

And just like that, they had killed Rick in front of him, and so had at least five others. Everyone in that little clump of homes by the marina was likely dead, and Derek had been powerless to stop it.

There was no sense to any of it.

What was her problem, anyway? The mere mention of Terrence hadn't caused fear—it had caused white fiery anger. *Bitter anger... like...* Derek's eyes widened.

A week ago, a woman had come to Terrence's door. Derek hadn't been there, but he had been on speaker phone, talking to Terrence about another solar project in Blind River. When the woman came to the door, Terrence had left the phone on and Derek could hear both sides of the conversation.

Now that he thought about it, the woman's name had been Cecelie.

He didn't hear the entire conversation, but Terrence had thrown her out. When asked, he also didn't want to talk about it. Something about...

"Hell hath no fury like a woman scorned," said Derek, his eyes widening.

"What?" asked Jeremy, shocked by Derek's sudden outburst.

Derek, with a sigh, turned to look at Jeremy. "Were you around when someone came to the door wanting Terrence? A blonde woman? French, possibly?"

Jeremy tilted his head slightly. "No, but I remember Shiloh being ready to climb a wall in anger. Something about a gold digger wanting the Manor."

"I think I just found her again," said Derek.

"Seriously?" asked Jeremy.

Derek shrugged. "I'll have to ask Terrence."

"What happened back there?" asked Jeremy, but Derek shook his head. "All right, fine. But I heard gunshots. Where are the others?"

Derek shook his head again.

Jeremy sighed.

It relieved Derek to see the gates of the Manor and hear the gravel crunch under the tires of the Jeep. Once Jeremy stopped the SUV and killed the engine, Derek slid out of the passenger side and walked into the house.

He looked around, noticing the increased activity and population. While the house could handle this level of activity—been designed for it— it never had been this full. They probably finally have every room and every bed full, he thought. Derek walked into the study Sheridan shared with Terrence and found Terrence bent over a table with a map of the area on it. "We've got a problem."

Terrence jumped and then stared at Derek. "Where the hell have you been? We've been worried sick."

Derek sucked in a breath. "Busy."

Terrence inspected him, and Derek wondered what he saw. Did the ex-military part of Terrence see the death he just experienced? See the guilt? He didn't have time to find out, as moments later both Marissa and Shiloh, Jeremy not too far behind his own wife, ran into the room. "Derek, you… you…" Marissa ran up to him. "What the hell happened?"

"Jeremy said something about a gunfight, and you being on your own," said Shiloh.

Marissa and Terrence gasped, and both of them stared at Derek. The gaze from Terrence was one of sudden understanding. "I think you should sit, my friend, and let Shiloh or Reese get you both some coffee, or something else hot," said Terrence, pointing back at the kitchen. "I don't mean to be a boss, here, but they could use it. Pour something extra in for Derek."

Shiloh blinked, but nodded. Marissa didn't follow, choosing to sit beside her husband on the leather couch in the study.

A few moments later, while Derek stared at his hands, Shiloh returned with two steaming hot mugs. Sheridan followed her, and she took one look at the both of them and then sat down across from them in a chair. Derek looked up, and a stray thought strafed across his mind, *She looks almost like a Queen, sitting like that…*

"Where do I start?" he said finally, after taking a few long drinks from the mug.

It was coffee, mixed with hot chocolate… and, if he wasn't mistaken, a good amount of Bailey's Irish Creme. The warmth hit him in the chest first and then spread outward from there. He hadn't even noticed the cold until he had something warm to compare it too. How much was due to what happened, and how much to what it was actually like outside, Derek didn't know.

"How about start at the point Jeremy left off," suggested Shiloh. "The part where you turned your Jeep around and pointed it back North to here and told him to take over the driver's seat."

Derek sucked in a shuddering breath.

"We went to the marina, and found Rick," he started.

"I was there for that," said Jeremy. "Something wasn't right. Rick was insisting we leave but come back later. With Terrence and Shiloh. We knew that was a call for help, but we didn't know why. So, we headed up and Derek turns around, and then he hides his truck and me up past the hill and around the bend. Not too far away, but not so close as to see easily."

"And then he took off on his own?" realized Terrence, looking over at Derek. "You went back on your own—alone, with no idea what you were up against. Unarmed, even."

"How the hell was I supposed to know they had guns? Let alone willing to shoot people?" asked Derek, and then he blew out a breath as he leaned back in the couch, ignoring Marissa's wide-eyed stare. "So, I went back to talk to the ringleaders. Used your name a bit to intimidate them and remind them that 'the law' might still exist."

"I'm guessing this is where things backfired," said Shiloh. "They didn't care."

"They did," said Derek, grinning. "I came out of nowhere. They saw no tracks, never heard me coming. I just popped up out from under a rock and said, 'hi!' and they almost shit their pants."

"Next time you pull that trick, take a gun with you," said Terrence, his tone dark. "Or have a sniper in the woods as back-up."

"Oh, trust me, I will," said Derek as he sighed before he continued. "That's where it all went completely sideways. I mentioned I was from up the road, and the ranch. There was this blonde woman. She didn't give me her name…"

"How did you know her name was Cecelie, then?" asked Jeremy, puzzled.

"Cecelie?" asked Terrence, his voice rising, and then he looked up at the ceiling. "That bitch doesn't give up."

"Who is she?" asked Sheridan.

Shiloh answered, "His girlfriend from high school—one that Gramma definitely wouldn't have liked."

Sheridan's eyebrows rose, as did Derek's. So, he had been right. "Hell hath no fury," mused Jeremy.

"No kidding," said Derek.

"So, if she didn't give you her name, how did you find out?" asked Shiloh.

Derek swallowed and drank the rest of his drink before he continued. "She ordered her people to 'kill them all'. And they did. If not for me ducking behind a woodpile at the last minute, I wouldn't be standing here... I'd be..."

He stopped and stared into the empty cup.

"Dear God," whispered Sheridan. "They killed *everyone?*"

He nodded.

"Even Rick?" asked Terrence.

Derek nodded again. "Right in front of me."

"That... I don't even have a word for her right now," said Terrence, slamming his hand on the table. "How the hell did you escape?"

"The same way I surprised them," answered Derek. "I vanished. And, let me tell you, she wasn't happy about that. That's when I overheard her yelling and one of her people call her by her name. I booked it back up here after that. The rest you know from Jeremy."

"Jesus Christ," breathed Jeremy. "No wonder you were quiet all the way back up here."

Derek looked up. "Whatever supplies you look for; make sure you add weapons to it. We have bigger problems than we thought, and we are going to need them. Not to turn into whatever dark hole she has dove, but to protect those who are counting on us. I won't lie. Even if I had been armed, I wouldn't have stuck around. I was alone. And that's one more thing. No one goes out without an armed escort... we need patrols. A wall."

"The wall we're already working on," pointed out Terrence, and he looked at Sheridan. "Aren't you glad I started work on that?"

She sighed. "All right, you were right."

\* \* \* \* \*

They built the community centre to hold twice as many people in it. But too few remained in the town. *I wonder if it's because the community hall is nearly a hundred years old—when the town was twice as large and bustling,* he thought. *Back when the mine was open and before the collapse.*

Before the closure when most of the town moved on.

*Or is this from that Kovach fellow dragging people out of their homes?* Garrett frowned as he leaned back in his chair.

A quick head count and some math in his head with how many houses still stood in the town betrayed the latter.

From his seat, he could see the entire room. He tried to keep from frowning, but he was not the only person to hang back and keep to the edges instead of heading for the seats near the centre of the room. More than one person kept casting furtive glances at the exits, and at him.

*Even after tossing Kovach out and they're still uneasy,* Garrett sighed again. *Can't quite trust me…*

*… I didn't toss him hard enough.*

Once everyone was there, Garrett stood up, the chair's legs screeching in the small space. Everyone looked at him, their eyes wide. "Right, where the hell are the police?" asked Garrett, looking from person to person.

"What police?" asked the same woman from before—the one that would have let him die. "They haven't been through here for weeks. Nothing exists out here. It's not like the city."

"Bullshit," said Garrett, pointing at her. "I don't know what I've been dropped into the middle of here, but we have laws. Taking people from their homes—or letting them starve to feed the city—is illegal."

"Are you really, really that clueless?" she asked, taking a step back before she moved in toward him again. "There's nothing out here. The law doesn't exist anymore—if it does, it's only in the city. Nowhere else. No one cares anymore about what happens to us, and even if they did, they don't have the support to do so. I can't believe you don't have a clue about what's going on out here."

Garrett took a breath and looked around. "This isn't a damn movie. The whole thing doesn't go poof."

"Pull your head out of your ass, man," she threw her hands in the air. "It didn't just happen overnight. We didn't even know until there wasn't a sign of a snowplow or a cop on patrol up here in longer than a week. By then they cut us off—and when that slaver showed up and started taking people we really noticed."

"The emergency line stopped working," said Mira. "I tried to call nine-one-one and got dead air. The phones went down completely a few days after that. Just dead."

"The power started winking out after," said the woman. "It was slow—but when Kovach showed up, we knew. After that, it was all we could do to survive."

"Did you try fighting back?" asked Garrett, and he saw them nod. "What happened?"

"You'll see in the spring," answered Mira, and she shuddered. "On the west road heading to Nairn."

"What did they do?" asked Garrett.

"They drew and quartered Mira's father and other men in the middle of the road using the horses from their farms. Slaughtered them while we watched for meat—and then dragged off her mother. They left everything there... right in the middle of the road. Didn't even bother to hide it," answered Roch. "We had hidden Mira in my cellar. No one they've taken... well... it's best we don't think about that."

Garrett stared at Roch, his mouth open as he tried to wrap his head around it. He couldn't even imagine it, but he had seen the scars on the trees himself. He looked around as he put his hands on his hips.

He couldn't say that Sudbury had been immune. Entire stores had shut down and boarded up. Grocery stores had strangely empty shelves, but much of what they carried had become locally supplied. Until a few days ago, it had been possible to find boxed food in the frozen section, but that had also ended.

Outside of that, he had noticed little. The power had gone out occasionally in Garson—usually at the worst possible moment—but that hadn't been too unusual either.

Odd things.

He blew out a breath.

"All right, fine," he admitted. "What if you're right?"

"Then you're as trapped as the rest of us," said Mira, shaking her head. "Kovach will be back and he will know to look for you."

Garrett's eyes thinned. "Oh, he will, will he?"

The rest of them stared at him.

Garrett spread his arms wide. "How many of them are there? Five? Ten?"

"When they first came, there were almost twenty," answered Roch, and he shrugged. "They haven't needed to use the same force once we lost our ability to fight back."

"So, expect thirty since I've probably really ticked them off."

"Are you planning to fight them?" asked the woman. "How? With what back-up?"

"You," he answered, and her eyes widened. "And everyone else. We can fight them off and make them think twice about it. The key thing is not letting just one person at a time try their hand at it. We have to hit them as a unit. Concerted… and not out in the open."

Roch took a step toward him. "Are you saying you're going to lead us?"

Garrett blinked, but then he nodded. "I don't see anyone else stepping up to the plate." He pointed at Mira. "Listen, they came back for her. She's one of you—and if they think you've hidden one young person, what's stopping them from thinking you've hidden others? Especially with me popping up out of nowhere. If you want them to stop, leave you alone, and not come back, we're going to have to hit them back hard and make them stop."

"He's right," said a man in the back of the room.

The woman nodded. "Okay, you have a point—but how are we going to manage that?"

He grinned. "With surprise. I mean, they know I exist now, but the one thing that knocked them over a real loop was the complete shock and awe of it all. We hit them with more of it and keep hitting them with it until they give up."

"But what will we hit them with?" asked Roch.

"Do any of you have any guns? Even bows or arrows. Sharp pointy things," he listed, looking at the ceiling. "Rope, chains, you name it. What do we have that we can repurpose? What can we use to make them move through town in the direction we want them to?"

The others looked around, and one shrugged. He could see more than one of them giving the idea real thought—and beyond it being just possible what they could do.

Roch took a breath. "We've got lots around. If not in the town, there is certainly plenty kicking around on the farms and the old mine site."

"Old mine site?" Garrett looked up and over at him. "It still exists?"

"Not much left since they shut it down and scavenged what they could take there—and the crater is a lake now—but we could find something there we could use."

Garrett took a breath. "You know, I think I've got an idea…"

# CHAPTER THIRTEEN

A log snapped, settling further into the hearth as it sent sparks flying.

The crackle was enough to startle one of the German Shepherds sleeping on the rug in front of it. Realizing the sparks hadn't fallen out onto the floor and remained in the enormous stone fireplace, the dog rested his head on the back of the other dog and closed his eyes.

"There is no sign of anyone from city works," said Marissa. "The phones are dead and even the emergency stations are out. Now, to prevent jumping to conclusions or panic, it could still be a military training exercise, but that excuse is quickly losing its credibility."

"I'm with Reese on this, Sheri," Derek pointed out. "This has gone way beyond anything allowed to the military as part of their training—and this is also way beyond an actual military exercise. There are simply no communications of any kind and no power. It's as if the infrastructure vanished out from under us. And now there's this Cecelie to contend with."

"Which means what? The end of the world happened?" asked Sheridan. "We're at war and the government forgot to tell us? Surely it's more likely to be a strike or something? Isn't that what usually happens just before Christmas? All the infrastructure workers go on strike to get more money for the holidays?"

"Yeah, true, that may have happened, but that doesn't explain why the mobile phones are out and so is the power. I mean, surely the news networks would still broadcast if it was only a strike," said Marissa.

"Maybe something's broken at the power generator?" Sheridan continued to list. "Maybe a line has come down somewhere?"

"If that's the case, then I'm sure Garrett is onto it. After all, that's his job, isn't? The power will be back on soon."

Derek glanced at the fireplace and the dogs before pacing back to join the two women.

"Or, I'm right and civilization has gasped its last breath," Marissa said. "How else would this Cecelie manage to take over the marina?"

"Marissa's right. Think, Sheri, what's the first thing lost when a government ceases to exist?" asked Derek.

"Their ability to maintain infrastructure in outlying areas… the ability to defend territory," she answered. "But, Derek, these are not the days of Rome and Byzantium. We have the Internet, phones, mobile phones and radios. The ability to travel hundreds of miles in a matter of hours instead of days. A civilization can't fall with no one noticing."

Sheridan looked away and into the fire. Derek tapped his fingers against the counter. "What if— what if civilization, as we know it, is now gone? What are we going to do? We shouldn't be arguing over what is and isn't possible. We should plan what we are going to do about it right now and for the future. There is a long, rough winter out there. Probably the worst we've had in years and we're still only in December, which means there is still January, February and March to think about. And, not to mention, what about burying our dead?"

Derek closed his mouth with a snap and looked over at Marissa, motioning for her to step in and say something. Marissa sighed heavily.

"Of course we haven't forgotten about Rick or the others we've already lost," said Marissa. "But we need to think of the living first."

"The dead can wait," pointed out Derek.

Sheridan thought for a long time and then looked back up. "You're right, of course. Reese, what is the status of our supplies? I know we won't have enough, but perhaps we can stretch them somehow?"

"Stretch, maybe, but not for too long. We'll have to venture out and get more supplies at some point. Our larger issue is going to be defending what we have. If civilization has fallen, many people out there will be desperate to live and they won't be all that nice about asking for help—like Cecelie and her cronies. They'll just take what they want," pointed out Marissa. "There's a reason they call it looting."

"And with no help from emergency services to prevent it," added Derek. "We're on our own."

"Wonderful," said Sheridan. "So, we need to supply ourselves and keep our supplies from looters. First things first—we need the defenses, then. I want anything glass, such as windows, boarded up."

"That won't really help," pointed out Marissa.

"Then what will?"

"Taking out the glass and bricking it up with solid timber reinforcement, and proper insulation, will do two things. One, it will prevent looters from getting access and, two, it will also conserve heat," Derek answered, blowing out a breath.

"What about Norse shutters?" asked Sheridan.

"Sorry, what?" asked Derek.

"You know when you see those movies about 'ye old medieval times'? The windows close by closing up wooden doors that swing inward on heavy hinges and bar from the inside like an old fortress gate... only in smaller scale?" asked Sheridan.

"It would be easy enough to build and add to the existing structure," mused Derek, interest in his tone. "And insulate. Should be more solid than boarding them up. You'd know about those... it would give Terrence something to do other than pace and fume."

"And we could open them back up later if this all blows over," Sheridan pointed out. "If this is nothing but a scare, it'd be one more curious but functional historically correct addition to our already near-historically correct English manor... in Canada."

Marissa coughed, although it was more to hide the bark of laughter at her goddaughter's comment. *The shutters would just add to the charm of the house if this whole thing is just a scare...* Derek thought, and he lifted a brow, but Marissa waved him off. *I hope it's just a scare—but Cecelie just proved it otherwise.*

*I will not let my family be one of them—and I'm definitely not going to let Cecelie take it all from me just because the police didn't survive this either...*

"So, if the world has suddenly ended, what other issues do we need to consider for the near future other than those with looters and lack of supplies?" asked Sheridan. "Not to mention medicine and some way to treat our own injuries."

"Spoken like a doctor," said Derek. "Without you, Sheri, we're screwed."

"I can't deal with this on my own," she pointed out. "We need those shutters on the windows now. False alarm or no, Cecelie is a threat. And we also have to think about a way to cook and store our food, especially what we already have."

"I wouldn't worry about what's in the freezer right now. It's cold enough in here, let alone out there, to keep," said Marissa. "But cooking it when we need to will cause a problem. We'll have to move that old wood stove from the barn to here and move the electric one out."

"No power."

Sheridan let out a breath as she plopped down onto the couch. Derek stared at her for a moment before looking out of the windows. While grey clouds still hung heavy over the trees, the snow had at least stopped.

*For the moment*, Derek thought as he tapped his fingers along the back of the couch.

"Unless—and this is just an idea because there's nothing we can do about it now—we move a solar panel or ten to the roof and set them up for net metering. That way if, by some miracle, civilization comes back, you won't run into the 'Dammit, the power's out again' annoyance," he suggested. "And still be supplying the grid with your extra power."

"That's why we bought a few extra panels." Sheridan chuckled as Derek's eyebrows rose. "I just haven't had the time to get them up there."

"What? Where the hell have you been hiding those?" asked Derek.

"Terrence bought them and put them in the shed," answered Sheridan, and she leaned her head back on the couch. "He never even took them out of the packaging."

Derek shook his head. "Well, all right then. I'll prod Terry and Jeremy to install those for you, Sheri, when we aren't in danger of breaking our damn necks. Can we use that massive fireplace for cooking for now?"

"Easily," answered Sheridan.

"Then we'll move the furniture around to accommodate," said Terrence as he walked into the room. "Now…"

There was a sharp knock, and Terrence and Derek stared at the front door.

"Hello?"

If the knock had not preceded it, Derek would not have heard her if not for the slight echo. Marissa's eyes widened as she spun to face the front door as Sheridan stood. Marissa looked at Derek, whose lips drew themselves into a compressed line.

Two people—one with hair that had at one point been a fiery red but was now turning silver—and a man that made Terrence who was over six feet tall look small.

"Don't mean to give you a start," said the man as he held up his empty hands. "Couldn't help but notice you have light and warmth where there really isn't any anywhere else on the road."

"And?" asked Terrence.

But then he winced as Sheridan jabbed him in the ribs with her elbow as she moved around him.

"You must be freezing!" Sheridan threw a throw blanket around as she guided the older woman into the living room. "Come by the fire and tell us what you've seen up the road."

Then the man took the other blanket from Marissa and knocked the snow off of himself as best he could before he followed Sheridan the rest of the way into the house.

"I'm Sheridan… the glowering darkness behind you is Terrence, and that's Derek."

"I'm Tyrell, and this is Helen," the man introduced as he looked over at Marissa and Derek. "I'm sorry if we just barged in on you, but Helen noticed the bell didn't work, and knocking wasn't having much effect."

"A little hard for a bell to work without power," agreed Derek, poking Terrence in the ribs.

*Can't blame him*, thought Derek, staring at the hallway. *After the marina, I'm a little gun shy over the idea of strangers waltzing in here too.*

Terrence had always been jumpy, and Derek didn't need the already on-edge Terrence to snap unnecessarily at neighbours, especially if they could help each other out. Derek caught and maintained eye contact with Terrence until finally the much taller man blew out a breath and sighed.

"When was the last time you ate?" asked Marissa, more to Terrence but also to the others.

"Yesterday," answered Helen.

Terrence stared at them. Behind his hand, Derek grinned. *Found the humanity behind the glowering darkness,* he thought. *Now to keep it found.*

"Can't have that," said Terrence, and he tilted his head to the kitchen. "C'mon, I know I think better on a full stomach."

"Well, we have a painfully obvious problem with our security, though," Derek pointed out, shrugging as they all walked into the kitchen while Terrence started searching in the fridge and cupboards. "Not saying that you two are going to be an issue. Actually, it being you instead of someone else not so friendly is a good thing."

"If you need a hand, I'm up for it," said Tyrell.

Terrence nodded and offered a jar of mayonnaise, and Tyrell opened it. He passed a butter knife to Tyrell, and the two men worked as a team in the kitchen. As they finished, Terrence turned around from the fridge to face Sheridan and the others. Sheridan looked over at Derek and Marissa.

"Well, you're welcome to stay, of course," said Sheridan. "If you can help with horses, it will be good news for my cousin, Shiloh. She will be more than happy to welcome the help in the barns."

"Barns? As in more than one?" asked Tyrell.

"There are three horse barns," answered Marissa.

"Is there anything else we can do?" asked Helen. "I'm not much use in a barn."

"I'm sure there is. I didn't think it would get to this point." Sheridan blinked and then turned to look at them. "Which way did you come from?"

"Up the road—close to where that little general store used to be at the fork," answered Tyrell.

Sheridan's eyebrows knit slightly. "Were there any signs of life or even a snowplow?"

"None, and the phones are dead too," answered Helen. "If you haven't noticed."

Derek chewed his bottom lip, and Terrence looked over at him. With a glance toward the barn, Derek hoped Terrence understood his intent. Terrence thought for a moment before his eyebrows rose.

"Come on, may as well introduce you to Shiloh and her husband, Jeremy," said Terrence. "The barns are plenty warm as well. We could use all the help we can get—if you're willing to learn about the horses, then we can't refuse anything you can do. Even if it's just making sure they're fed and watered."

Tyrell was the first to stand. "Never got too close to a horse. Always wanted to learn to ride. If it means helping in a barn, then I'll do it. I'm better at blacksmithing, though."

"Are you?" asked Terrence, and he broke out into a grin. "Let me tell you, there's lots of work for a good blacksmith in a barn."

Helen followed the two of them and her voice faded as she said, "I wouldn't even know what to do, but they've always looked pretty in pictures…"

"Get dressed warm," said Terrence as he took them down the hall and out of sight.

Derek waited until they were around the corner and into the mudroom. He shuddered as if in a sudden draft, rubbing his arms as he looked at Sheridan and Marissa.

"At this point we'd best call it for what it is," began Derek. "With no way to confirm whether we still have government or order, we are on our own and we need to think that way—and, like I said, there's still Cecelie to contend with."

"As much as I hate to admit it… I think you're right," agreed Sheridan. "You and Marissa were right—we need something for defence. Tyrell and Helen may be friendly, but that they waltzed right up my driveway and through the front door of my home clarifies that we need some way to prevent Cecelie from doing the same."

"I have an idea. Since you're blessed with natural barriers here, they may just save us," began Derek as he laid out his plan.

Sheridan's farm occupied its own little valley with an escarpment that ran along the north property line. The road, with the river on the east side, cut a climbable path up the cliff. The

Vermillion River ran along the east property line before looping around the south and following a line of low mountains further south and was both deep and wide. In recent years it rarely froze completely over, but this year was an exception.

The property had once been a golf course, but Sheridan had snapped up the property for a reasonable price. The northern half had been another horse ranch owned by someone else. A few short years later Sheridan bought that property, too.

Sheridan's house was on the northern half where the old ranch house had been. The southern fields that formed the old golf course still lay mostly empty. Sheridan's aunt and uncle lived on the other side of the river on the Whitefish First Nation Indian reserve.

"With no help from authority, we're going to have to be the authority. There are going to be a lot of scared people out there that aren't road trash. We start something here instead of watching what's left of our civilization vanish like a puff in the wind. We can do something very real to drag ourselves out of the dark ages," he finished.

"Is this what it is?" Sheridan mused, lifting a brow. "The dark ages?"

"Well, I wouldn't know."

"No, I think you're on to something there," she pointed out. "Rome was very much like the modern world. Marissa and I have often seen the parallels. The US even modelled their society on it.

The White House looks like a Roman villa with its columns, and most of the traditional homes along the east coast had those same Roman columns. But even Rome fell on itself and was reborn. I think, unfortunately, history just has repeated itself."

"If that's the case, what are we?"

"I don't know," she shrugged. "Celtic England before we called it that, perhaps? After all, it was the remnants of Rome that intermarried and set aside their Roman trappings in Britannia, and eventually it became Britain. The ancient reborn into something new built on top of the old."

"So Rome has fallen, so does Canada?" asked Derek darkly.

"Canada was supposed to be a colony of Britain, and was created the same way Britain was," said Marissa.

"Yeah, through invasion," murmured Sheridan, and Marissa sighed as she looked over at her goddaughter.

"… And still is still part of the Commonwealth… Was… who knows until we can confirm that the government either doesn't exist or has lost grip on the rest of the country. Rome did the same—it simply lost grip on the outlying areas and collapsed on itself," Marissa finished, and she pointed at Sheridan. "Rome invaded Britain, Britain repeated the same mistake on Canada. Rome fell, perhaps now its remnant has and we are in the modern equivalent of ancient Britain—we failed to learn… and now we're repeating that history."

Sheridan eyes widened, and was about to say something but before she could Shiloh said, as she walked in, "Since that's the case, where's did you put Terrence's broadsword—because he's going to need it. What's this?"

Shiloh looked down at the paper where Derek had drawn a rough sketch of the area and his plans. "An idea I have—if 'Rome' has indeed fallen."

"I would hope we won't repeat the same tired old mistakes," said Sheridan as she watched Derek spread the papers across the table. "Colonization— conquering settlements and taking them over when they were doing just fine on their own before we got there isn't necessarily a mistake worthy of being repeated. Perhaps this time we can do better." She looked at Marissa, who leaned back in her chair. "Perhaps, in that way, we can change another civilization's fate down the road if we break that chain."

Much of what he had was little better than random scrawls. Sheridan was familiar with the way Derek processed information, especially when he had a plan in mind.

The scrawling notes and scribbled diagrams sprawled across the desk. Derek's own hand could not keep up with how fast his ideas came to him when on a roll. This translated into the just barely legible mess he had in the notes early into a project.

"Okay, you need to walk us through this," said Sheridan, trying to make heads or tails from the notes.

"Right now, all I have is what I did to keep myself from being bored silly," pointed out Derek, scratching the back of his neck. "It's not really that much. Just ideas at this point."

"We can tell," said the three women.

# CHAPTER FOURTEEN

Concrete dust continued to fall, and they looked up nervously. There were other thuds and things continued to shake. Daniel motioned to the others and pulled the Mayor along behind him. "We can't stay here," he said. "The building could come down on top of us."

Victoria tugged back and pulled them all back into the stairwell and then across into the exit he and Lescelle had noticed before. Once they were all in the tunnel, Victoria used a lever.

Another door, one far more solid, slid shut after a short bark from an alarm system.

The thuds still shook the ground, but there was no sign of the dust or shaking—at least not to the same degree—within this new tunnel.

"This is a panic path, isn't it?" asked Daniel.

"Yes," she answered. "I'm guessing you need to head back to the police tower."

"Yes… wait, does this?" asked one officer asked. "Is this a direct escape tunnel to the police tower?"

She nodded her head. "Yes, and another branch will also eventually lead out to underneath the arena, but it, too, branches off. There's an exit in the pedestrian tunnel between the downtown and Riverside."

"Are you serious?" asked Daniel. "When the hell did they build that?"

"They made the plans for it after Nine-Eleven," she answered. "Not sure which mayor decided actually acting on them would be wise or when it was actually built… it's before my time. I heard rumours of a direct tunnel to the Skybox for the arena maybe getting built and taxpayers being more than upset about 'yet another frivolous spend' by city hall."

"That was probably the cover for this," said one officer. "Judging by the obvious exit sign behind the desk, I think they meant it as a general escape route for the entire council, maybe even as many people in the council chambers as possible. Although, what would make it even useful…"

"Riot," suggested one officer, pointed back up to the council chambers. "All that glass wouldn't protect a damn thing."

"Attack, for the same reason," said another.

"Doesn't matter," said Daniel. "All that matters now is that we're standing in it and where we come out… and then how we get back to the police tower if we're not already there."

Victoria led them through, her heels echoing in the underground passage. "If memory serves, we go this way. The other way is the as yet uncompleted connection to the arena."

They followed her, and it amused Daniel that out of all of them, her footsteps were easily the loudest and she had to stoop the most to avoid the emergency lighting except for a tall officer. Finally, they reached another set of stairs and climbed up and to another landing. Victoria took out a keycard and scanned it.

The door opened, and they walked out.

"Jesus Christ, isn't this handy?" Asked one officer as they stood outside the second door in the police parking garage.

The other team, who had got back and through the gate, stopped and blinked in surprise as they materialized out of the wall. "When the hell did they build that?" asked the other team leader.

Daniel shrugged.

Victoria stepped forward. "Perhaps it would be best to talk inside, rather than out in the open?"

He led them upstairs and to the boardroom. For a moment he paused before he entered, but then he opened the door and let her head in first. A few of the others milled around and Daniel looked at them. "What's up?"

"If it's all the same to you, we're going to head downstairs and see if we can find some food. Maybe even see if we can find anyone needing us," said one other. "Take care of the Mayor. I know that look in her eyes. I think we all do."

"Can you do me a favour?" asked Daniel.

"Shoot."

"Lescelle was looking for someone for me—"

"Fitz?" asked the older man, and Daniel nodded. "Yeah, that's one survivor we're still looking for. We'll let you know if we find anything."

Daniel nodded before he walked all the way into the room and closed the door behind him.

The boardroom hadn't changed. It still overlooked the construction sites on Brady—and the holes that had once been the arena and the parking lot that was supposed to be a condo. The walls hadn't changed. The same distinguished officers, in framed pictures, still hung on beige walls. But lit from only the grey skies outside, the boardroom seemed darker.

Sombre.

*Pure coincidence*, thought Daniel. *But strangely appropriate.*

At the head of the table, her fingers intertwined together in front of her, Victoria stared at her hands. Although staring at them wasn't quite accurate. He doubted she was actually looking at them, or even seeing them. They were in her field of vision.

He didn't know what she was looking at or if she was just deep in thought.

*Lord knows I have my own 'processing' to deal with*, Daniel blew out a breath as he glared at the sky. *Especially after yesterday.*

"He won't give up," she finally pointed out. "His type never does."

There was no doubt which he she referred to.

"I know that, 'Madam Mayor'," he answered.

Victoria sighed heavily and glared at Daniel.

"No more of that—if there's no Canada... or anything else... then I'm hardly the mayor anymore. And even if I am, what am I mayor of? A crumbling building in the shadow of a city of ghosts," she answered grimly. "Despite every effort we make, we will fade into obscurity."

He turned around to look at her. "So, you want us to what? Just give up?"

She snorted. "Hardly."

She rose from the chair and leaned on the table as she crossed her arms. "We survive and we note history changing around us. Like others did when they found themselves in the same situation, I'm sure."

*Spoken like a real politician,* he mused. They were all about making a mark on history. Now that he thought about it, Victoria had always been a bit of a ringleader with the other children in their neighbourhood.

She still had a point, though. He continued, "Easier said than done, given our present situation, Victoria."

This earned him another sharp glare in response. He shrugged his own response. Part of him yearned to be involved in making sure the core survived, but an enormous part of him knew they had already lost it.

She just didn't realize this yet.

"Who have you left behind out there?" she asked.

"In what way?"

"I can clearly see a troubled mind when it's before me, and yours is plainly fraught with something," she answered. "I'm guess Sheridan and the rest of your family?"

"Yep," he answered. "I have no idea if they're all right or if they're as dead as most of this city now is."

She sighed and looked up at the flags that hung behind the Mayor's seat. "You're not the only one. When I left my house this morning, it was just like any other day. I had no idea what would unfold today and to remember hugging my husband on the way out, it kills me to wonder if that was the last time I will ever see him alive. I imagine it is much the same for you."

"You have no idea," he answered as he turned back to face her. "I wasn't even supposed to be here today. If it weren't for Fitz or running into you, I wouldn't be. And now we're stuck here like everyone else."

Victoria leaned forward, and they both looked at each other. "Have you found Fitz yet?" asked Victoria.

"We're looking," Daniel reassured her. "I haven't forgotten about her at all… and I'm just as worried."

Victoria blew out a breath, her eyes closing slightly as she let herself fall back into the chair. "Good," answered Victoria. "Because I haven't forgotten either."

\* \* \* \* \*

Derek twitched his nose as he opened his eyes, staring up at his wife who was sitting on the edge of the bed with a steaming mug in her hand. "That coffee?" he asked.

She nodded, getting up from the bed and walking over to the table in front of the sliding door to the patio outside. He groaned, but temperatures outside had been creeping up over the last few days. He wasn't surprised to see grey and cloudy skies instead of a blue sky. Marissa left the coffee, and without saying a word—she only smirked a bit—she disappeared from the room and into the house.

He sighed as he went through his morning, and finally found himself downstairs in the kitchen, the now empty coffee mug in his hand. "Morning Lorraine," he greeted.

"Good morning, Derek," said Lorraine.

Lorraine had a morning routine. While she didn't make coffee for the entire ranch, she made enough coffee to fill at least three self-serve containers that would keep it hot for hours afterward. All three were taken out to the barns where ranch hands and barn helpers could have coffee first thing in the morning, and throughout the morning.

Lorraine was in the middle of filling these containers, but he noticed they had taken an additional two out. "We're going through more coffee, eh?" noticed Derek, and he wondered how long the supply would last.

"Thankfully, with the scavenging runs you set up we have been able to get more. For now," she answered, but she motioned to the other two. "We have had to figure out other methods to get the same result. So, two of those are for tea instead of coffee. We'll still have coffee first thing in the morning, but after that it will be just boiling water for tea or bone broth."

Derek felt like someone stepped on his chest, and he looked down at his own cup. He never felt quite human without his morning coffee, and the thought of running out was not a welcome one.

"I wouldn't worry, we have lots for now," said Lorraine, seeing his wide-eyed look. "Here, take this to Terrence, will you? He'll be calling for you soon enough, anyway. May as well nip his shout in the bud."

Derek took the other mug and walked through the kitchen to the back of the house. Behind the garage was another office, one more secluded and away from the hustle and bustle. A long time ago, this office had belonged to Russell Wither, Lorraine's husband and father of her three sons— Russell Junior, Garrett, and Daniel—but now it belonged to Terrence.

After Terrence, who knew? He and Sheridan had no children of their own. There were the younger Russell's children—including his son— but they were still in Toronto and with the way the world was they could be alive or dead but no one here had any way of knowing. Garrett had two children, Michael and Shiloh. Shiloh was here, and she had her own son—Eric—but Michael had always lived in Wahnapitae. Since no one from that direction had made it here, they could only assume they likely lived but, like Russell and his children, they had no actual way of knowing.

Perhaps it would be Eric's after Terrence no longer needed or wanted it.

Or even Shiloh's.

Derek sighed as he set the mug down on the desk.

There was no point in getting caught up in that rabbit hole of thought. What would happen would happen, and that was the end of it. "Terrence?" called Derek.

Lorraine had said he had come this way.

There were a few places he could have gone. This wasn't the only room this way, but they weren't ones he frequented or would be in for long. It was just off the mudroom and by the entrance from the garage, and there was a bathroom and laundry, but that was pretty much it. The bathroom door was open, so he hadn't gone in there.

Derek moved around the desk.

He stopped.

"Terrence?" Derek called, and he knelt by the younger man, rolling him over. "What the hell happened?"

"Cramping," grit out Terrence. "Really bad."

"What did you eat?" asked Derek.

Terrence shook his head and pointed to the drawer. Derek opened the drawer and pulled out Terrence's various medications. In it were a few bottles of metformin, both empty, and... Derek set the kit down and looked down at his friend.

*Mothering goddammit*, thought Derek, his eyes wide.

Terrence was out of his heart medication.

Derek didn't know what to do, but Terrence wasn't dead yet. He wasn't comfortable—but he wasn't dead. "I have no idea what to do…" said Derek, and then he stood up. "Sheridan… she will."

"No, wait!" called Terrence weakly, but Derek ignored him.

This was no time to hide health issues from the wife. Derek tried not to swear at Terrence, even silently, for being so monumentally stupid and letting that slip when they could have tried to help him. Derek didn't know if they were too late or not, but Sheridan — as a doctor — would know.

He skidded into the kitchen and asked Lorraine, who was still filling the containers. "Have you seen Sheri?"

Lorraine crinkled her brows. "She said something about going to see a new foal in Barn Two."

"Can you take some blankets and a pillow to Terrence in his office?" asked Derek, pointing back down the hall as he grabbed the closest coat he could find, and started pulling on boots. "I'm going after Sheridan."

"Wait, I'm already dressed," said a young woman. "It's the doctor lady, right? With the really long hair and glasses?"

"That's her," answered Derek. "Can you get her and tell her Derek says come to the house now — we need her as a doctor."

Derek tossed the boots aside and helped Lorraine grab the blankets and a pillow. He returned to Terrence's side and made him as comfortable as he could. Terrence opened an eye. "Thanks," he mumbled.

"Don't mention it," said Derek.

The back door slammed open, and Derek shivered with the sudden blast of wintery air. Sheridan looked into the office and came running over. "What's going on?" she asked, as she looked at the bundle on the floor.

"He's out of his meds."

"What?" came Sheridan's shrill reply, and she threw open one drawer of the desk. "No, no, no... you went the pharmacy in Lively not two days before this happened for a month's supply."

"They were out," said Terrence.

"What about the extras you always have?" she asked.

"Also out—Sheridan, listen..." Terrence tugged at her pant leg until she sank to the carpeted floor. "They've been out for weeks. I've been rationing... and now I'm out."

"We can find more," she said, and then she looked up at Derek. "There's a Fire Hall at the end of the road. It's also the dispatch point for a few ambulances—if they were there when all this went down, they could have at least that."

"And then what will happen when that runs out?" asked Terrence, his voice stronger again. "You raid another one?"

"We'll sort something out by then..." she said, and then she looked up. "We find our Aunt Niala. She might know a way."

"If we were going to find her, we would have by now," said Derek quietly. "And she lives down that same road as Rick did."

Sheridan glared at him. "No, I won't accept that. If we didn't see her, then she wasn't there. There's another end of the Reserve just past Naughton and a clinic there. Maybe she's even in Lively. But, until we find her or anyone else, there could be more than just insulin in those ambulances. We may even find more survivors."

Derek sucked in a breath, knowing what was coming. She hadn't asked him. Maybe she hadn't even thought to send him in specific. Even still… Derek stood up and he looked over at Shiloh. "That sounds like a mission to me."

Shiloh's eyebrows rose. "What are you thinking?"

"That Sheridan has a point," he answered, and then he sighed. "But, first, we need to get this lump of jellified bones to at least a bed."

# CHAPTER FIFTEEN

The garage door was closed. Even through the thin insulation on the metal doors, Gina could feel the cold seeping into the room. Vince leaned against one wall, sipping at his tea as he did. "Well, he should be happy."

"Not doing it for him," said Gina, pointing the screwdriver in her hand in his direction before bending back to the snow machine. "Doing it for us. If what he said about his Uncle is true, then finding the old bugger and dragging him and his stuff back here will help us, too."

Vince watched her for a few more moments, taking sips out of his cup.

"There," said Gina, dusting herself off as she stood back up again. "That should do it."

Vince walked over and lifted his brows. It was the machine Paul had loaned her when they had first rescued Russell—and Gina had stitched the cowling back together using black zip ties and duct tape. "It would impress Red Green," said Vince. "Or Frankenstein."

He swallowed, his eyes widening as Gina's thinned while she slowly turned her head to look at him. "I mean, given what we have at hand and all, it's really not that bad…"

"Keep going, you're digging yourself deeper," she pointed out, her voice low.

"Uh, well…" he grinned. "It may not be pretty, but at least it works?"

She rolled her eyes, throwing her hands up in the air before pulling the door from the garage to the mudroom open. She came to an abrupt stop, as had she taken another step, she would have bowled Russell over. Holding a hand over her chest, she said, "Jesus Murphy, Russell, were you trying to give me a heart attack?"

He sighed and shook his head. "No."

"I'm headed out first thing in the morning." She clapped his good shoulder with one hand. "I just had to make sure that one sled was going to make the trip there. It's not like it's an easy ride there and back."

"That's why I'm here," he said. "I wanted to know if you needed any help... I at least owe you that for what you're about to do."

Gina blinked, and then she shook her own head. "Nah, she's good. Thanks for the thought, though... really."

Russell stepped out of the way, and she walked into the living room. She closed her eyes as she sank into the couch and put up her feet.

"How'd the machine get damaged?" asked Russell.

"Looking for you," answered Gina. "Came down that same little gap you climbed down, only Paul and I came down it on the sleds. I zigged when I should have zagged and that was it for that side of the cowling."

Russell's eyes widened again, but Gina waved it off. "Nothing a few zip ties and five hundred mile-an-hour tape couldn't fix for now. I'll see if I can find some actual parts for it with when I get to that store at the Four Corners near your uncle's home."

She stretched as she then got up and headed to her bedroom. "Anyway, have a great night, fellas, I have an early start tomorrow."

Gina walked through her door and leaned on it, blowing out a breath as she did. *You're an idiot, you know that?* Gina shook her head. *First winter in Canada... first winter period... and you volunteer for a kamikaze solo trip into the danger zone.*

*Great decision maker, you are. Where is your survival instinct? Did you lose it? Yep, great decision.*

It was too late now, though. She had committed—not that she'd back down now.

*Snow is another kind of desert,* she thought. *Cold can kill as quick as heat, but if I'm prepared, I should be all right. That's the key—have to make sure I have what I need.*

She flopped on her bed and closed her eyes.

A long time ago, her martial arts instructor in college had taught her how to breathe. How to react—how to stay calm. As she breathed in and out, she focused on relaxing each muscle one by one.

Finally, she opened her mouth in a near jaw cracking yawn.

*No rest will kill me by making a mistake from fatigue, sure as heat or cold.*

*… And the morning comes early enough as it is.*

\* \* \* \* \*

There were seventeen two foot by one-foot slate tiles in front of the fireplace to keep the sparks and heat from damaging the wood floors. Derek had counted each one—had even noted the flecks and oddities in each tile. *I'm surprised I haven't worn some of it smooth,* he thought, with a snort. *Were that even possible.*

Counting the tiles could not dispel the image burned into his mind.

Rick and the people at the marina.

Killed by Cecelie with no one to stop her.

Terrence, who didn't have the medication he needed and would probably die—and who many others simply dead because they froze to death?

*How many more before we put a stop to it?*

He asked himself this same question over and over again.

Marissa walked into the living room and crossed her arms. While he didn't look up at her entrance, out of the corner of his eye he could see her gaze follow him as he walked from one end of the tiles to the other and back again.

How long before something took her from him, too?

How long before he found himself in a snowbank?

"What do we do now?"

"There is still that Fire Hall." Marissa lifted a brow. "In case you've forgotten."

He waved that off. "I haven't."

"Then what's wrong?"

He stopped, staring through the picture windows over the fields and to the barely visible Vermillion River in the distance. Not that there was much to see. This section of it was slow and had frozen over. With the snow, it looked like an extension of the fields. "What kind lunacy have we found ourselves in?" Derek crossed his arms, and then he looked at his wife. "And why me?"

Marissa tilted her head. "Can you do something?"

Derek sighed and ran a hand through his hair.

"Yes," he said. "I can."

"Can someone else?"

"I have no idea." Derek sighed and then looked up at the ceiling. "You've made your point."

"I know you already have a plan." Marissa took a step toward him. "Why torture yourself now?"

"I already watched someone die in front of me because I assumed something and was dead wrong," said Derek, and he blew out a breath. "I can't do that again."

"And if you don't go, who will?" she asked again.

"Shiloh."

Marissa sighed this time. "She can't go alone either."

"So, what are we looking at?" he asked, pulling out his notebook.

It was at this point he stared at the little book and blinked. Marissa looked from the book to him and back again. Derek opened it, flipping through the pages. He had started this notebook—one of many in a long line of filled notebooks, eventually discarded as the paper yellowed and aged beyond the ability to read them.

What would happen to this one?

It wasn't as if he could run to the nearest store and replace it. Once he finished filling this one with notes, that would be it.

No more.

He slid the notebook back into his pocket.

"What's wrong?" asked Marissa.

"Unless we have a secret stash of notebooks, it'd be best to save the one I have for the important details I can't afford to forget," he said, tapping his pocket. "I don't need to write everything down."

"Or perhaps we should," said Marissa. "Just not in a notebook. If this is truly the end of everything, we should put something down. People will follow us. They will want to know how we survived."

Derek shook his head. "I'm not worrying about that," he said, stepping forward to kiss his wife quickly. "You can, if you want to. I have to make sure we survive first."

# CHAPTER SIXTEEN

The scrape of metal shovels digging into ice filled the air. Garrett leaned on his, blowing out a breath as he did so. The others continued their work— digging holes in the frozen ground where they could and creating traps and other obstacles. *I hope this is enough,* he thought. *Even to just slow them down.*

He bent over; his shovel poised but paused.

A familiar wail had risen to the west.

*Already?* he thought. *We're not ready!*

His eyes thinned and he threw the shovel to the side as he jogged back to the row of houses, whistling in a set pattern as he did. Roch stepped outside of the house, and Garrett caught the shotgun Roch threw him, and he loaded it as he ducked behind the nearest house.

"Warn the others!" shouted Garrett.

Roch nodded and disappeared around the corner of the house.

The rider of the first snow machine that came around the corner didn't see the wall of ice.

A crunch of plastic and steel, and the whine of the motor came to a stop.

The rider slid, launched over the wall and from the machine, down the street.

He tried to push himself up, but the street had been covered in water days before and now was glare ice with the barest dusting of snow.

He tried multiple times but kept slipping back to completely prone.

The echo of a single shot from a rifle filled the valley.

The ice became stained with blood from the slaver.

Mere moments had passed.

Another snow machine followed by a third came around the corner. Seeing the stricken rider and machine, they swerved to avoid it. One dropped into a pit, and the other skidded sideways down the road as it hit the ice.

Garrett watched as the group on snow machines grew, and eventually one snow machine stopped well outside of town. Others circled him, stopping before they came into town.

Out of the ten machines, some with over one rider, only four remained intact.

The lead rider motioned to the others, and they turned the machines off and dismounted them. The riders opened rifle cases, armed themselves, and they cautiously picked their way toward the town using the trees as cover.

Garrett blew out a breath but picked up the flare gun taken from his truck and fired it into the air.

The motion in the trees stopped.

Garrett suspected this had given them pause. The flare was too obvious—too easily seen in the area. If he were Kovach, he'd be wondering not only where Garrett had come from, but now if he had brought others. How many would he have to fight? What did they have for arms?

Where had he come from in the first place?

*I'm making you sweat now, you bastard*, thought Garrett. *Good*.

As planned, Kovach split his forces—sending them to either side of the town.

A loud snap, followed by a scream, sounded from the south side of the building Garrett hid beside. "They've got bear traps!" shouted one slaver.

"I don't care what they've got, there aren't as many of them as he wants us to think there is," said Kovach. "Cunning move, sir, you've divided us to conquer. But we've got numbers you don't."

"If you don't go back to wherever the hell you came from after," shouted Garrett. "Then the snake is without a head, isn't it?"

Kovach was quiet. "You son of a bitch—you play for keeps, don't you?"

More snow machines came up the road, and Garrett ground his teeth. With another whistle, gunfire rained down on the other machines.

This time they skirted the traps and ran into the town past them.

Only half made it, but half of the riders were enough.

Garrett blew a whistle twice in quick succession and the sound of the guns fell back toward the east road, back into the valley below, and to the mountains where they could force the slavers off the machines and on foot.

To his relief, as he also fell back, he didn't see any of the townspeople on the ground—only slavers who had been foolish enough to be caught out in the open.

He came up on a slaver on a snow machine, and the man went to stand up. Garrett barrelled into him, knocking him off the machine and to the ground. Garrett dragged him, kicking, head in a choke hold off to the side of the building and out of sight. The slaver used his feet to push himself back, and Garrett into the wall.

Garrett saw stars as it knocked out his breath of him, but his arms clamped down even harder.

There was a sickening snap, and the slaver went limp in his arms.

Garrett dropped him, heaving as he tried to catch his breath.

Scowling, he relieved the dead slaver of all his weapons and tools, plus the snow machine key. Another slaver came around the corner, but Roch stepped around from another corner and threw the axe, and the blade buried itself deep into the slaver's chest. He fell back on the ground, his blood already frozen before it hit the snow, bouncing like beads on the ice.

Garrett looked around, his eyes thinning.

He pulled the hatchet from the slaver's chest, wiping it off on the slaver's jacket, grabbing the guns he had as he went.

One thing was on his mind—Kovach was the key here.

Eliminate him and the slavers would crumble without their leader... and Garrett was done playing games.

"All right, you bastard," came Kovach's voice as he moved out into the street.

Garrett was about to advance, but he stopped mid-stride.

Kovach held one of the townspeople, a gun to her head.

"I'll make you a deal," shouted Kovach. "You wanna try your luck at evening the odds? Fine. We sort this out one on one. Whoever walks out of this chooses what to do with this rat hole. But I'd think quick."

Kovach turned around, pulling the hostage around with him.

Garrett's blood turned to ice.

It was Mira.

# CHAPTER SEVENTEEN

Gina slowed the machine to nearly a stop and then stood up—her hands still on the control yoke—with one knee on the seat. The ride from the house she shared with Vincent and boatyard had taken less than ten minutes. Walking, even on snowshoes, would have taken hours.

The parking lot of the department store and the surrounding strip mall was quiet, but, like everything else, snow had filled in the streets and parking lot.

*There's a ditch hiding under all that snow,* thought Gina. *Usually has water in it too. Probably frozen, but if it's not, there'll be just enough to cause problems.*

Fencing surrounded the doorway, and it reminded Gina of riot fencing. She compressed her lips. *That's a bad sign, if they felt they needed that kind of control. Especially since half of it appears to be down...*

She looked down at the machine.

While it had certainly been faster to travel on it, a snow machine had a loud and distinctive whine. Everyone in the area could probably hear it. One lone machine and rider did not stand a significant chance of defending herself, as tough as she was.

The one advantage she had with the machine was how fast she could get away so long as her path was reasonably clear.

*The problem is...* she thought. *The problem is that they are so bloody loud. They could probably hear them from the lake, and now I've packed a fantastic trail right there.*

*Damn.*

Nothing could be done about it now, and they needed the supplies.

She slid back down onto the seat and opened the throttle, choosing to take the street that curved up and over the mountain before cutting between the strip mall and the department store to get into the parking lot.

She drew closer and hissed through her teeth.
*Double damn.*

The glass doors, windows, and all the shelves in the store were smashed in. The riot fencing—what still stood—now hung uselessly against the wall.

Gina looked back the way she came and back to the store again. Blowing out a breath, she leaned one hand on her chin. *I could walk into a trap in there, she thought. Or they could have moved on…*

*… Or I could find a bunch of survivors clinging to what little they can who think I'm going to steal what they have.*

Even if the food and supplies were gone, the department store could still have plenty of what she and the others could use to survive the winter. A stray thought—one from the conversation the day before with Russell—popped into the forefront of her mind. Something to fix the cowling on the machine. Not very many would want or need that.

Still, something was making the hair on her arms stand on end and it wasn't the cold.

*Nope, to hell with this, she thought. I came here to find Russell's Uncle as well. It's time to move on—before whatever is making me have second thoughts materializes.*

Gina turned the machine around, running it in a lazy circle in the parking lot. A glint of metal caught her eye across the parking lot by the liquor store, but it disappeared just as quickly. Her eyes thinned.

That had been what, or rather who, had made
the hair on her arm stand on end.

*Company.*

While it could be friendly—and just as afraid
of her as she was of them—the chilly hand on her
spine said otherwise.

Gina grinned beneath the helmet before she
throttled up and rode back the way she came, only
this time she followed the curving road as it went
up, around and then back down into a small valley.
There was a community arena on this side of the
overpass between Long Lake and the rest of the
Four Corners. A sprawling subdivision filled with
houses both older and newer—some less than a
year old—filled the low valley.

Russell's Uncle lived in the older part.

Relatively older.

While the house was older than thirty years
old, and old by the standards of the houses she
rode by that had just built, Sudbury was not a
young city. The houses here were at least a century
or newer than the downtown core and even into
Copper Cliff.

The house came into view, and a lazy curl of
smoke rose from one chimney.

*That's promising,* she thought, as an eyebrow
rose. *Russell was right—if his Uncle is alive in there—
that the old man was more than able to survive on his
own if he needed to.*

She slowed the machine, again moving up to
one knee on the seat, just as two people came out

from between the houses. Gina stopped the snow machine and held up her hands—not that she could do much else.

They had rifles.

She didn't.

*＊ ＊ ＊ ＊ ＊*

Garrett held Roch back and shook his head. Roch hissed, "It's Mira!"

"I know, but you walk out there, you're dead."

Roch lifted an eyebrow. "If you do the same, it's the same result... and we need you."

There was a long moment of silence as Garrett considered this. *He's right*, thought Garrett. *I go out there and I'm an easy target*.

If he didn't, they would kill Mira to spite him, or they'd drag her off. The morale of the town would sink. *They could even give up*, thought Garrett. *I'd die anyway, like Mira's father*.

*I'm dead either way*.

*What way would I rather go out?* Garrett sighed. "I can take him."

Roch's eyebrows lifted until they nearly met his scalp. "You can what?"

With a grin, Garrett handed Roch the rifle liberated off one of the two dead slavers, removing some things he wore Kovach could use as a handhold. He pointed at the rifle. "If he pulls anything funny, the deal is off. Shoot him."

Roch nodded his understanding and Garrett yelled out, "All right, Kovach, you've got yourself a deal. Let the girl go, and I'll gladly take you up on that offer."

With a grin, Kovach pushed Mira to one of the other slavers. Garrett couldn't catch what they said, but the slaver—who had been about to move off with her—only moved off a few feet. His hands stayed where a father would prefer them to stay instead of straying elsewhere.

Kovach stripped off the same amount, and probably for the same reason, as Garrett had.

Garrett grinned and charged at Kovach.

Kovach's eyes widened, and he dropped to one knee. The air above his head whistled as Garrett's fist missed him by inches. Garrett saw his eyes widen again as his other leg slid out from under him and he fell sideways, rolling to his back.

His legs lashed out, and Garrett felt his world tilt as Kovach swept his feet out from under him. He landed on his back—relieved that the air hadn't been knocked out of his lungs. With a snarl, he rolled over.

The ground was icy.

He had a choice—stay on the ground or try to stand again.

Garrett grinned, and in a move ground into him from years of wrestling in high school, he got to his knees and reached for Kovach only to be rewarded with only air.

*Fast little bastard*, thought Garrett as the younger man all but slithered out of reach. Had he not been in the middle of a fight, he would have been amused by his own metaphor, but he pushed aside the thought as fast as it had appeared.

However, in the try, Garrett landed on his back again.

Kovach was not out of the reach of his legs, and Garrett kicked out—using the same move Kovach had used on him.

With a snarl of frustration, he watched as the still wide-eyed Kovach avoided his legs—if barely—and seemed equally surprised as he moved back and out of reach.

"You're fast, and you're lucky," said Garrett as he pushed himself to his feet. "I'll give you that."

"Yeah, wasn't expecting someone who knows how to fight both on their feet and on the ground," said Kovach.

He grinned as he reached behind him. The knife gleamed silver white in the sunlight.

Garrett's eyes thinned. "It would figure you'd cheat."

"Cheat? No—evening up the odds, old man," answered Kovach. "I'm clearly at the disadvantage here."

Garrett hesitated. He had nothing to prevent Kovach from gutting him like a fish, and he had nothing to fight him with other than his fists. *Stupid, stupid, stupid*, he chided himself. *You should have known he wouldn't play fair…*

He grinned and cracked his knuckles. "You're going to need a lot more than that little knife to keep me from pounding you into the ground like a nail."

Kovach's eyes widened, and then he laughed, but the laugh sounded hollow—like he didn't believe himself. "If you say so, old man."

Kovach jumped forward, the knife flashing in a silver arc in the light. Garrett jumped back. Garrett glanced over toward Roch but wasn't able to see him clearly. There would be no help there. The two had wandered out of the other man's line of sight.

Garrett took another step back, hoping to draw Kovach back out to Roch's cover, but Kovach didn't follow. The younger man crouched slightly as he stepped sideways and then back to where he was—but he didn't take a single step forward.

The sharp crack of a rifle echoed, and bits of lumber, vinyl siding and insulation rained down on Garrett and Kovach—mostly Kovach, though. Roch had tried to take a shot, but the angle and the house were too much. Kovach's eyes thinned.

"And I don't fight fair?" he said, his voice quiet.

He grinned, and he stepped back between the two houses. Any further and he would be on the primary road between town, but away from Roch.

Garrett didn't want to follow him. The primary road meant Kovach had his own back-up and the sound of rifles and guns as the few remaining townspeople fought for their own freedom was heaviest in that direction.

A shriek—masculine—from behind him, and then shortly after he heard Roch call, "Are you okay?"

Mira answered, "Yeah."

Garrett grinned as Roch yelled, "Take his guns then."

Kovach glowered and screamed in rage, lunging for Garrett again, but Garrett moved out of the way.

Garrett stepped down, and under his foot he felt something give way and then stop. He looked down, and, taking his foot off it, he pulled the short length of lumber out of the snow. It was only a three-foot-long length of two by four construction lumber, but, after giving it a few swings, Garrett knew exactly how he was going to use it.

*Batter up*, he thought as he stalked Kovach.

# CHAPTER EIGHTEEN

Derek paused at the top of the steps, one hand on the makeshift railing made of two-by-four lumber on the platform leading from the garage into the mudroom and the rest of the house. It was just after dark, and the rest of the Manor and everyone else within the house had retired to their rooms, perhaps even to bed and sleep. Instead of the buzzing hive the Manor had become over the past few days, Derek had a peaceful quiet.

Except for one other person.

"Are we ready for this?" he asked. "Truly ready for what's out there—or what's not out there?"

Shiloh looked up and shook her head. "I don't think any amount of planning or packing could possibly make us ready enough. Not after Rick—not after the Marina. It's one thing to hope trouble doesn't find you, but it's a whole other thing to know it's coming."

"Just when," mused Derek.

She nodded. "Yep."

With that the conversation ended, and he and Shiloh packed in silence.

They were of a similar mind.

Derek sat back on his heels once he had the very basics settled, and into the various saddlebags and packs.

Derek's pack contained everything he could need for at least five days out in the bush in the middle of winter. Shiloh packed her backpack similarly. This offset each other's skills, although it assumed that they would not likely be eventually separated.

It was not the absolute best idea.

Especially since part of the plan included splitting off.

He blew out a breath. "Shiloh, we've a problem here."

She looked up from her packing.

"We're assuming we're sticking together from beginning to end. Your pack complements mine, and we both know that once we're past a certain point that you're heading off on your own."

"That's not exactly true anymore," pointed out Shiloh. "Sheridan and I had a chat. We realized that it's suicide for me to head off alone—suicide for you as well. So, we're going to be sticking together."

Derek blinked suddenly, looking at his pack that comprised the same basics as hers did— sleeping bag, winter cover for the sleeping bag, and their respective covers for carrying. Emergency 'foil' blankets—two each and enough dry clothing and spare dry socks to last more than a few days. Dry clothes were the make or break of survival, especially in the winter when wet and cold could literally mean a very swift death.

Other things in his pack were enough dry food and other edibles, just in case foraging or hunting failed while out there. He also made sure he had what he needed to hunt with ammunition that was easy to replace and regular rifle ammunition. He had both a hunting rifle and the compound bow Sheridan gave him.

Shiloh was not much of a hunter.

Where she excelled was at trapping, so her pack leaned heavily on that nearly lost art instead, although she also carried a shotgun just in case Cecelie made another appearance.

"I'm guessing our surprise guest at the Marina has something to do with that decision?" he asked, and after Shiloh nodded, he asked, "Why wasn't I included in this?"

"You were already in here," said Shiloh. "Sheridan caught me in the hallway before I came in. That's why I was a little late."

"Oh," said Derek, and he shook his head. "Well, she's right. It was sheer folly to send either of us alone and I'm glad for the back-up."

She grunted once and returned to backing her bags. Now that he knew they were travelling together, he found he could breathe a little better. *I didn't want to lead this all by myself anyway*, he thought. *While I would have preferred they consulted me… No. I was consulted and we all decided it was possible for me to go alone, even if I said I would rather not go alone. She was right to take my advice without further consultation.*

Cecelie was still out there. He knew it. Shiloh knew it.

Everyone knew it.

It was just a matter of when she would return and expect them to roll over like Rick had. *Rick hadn't been prepared though*, thought Derek, *his lips set in a grim line. We are.*

Thanks to Rick, come to think of it. And Derek—if Derek and Jeremy had not gone to the Marina when they did, who knew what could have happened then. Could Cecelie had wandered up the road to the Manor? He shuddered.

The two from up the road had been at least friendly, but they had still wandered into the house. No one had known they were there until the man had called out to announce their presence. That it could have been Cecelie and her raiders instead...

He pushed that from his mind.

It had not come to pass.

He had found Cecelie first and with that all advantage of surprise she could have had went up in smoke.

*Luck*, he thought. *We've had nothing but good luck so far—everything we have had so far is due only to good fortune.*

That could change.

*No, our luck will eventually change. There's no 'could' about it*, he thought.

He paused, one of his camping knives in his hand as he tapped the sheathed blade against his lips.

*But our 'luck' could become simple good preparation*, he thought, putting the blade on top of his pack with the items he would wear tomorrow. *Which, honestly, has been the source of our luck.*

With a sigh, he stood up and stared down at the three bundles. Two would go into his saddlebags, and the third would be another saddlebag that would be draped over the other two. He had been leery of the English riding style and the ability for the saddles to handle travel and packs, but Sheridan and Shiloh had maintained that not only were the saddles more comfortable—if riding on a hunter style saddle—but also lighter and more comfortable for the horse as well. They were also lighter and easier to carry and move around if he had to take the saddle off for any reason. The straps were simpler, but as secure.

The first time he rode on a general English saddle, he had changed his mind. While no saddle was perfect for pressure points, the hunter saddle seemed a bit more comfortable. It was just strange to not have a saddle horn or any of the other bits the Western style saddle was known for.

The other difference from the racing saddle was that he could comfortably allow his legs to hang, if supported by the stirrups. Like many others before him, he had mistakenly assumed that English saddles meant racing and having to use his knees to support himself. If he sat in the saddle, his legs would have been curled up almost under him.

He remembered Sheridan's laughter when he had expressed his surprise when he learned otherwise.

"My horses are event horses, Derek, they have to jump fences. While I wouldn't recommend having your butt on the saddle when they jump, the racing posture would see you headfirst over the fence before the horse even landed," she had answered. "While we don't hunt real foxes—I wouldn't even if it hadn't been outlawed—we train the horses to handle that kind of ride, anyway. The riders here go on to events."

Derek had never really been into horses or riding them. He enjoyed it as much as the next person. Excursions to local riding stables for a half-day once in a while, but never enough to own a horse let along let himself get roped into riding and caring for horses every day.

Until the Withers.

And now both of his goddaughters were so horse crazy that they owned the ranch fifty-fifty, although the house was Sheridan's.

Derek sighed, pulling himself back to the present.

They had packed the saddlebags. He didn't even need his own backpack, which would make him more mobile once on the ground. All that remained would be to saddle the horses in the morning.

"Well, that's it for me tonight," he said as he looked over at Shiloh, and she looked up at him. "Early start—I'd like to be out of the gate at dawn, so we're going to up before it. If you're all right with that?"

"I'm fine with it," she answered. "Have a good night, Derek."

With a wave, Derek returned to the house, following the hallway between the kitchen and garage, back into the central part of the house and up the stairs to the second floor. He paused just outside the door to the room he shared with his wife before slowly opening the door. Slipping inside and closing the door as quietly as he could—even going so far as to not let the latch click—he slowly let the knob turn as it shut instead. He tip toed his way across the floor to the bed. Marissa was already sleeping, and the room was dark except for the fire in the fireplace.

Not for the first time, he gave silent thanks for that quirk of Sheridan's that loved classic architecture. Instead of updating the house and the fireplaces from actual wood burning to natural gas like many other homeowners had done, she kept them the way they were.

It had cost far more in upkeep and for house insurance, but the difference was that the house now had heat where millions of others didn't. Not that it was still cold in the room—it was. Updated insulation or not, it was still freezing outside and at least thirty to forty degrees below in both Celsius and Fahrenheit. It was cold enough to freeze wine and less distilled alcohol, including fuel for cars.

The fire kept the room livable, but he was still going to welcome the respite from the many layers of warm blankets and the heavy coverlet would give them.

"You pushed that a bit late, didn't you?" came Marissa's voice.

"Had to be ready for tomorrow or we'd be packing when we should move," he answered, and looked at the clock. "It's not that late. It's just because it's dark so early that it seems it."

"Late enough if I'm in bed, Dare," came her response as she shifted to lean her head on his shoulder. "You will be careful, right?"

He smiled slightly, even though he knew she couldn't see him. "Always."

* * * * *

Gina looked from one to the other, her hands held out to show that she was no threat to them but not above her head. They looked from her and then further down the road. "How many others are with you?" asked the woman.

"No one else," she answered. "I'm alone."

"Were you followed?"

"That I could say... probably..." answered Gina. "And, no, I don't know them. They picked up my trail at that Walmart back there. However, I easily outpaced them on this thing."

"Why did you come this way?" asked the older man.

Gina looked up at him, and her eyebrows lifted as she had to crane her neck a bit. "I was sent here by a man who landed on my doorstep a little over a week ago... he's hoping his Uncle is still alive."

The man's eyes thinned and he looked at her sideways a bit. "Here?"

Gina nodded to the house just past them. "There, actually."

The man looked from the house and then back at her. "That's my house, young lady."

"Then you must be Russell's uncle," said Gina.

He relaxed a bit and nodded to the other woman. "I had wondered what held him up.

Figured he stayed back with his Mom when the weather turned really bad. But you're telling me he's at least somewhere up the road a bit, eh?"

"Middle Lake," she answered. "My name is Gina, and yours is Kirk, right?"

The woman looked over at the older man, one eyebrow raised. "Still think she's here to loot our stores?"

Kirk shrugged. "S'pose not," he lowered his rifle, leaning it so he held it in the crook of his arm but pointed at the ground. "So, where is he?"

"Russell is back at my house," answered Gina. "He sustained a bit of a head injury when his SUV left the road. I thought it better I come instead of him—the last thing he needed was to be out here and to have a dizzy spell or something."

"He is all right, though?" asked Kirk.

"With time and actual rest," answered Gina, and then she grinned. "Which was a bit hard to convince him to do when his elderly uncle so clearly needed his help."

Kirk snorted and shook his head. "I'm quite fine, thanks."

"So I see," said Gina, and she settled onto the seat of her snow machine. "I guess I could head back now?"

Kirk stared at her and sighed. "You came all this way just to check up on an old man and you're going to head back, just like that?"

"I came to see if I could convince you to come back to Hannah Lake with me," answered Gina, but she motioned to the house and the others with him. "But I can plainly see that it's not likely to happen. Russell sent me here to rescue you."

This was rewarded with another grunt. "Yeah, well, I don't need a rescue, thanks."

"I can see that."

The younger woman poked Kirk in the ribs. "She came all this way as a favour to someone she barely even knows and the best hospitality we can offer is to have a chat in the cold?"

Kirk rolled his eyes and moved out of the way of the snow machine. "Park that thing in the drive, miss, and we'll be there in a minute."

Gina closed the face cover of the helmet and rode the machine the scant hundred feet to the driveway. As Kirk said, it didn't take long for them to catch up. She pulled off her helmet, grabbing the smaller of the packs on it and followed Kirk into the house.

After they silently peeled off the outer layers of winter coats, scarves, and—in Gina's case—snow pants and their boots, Gina was glad to have a cup of hot tea while sitting by Kirk's wood stove in the living room he introduced his wife.

Gina sipped her tea as she looked at the pictures on their wall.

One picture was a university degree in economics, but it was clearly a son as the first name wasn't the same but the last name was. The picture of said son sat on the bookshelf—a smiling young man in a cap and graduation gown. There were other family pictures, including one taken in one of the world wars of a young man in uniform.

She motioned to this one and looked at Kirk, "You, I take it?"

He shook his head. "Brother. Didn't make it back."

"Sorry."

He shrugged. "Don't be. It was a long time ago. I guess a whole other world ago, now."

Gina sighed as she sipped her tea.

His wife came in with a teapot full of more tea, and Gina's eyes widened. She recognized the amused look from his wife. "I can see Kirk forgot to introduce us. I'm Jen."

"Gina," answered Gina as they shook hands.

"Gina here thinks we need a rescue," said Kirk. "Russell sent her."

"Whitefish is a bit far for a rescue," pointed out Jen.

"That's the second time I've heard that," said Gina. "I take it that's where he was coming from?"

Jen crinkled her brows and looked at her husband, and he smiled. "Gina here is from Middle Lake—that's as far as Russell made it before he ditched his SUV. From what she told me, I take that as literally putting the damn thing into a ditch."

"Pretty much," answered Gina. "He all but fell face-first into my driveway."

"Well, maybe we should go with her, Kirk," began Jen, but Kirk cut her off with a motion from his hand. "We are kind of close to where we heard all of that noise. Putting some distance between that may be prudent."

Kirk looked up at his wife and then at the wall of pictures. "This is our home, Jen, you want us to just pack up and leave it?"

"Well, no, but we could come back to it later," she said.

Gina sighed as she listened to them argue about it. This must have come up before, she realized. I just reminded them enough to discuss it again.

She was about to get up and ask where she could go now that she was full of tea, but the young woman who had stopped her—the same one that had been with Kirk moments before—came running into the house. "Kirk, we have trouble."

He looked at Gina, but the woman shook her head. "No, other direction."

Kirk sighed heavily and looked at Gina again. "Don't even ask. I'll do what I can," she answered.

His eyebrows rose. "You don't even know us—and my nephew hasn't been around you long enough yet…"

"I'm emergency services," she answered, and his eyebrows rose further. "Firefighter, sure, but not about to leave civilians without some help if I'm here."

He nodded. "All right. I'll get Sam to see if she can find you a spare rifle."

# CHAPTER NINETEEN

A low rumble shook the building, but it wasn't until the second one that Daniel opened his eyes. Desperately rubbing the sleep from them, he stumbled over to look out the window and down to the street seven stories below.

Without his glasses, he could barely make out what he was seeing.

A third rumble nearly knocked him from his feet.

The door to the office he was using as a bedroom opened, and Victoria rushed in. "Harnet is not satisfied with running."

"What is he doing now?" asked Daniel.

"So far? Nothing. The other police officers tell me it's only flash bangs," she answered, and she stood aside.

Daniel walked by her, pulling his arms through his shirt as he did so.

Another office, also now a bedroom, was on the other side and he walked through to look out the windows. This one faced the central courtyard and had an unobstructed view past the other office towers and to the mall beyond.

The rumbles ended, and they all waited.

But it stayed quiet.

Daniel shook his head. "Either he ran out, or he had his attention on something else," he looked over at one of the others. "Lars, can you set up a post on the roof of each tower on this block we can access?"

"Yep," answered the other officer. "In fact, already on it."

"Fantastic," Daniel rubbed a hand over his face.

It was dark.

It was the one thing he could not get over—especially in this part of the city. Normally, even when at its most silent when everything was closed on a holiday, there was something for light. With no power anywhere, the streetlights stayed dark.

There were no windows lit up.

No cars moved.

What did not help was that the blizzard, the second in as many days, blotted out the stars, and the moon—assuming the moon was full or partial. He had no idea, as no one had seen the moon in days.

*Like being buried under three dozen blankets,* thought Daniel. *And just about as oppressive.*

"Aren't you going back to bed?" asked Victoria.

Daniel looked over at her and shrugged.

"Don't be foolish and stay up," she chided. "Everyone seems to have picked you to lead us— but you saw what happened and led them to retake the tower after all. If you don't rest, you won't be at your best. All things considered."

Daniel lifted his eyebrows and then rolled his eyes, but a small smile was on his face. "Yes, Mum…" he said as he walked back into the office.

It felt like he had just closed his eyes before a new set of rumbling, from the same area, started up all over again. Daniel threw the blanket off and ran back to the other office. "What in the name of hell?" he exclaimed, and he turned as the same officer stomped in.

"Bloody bastards are doing this on purpose," Lars said. "Started right back up again exactly sixty minutes from when they first started. I'll eat my hat if it stops at the same number of explosions."

"Flash bangs again?" asked Victoria.

Lars nodded. "Yep."

Flash bangs were a nominally a type of grenade. However, instead of dealing lethal or truly destructive damage, they were mostly just for show. A bright flash and loud noise, sometimes smoke, was usually the worst they could do. From this far, they were harmless.

Except for the light and noise.

In the middle of an otherwise completely silent night.

"It's psychological," stated Daniel quietly. "They're doing it to keep us awake—off balance."

"It's working," said Victoria.

"That's the point," said Lars, and he blew out a sigh. "It's not as bad for some of us. We know it for what it is."

"Set a patrol and watch between the towers," said Daniel. "But make sure people have set times to rest. It would be stupid to assume it's just that... he's up to something, and he wants us too tired to do anything about it. Find some earplugs or something to block out the worst of the noise and move them as far from it as possible so they can rest up without being disturbed too much."

Lars nodded and then went back downstairs. Daniel touched Victoria's arm. "Hey, what's wrong?"

"We have the benefit of the tower," she said. "I just realized there's no one else but us—and those other officers—here. What about the rest of the city? There have to be other survivors."

"And we'll find them," said Daniel. "That's a promise."

Lars came back upstairs and caught the end of the conversation. "We have a different problem. We'll have to venture past them sometime. What's left inside that cafeteria and the vending machines is now running dry. We're out of food."

Daniel closed his eyes and sighed heavily and threw off his own blanket as he paced. Victoria picked it up, smoothing it out as she did. "We can't keep hiding in here and reacting to what he's doing to us," he said. "If we do that, he'll eventually get back in and this time we'll be on the defensive. Not to mention, if he waits long enough while doing that," he pointed outside as the rumbles stopped again, "we'll be both too tired and too hungry to fight him off. We're going to have to take the fight to him."

Victoria's eyes widened, as did the other officers. "How do you propose to do that?" she asked.

"This is the police tower. We have SWAT here. We have the benefit of everything a fully equipment police department has," said Daniel, and he stopped to look at her. "And they trained us to use it all. He's not the only one with trained a trained para-military force. Except we have something he doesn't."

He stalked back to her, staring at her. "Me?" she asked, raising an eyebrow.

"The last living—"

"—That you know of," she corrected.

"… Duly elected official in the city," he finished, as he waved an arm toward the window. "We work for you, and they do not."

\* \* \* \* \*

Eric Kovach took another step back, and Garrett held his gaze. He lunged forward, forcing Kovach to retreat again. While the space between the two houses was open, it did still mean there were two houses blocking any gunfire from either direction on the road. If someone was taking a bullet, Garrett wanted it to be Kovach.

With a snarl, Garret surged forward, swinging the two-by-four straight at the knife in Kovach's hand.

Kovach jumped away—turning to his side and letting slip a small yelp as he did.

While the knife was still in Kovach's hand, the other man groaned as the lumber hit him across the back.

Garrett held the lumber in both hands and followed that with another sweep to Kovach's knees, but Kovach moved out of the way.

With a shout, Garrett lifted the lumber and ran straight at Kovach.

"Jesus Christ!" yelled Kovach. "You're crazy!"

This time Garrett's sweep with the lumber hit him just under the knees, and this time it was Kovach in the air as his arms flailed wildly in the air—finally landing flat on his back in a snowbank. Garrett grinned, but it was not a grin of mirth. Kovach pushed himself backward and away from Garrett, his eyes wide.

Garrett lifted the lumber high.

Kovach's eyes widened, and he pulled a small handgun from under his jacket as he aimed it at Garrett.

Garrett jumped to the side and rolled behind a car, still buried in snow, as Kovach fired wildly in his direction until the telltale click of it running out of ammunition echoed across the snow.

"Goddammit," breathed Kovach, and the crunch of snow as he ran behind another car told Garrett he had moved away.

"If I'm not mistaken," shouted Garrett. "You lose."

"I don't lose until you lay me flat on the ground…" There was a pause. "Dead *and* flat on the ground, old man."

*Should have known he'd cheat*, thought Garrett. *And not just bend the rules—outright break them all.*

He blew out a breath. It would not be a mistake he repeated.

A low whistle caught his attention, and he looked over. Mira slid a shotgun over to him before ducking back behind cover, a rifle still in her hands. He frowned.

It wasn't that she had a rifle.

*She shouldn't need to be in the middle of this*, he thought. *None of us should have to be in the middle of this.*

But they were.

Garrett blew out a breath and let his head rest against the car. He checked how many shells he had.

Two.

*Two more than I thought I had*, he thought. *But I'll still have to make them count.*

There was a crunch of an ice shard crushed under a boot just to his left, and he looked up. Kovach's knife buried itself into the car door centimetres from where his head had been as Garrett rolled to the side. He aimed the shotgun.

With a roar, Kovach kicked his arm, and the first shot went too wide.

So did the second.

"We're both out of ammo now, old man," snarled Kovach, shifting his knife to the other hand as he stood above Garrett. "And you've nowhere to go now. Who won this one again?"

Garrett stared up at Kovach. The younger man flipped his knife from one hand to the other and back again, a smirk on his face. *Knife fight in the middle of the road on the way to work*, Garrett thought. *Not the way I thought I'd go…*

He couldn't risk glancing at Mira or looking for Roch, so he kept his eyes on the knife.

Garrett tensed, feeling the ground beneath him for grip.

Sand.

Gravel.

Not ice and not snow.

He pulled his lips back and stared at Kovach.

"If you think I'm going to let you keep taking these people, you've another thing coming," ground out Garrett.

"From where? The ground?" asked Kovach, and he chortled. "Flat on your back like a turtle with nowhere to go. What are you going to do, old man?"

Garrett closed his fist around a handful of sand and gravel, flinging it into Kovach's face. He rolled and kicked out one leg as he did. Kovach fell hard to the ground.

Instead of getting up, Garrett pressed his advantage from the ground.

*Thanks, Dad, for paying for those judo and wrestling lessons*, he thought as he wrapped his arms around Kovach's neck in a choke hold and pulled him toward the car.

Kovach threw himself against Garrett, pushed them both into the side of the car. The metal crumpled in a bit, and Garrett gasped for breath, but he held his grip.

The younger man switched his grip on his knife to point the blade down in his fist and stabbed Garrett in the thicker part of his thigh. Garrett gritted his teeth but didn't let go.

The knife was flimsy—or had seen too much use—as Kovach pulled back and the hilt came off the blade.

He flung his arms around, trying to get a grip on Garrett.

Garrett bear rolled so that the blade, still in his leg, could not be pushed in further.

His grip slackened slightly, and Kovach used the opening to his advantage to slip out of his grip enough to elbow him in the ribs.

Garrett let out his breath in a whoosh, and he lost his grip.

Kovach rolled out from the hold, laying on the ground as he also tried to regain his breath.

*So close*, thought Garrett.

A few seconds longer and the hold would have rendered Kovach unconscious—but now that opportunity was lost. Despite the knife in his leg—which only fuelled the sudden fiery rage that spiked through him—he pushed himself to one knee as Kovach pushed himself up to his own. Kovach's eyes widened as Garrett came at him again.

"Who are you?" wailed Kovach as Garrett knocked him to the ground again.

"My name is Garrett Wither, and you'd best remember it," growled Garrett. "If you walk away from this at all."

Kovach's eyes widened again, this time as recognition flooded through him as he paled. Garrett was well aware of his reputation among the other mine workers and their support. He was known for his reliability and his skills, but he had another less savoury reputation.

No one crossed him.

No one *dared*.

That history was far behind him, but there was always a rumour that perhaps not that far behind him.

After all, he still rode his motorcycles.

But Garrett had left that behind decades ago after getting married and having children. It was something he never wanted them to be involved with, so he had walked away from it all in favour of taking a trade to provide for his family honestly.

Kovach didn't know that, though.

The moment of hesitation—of fear—from Kovach was more than enough For Garrett.

He pounced on the other man, his fist squarely landing on his jaw.

Kovach collapsed to the ground.

He didn't get back up.

Garrett blew out a breath and looked around as Mira came running up to him. "Your leg!" she exclaimed, wrapping her scarf around his leg. "Sit down before you fall down."

"I don't hear any more gunfire," he said.

"The fighting is dying down," she said, and she grinned. "We're winning."

Garrett stared down at Kovach. "Good, gag him and tie him up. Drag his sorry ass into the town square."

"Are you going to kill him?" she asked, her eyes wide.

He shook his head. "No."

"Why the hell not?" asked Roch as he joined the two of them. "After all he's done?"

Garrett looked at Roch, and then down at Kovach, watching as Mira did as he had requested. "Let him tell others what happened here. He got his ass beat, Roch, that's not something he, or the others, are going to bounce back from. We're off limits."

Roch sighed heavily and then nodded. "All right, fine. You haven't led us wrong yet. I hope you're right on this too."

Garrett ground his teeth as he and Roch half-carried and half-dragged Kovach through the driveway and onto the main road through town. Once there, he nodded to Roch, who let the bound Kovach fall to his knees.

What few remained of Kovach's people stared.

"Is this your fearless leader?" he shouted, looking at each one of them in the eyes. "Taken down by an old man who wandered through town."

He pulled Kovach up to his feet and gave him a push down the road.

"Next time I see you, Kovach, it had better be for some honest trade," growled Garrett before he was too far. "Because if it's not, you won't be walking out of here at all. You'll be six feet under. Do I make myself perfectly clear?"

Kovach's eyes thinned as he pulled the gag from his mouth. "Crystal."

"Good. Now, get the hell out of here."

He looked at the others and raised his voice. "I let you live—don't make me regret it. If I even so much as see your shadows in this town again and it's not for honest trade, you will die. Now, get out of my town."

The slavers turned snow machines back over, and some other machines they turned around. Kovach clambered shakily onto one machine, turning once to glare at Garrett.

Garrett crossed his arms and returned it.

The whine of snow machine retreated into the distance.

Moments later, a cheer erupted from the people of Worthington.

Roch slapped him on the shoulder. "Good show, Garrett. I wouldn't have believed it if I didn't see it with my own eyes—but they're really, really gone!"

Garrett finally grinned. "Yeah… now… I think we should see to my leg before I fall over."

# CHAPTER TWENTY

For the first time since this started, Daniel wished for snow. A blizzard would have given them cover. *A good, old-fashioned white-out would be perfect,* he mused.

But the sky was clear.

There were a few ways to pop back out to street level from the parking garage, or from the building. The design of the building had that all three towers, even if completely separate from each other, had a surface level connection. Only the first two floors between City Hall and the Provincial Tower connected to each other, and the third was a rooftop garden, however, once past City Hall and to the Police Tower, there was only a hallway. With City Hall, it was the same first floor making for effortless movement between the three different government buildings. However, the slope and grading between the buildings made for an interesting connection from that point, with the main level of the police tower two floors below the main level of City Hall. The street level here faced the corner of Minto and Brady, and on the opposite corner sat where the arena should have been—still was, if under major reconstruction.

There were entrances and exits on each corner the towers sat on, plus three more into the central shared courtyard, not to mention the entries and exits for the public parking garage beneath the three towers.

It was a glass—the old regular glass replaced with hardened glass since the early 2000s when fears of terrorism ripped through North America—ant hill for most of the city's business.

Daniel had always liked this—especially when it was the coldest during winter and the hottest in summer. He could park his car and then step immediately into a comfortable building without going outside… when he was lucky enough to get a parking spot. It was a popular and often full parking lot for this very reason.

He had been looking forward to the recent development on either side of Minto, with two levels of parking beneath both the arena and the condo directly across the street. The planned pedestrian tunnel above the street—much like downtown Toronto—would have been great in winter.

Neither of these existed which created part of the problem.

There was a distinct and alarming lack of cover for his own people to move downtown enough to get around Harnet and his people.

*Funny how he knows Sudbury as well as any of us,* thought Daniel.

Most of what Harnet had used to his advantage could have been gleaned from a simple search on the Internet, including the comprehensive maps and street view ability of one search engine in particular. However, Harnet's knowledge seemed beyond that. It was almost instinctive.

*The man had clearly spent time in Sudbury, possibly even raised here.*

Not for the first time, Daniel felt Harnet was familiar. He couldn't put his finger on why, but there was something familiar. *Then again, it would have been handy if I actually saw what he looked like,* thought Daniel. *I've heard his voice somewhere, though...*

He pushed it out of his mind and looked behind him. "There's only so many places he could hide and still be close enough for the light show," said one officer. "But the best guess would be the Provincial Tower... one of the first few floors. They locked the rest of them to even stair traffic. Can't get above the first floor any other way but by elevator, and they'd be shut down right now."

"He could climb up and down them," pointed out another.

The first officer shook his head. "I doubt that. Too risky for regular traffic. I'd check the doors to the stairwells, though. If they look tampered with, we're going to be digging them out of there like cockroaches."

"Thanks for the visual," said Daniel.

"Sorry," said that officer.

Daniel sighed and rolled his eyes. "We can't afford to assume they haven't gained access, though," he admitted. "Okay, you and you check all the accesses to the upper floors. Together— monitor each other's backs. Meet up with us in the lobby facing the street."

Going out of the provincial building facing Paris was risky, but ironically had more secure cover as solid cement and granite walls. They blocked the worst of the frigid wind as people exited and entered the building, and privacy, but now it served as cover to prevent his team from getting picked off by Harnet and his people.

Daniel stepped through the double doors into the Provincial building. This section was older, and it was easy to tell. The floors were scuffed with dark sole marks from more shoes on its floors over more years than City Hall or the Police Tower.

Or the budget wasn't the same. Daniel was never sure which, or if it was a mix of both. Whether by design or accident, the provincial side of the government here either forgot to spend money on keeping it up than other buildings, or even other parts of the building.

There were no corners to hide behind here— unlike on the city side.

If one of Harnet's people popped out and started shooting, they were all going to get hit. Daniel held his breath as they moved—as silently as possible—through the hall and into the lobby.

His footfalls were as far from silent as they could be. Each step on the hard linoleum echoed in the enclosed and spartan white painted corridor. He could hear his own breathing. If any of Harnet's people were in the building, they would not need to see them—they could hear them.

Each one of them tried to be quiet, stepping gently on the floor, but it didn't matter.

Daniel swallowed.

Finally, they stood on another set of hexagonal tiles, the same used in the building of City Hall, only here they matched the dark tones of the lobby—unchanged since they built the complex in the early seventies.

No one was here.

Daniel blinked, and then looked back at the others, relaxing marginally.

"Did we come prepared for a fight," asked one. "And the guests of honour couldn't be bothered to grace us with their presence?"

"Appears so," said Daniel, crinkling his brows. "This was too easy."

"Oh, there you go," said another one. "You cursed it. Now everything has to go wrong."

Daniel blew out a breath. He motioned to the elevators and then to the stairwell. "Check them."

He moved over to the glassed-in part of the lobby. This faced Larch Street, and the walkway in the gardens led to a crosswalk by the condos and the corner of Larch Street and Young Street. The short two-block street ended at another cluster of buildings surrounding a cramped parking lot. A liquor store and a fast-food coffee chain that was always busy shared the parking lot.

*Well, guess it's not so busy now*, he mused.

He couldn't even remember when he last had a coffee. They had run out a few days before.

A blur of motion had him and the others raising their weapons.

A single gunshot rang out in the confined space, and the person dropped to the floor. "Jesus Christ! Don't shoot!" shouted a woman.

Daniel had the curious sensation of having his heart leap at the sound of her voice and drop at the same time. "Hold your fire!" he shouted, holding up his off-hand. "Fitz!"

She poked her head up from behind the security desk, but then her eyes travelled past him and the officer with his hand on the stairway door. Her eyes widened, and she sucked in a breath.

"Don't touch that door!" she yelled just as the officer jimmied at the door.

Fire erupted, blowing the door clean off the hinges and across the room. A helpless officer was carried with it. Daniel jumped into a corner, but mid-jump the super-heated air blew him across the room and into the glass windows.

Felicia Moss ducked, taking cover behind the security desk while others scrambled for cover in corners and back down the hall.

Daniel slid down the window, falling into a crumpled heap. Darkness began to swallow him, the edges of his vision blurring. Gunfire broke out over and around him.

*The bastards were waiting for us*, he realized.

"You bastards!" shouted Felicia as they pulled her out from behind the desk. "How could you do this?"

"Take her back to the mall," said the one mercenary. "Quick, before those cops rally."

Gunfire was erupting again.

His people, not Harnet's.

Darkness finally claimed him.

* * * * *

Kirk was on his feet almost faster than Gina was. She lifted a brow but fell in behind him as he walked into his kitchen and to the door. Gina was silent beside him as they dressed for the outside again.

With his rifle in hand again, and Gina handed one as well, they went outside.

"Which direction?" asked Kirk.

One other pointed down the street.

Gina followed his gaze. It was the other direction than where she had come from. *If I remember right, that's the other way into town from here,* she thought. *The one by the automotive place.*

Kirk sighed. "Dammit."

"Don't blame me, I didn't bring 'em," groused Gina.

"Wasn't going to," said Kirk. "But it means we're in a bit of trouble… and you're here with us for it."

"Don't apologize. I like a good fight."

He grinned. "Well, fine then."

Gina leaned on the rail of the balcony and tilted her head. From here, she had a fantastic view in both directions. *Small wonder I had the greeting I did—when I did,* she thought. *From up here, he can see everything.*

She didn't have time to enjoy the view, even though it was at the back of her mind. The idea of taking time out with a newspaper and a coffee in the morning on the deck above their garage and just watch traffic go by—just watch life—must have been peaceful.

Now it served as a watchtower for the street.

The younger woman who had been with Kirk when Gina first came up the street pointed down the road. "They're coming from there," she said.

Gina's gaze followed where the woman pointed.

*They're not close*, she thought, her eyes thinning. *Not yet. But they will be…*

Her eyes roved over the group as she counted how many of them there were. "I can see at least ten of them," she said, looking at Kirk. "There's more of us than of them, but their intent is unmistakable."

Kirk nodded, and he brought his rifle up. "Don't need numbers when you have intent and the people you're attacking have nothing to fight back with."

Gina blew out a breath. Kirk had a point—even she could see that.

She looked back down the road, and one of the incoming looters looked up at the same time. A smile spread across his face, and he pointed up at the balcony. Gina's eyes thinned.

*So, that's their leader*, she thought as she committed his face to memory.

"What do we do?" asked someone from behind them.

Kirk shook his head, and he looked at Gina. "I take it this is a first?" she asked.

Kirk nodded.

Gina closed her eyes and then opened them again. "Hold your fire until we are absolutely sure there's no other option," said Gina. "Don't know how much ammo we have, and if we conserve it, it lasts longer. Maybe for hunting or something rather than fighting off a bunch of jerks who went all Mad Max on us."

There were a few nervous titters. "C'mon, you guys, we can do this," said Kirk, as he settled his rifle. "These are our homes and families. We tried the peaceful solution. They rejected it."

Gina smiled then as this made a few of the others finally stand a little straighter.

The group of looters had moved closer.

*If the weather was more reasonable, they'd have been on us already*, thought Gina. *At least the snow will slow them down—and us.*

Their leader—a burly, barrel shaped man no taller than she was—lifted his own rifle.

"Oh shit," breathed Gina, ducking behind the wood rail.

The others followed her lead just as bits of wood exploded from the rail, raining down on them.

"So, they made their choice clear," said Gina.

Kirk answered, "I said that, right?"

Gina shouted, "Drop your weapons! No one has to get hurt."

"You first," shouted back the leader, and she heard the next comment.

He didn't exactly mean for her to hear what he called her—but then again, perhaps she was. *Racist prick*, she thought before shouting back, "Five out of ten for lack of creativity! I'd tell you to come up and say it to my face, but I don't think you've got the guts to do so! My little brother did better when he was five!"

There was a snort from Kirk.

Gina looked over to the top of the stairs and then looked at Kirk before she took what would have been three steps to the left to the stairs. On her knees while avoiding shots by the raider meant a half crawl. *Now at least I can see down the driveway,* she thought.

More wood, this time closer to the far corner, exploded off the deck.

"If he keeps firing, I'll have to redo my deck again," groused Kirk.

Gina scowled. *That's it. He made his choice. And he's in range.*

Aiming her rifle, she stared down the sight and—once she was reasonably sure she could hit the looter—she fired.

The leader stopped as snow exploded into the air not two inches from his foot, staring up at the balcony.

He stared up at her, his eyes wide, and she stared right back.

There was silence.

*He wasn't expecting us to fight back,* realized Gina. *He honestly thought he could roll right over us.*

And then, with a howl of rage, he ran forward.

"They made their choice," called out Gina. "Let's show them what we've got."

The first of the looters stepped into the driveway and took a half step to run up the hill. Gina took a breath and then fired. The looter went down—the snow stained red from the spray. She barely noticed as bits of wood rained down from around her, but she moved to hide as another looter picked up the first one's crowbar and threw it at her. Metal against stone echoed as the crowbar bounced off the stonework and onto the deck.

She heard someone grunt from behind her. "Get our wounded inside the house," she barked.

Only a few of those with her and Kirk had rifles or actual weapons.

Some fought with broomsticks. Hockey sticks… anything that they could grab from within their homes.

Gina fired on the second looter. His eyes widened as he clutched his stomach, staring at her in the eyes as he crumpled.

She sucked in a breath.

The looter rolled down the driveway, smears of red trailing behind him.

Bile rose in her throat.

His eyes had been a sky blue. That was all she would remember about him.

She pushed her back up against the wall and looked at the rifle. It took a few seconds for it to connect that it was out of ammunition and needed to be reloaded. She sucked in a breath. *This is not the time to regret things*, she thought. *More people will die… good people. Pull yourself together!*

She had no choice but to pull herself together as the scrape of boots on wood alerted her. She looked up and stared up at another looter—this one above her with a metal bat in his hands.

She looked at her gun and then pulled out one of her knives as she threw herself to the side. The clang of the bat striking the wall echoed. Gina pulled herself to her feet, her knife held defensively—edge of the blade out and held in a reverse grip as she crouched.

The looter raised his bat and was about to strike, but a blur of motion barrelled into the looter and the two men rolled down the driveway. Gina blinked in surprise, seeing Kirk as he grappled with the younger man.

With a cry of pain, Kirk clutched his side, and the looter stood up, bat held up.

Gina flipped the knife and threw it.

The looter half turned to stare at her in surprise—the knife buried deeply into his back— before he fell, and the bat clattered to the pavement.

Kirk struggled to stand but couldn't quite get his feet underneath him.

Boots crunching on snow made her whirl, and she caught the bat Kirk rolled to her as she held like a police baton.

"You're not like the others," said the man, and she stared straight into the eyes of the leader of the looters. "From the training, I'd say either military or police."

"Close," admitted Gina. "Firefighter in the military."

"Figured," he said as he flexed his neck. "Well, guess you win this one. But… I'm not leaving without at least one prize…"

He turned and ran down the hill, and too late Gina realized what he was going for. She darted down the hill after him, but by the time she was close enough he had started her snow machine.

All she could do was watch and swear as it tore down the street and away from her.

# CHAPTER TWENTY-ONE

Dawn hinted in the sky, just staining the early morning with shades of deep violet and burnt orange instead of the grey that previous mornings had given them. Derek could see his breath—and the breath of others as it condensed immediately on exhale. He wrapped his scarf around his face and pulled the toque and wide-brimmed hat down closer around his ears, shivering through the layers.

Had it been any other day—any other circumstance—he would have called it until the weather yielded something better for riding and outside than this. It was not only a risk for them but also the horses.

But they didn't have that luxury.

He noted with relief that it was not just him and Shiloh. Helen, one neighbour from up the road, had already packed although she had not yet mounted her horse. With a bit of curiosity, he noticed she had picked a saddle he wasn't that familiar with. Shiloh leaned in, "It's a crossover between English and Western. Australians love them. I can see why. They aren't so fancy as Western, but comfortable for long rides like them. Light like English trail and hunting."

"Oh," he said, wishing he had had the same option.

But now that he was used to the English seat, he wasn't sure if he wanted to learn a new saddle on a ride like this. *Better to keep the one I know how to sit on. I can learn that one later.*

Before Cecelie, he would have questioned Shiloh on her choice of taking rifles and a few other weapons from Terrence's private stock. Now, though, he knew he might enter a hostile situation. *She was out there somewhere. A little off-putting having that hanging above us*, he thought. *Like the sword of Damocles, that.*

Derek ran a hand over the horse after letting it 'get to know him'. Most of the horses already did as he had been in and around the barns enough, but sometimes Sheridan surprised him with a horse he had never seen before at the ranch. The horse was massive, but with sturdy legs and, from the relaxed but curious flicking of ears, easy-going but, like all horses, alert. She didn't shift around but only shivered a bit as the morning was not just cold for him.

"Which one is this?" asked Derek, running his hand down the mare's neck.

"Her name is Maya," answered Shiloh. "Sheridan's favourite horse and one of the signature mares of this ranch. Well suited for riding, equestrian show jumping and eventing. Has given us some wonderful foals, but she's retired from being covered. I mean, she still could, but Maya needs a break, right, sweetheart?"

The horse seemed to agree. Derek knew why Maya was a favourite. Her personality was one of enduring patience. "She's not the classic choice for fox hunting, which is what Sheridan loves to do, but a wonderful alternative given the breed's other strengths and size," continued Shiloh.

Derek saw Helen had tensed, and her horse had picked up on it. "Everything all right?" he asked.

"I didn't realize the ranch had fox hunting," she answered.

"Oh—*no*, not real fox hunting," said Derek, but he noticed there was a snort of laughter from Shiloh and he paused before and continuing. "No foxes actually hunted. More like… how the hell do you do it again?"

"A synthetic brush and a drone," said Shiloh. "A human controls our flying fox."

"I've ridden in these 'hunts'. They're fun—if you're into that kind of thing," he answered and turned to Helen. "If things return to normal, and even if they don't, you'll have to try it. Sometimes we take a turn as the fox, too."

"That actually sounds like fun," said Helen. "On both counts. Tricking the hunters sounds like a real riot."

"That's for sure," said Shiloh.

"Forgive me for being lost here—not familiar with anything and I've never really ridden a horse, but why do some of you have different saddles? Mine looks a lot like those saddles in the movies and at the local ride-a-horse for-a-day place," said Helen, eyeing the horse again.

Derek looked over, noticing for the first time that Helen rode one of the dappled grey geldings and not one of the prized Friesians like the rest of them. Partly Cloudy was known well—he was older, but not old. When Derek had first ridden a horse here, that had been his horse.

Partly was known for two things—he loved his stall and he was the least likely of all the horses to bolt, let alone gallop. The more he had gotten to know the dappled old gent of a horse, the more he had bemoaned the fact that Sheridan should have named him Lazy Bones and not Partly Cloudy.

Except when he was with other horses.

Partly had a bit of a competitive streak in him and would pick up his feet and keep up with—or at least attempt to—the other horses in a group.

Considering Shiloh was riding one of the more famous horses at the ranch, Partly had reason to pick up his feet. It was hard to mistake the majestic, but striking, midnight black horse that was the largest of the four horses. Northern Tempest was like reality blanked out in the shape of a massive Friesian horse, a classic Baroque style Friesian. The classic version of the breed was large, with sturdy legs and ankles. Almost as large as a Clydesdale, but with only a light feathering of hair on the lower legs.

He stood in stark contrast to the snow that surrounded him.

He was calm now, but under the right rider he earned his name.

Shiloh was one of those riders. She could keep him in check, but also encourage him—not that it took much—into feats of great speed and agility. The first time Derek had watched him in action was during a jumping event as the horse's explosive energy propelled him over fences as easily as Derek could climb a low step. They well knew him for almost liking the colder weather, or at least more able to handle it.

While Partly Cloudy looked small—almost pony-like—beside the larger Northern Tempest, Partly was like a small dog with an inferiority complex.

He'd pick up his feet for Helen when he had to. Partly was competitive at heart. He would keep up to the pitch hued horse.

"I picked an Australian saddle for you," answered Shiloh. "It's a good all-round saddle. Comfortable for longer rides for both you and the horse. Not as complex as the Western, but a little more of a foundation on it than an English saddle. We do prefer the English saddles here, but that's because of the ranch's specialty of dressage and eventing."

"I imagine the lack of horn and other components means the horse is better able to move?" asked Helen.

"They also made these to conform to the horse's back contours without creating pressure points," explained Shiloh. "Not that a good Western saddle—made by a reputable company—won't also do that. The big difference is like comparing a steel frame camping backpack to a lighter one of the same, but only without a frame. You can't get the same amount of stuff onto or into a smaller pack that lacks a frame that you can the framed one, but you get a trade off on how much you're carrying. The hunter saddles, by their name, suggest that they have more to them. Naturally, the point to them is as it suggests in their name."

"Given what we're about to do, would it not be to our advantage to use the Western?" asked Helen.

"Normally, yes. However, these horses are English trained—except for old Partly, who is trained with both English and Australian. If we suddenly changed saddle and tack type, they would need a few days to get used to the feel. This isn't a good time to wear a brand spanking new boot without giving them the time to break them in first," she answered and motioned to Helen. "You first."

Helen let Shiloh boost her into the saddle. Once she was in the saddle and settled, she immediately felt the difference in her riding expectations and settled with a contented sigh.

Shiloh grinned. "Not all hunter saddles are created equal. These are top of the line saddles meant for long periods of time on horseback, but you can very quickly dismount and remount the horse."

Helen slid off in a graceful dismount, surprised and pleased by how quick and easy that was.

Moments later she stared up at the saddle, wondering just where she was to grip the saddle to remount. Shiloh patted where the horn normally would be, but a small rise and roll of leather was all that presented itself.

Her first try was rather embarrassing—the saddle slid sideways, and the horse nickered his displeasure.

Shiloh took that moment to show her the differences in adjusting the saddle. Helen tried again and this time, while not as graceful at the dismount, she could mount the horse on her own.

"As a hint, because he's huge, sometimes leading him to someplace where you can get some height advantage on him goes far. But knowing how to do it from the ground is helpful," said Shiloh.

"The big difference is that I have to put more of my upper weight over him first before I put my feet in the stirrups," said Helen. "I wasn't expecting that. I mean—you still have to with Western—but you can get away with more on the stirrup than English. You almost have to lie over him and position your butt first before putting your feet in the stirrups."

"The good news is that riding after that is nearly identical. The tack and bridle, again, have less to them and you need a gentle touch—but everything else is the same. Watch and listen to his cues," said Shiloh. "They're trained for riding over terrain and jumping stone fences chasing after a fox. They will see and hear things before you do, but they're trained to let you know so you have the tools to respond."

"Like any horse," said Helen with a smile. "It's not the rider…"

"… It's the horse," smiled Shiloh. "Good, you'll be fine."

Shiloh and Derek mounted their own horses and Shiloh, once she herself mounted, took the leads of the packhorses. Jeremy waved a hand as they passed through the doors and closed the barn door after them. With one last look at her own husband, Shiloh led them up the hill and through the gate of ice. Someone had connected the two sides with a bridge made of planks that had them buried on the two sides in snow. Thankfully, the gate was now tall enough so someone could ride under it on horseback without having to duck. On either side, there was now a tower made of snow and ice.

Derek had concerns on the stability of the towers, as snow had the tendency to topple and collapse without some sort of structure. But there was little he could do about it now other than ask Terrence once they returned. He was sure he would not leave it unstable.

Unfortunately, they still had not figured out how to make an actual gate to put in the opening. All the gate did now was restrict flow to two horses at once with a bit of space in between.

Still, it was better than nothing.

Life inside the wall was vastly different from that outside, and it was swiftly apparent. Inside, they had almost forgotten that civilization had ended once everyone had sprung into gear. The roads and driveways perfectly cleared—sure, that was mostly because of the need of snow to build the wall. Now people were throwing their efforts into keeping it clean, even if they removed snow to build something else.

Activity was also high inside the wall. There was light in the windows and warmth in the houses, even this early, and something seemed to say 'civilization still exists here'.

Once past that gate to the North, all hints of life vanished.

Houses were dark, cold and snowed in. Windows frosted to where the glass was opaque with rime. The roads completely hidden and the only hint of where they could be was the clearings between the trees. They stopped just outside the wall and looked at each other. Helen swallowed thickly. *This could have been her and Tyrell if they had not made for the farm*, Derek realized. *I think she just figured that out*.

The search parties had been through here and found only death and the occasional hermit that had always been off the grid to begin with.

"Well, we can't do anything by staring at it," said Derek thickly. "Let's get this done and get back."

They were in silent agreement as they rode out of the gate and back down the other side of the escarpment. It was not as far a ride down the other side. Sheridan's side of the valley was lower than this side, but the ridge still served as its own natural wall sheltering the valley.

The snow made it almost impassable as the horses laboured through the drifts. "It's going to take longer than I thought," said Derek with a heavy sigh as the morning sun came up and tracked through the sky. "What time is it? Nine, ten?"

"Quarter after nine," answered Shiloh. "And we're only a third of the way."

Thankfully, the ride so far had been uneventful. The snow did not bother the horses. As they rode into the flat farmland, it became apparent by the drifts that it would be both harder and easier to get through the road. The drifts were like sand dunes—they had tall sides and low sides, and the wind would blow the drifts into rippling waves. Like a desert.

On the low side, the ground was almost visible and easily ridden. It was the navigating through the tall parts of the drifts and trying not to break the leg of the horse if the snow gave way beneath them that was challenging.

While Derek rode, he kept his rifle at the ready. Helen did the same to his left, but they encountered nothing. No signs of life or other noises greeted them. There was nothing but the howl of wind over the frozen snow drifts.

What remained was the crunch of the horse's hooves as they pushed through the thin crust to the soft snow beneath and their own low conversation.

The wind whistled, and the snow settled with a gentle sigh—like paper ruffled in a library. Trees snapped and crackled in the cold as they swayed in the wind. Birds that had not migrated south chirped and tweeted in the branches of the trees.

There was no one—not a single living person—to disturb the wild symphony left in their wake.

# CHAPTER TWENTY-TWO

The ringing in Daniel's ears was driving him crazy, as was the low buzzing. Light was the last thing to penetrate the dark haze he floated in. Finally, he took in a breath. His eyes widened as pain lanced through him.

His eyes widened, and then he stared in confusion at the ceiling.

The Provincial building's ceiling had a similar pattern to the floor. This ceiling was basic drop ceiling, although the fluorescent lighting was off. Not that they had been on since the world went crazy.

He looked to one side, watching it snow outside the window.

The apartment building, built half into a rock, was visible outside.

Daniel looked around.

*I'm in the Mayor's office*, he realized, and he tried to sit up.

"No, no, no," said Victoria, as she moved into his range of vision from somewhere behind... *above?*... his head. "You're still too injured to move around."

"The others?" he asked, his voice rough.

"We lost five—one of them staff—the other four all good officers," she answered, and he clenched his eyes closed. "Hey, no, there was no way any of us could have known. You were prudent. If you hadn't thought to check, it could have been another place we would fight over floor by floor."

"If not for Fitz's warning..." his eyes opened again. "*Fitz!* She was there! She warned us! They took her somewhere."

"If she's been surviving between here and wherever Harnet has hidden himself without being captured before now," said Victoria. "Then she is everything you said she is. Unfortunate they took her captive. Curious they did instead of killing her..."

A thread of worry wormed its way into the back of his mind. He wasn't so naïve to think about what a group of men, if not perfect gentlemen, could do with a lone woman—even if Fitz was likely to fight tooth and nail to prevent it. *She'll probably kill a few before they finally take her down*, he thought.

*Small consolation.*

"I have to get her out of there."

"Daniel, you're still too wounded to stand up, let alone walk into wherever it is Harnet has used as his stronghold to for a rescue," insisted Victoria, and, at his look, she sighed. "Look, if what I think has crossed your mind, I can definitely tell you it's crossed all our minds."

"Then you know why—"

She held up a hand. "What good would it do for you to storm into wherever he is—and we don't even know that yet—in the shape you're in? You can't even stand up."

Daniel lay back. The hard surface, padded as it was, was still on the top of her desk. Considering the alternative, he was glad it for her desk. He had never noticed how plain it was compared to the rest of the room.

With a sigh, Daniel closed his eyes.

*I hate this*, he thought. *This is not why I changed careers to do this instead of welding.*

An old memory, one dredged up from the very depths of his mind, pushed its way forward.

Victoria patted his arm and tiptoed from the room. She closed the door behind her. Daniel realized she must have thought he had fallen asleep but couldn't raise the wherewithal to correct her.

Decades ago, he had found himself in a similar position as he was now.

He had not been wounded, no, but he had found himself similarly struck helpless. Back then, all he had to defend himself — and his family — was a steel baseball bat.

His daughter had been barely into her teens. He had been between contracts then, and money was difficult to come by. Work had been scarce. They had laid Fiona off from the tree nursery, and as a botanist it was not as if she could find a similar position anywhere else.

*We could move*, she had said then. *Somewhere with more work — Sheridan is still young. She could go to a better school…*

Daniel could not remember what his argument had been against the idea. Probably about Sheridan not having to uproot herself from her friends and that she was in a good school where they were. Living on EI was not the greatest solution, but it was short term. Things would bounce back.

They always did.

*And they still should*, he thought. *We can bounce back from even this situation… maybe not now. Maybe not tomorrow. But eventually*.

The problem was that he still had to stop, wait, and let others do for him instead of out there with them. Daniel sighed again and let himself relax. He would get Felicia out of wherever she was. He may not be out there, but he could organize his people into teams to cover more ground.

Mind made up, and his conscience—at least temporarily—soothed, Daniel let himself drop off into sleep.

\* \* \* \* \*

Shiloh dismounted, and they looked around. "We can't stay out in the open, we'll freeze and so will the horses."

"I know, but we can't keep going either," pointed out Derek before nodding at the horses. "If we can't see, then neither can they. And we'd risk them falling into something and breaking a leg. Not worth it."

Shiloh blew out a breath and looked around. She then pointed to a deserted house that had a sizable garage attached to it. "What about there? It's large enough for both the horses and us. If it has a cement or dirt floor, we can make a fire pit and keep the doors open enough to allow the smoke to escape. Between the fire and the windbreak, we should be fine."

Derek and Shiloh checked the deserted house to see if there was anything suspicious inside. They then checked the garage for non-human habitation. Not that bears would be awake at this time of the year, but it was better to be safe than sorry. "Clear," said Derek, and Shiloh nodded her agreement.

"We could check the house for supplies," suggested Helen.

"It was probably checked already," pointed out Shiloh.

Derek sighed and said, "Can't hurt to double check it."

He and Helen entered cautiously, finding signs of forced entry, and walked through the rooms. The very first room off the garage was the kitchen and mudroom. The sight before them stopped them in their tracks.

Huddled around an electric oven was a family of four. In their desperation they had turned it into a wood stove.

Their bodies frozen in the same position in which they had died.

*Hypothermia, or even carbon monoxide*, thought Derek. *Tried to burn something in that oven.*

Derek paused, staring at the frozen child. Helen touched his shoulder. "Snap out of it," she said, her voice low. "Nothing we can do for them now—but we have a house full of people with kids back at that Manor and we can help them."

He blew out a breath, watching as it fogged in the air. "The oldest one can't be older than eight."

Compressing her lips, Helen stepped in front of him. "And how old is Eric?"

Derek blinked. *What does Shiloh's son have to do with... oh.* He sighed. "Yeah, good point."

He cleared his throat and looked at Helen again as they silently moved past them and to the fridge. It felt wrong to rifle through their cupboards with their silence watching them, but to leave something there that could otherwise feed the living would have been a waste.

"Who puts a can of paint under a kitchen counter?" wondered Helen.

Derek shrugged his shoulders and while he checked the bedrooms, she checked the living room, den and bathrooms.

There was nothing useful for them to pick over. "Take a note of the house," he said when they returned to the garage. "We'll have to send burial teams when the weather isn't as bad to cremate the dead."

As the last of the light from the sun faded in the twilight, the sounds of the animals and birds along with the wind outside faded. Not even crickets dispelled the frozen silence.

Once the surroundings grew quiet, they stopped their conversation, almost as though something held them quiet. He could not put it into words if he tried, but it was not fear. At least it was not for him.

The only thing that broke the silence was the crackling of the fire.

It was as if all that remained of the world—even though they knew that just over the ridge was Sheridan and the farm full of survivors—was the small space in that garage. It was humbling and, while terror wasn't applicable, there was a certain amount of trepidation of what the next days could hold.

Logic said that they could not be the last of everything. Someone else—somewhere else—had to have also survived this, but where they were and how they did may never come to light. They could be the next town over and no one would know until someone got curious enough to range out and find out if it were true.

It was humbling to see just how large the world really, truly was. Life before…

Derek stopped himself at that very thought.

*… Life before… life before what?* What exactly had ended everything as decisively as it had?

Had it been a nuclear war and now they would have to deal with fallout and nuclear winter on top of the typical Canadian winter? Did a virus wipe out most of humanity?

He discounted these since there would have been some hint even among the survivors had that been the case. It had to have been something significant to bring civilization to its knees, but he could not figure out what it could have been.

Derek thought about the weeks leading up to all of this.

Gas prices had been going up sharply—this had been all over the news. But it meant little. Prices always went up and fluctuate around. It was one of the primary reasons that cars like the Smart car and Tesla had come out as an alternative to petroleum-based fuel. It also was not the first time gas prices had spiked. The seventies had been infamous for a rather large spike in gas prices, as had the early 2000s.

He almost dismissed it.

But something set its hooks in the back of his mind and refused to let go.

Gas prices had not been the only hint of trouble. Much of the furor over going solar and other alternatives was everyone who cared about it had been up in arms about carbon in the atmosphere and other greenhouse effects. But where before it had been mostly token efforts lately it had turned into a major industry.

So major that some companies well-known for oil and other fossil fuel exploration had turned to alternative sources of fuel and re-branded themselves as the purveyors of 'energy' versus oil or gas.

Derek sat bolt upright, nearly knocking himself out on a hanging tool on the workbench. "It's the end of oil…"

He winced as he spoke, his voice loud in the silence.

The others jumped, startled. "What in the name of Christ, Derek?" asked Shiloh.

"What brought all of this on," he said, motioning around the room.

"The end of oil?" asked Helen, and her eyebrows rose as she looked over at Shiloh, who only shrugged. "Why did you even… what gave you that idea?"

"Think about the news lately," he continued. "Gas prices soaring to unreal levels. Natural gas and the cost to heat a home at the ridiculous point... Some people even gave up on their gas furnaces and were using electric space heaters because even hydro was less expensive. If you had an oil furnace, forget it. I worked for a solar panel system installer—we had more calls for panels so that people could net meter... We had far more calls than we could sometimes handle. We had insurance sales people jumping over to our industry because it was the hot ticket to sell."

"So... we just ran out, and the world toppled?" asked Shiloh. "That makes little sense. The government would have warned us it was going to happen."

"Shiloh, you worked for Ontario Shared Services while in school... would they, really?" asked Derek.

Shiloh looked down at the ground. "It's not as if they'd go out of their way to not tell people. Well... at least the government workers and office administration wouldn't. If they had the information to give, they'd give it."

"... But?" asked Helen.

"Well, I don't work for them anymore, so I wouldn't have heard anything, anyway. I can tell you that with bureaucracy even if they had the information there were always approvals needed and, well... It's not that they'd try to not get the information out, but whether it would be useful by the time anyone got, it is the real question. And they'd have to know about it first. Can't supply a public service information bulletin without the information in the first place," she answered. "If all this were true, and the government knew it wasn't 'the government' that would know per se. Just those in office with that decision-making power to pass the information along."

"Would there be a report somewhere?" asked Derek.

He knew Shiloh's point, having dealt with the government more than once. He knew, however, that the others didn't understand. Helen looked particularly confused.

"Okay, say your theory is right. If there was a report written that our resources in oil and natural gas were about to run out and we were all, globally, at that critical point… then, yes, there would be," answered Shiloh. "However, not all government offices would know that even existed. Government and the bureaucracy just don't work like that."

"How do they work then?" asked Helen, still confused and her brows crinkled.

"Well, there would have to have been a study or a report on something that someone noticed. They'd write a report and send it to a supervisor in whatever office they were working in for whatever ministry that office was part of. That one report would have to cross a few hands to finally arrive at the Minister of whatever office in question; and it would be up to that minister to decide what to do with it. He or she could either sit on it and not pass it along at all... Or it could get sent to a committee of yet more ministers to decide on what to do about it," answered Shiloh. "Once they had finally decided, they'd send to yet another committee to decide on what policy needed instituting and they would then create a policy. Only at that point would word trickle back down the same channels through to the various ministries that need to know. If a public service announcement was deemed necessary, only then would a bulletin get released—after they had sent it for drafting, anyway."

"The problem is that we don't know what ministry would have known and if they even did," mused Derek.

"And what's the point of worrying about it now?" asked Shiloh. "It's too late."

"She has a point," agreed Helen, as they turned to Derek. "Why bring it up?"

"Because if we know what caused civilization to topple, we know what we're working with and approximately what it will take to survive in the future—and what others are going to be eyeing for supplies."

*Not to mention Sheri would want to know—no,* need *to know,* he thought. *She'd need to know why 'Rome' had fallen so that she wouldn't base our new bastion of civilisation on shaky foundations.*

"There's nothing we can do about it now," said Shiloh. "We may as well focus on the mission at hand and tell Sheridan your theory when we get back."

"Theory?" asked Derek dryly.

"Well, it's not as if we can prove it—even it makes sense," she answered.

He nodded, and silence descended on them again. Even though it was quiet enough not to need it, they agreed on setting a watch and Derek decided he should take that first watch. His mind refused to let go, and he needed time to think and process his conclusion. Sitting a watch would be perfect to allow him to do that.

# CHAPTER TWENTY-THREE

Derek's eyelids refused to stay open. It didn't matter how many times he got up to walk around, stretch, or even get a breath of freezing cold air to wake himself up with. *I'm going to fall asleep before my watch is up*, he thought, watching his breath fog the air.

Going outside of the carport had been the only way to wake himself up.

He sighed, looking up into the sky. The stars above him lit up the sky.

With no light pollution from the city, there was nothing to make them seem dim. Nothing to filter the dark but more darkness and the reflection from the snow itself.

And the flicker of something yellow in the distance.

Derek tilted his head to the side.

*Didn't realize there was a set of stars this close to the horizon*, he thought. *At least, not yellow ones…*

The light flickered out, and then another flickered on, but slightly to the left of the first one. It disappeared, only to reappear with the first.

*What in the…?*

It dawned on him.

They weren't stars but lights in a structure across the field.

Derek rubbed his eyes and stared again.

*No mistaking that*, he realized. *There are people over there. But what the heck is even over there?*

Rubbing his arms, he moved back into the carport, and the warmth afforded by the fire. As he rubbed his hands as close as he could handle over the fire, he sucked in his lower lip. It was then his eyes widened.

There was an electrical contracting company on the same road as the ranch. If he wasn't mistaken, and he was sure he was not across that very field, was the warehouse and garage for the trucks for that same company.

*It doesn't make any sense*, he thought. *The owner of that place doesn't even live there. He closes that up every winter holiday to take just that—there's no reason for anyone to…*

"Sons of a bitches," he swore under his breath, and then checked to make sure he hadn't woken the others.

Breathing a sigh of relief, he took in a steadying breath.

Cecelie.

The warehouse was on the river which led past the very outer edge of the ranch and down to Rick's.

*That's one mystery solved.* His lips compressed into a thin line.

*They still seem a touch too organized for comfort. This doesn't make sense at all. There's no way she could lead this many this well. She doesn't have that kind of leadership capability.*

The only other option was too worrying—and that was if she were working for someone else. *Who, though? Who would even take her? Who would let her lead that many?*

*Or was she just another underling?*

*That's a scary thought.* Derek looked at the wall, almost imagining the ranch and Manor down the road on the other side of that wall. If Cecelie was only a symptom of a much larger problem, then there was little chance they could fight them off.

*Don't think like that, Derek,* he chided himself. *If they could have taken the ranch, they would have done so already. They wouldn't have bothered to negotiate with Terrence or try to cut us off on Panache Lake with Rick—we'd be like them already.*

The alarm on his watch cut through the silence and echoed off the carport wall. Shiloh rolled over and sat up as he silenced the alarm. Helen snorted, opening an eye, but when she saw Shiloh already up and moving and Derek settling by the fire, she rolled over and fell back to sleep again.

"Anything interesting?" asked Shiloh, her voice soft.

Derek nodded. "Watch for lights to the east and a bit to the south. I think there are people in the electrical place."

"People?" Shiloh lifted a brow.

Derek looked at her, lifting a brow. "Cecelie."

Shiloh's eyes widened, and she mouthed, *Oh*. She took a breath and said, "That could be trouble."

"I don't think they know we're here," he answered. "Which gives us the advantage. We'll leave before first light tomorrow and keep to the treeline. With any luck, we'll be past their line of sight and to the Fire Hall before they know we were even here."

"Good idea," she said, and she patted his shoulder. "Your turn for some sleep. It looks like we're going to need every ounce of rest for tomorrow."

Derek nodded, and he slipped into his sleeping bag.

Sleep yanked him down into oblivion before he registered a second thought.

* * * * *

His nose twitched first, and then his eyelids flickered. Garrett sucked in a breath, letting the scent of coffee pull him from slumber. He cracked an eye open and groaned.

*I don't even like coffee,* he thought.

The problem was that coffee was the harbinger of mornings. His mother, and his grandmother, had always brewed it right before the first hint of dawn—it had been their way of waking up. His grandfather never drank the stuff, but his mother! She would drink it all day, if it was available.

Garrett sighed, groaning again as his leg protested moving.

Mira pushed the door open, and he pulled the blankets over himself again.

"I'm awake," he said.

"I know," she answered. "Your groaning gave that away."

He snorted, letting her put a stack of pillows behind him to support his back as he leaned against the headboard. Another set of pillows—where she had found them all was a mystery—supported his leg. "I know you're not much for coffee," she said. "But if you want tea or something else, I could make it."

"Nah," he answered. "Although a bit of broth would be great."

She smiled and patted his shoulder. "I'll see what I can find. I'll let my grandfather know you're awake."

Garrett sighed, leaning his head back into the pillows.

When he opened them again, the shadows had changed angle. Garrett stared at them and shook his head. *Fell asleep again*, he mused. *I think I lost a few hours, at least*.

Roch walked into the room and shook his head. "Awake again?"

Garrett snorted, rubbing the back of his neck with one hand. "For now, it appears. What time is it?"

"Around noon," answered Roch. "With that leg injury, it's not surprising. He got you real good with that knife of his."

"Yeah, it didn't tickle."

Roch sat down in the chair by the bed, shimmying it over until he was at the very edge of the bed. Now close enough to poke Garrett in the shoulder which he did, Roch said, "You didn't even know us from a hole in the ground and you put your life on the line. The rest of the town is of a mind to ask you to stay."

"I'm not going anywhere for a while," pointed out Garrett, looking down at his leg, although it was covered by a blanket. "I'd have to walk out of here first and I don't see doing that soon."

"Four weeks," agreed Roch. "At least. Which means you aren't leaving until February at the earliest. Listen, why don't you stay? We could use you. I don't know what brought you here in the first place, but if they can survive for a month, then they don't need you. We do."

Garrett chewed his bottom lip.

Roch was right. He would be lucky to make the trip before January was out, and it was still not quite past Christmas—unless he had lost that much time in recovering enough to wake up. *It doesn't feel quite that long*, though, he thought. *A day, maybe. But not more than that...*

"I don't know," answered Garrett as he looked up at the ceiling. He blew out a breath. "That's a big thing to ask. Even if they can survive without me—and I have no doubt that they can—what I was going up there for hasn't changed. And then there's my family to think about too."

"And how far are they?" asked Roch, lifting a brow.

"My daughter lives just outside of Whitefish—on Panache Lake Road, actually, so not that far," answered Garrett. "Although, it is a bit far to walk. Especially in winter and all. As to where I was going, that's High Falls."

Roch's eyebrows rose. "Why would you need to head there... *oh*. You're here for that. They sent you to see to the dam, weren't you? I never found out what you even did before everything went to hell, but if you're going up there then... are you a power engineer?"

"Electrical engineer," answered Garrett. "With power generation as my specialty. I was, when I started, an electrician like my father. Mining and industrial—just like him and his father before him."

Roch's eyes were still wide. "You could be the one that turns it all back on."

"I dunno," said Garrett, shaking his head. "If everything is off, the best I could do is see to Worthington's needs, maybe even Nairn. Further than that would require more than just that dam if the entire grid is down… and even then, because we're a grid, it's still not that simple. I'd need to restart the whole Eastern seaboard and I can't do that all by myself."

Roch sighed, looking down at the ground. "Ah."

"Sorry to disappoint."

Roch shook his head. "I won't lie. I had hoped that it would be as simple as someone like you just flipping a switch, but you're no miracle worker… outside of giving some slavers the ass whoopin' of their lives."

Garrett grinned. "Well, that was just a small group. All I did was remove a tiny sliver out of a hand. I didn't take on an entire army."

"Listen." Roch put a hand on Garrett's shoulder. "At least give us until you fully recover, until you decide to move on or not. I know you don't owe us a damn thing—the opposite—but…

please. You're the brightest spark of hope to walk into this town in months."

Garrett nodded. "I can at least give you that much."

Roch stood up, and Garrett watched him leave. He blew out a breath once the older man left.

*Stay here?*

There was no way he could. He still had a job to do at High Falls. Maybe after it was done, he could come back and stay, but he had to go there first.

*There's no straightforward way out of this one*, he thought. *I don't want to leave them either, but I can't leave the job they sent me to do undone. Given the situation, though, I don't know if I even can do the job they sent me to do.*

But, with enough of the local grid cut off from the rest of the bigger grid, he could use what the dam generated to give High Falls and Worthington their electricity back. That was possible. *It won't be easy*, thought Garrett. *I would have to oversee the very hydro lines linking us to the rest of the Eastern Seaboard cut and terminated properly... and then control the supply so that we don't get surges.*

He blew out a breath.

*But first I have to get to High Falls...*

And for that, he needed two good legs.

# CHAPTER TWENTY-FOUR

Gina felt like someone had dipped her in ice. All she could do was stare, the bat held loosely in her hand, as the surviving looters fled on foot while their leader rode her machine away.

A few moments later and it had disappeared around the corner.

*Dammit, no…* she thought, grinding her teeth. *How am I going to get back to the others now?*

"Gina!" shouted one survivor. "Kirk's hurt."

Gina sighed and trudged back up the hill. She kneeled down beside Kirk as he leaned up against the wall of his garage. "Well, that could…" he caught his breath. "… Gone far better."

"No one died on our side," said Gina, running her hands up and down his side. He grunted when she touched his side. "Can you walk?"

"I think so," he answered, and she helped him up to his feet. "Dammit."

It took both Gina and another of the survivors to walk Kirk back to his house and inside. Jen came running upstairs from the basement. "What happened?"

"One of the…" Kirk paled, sucking in another breath. "Ow."

"Sit your fool ass down before you fall down," barked Jen, and she looked up at Gina. "Well, you sit too. Judging by the bruise on your eyebrow, you've taken a few good hits too."

Gina felt her eyebrows lift, and then she winced as she lifted a hand to her face. When she pulled her hand away, her fingertips were shiny and red. "Oh," said Gina as she sat down heavily.

Jen looked back up and pointed to the others. "Catch her."

Gina looked back up, this time her eyebrows knit together. "I'm fine."

"I'm sure," answered Jen, as she turned her attention back to her husband. "The good news is that I don't think they're broken and I don't think there's any internal bleeding, but you'll be some sore for a while. What the hell were you thinking?"

"That I needed to protect our house," answered Kirk, and he looked up at her. "And you."

For all of a moment, Jen's expression softened, but then her eyes thinned as she pointed at him. "Don't you dare try that on me, you old smooth talker."

Kirk tried to shrug, but his eyes widened as the movement pained him. "Was worth a try."

Gina leaned back in the chair, watching as Jen settled her husband into his chair and as the pinched look on his face eased. Kirk watched as Jen fussed over Gina. "I don't think it's shock, sweetheart, I suspect what you're seeing on our young friend's face is worry."

"They took my snow machine," said Gina.

Jen paused, her lips compressing. "I thought I heard it leaving. At first, I admit I thought it was you leaving us, but when you came in with Kirk, I knew what must have happened."

Kirk took a breath, wincing, and then released it. "What will you do now?"

"Look, I came to see if you'd come back to Middle Lake with me—to Russell," said Gina. "That's still on the table. You'd be a lot safer at Middle Lake, given the distance, than you would here."

"This is our home," Jen's scrunched up her face, almost as if she had bitten off something sour. "We're not about to pack up and leave it."

"Wait," said Kirk, lifting his hand. "Gina has a point. If we stay here, we're just going to keep fighting them off. Eventually they will overwhelm us. It's simple math, really."

Jen whirled to face her husband, pointing at him as she did so. "Kirk Reginald MacIssac, you look…"

"No," he answered, his voice soft. "I went out there to make sure you were protected. If that means we pack up and leave, then we leave."

"And go where?"

Kirk looked up at the ceiling and then over at the pictures on the wall. "Our son lives near Long Lake. I imagine it must be like Middle Lake?"

They aimed this last toward Gina, and Gina's eyes widened. "Long Lake is farther out than Middle Lake, yeah. So, it's probably a hell of a lot better. Better lake to fish on, too. Farms. Good family."

Kirk grinned as he stared at Gina, and then he pointed at her. "I have a counteroffer. You go back to my nephew and you tell him to get to Long Lake. He won't know how to get there, but I imagine someone in your little community on that lake does. You come join us in Long Lake."

Gina's jaw dropped as she leaned back in the chair as she thought, *Well, that was bold.*

But was it really? Kirk had a point. Long Lake was a far better area than even Hannah and Middle Lake to survive on. Jagged cliffs surrounded it to prevent invasion… *And part of me still keeps wanting to skitter off and away from that concept. Invasion. We're weeks into this and I still keep looking outside expecting to see normal life.* She fought the urge to snort. *But Long Lake has the mountains, the cliffs, the clean lakes… the farms… it'd be better than Hannah and Middle Lake.*

It was further from the city as well—practically cut off from the rest. Walking there, even in summer, could take a full day.

*The old man has a point*, Gina finally sighed as she looked straight at Kirk. "Look, all right, I might agree with you but it's not just my decision to make. When I get back there, I'll definitely tell Russell where you headed and let the others know you've invited us."

"Good," said Kirk, and he nodded. "Now, Jen…"

"We raised our sons here," she said, her voice quiet. "You built this house."

"I customized the house based on a contractor's plans for an entire neighbourhood. It's not exactly unique."

"You still gave it a vision the contractor couldn't." She looked around and sighed. "But what is the point of it if we're not here to see it. You're right."

"I don't like it either," admitted Kirk, running a hand over his head. "We're not leaving it all here. It will take us time to pack our best, and most portable memories and lock up the rest. Same with the others… and then we're going to have to figure out how we're getting to Long Lake."

"I saw a truck at the bottom of this driveway," pointed out Gina.

"Yes, well, it's not exactly four by four, but it'll do in a pinch. At least we should be able to get some of our stuff out of here if we follow in the ruts the others will leave," said Kirk, and he leaned back. "So, are you coming with us?"

"No," answered Gina.

Kirk's eyebrows rose and Jen stared at her.

"But I thought—" began Jen.

"—I said I would take it to Russell and the others, but I have a large score to settle and a snow machine to get back. I had supplies and a toolkit I want back on that snow machine," answered Gina, and she grinned although it didn't quite reach her eyes. "You could say I have a debt to repay."

"You're going after them?" asked both Kirk and Jen.

"That's suicide," said Jen.

Kirk nodded. "I'm with my wife on that one."

"I will come back," Gina said.

Kirk blew out a breath. "Listen, I can see you're very capable. You've got training—that's plain as day. But you're still all by yourself."

"My people have a long history with the bush. I can find my way around with no one knowing I was there," said Gina, and she stretched. "Just maybe not today. It's late as it is, and I would like to rest and recover a bit."

She smiled sheepishly.

Kirk nodded. "Jen will set you up a room. You're welcome to stay as long as you like—at least until we leave here ourselves. I won't leave a woman by herself in this world. Not even one who saved my ass."

* * * * *

The day was as grey as Daniel's mood. *I shouldn't be here*, he thought. *I should be out in Whitefish, stuffing myself silly on my Mom's turkey dinner*. He glowered through the window, shifting the sling. He held a hand on his shoulder and arm as pain lanced through him.

*I should also be out there—not stuck in here.*

That was the real crux of the matter.

Daniel hated being stuck inside.

Hated being sidelined.

Now, in the most critical moment, he had no choice but to sit, wait, and be on the sidelines while others went out.

Each day more people flooded into City Hall. The story was the same.

With the power out, they had no heat. With no transportation into the city, or out of it, food was running out. Fresh water was ending as the pressure in the water pipes ran low—or froze entirely. People were dying as medications required for life ran out.

Some of those who made it to City Hall died soon after, just on that last point alone.

*Each day we lose the old wisdom. Those who remember further back*, he thought, shifting the sling on his shoulder again. *With each passing day, our own history vanishes.*

He sighed, pushing that out of his mind. That was not his problem. If that problem belonged to anyone, it would likely be Victoria and whoever she decided should carry it with her. Once he healed, and ready to go back out, his problem would make sure she lived long enough to hold on to that.

Victoria came into his room, her hands on the shoulders of a younger woman, although this was inaccurate.

The girl was in her teens, but not by much. Her eyes were wide, and she looked from Victoria to Daniel and back again. Victoria nodded and gave her shoulders a slight squeeze. "Go on, tell him what you told me," said Victoria.

Daniel moved over to the overstuffed armchair, using one arm and the pillows they had found to take the pressure off his shoulder. "Have a seat," he said, his voice soft. "I swear I won't bite."

"Can you really do anything?" she asked.

Daniel lifted his brows as she finally sat in the other chair across from him. Victoria didn't stray far. In fact, she reclaimed her own chair behind her desk, folding her fingers together on the desk and leaning her chin on them.

"I can only try," he answered. "What do you need done?"

She shook her head. "Nothing that you haven't already done."

He looked at Victoria, and she shook her head. "It's what she can do for us—or rather, what she has to tell us."

Daniel looked over at her again but said nothing. From what he remembered when Sheridan was this age, it was remarkably easy to spook a young person—any young person. The only ones he didn't spook were those who usually were destined to be become officers themselves or were interested in policing. It would never matter what situation they found themselves in that brought them into contact with police, they would be far more curious than nervous. Others were apprehensive, and if approached the wrong way went from that to downright nervous.

It was then they would clam up.

Daniel was one of those—perhaps from as a parent himself—who the others had always sent in to talk to children. Maybe because, as his mother liked to say, it was because he was little more than a big kid himself.

*A big kid who would love nothing more than to have the bullies brought to justice*, he thought. *If I had to say it that way.*

"Okay, what's up?" he asked.

She blinked. "That's not how everyone else asked me."

"I'm not everyone else," he pointed out, leaning back in the chair.

He cringed as he hit his shoulder the wrong way, closing his eyes as pain—white hot and sharp—tore through him again. He heard two chairs scrape the floor. "Dan?" asked Victoria, her voice low and close to his ear.

"Is he okay?" asked the girl.

"Dan, talk to me here," said Victoria again.

He sucked in a breath and opened his eyes. "I'm fine," he ground out, and that ended on a groan. "I just leaned the wrong way, and it hit me like a hammer."

"If you would rather wait," said Victoria.

He shook his head, seeing the girl at his elbow. She had moved the pillow to sit behind him and another one to cradle his arm. He patted her arm. "That's much better, thanks," he said.

She moved back to the chair, but she seemed as ready as Victoria to jump back to help him.

Once she sat down again, he looked over at Victoria. Instead of sitting behind her desk, she had moved around to the same side of as they were. She leaned against it, her arms crossed over her chest as she stared down at him.

He nodded at the girl. "Okay, let's try this again. Victoria said you have something to tell me."

"I live in the condos with my parents," she said, pointing toward the mall. "In the mall."

He tilted his head to the side, not sure what her point was. He crinkled his brow. The mall was an unusual anomaly in the middle of the city. When it had first been built, they had meant the tower for offices. The mall itself had sprawled across two levels with every known chain retailer. At its height in the sixties, it had been as busy as the Eaton Centre and Yorkdale in Toronto—and as high end. Everything those two malls were known for had been in the Downtown Shopping Centre.

But it was not to last.

Starting in the nineties, once the New Sudbury Centre and Four Corners Mall opened, business slowly died. It hadn't helped that in a city where pay-to-park was not well received, that parking had been expensive.

This change drove shoppers and mall wanderers away from the downtown mall and to the other two centres.

As retail itself moved online, and parking became more and more expensive and harder to get downtown, the stores closed as businesses had no choice but to close. The mall shrank—not physically as the building outside never changed— but to rescue the space mall management turned to renovating the upper floor into office space as the demand increased. Where once were stores became a call centre, and then two call centres and a school.

The major department store that had taken up over ten thousand square feet and two floors became a government office, and when it moved, another call centre and data centre moved in.

This had helped the retail spaces—those that survived—as they turned to supporting the office workers now occupying three quarters of where mall used to be.

Nearly a decade later seen a whole new shift.

The office rental market died.

No one could put a finger on exactly when things shifted from working in the office to working remotely and from home. There had been a few severe flus to go through. People spent more time sick or avoiding getting sick. With high-speed internet now standard, and security protocols enabling working from home as easily as working from the office companies shrank their office footprint. Some office remained, but instead of needing to house four hundred employees in a call centre it was easier to send them home with a laptop—if they had the office at home to work out of—and have perhaps only fifty to a hundred in the call centre and the other three hundred or more work from home. Overhead on renting an office dropped for the company and they could afford a few more employees that rent would have rendered impossible to have without cutting into profits.

Suddenly the mall found itself in the middle of a second crisis—what to do with an empty office tower?

One developer, after visiting Toronto, saw many buildings turning to mixed use. The top three quarters or third the building became condos or apartments. In a growing city where living space always was in high demand, it was a working solution and Sudbury was no different.

The entire office tower of the downtown mall, which had changed names a few times to the point where even he didn't know what it was called anymore, became a new condo development. Where the Eatons had sat before going bankrupt facing Paris and Notre Dame became the new home of an expanded grocery store. The college expanded, using the old entrance of a dead call centre as its new entrance and the remnant of the old food court and fountain revamped so it had a more impressive entrance.

The entire second floor of the mall became office space.

The first floor saw new life as a mall again—the condos in the office tower feeding a new generation of shoppers into the mall who didn't need to pay for parking as they already were in the building.

This girl lived in those condos.

However, how that related to things was a puzzle.

"I'm sorry," he said, shaking his head.

"People in uniforms pushed us out of our home," said the girl, and Daniel found himself riveted.

*Harnet.*

*So, that's where he went,* realized Daniel.

"These uniforms were they like ours?" asked Daniel.

She shook her head. "No, they didn't have a country flag on them. That's how I knew they weren't really real—the real ones have a Canada flag on them."

"After they forced you all out, what then?" asked Daniel.

"I don't know, but we couldn't go back. We were shot at or told we couldn't go back. It wasn't our home anymore—not unless we would swear loyalty to the Colonel."

*Gotcha*, thought Daniel. *Now I know where you're hiding.*

He leaned back, sucking in a breath. This time it was not in pain.

He nodded at the girl. "Thank you both. You're right. That is something I needed to know."

Victoria nodded to her, and she left the office. Victoria crossed her arms and looked over at Daniel. "Now you know where he is," she said. "However, there is something else you need to think about."

Daniel looked up at Victoria. For the second time, he was puzzled. "And that is?"

"He has the library."

It was in her tone. Daniel could not think of a reason, other than the books themselves, of why the library would be so important. By itself—yes, the books were important. Eventually, if they were to rebuild, what they housed in the library would be critical to their success. Their history was there.

But it would not help them now.

Not unless it had a way to conjure food out of thin air.

"I know we'll need to get it back eventually," he admitted. "That's our history, not his..."

"No, Dan, you don't understand," she said. "That branch of the library not only has reference material on survival and everything else, including our history—but maps of the area. Topographical ones."

Daniel's eyes widened as it sank in. With those alone, Harnet had full and complete picture of the actual terrain. The only thing better than that would be Google Maps, which no one had anymore. He did not need anyone local to tell him anything—he would just know.

"Son of a bitch," he breathed. "We can't have that."

"Not to mention that if he's holed up in that tower, he can see us coming."

He looked up at Victoria. "Have any other good news to tell me?"

She lifted a brow. "We know where he is now."

He sighed. Despite everything, that alone was miles ahead of where they had been a few days ago. They didn't have to hunt for Harnet anymore. Daniel tapped his lip. "Any chance of there being a tunnel like the one out of this office to the mall, is there?"

She thought for a moment, and then her eyes widened.

"You aren't serious," he said.

"Back in the sixties, but I don't know if they exist anymore. There were pedestrian tunnels from one side of Notre Dame by the church and

Hnatyshyn Park," she answered. "There was another set by the apartment buildings on Anne."

"That's what those structures are for?" he asked, surprised. "I always thought they were hydro boxes."

She shook her head. "I think they were closed off—bricked up. The tunnels may have even been filled in."

"They're worth checking," he said. "Anything else you can think of?"

"Well, there's the new pedestrian bridge from the downtown bus terminal into the mall itself," she said. "But they'll see you coming through that. It's a glassed-in bridge over the street."

"Either way, we have to get into that tower," he said. "I can guarantee you that's where they're taking shelter—and that's where he took Fitz."

Victoria touched his shoulder. "You still need to heal."

"I know that," said Daniel, and he flicked an imaginary piece of lint off his shirt with the hand on his good side. "We need more intel on this—I need a way into that tower first."

He stood up, clutching at the arm of the chair to steady himself as Victoria grasped his good arm for the same reason. He sighed heavily. If he couldn't even stand up, there was no way he could rescue Felicia. *I also have to consider she may not even need saving, but I'm going to at least attempt to make her own rescue that much easier for her*, he thought. *Even a path out would be useful to her.*

"I think I'll take your advice," he said as he moved over the cot she had made up for him. "But tomorrow, I'd like to meet with the teams going out there. We need a new strategy—now that we know where they are."

"I agree," she said, as she helped him lay down. "But you need to rest first."

# CHAPTER TWENTY-FIVE

January in Northern Ontario swung between two extremes, or so Gina had noticed in the year and a half she had lived there and from what others had told her. On one hand, enough snow could fall to eradicate any sign of passage within a few hours. Enough to bury compact cars and clog streets, rendering them impassable by normal vehicles or even by walking.

And then, almost with no warning, the snow would at least stop.

A false spike in temperature and the sun, off the snow, was enough to be blinding.

Gina frowned, making sure the straps were tight on her snow goggles — tinted with UV protection. They had to be.

Snow blindness was a real risk. The unending white wasn't a matte flat. The crystals within the snow reflected the same sunlight up from the ground. With no clouds in the sky, there was no respite from the glare.

The single advantage the sudden break in the near continuous snowfall and the slight increase in warmth gave her was the clear, crisp, track the snow machine had left behind as the snow changed slightly from light and fluffy to still fluffy but easily packed and kept that shape.

She still only had so long before the track disappeared — but unless it snowed a few feet in the next week and a half, the track would still be obvious enough to find.

*Still, the fresher it is, the more likely I'm tracking the right one*, she thought.

The track had followed a snaking path up Kirk's street to another winding boulevard street leading back to Regent past an industrial park with a motorcycle dealership and other mechanics shops before it came down a small hill by the second largest Canadian Tire in the city, but it didn't go there. Gina knelt as she looked up at the intersection where it led to the mall at the Four Corners.

*Now, why would you go that way instead of this way?* She lifted a brow.

The only thing that way was a mall, but there wasn't much in that mall. A farming supply store — and she somewhat chortled at this. Farms and farmland were not as pronounced at this end of town. This store would have made more sense to locate it closer to Notre Dame and Lasalle in the North end of the city where most of the farms were actually located in Azilda, Blezard Valley, and Val Caron by following Notre Dame right until it became Highway 69 North.

Here, it was technically on Highway 69.

South...

... With an entire city in between unless the farmer felt like taking the bypass loop all the way around the city in either direction. While there were some farms south of the city and to the west, the greatest concentration of them lay to the North.

She shook her head.

*Could have been cost-related*, she thought. *This mall isn't exactly a mall anymore... hard to be with barely any stores in it.*

It was a shame, really. The closest mall to the Four Corners and the South End was in the downtown core, but before the downtown mall had revitalized itself by turning its office tower into condos, it had been just as deserted as the Four Corners mall.

She stood up, tapping her fingers against her thigh.

What was in that mall again?

Rumour had it there used to be a Metro, but it had closed—much to the horror of the shoppers in the area—which had become another store with groceries within it but it was mostly a discount department store. Gina had only walked into this latter discount store twice as she found that it never had what she needed or even wanted.

Or the quality was a little iffy.

There was the farm supply store—which, for those now forced to survive on little to nothing, could be useful but Gina would have gone for the Canadian Tire first.

A liquidator—again, mostly hit or miss and usually picked over.

One Chinese restaurant—which had been actually decent for a mall food court which she had frequented—a sub sandwich chain, and a Laura Secord. A few smaller stores, most independent, and a dollar chain store.

Again, if Gina had been leading them, she would have headed for the corner she stood at which had a few hotels, the Canadian Tire, the more famous of the Canadian coffee chains, and a better selection of restaurants even if they were mostly fast-food ones.

*There is that call centre*, she thought, and her eyes opened.

Gina had never walked within the doors of the call centre, but she had heard rumours. The security in the place was like the fabled Fort Knox, with hardened infrastructure meant to withstand threats both physical and cybersecurity. Workers were subjected to a series of security and financial checks before even allowed in for a second interview, and those who made it into training sworn into nearly intelligence agency level secrecy on what they actually did.

Not just what project, or what company—like in a normal call centre—but their very jobs were subject to secrecy.

The rest of the city called it a call centre, but the reality was no one really knew what it was.

But the snow machine plainly headed up to that mall.

*Could our looters be survivors in that bunker of a call centre?* Gina blew out a breath, but followed the track.

She almost stepped out from behind a tree when she caught the wide-open expanse behind the mall and she ducked back behind it, crouching down behind one boulder. *Wow, if I walk out there, anyone watching will know I'm here.*

With a sigh, Gina resigned herself to waiting.

While her clothes were lighter, and would fade against the snow, in the bright sunshine she would stand out like a stain of ink on paper. If she waited until nightfall, the dark would cover her movement as she moved between the piles of sand and loose boulders in the vacant lot.

Years ago, the mall owner before the current one had planned on building a condo. She didn't know what happened, but it never moved forward.

All that remained were hints of streets that had never been built. Buildings never raised… and the fill brought in now grew trees and grass behind her.

This one area, however, was empty but for a few boulders and two piles of gravel.

She sighed again and looked up at the sky.

*At least, with the days being short, I shouldn't have to wait too long…*

While the day did not last very long, a false spike into warmth followed. Gina shivered, even though the heavy layers of leather and insulation that made up the snow machine suit. *Rated to minus forty, my arse.* Gina blew out a breath. *Sure, it cuts the wind chill, but it could still use an extra layer or two.*

She had not seen a bit of movement around the mall, but they could have been on the other side of it.

She had been sure she heard the scream of her snow machine, and she winced.

*Every second that yobo rides uses more fuel,* she thought. *If it's empty by the time I get to it, they can have the useless machine.*

That wasn't an option.

While it was a brief ride on a snow machine through the snow back to Vincent and Russell, especially if she had to ride by Kirk's it was a long walk through at least two feet or more of snow without the benefit of skis or snowshoes.

She moved to the first boulder and looked around—and up to the roof.

*So far, so good*, she thought as she darted out and moved to the next boulder.

A flicker of movement near the door of the mall, right close to the entrance in the crook of the V that made up the mall, brought her to a stop. She strained her eyes, but it was too dark to see anything. She took a breath, and then moved to the last boulder.

From here, there was nothing for cover but for the building itself, and it was a good three hundred feet before she had even that.

Gina took a breath and released it as she looked around.

There had been a person, but they were heading back into the mall from the doors they had come out of.

*Did they see me?* Gina couldn't tell. *Stuffed if they did. Nothing I can do about it now, though…*

She ran to the side of the building and pressed herself against the wall, hiding and she could in a tiny gap in the cement. She released the breath she was holding as she looked around the parking lot.

Except for the holes in the snow from where she had run—or fumbled, as running in snow was never graceful—through it there was so sign of anyone having been to this side of the building in days, if not weeks. She felt fingers of ice up her spine. *Did I not see the tracks coming here?*

They had—she knew they had. The tracks had clearly run through the vacant lots straight for the mall. So where did they go?

The call centre was on the other side of the mall, on the side that was set into the mountain. The grade here was higher—on top of the mountain that had been blown apart decades ago to make room for the growing city and the mall itself—while on the side facing Long Lake Road, it was far lower. *Three stories lower, if I remember correctly*, thought Gina as she inched her way through the drifts of snow.

The wind had blown the snow up into a drift, leaving part of the pavement exposed. Walking was easy, and she kept one hand on the wall as she followed it.

It was dark—but the sky was clear and the moon and stars gave her some light, but without streetlights or any lighting at all she could barely see past her hands.

Sound carried, though, with the snow covering anything that could absorb it.

She picked her way slowly, wincing each time her boots made more noise than she wanted them too.

After the fenced area there was a loading dock, and then, once around this corner, she could see down and over the parking lots to the area below.

And it was here she found the tracks left by her snow machine again, and she grinned. *Gotcha*, she sing-songed in her head as she grinned, crouching to see where the track led.

Unfortunately, without daylight she couldn't.

Or, rather, shouldn't be able to.

But the light was still present—from the call centre. *Well, I'll be,* she thought. *I was hoping they weren't coming from there...*

The snow machine's tracks definitely went in that direction, and Gina followed the edge of the building. Now, though, instead of flat pavement she had to pick her way across exposed rock. A single misstep meant a broken ankle or a fall.

She couldn't afford either of these.

Gina slid down to the pavement level, leaning against the wall and using the last of the small outcroppings to hide herself in a patch of shadow.

She leaned down again, putting one hand on the ground.

*I'm not imagining it,* she thought as she looked up and at the razor wire protected steel and concrete structure outside of the building—once hid by wood fencing and flower gardens. *Independent power plant... big one. Diesel generator?*

*That's a massive set of generators, if it is...*

Between whatever was left for pressure in the natural gas pipes and this generator, the call centre could run independently of the grid for months.

*They'd need food, though,* she thought, frowning. *Which would explain why they're resorting to raiding... wait...*

Gina pressed herself into the shadows further, pushing herself close enough to the power plant to smell the diesel and feel the ambient crackle of electricity as it made the small hairs on her arms raise.

The snow machine slid sideways into the parking lot, and the same looter, now grinning like a loon, stood up on the footrests. From a basket he had tied to the seat behind him, he threw rocks and bricks at the windows of the call centre.

One barely missed her as it ricocheted off the wall.

From an upper window, a voice shouted, "What do you want now?"

"You can't stay hidden in your ivory tower forever, you know," said the looter. "Eventually you'll have to come back out. Food and that, right? Bet you're getting starving up in there."

Gina couldn't hear the call centre employee's sigh, but she imagined there must have been one as his tone when he answered said everything, "Go home."

"Nah, man, you're in it," said the looter. "That's just the thing. You see, I have food, water, people to help me defend it… and now I have this shiny beast which means I can go anywhere I want. The one thing I don't have is shelter with heat and power. You do, though."

Her eyes widened.

"And you expect me to believe you'll move in and let us live? Yeah, right."

"I don't care if you leave or die, but that place will be mine and you can go to hell," said the looter. "It's high time you had yours."

"I don't know what you have against us…"

"Everything! Anything! You all sit up there high and mighty—even before. How many times did my daughter apply to work there and you turn down her application? Your ads said anyone welcome to apply!" the looter sat back down on the machine. "No, no… she had all the things you wanted, but you never gave her the time of day. Never even called her for an interview. And she's not the only one."

"I don't know who or when she applied, but we've been interviewing everyone until we lost our HR…"

"Don't give me excuses."

*You're not just racist as hell,* she thought. *You're a jealous bastard too.*

Finally, he lost interest in tormenting the people in the call centre and rode the machine down the hill.

*Stop wasting my fuel!* Gina screamed internally as she came out of her hiding spot.

Picking up the rock that had nearly hit her, she tossed it into the parking lot before heading to one door to knock.

The window opened again. "What now?" asked the same voice. "Wait, you're not that idiot. Who are you?"

"The unfortunate soul who had a snow machine stolen from her," she answered. "It seems we share a problem."

For a long moment there was silence, and the window closed. Moments later, though, the light above the revolving door turned green. Gina pushed her way into the darkened lobby, and warmth immediately sank into bones as a beep and a solid click sounded behind her.

\* \* \* \* \*

Garrett sipped on the hot fluid in his cup. It wasn't coffee, nor really anything else anyone could find in a store. Normally, he wouldn't have even bothered with anything in the morning, but January was always colder than December.

He knew, and he rubbed his leg absentmindedly while sipping on his tea.

Roch pushed open the door, and Garrett flinched from the sudden influx of freezing cold air and a few flakes of snow. Once the door closed, and Roch started peeling off the multiple layers, he said, "Mira said the supply of leaves for her Labrador tea is getting low."

"Yeah, I've been hearing that from everyone," groused Roch and he looked up. "The problem is between hunting and chopping trees, we don't have a lot of time to forage to find the right plant for that tea."

"Is it hard to find?" asked Garrett.

"Not really," answered Roch, leaning against the wall while pulling his boots off. "It's not exactly rare—more of a weed—even if native to the area. But it is half buried in the snow at this point. The issue is digging for it now and, even if you find it, finding good enough leaves to use. By now, they'd be brown and dead and what you need is when it's green."

Garrett blew out a breath as he watched Roch walk toward the kitchen. "Damn."

"We'll figure something else out," said Mira as she walked in midway through the conversation. "We have lots of brown rice, and from what I understand, that's not bad when roasted and used in tea. Could even stretch what we have with the roasted rice. It wouldn't even take that much of it."

It was here that Roch paused, turning to look at where Garrett stood in front of the large picture window in his living room. His eyebrows rose, but all Garrett did was sip at the tea in the handmade earthenware mug.

"Your leg," said Roch finally. "You're walking on it."

Garrett lifted a brow. "Yes. That's normally what you do with legs."

"No, I mean…" Roch groaned as he waggled a finger at his friend, but Garrett only chortled in response. "Very damn funny, Garrett. You know what I mean."

"Yes, it feels better," he answered. "Fine, actually. Even when I go outside."

Roch was quiet as he stared at Garrett. "I see."

"Disappointed?"

"No," answered Roch. "No, it's not that. I'm glad you're back on your feet, truly. But I suppose that means you're going to be leaving us soon—unless we've convinced you to stay?"

It was hard not to hear the hopeful tone in Roch's voice.

Garrett sighed. "I wish I could, but I have to at least check on that dam. I may not work a miracle, but I can't give up now. Hopefully, they've survived up there."

"If that's what you really want to do…" Roch shrugged finally and then smiled. "Look, I get what you're saying. You don't want to abandon them either—like you couldn't abandon us. If you're determined to go, then let me just say that you're always welcome back here."

Garrett held out his hand, and Roch took it as they shook hands. Garrett dropped his hand, and—still sipping at his tea—looked out the window. "It's a nice place to settle down in. If things don't work out up there, you wanna believe I'll be back down here. Or even if they do. Maybe I can't do anything, but I have to see."

"It'd be kind of late to leave now, though," pointed out Mira.

"Wasn't planning on it," said Garrett, glancing over at her. "First thing tomorrow after I've said my goodbyes around here today."

# Chapter Twenty-Six

Gina stopped and looked from one person to the next. Three people faced her—two security guards and a man in a wheelchair. "So, that's where he got the snow machine. We had wondered," said the man, moving himself out of the way so that Gina could sit on the couch by him.

She did, and for a moment they considered each other. "I'm Gina, by the way," she said. "Greater Sudbury Emergency Services— firefighter, if you want specifics."

"Mark," he answered. "As you probably can guess, I work here and my job is classified."

"Didn't think this was a government facility."

He lifted a brow. "Classified isn't limited to government."

"Good point," she admitted, and she looked at the heavily tinted and translucent instead of transparent glass separating the lobby from the rest of the centre. "And what is that?"

This time he lifted both eyebrows, and he grinned. "Well, I can at least tell you it's financial and global. Beyond that, sorry, no." His smile dimmed, and he sighed. "Or, at least, it was."

"Was?" she asked.

He looked at her and then sighed again as he stared at the windows as if he could see through them. *At least he has the advantage of knowing what's there,* she thought. After a moment, he answered, but his voice was quiet, "Because there's nothing out there anymore. It's all gone. Wiped clean like it never was."

She stared at him, her mouth opening a bit. *"What?* How?"

He shrugged. "Not sure, but we all had the dubious distinction of watching everything zero, and then just go offline. I can't even hazard a guess on how, why, or who might have done so. But everything, everywhere… if they had access to it… will now find their bank accounts drained of every last penny. But, that's not the worst part. That would imply it went somewhere."

Mark looked up at the ceiling and then back at her. "Databases went dark—vanished. We could see the traces of where they should have been, had they existed, but it wiped them out. Now… well… you can see the after."

"Are you sure someone just didn't pull the plug at another end of it and it just look zeroed?" asked Gina, and Mark looked at her sideways.

"Well, I guess, but it still means everything has gone down… possibly for good. Rumour had it that only eight people in the world could ever get the internet back up and running were it all to shut down and I can tell that's exactly what happened," he answered, and he shrugged. "I can see that much. We all did."

"So, you're saying this is our life, now?" she asked as she stood up, but then she stopped.

*You knew this already when the radios stopped working. Even Russell knew when you told him. Stop acting so surprised.* Gina sank back down onto the couch and leaned back. *Now just deal with how to move forward from it…* "Damn," she breathed, and she looked at Mark. "I came over here on a temporary assignment to learn how Canadians fight forest fires and teach your blokes our methods. I'm from Australia…"

"… Figured from the accent," said Mark, and he shrugged when she stared at him.

"Now you're telling me I'll never go back home. I'll never see country again."

"I wish I had better news," he said. "Really did."

"And now those yobos want in here to top it all off."

Mark nodded and looked out in the generator's direction. "The problem is that the generator has been running nonstop since this happened. We had enough to last a month. Unfortunately, we've been running it for nearly a month and we've only a few days left... tops... before we lose what we have."

Gina stopped and stared at him, realizing that the reason the call centre was dark wasn't that it always was so. *They turned off lights to save power*, she thought. *To make it last. Just kept what they absolutely required to avoid tripping in the dark on and nothing else...*

"What happens when that stops?"

He looked at the other two and then at the ground. "We need at least some power to run the furnace and to control it. Once the generator runs itself dry, we'll have half a day of heat left before this office turns into the city's biggest walk-in freezer," he motioned to his chair. "And I'm not exactly in the best position to make a run for it with all the snow out there."

"Jesus," breathed Gina, her eyes wide. "But if you stay here, you'll freeze to death."

"And so will everyone else, since they've refused to leave," he answered, and then he snorted. "Not that we can with our snow machine thief out there with a chip on his shoulder."

Gina tapped her fingers against her leg and then her eyes widened as she stared at Mark. "Have you ever ridden on a snow machine before?" she asked.

"When I was younger, yeah, why?" and then his own eyes widened. "I think I could hold on long enough to get out of here if you got it back from him. But... how will you do that?"

"I came to get it back," she answered with a grin. "And that's what I'm gonna do... and then I'll come back and get you. All of you. I can't say exactly what my plan is, but I promise you and your people will survive this."

Mark nodded and smiled slightly. "That's more hope you've given than what we've had since this started."

"First things first, I think I have to loot a department store upstairs..."

\* \* \* \* \*

The sigh as he sank into the chair was audible, and Daniel saw Victoria raise a brow. She smiled slightly, but then turned to face the others in the room. *Where were they hiding this chair?* Daniel let his eyes close slightly as he, for once, didn't have to find a comfortable position as pressure points he didn't know he had unwound. *What corner did they dig this out of...*

*... And are there more of them?*

The height of the padded arms was just perfect to support his injured arm. The Mayor had moved off to the side, staring out the window and over the half-built arena across the road.

He blew out a breath as he looked over the scant few volunteers.

Some of them he had concerns whether they would even come back if he made them go out there. Not from them deserting, no, but from surviving out there.

The group was mixed.

Some were now former police officers, and like him, had stopped wearing their uniforms even if they still had them. Daniel had done the same. *What point is there? Who, if anyone, are we organized to serve and protect anymore? There's no government. That's our new normal. The symbols and insignia are for a dead civilization.*

Others were from other branches of emergency services. This was no surprise. The primary fire hall was two very small blocks away from City Hall. It had not been a matter of if the paramedics and firefighters in that building would come over to City Hall if lights and noise here had been noticed, but when.

It was these others that had prompted the meeting.

He knew a few of the faces in passing. It was hard to work in emergency services, even in a major city, without running across others. Sometimes repeatedly. Sudbury was big enough that he could not possibly know all of their names or faces, though.

"So, this Harnet never got over to the Fire Hall?" asked Daniel.

The one paramedic shook his head. "No, I'm guessing once he was hung up here that he didn't have time to consider it."

"That might have changed if he went South instead of North to the Mall," pointed out Victoria.

Another firefighter shrugged his shoulders. "It's a moot point now. He didn't. However, that leads to some issues you may not have thought about."

"Food and water," said the first paramedic. "He went North because that's where the grocery stores are — and he has at least three he can ransack. He didn't need to really push hard. Starvation will push us to surrender or we'll just drop like flies, anyway."

Daniel leaned back in the chair and looked up at the ceiling.

*First, Harnet had the library and all the maps. Now, he had all the food and water. Or was that the other way around?* Daniel crinkled his brows, but pushed this aside. *I'll talk to Victoria about it later.*

"Is there anywhere he may not have known about or been able to get to?"

"The South End," pointed out one. "But, considering the situation, that's a long way from here."

"There's that grocery store on Lorne—the one across the tracks from here," said Victoria. "Not saying he wasn't able to get there either, but we could try there as well."

"The restaurants and cafes downtown," suggested Daniel. "Houses… as much as I hate to say this, but we're living in a time where any resource is one looking into. First, we need to find the other survivors and make sure they're not left behind. They're our citizens—and whether there's a Canada or a Sudbury to speak of anymore, I won't sit on my ass and do nothing about making sure those we can help get that help."

He took a breath and looked around the room. "Second, we need to liberate any supplies we can get from those who didn't make it."

"What about the bodies?" asked someone, and Daniel tried to place him.

They weren't in emergency services, or at least they were not anyone he knew. He looked over at Victoria and he could see her eye twitching. This had been on the forefront of her mind as well, he knew. The thought of so many of the citizens she had run for Mayor to serve just *gone* had to be like a knife to the heart.

And a dull one at that—slowly pressed in and then twisted.

Daniel sighed heavily. "The living will have to come first," he said, holding up a hand when the man opened his mouth again. "It's not that we don't care about the dead. But if we don't do something for those still breathing now, we'll have even more dead. Once we are reasonably secure in our survival, we can think about proper burials and funerals. Taking note and remembering—but we can't let everyone here add to that list. It's already too long as it is."

The man nodded and then backed off a bit.

"You had called us up here for a reason?" asked a firefighter.

"I had asked for volunteers," said Daniel. "You are going to form the first of the groups to go out there and find what we need to keep surviving—even if that means moving to a new base. That's your entire mission, so to speak. Priority is to find food, water, and medicine. We've had too many run-ins with Harnet and his group, and without even basic first aid supplies, we're going to see people down with infections from wounds that could have been treated. The other half of your mission to find a new home. No one meant Tom Davies Square to house people overnight. It's drafty, cold, and some areas are getting dangerous from water penetration—especially since we don't know what other 'surprises' Harnet left in the Provincial Tower."

The group was silent throughout the entire explanation, and once he finished, Daniel saw a few of them looking at each other. However, none of their expressions changed.

One even shrugged.

"I'm getting the feeling you were expecting me to tell you this?" asked Daniel, smiling slightly.

"Had our suspicions this was where things were leading," said the first firefighter. "The first part was obvious, but the second half of it isn't really that surprising given where we are. The other thing is that, if we head to the South End, is that it gives us a bit of distance between us and Harnet."

"Any idea on what kind of resistance we'll get if we do that?" asked Daniel.

The first firefighter's eyebrows rose. "Wait, did you ask me what I think you just asked me?"

"With everything that has been happening in the last month and a half, are you really that surprised?" asked Daniel. "Look around us. There's not one iota of a hint of anyone coming to make sure we're still breathing, let alone reassert the law but us. Not even so much as a query. And even when we try to contact someone in Toronto or Ottawa, all we get is static. No one is coming—everyone knows that. The worst part is the first person to even know is that power mad invader Harnet."

"That's the kicker, isn't it?" said the man who had asked about burials. "He knew, and he chose here. Why?"

Daniel shook his head. "Not important right now. We get some distance between us, a chance to rebuild our base, not starve to death—and then we'll discuss the who and the why he's here and why Sudbury."

He struggled to his feet, and no less than three people rushed to make sure he could stand. One of those was the man he had never met—the one so concerned about people. He tapped the man's shoulder in thanks.

"As you can tell, Daniel isn't in any shape to go out with you himself," said Victoria, finally speaking as she turned to face the rest of them. "But he does this with my blessing—if my word still has any sway at all in Sudbury anymore. It is as he says. And, since it is, I am no longer your Mayor."

"Ma'am, if I may," said one officer. "We, as a city, voted you into office. It doesn't matter if the Ontario government or the federal one is gone. That's what we did directly. If you're still breathing, that makes you the Mayor of Sudbury... even if we're all that's left to make that decision."

"I quite agree," said the third man.

The firefighter and the paramedic from the Fire Hall nodded their heads as well.

"With that said, ma'am," said the firefighter. "If you tell us that, for Sudbury, you need us out there to find supplies, survivors, and a new emergency shelter because this one isn't secure—guess what we're doing. We're going out there to find just that. If Daniel here is your deputy and he has the plan that came from that order, then we're doing what he says."

"Then that is what you will do," said Victoria. "Daniel is right—no one meant Tom Davies Square for this. Those glass windows don't hold in heat. None of the windows do. Without the furnace, all they do is block wind. And while I realize that is plenty more than what out there does, it doesn't keep us from freezing to death or going through more fuel and wood to keep us warm. The problem is just that—we do not have a large enough supply of wood and fuel to burn to keep us from freezing to death. The mall would have done, but Harnet took it from us before we realized what was happening. However, there is another option, but it means leaving City Hall."

"It will be a hard move but if we head across the lake, or even to the other end of Bell Park, we have the option of heading to the University or to the science centre and hospital," said Daniel. "But we need to know what we're getting into in either situation first. The hospital has emergency power and heat, but I don't want to push out any patients. If people are breathing, we keep them that way. However, the science centre is well insulated and has the same heat as the hospital. It's easier to defend too. Same with the University."

"They might help us as well," said one paramedic. "More help from trained emergency services from various branches to keep Harnet out. If what you say about him is true, he has zero issue with pulling the plug on people in that hospital."

Daniel and Victoria looked at each other, and Victoria shook her head. "He murdered everyone he could find in City Hall. I still hear the screams of the staff and a few of the councillors," she took a steadying breath and then opened her eyes again. "We must stop him. Sudbury depends on it."

With a nod, Daniel said, "Unless you've questions, I'll leave you all to it. You'll have stuff you need to prepare before going out there. I wish I could join you, but until this arm heals, I'm stuck inside."

The room emptied. Victoria pushed the door closed and looked at Daniel. "What's on your mind?" she asked.

"There's something not quite adding up," he answered, motioning in the vague direction of the mall. "I know he has maps at the library, but it's almost as if he knew where to hit and when to do it. That takes knowing the city—and knowing it before even getting here. He didn't even head south of City Hall. He went straight to the mall and the library. Before that, he went straight for the grocery stores like he knew where to find them without the benefit of an Internet search or maps."

Victoria paused and then tilted her head as she thought about it, and then her eyes widened. "Now that you mention it, I do remember something. While he was 'discussing' how he would run the city, I remember him mentioning Lasalle Secondary School—like he went there."

"He's from here," realized Daniel. "That's how he knows everything he needs to know. The rest he has support to find out—and now he has the library. Was he familiar? You went to Lasalle and you're around the same age, aren't you?"

She shook her head. "No, I think he's older than me. I mean, now that you mention it, he seems familiar, but I can't put my finger on it."

Daniel shook his head. "It's not important. What is important is now that we know he's from the area, we can expect his next move. What would another local do? I know where I'd go if I wanted to take over—and he's in the middle of it. I also know you would be the next logical target is City Hall."

"It's the symbol," she realized. "If he controls it, then the rest of the city should follow."

"Exactly," said Daniel, rubbing his arm. "Which means it's him… or us."

# CHAPTER TWENTY-SEVEN

Derek stretched and huddled closer to the fire with the others as Shiloh filled their enamel-covered metal cups full of steaming tea. The horses shivered slightly beneath their blankets as the first horse first woke and stood himself up, followed by others. "Jesus," muttered Helen as the third horse to get up jostled her.

Shiloh smirked at looked at Derek, who only shrugged. "I thought horses slept outside?" asked Helen.

"Not when it's this cold," answered Shiloh, pointing at Helen with the ladle she had used to dole out the tea. "Count your blessings. Their body heat kept us warm last night. Wasn't just the fire."

"Well, remind me to sleep a little further away so I don't get stepped on next time," said Helen, and then she crinkled her nose. "Or… other things on me."

Derek looked at Shiloh and lifted a brow, but Shiloh shrugged again. "Joys of winter camping with horses," said Shiloh. "Share resources. Share shelter—or wake up frozen."

Helen sighed but drank her tea in silence.

Derek stood up, stretched again, and clicked his tongue to get Maya's attention. The mare perked up her ears and let him settled the bit and bridle back on her as he led her outside. As he smoothed the blanket, he looked up at the sky. The sky was a brilliant shade of blue the next morning without a single cloud in the sky. "We should probably get a move on," he said. "The weather looks great, but the problem is that it's likely going to be freezing and we have another day of riding ahead of us."

Helen was the next one out, Partly Cloudy in tow. Derek fought to keep the grin off his face when Partly almost refused to leave the warmth of the carport, but when Northern Tempest, led by Shiloh, strode out of into the sun he changed his mind and followed the other two horses.

Helen mounted Partly and then shivered as she looked over at Derek. "Yeah, it's bright out, for sure. But the chill is definitely sinking in."

Shiloh grunted, wrapping her scarf tighter around her face. Derek watched her adjust the special leggings on the horses. They weren't exactly for warmth, but to prevent the sharp edges of the ice and snow from scratching and cutting into their legs.

Like in a desert, those drifts moved, shifted and were always changing. They were not as high as a dune in the Sahara as the sun had a tendency to melt the snow. They were high enough to create a hardened crust on top and loose snow would blow and settle, starting the cycle again.

They rode the horses around the higher part of the dunes instead of forcing the horses over and through them. While their path was in a zigzag, it conserved energy—both theirs and the horses.

Finally, at midday, they reached the Fire Hall and pulled up short.

There were definite signs of life around it, with tracks in the snow and near the entrances. The only question was how happy those inside would be to see them and how wary they would be. They cautiously rode up to the parking lot, which appeared tamped down by someone's repeated pacing. Derek took a rock and knocked on the side door. *The people inside probably are wary of strangers. At least if we don't surprise them, it could help smooth over any rocky beginnings caused by just showing up unannounced.* Derek sighed as he looked at Shiloh, who only shrugged. *Granted, with no communications, there's no way to warn them we were coming.*

Their answer came from above them. "Where in the name of hell did you come from?" asked a voice from the roof.

"My cousin has a farm up Panache Lake Road," answered Shiloh.

"I'm guessing the one with horses," said the same voice, a man, and the tone sounded facetious.

"Yes," answered Shiloh.

Derek looked at the door and noted that nothing appeared to be broken into. "I'm guessing because the doors are actually locked and there's no sign of break and enter that you're someone who actually works here."

"Yeah, I am," he answered. "Constable Zachary Radzinsky, Greater Sudbury Police Service."

"Derek Moss, Dr. Shiloh Wither, and Helen Mitchell," Derek answered.

Radzinsky thought for a long moment and then looked from Shiloh to Derek and back again. "Why'd you come this far?"

"Medical supplies," answered Shiloh honestly. "We didn't expect to find survivors. All we've found so far has been a lot of death between the farm and here. Saw one smoke column coming from a house. It didn't look burnt, so we're guessing someone there is alive."

"And that's all you saw?" asked Radzinsky, a worried look on his face.

"You?" asked Derek.

"What few made it here I let in," he answered gravely. "Me, one paramedic and a few of the firefighters in the hall, plus a family from the highway, are all that's left. The other paramedic and the other firefighters tried to head back to Sudbury. I don't know... I doubt they made it."

For a long moment, they fell silent.

"There's very little food here, so if you're after that expect disappointment," said another voice, this time coming from the side of the building.

They turned to face the other woman, still dressed in the winter clothing of a paramedic.

"Didn't come for food," answered Derek. "We came for what's in your ambulance and fire support vehicle."

"And that's Emilie, but—medical supplies?" asked Radzinsky, his eyebrows rising. "Those are advanced for the layperson."

"My cousin is a doctor—a surgeon to be downright technical," answered Shiloh. "She's the one who sent us."

"I thought you said you were a doctor?" asked Radzinsky.

"I'm a vet," she answered.

"If they've got a doctor, Zack, our best hope for surviving this is going with them," said Emilie.

"She just said she was a vet..."

"My cousin's the doctor; and she's the one still at the farm," pointed out Shiloh.

Zachary thought for a moment and then nodded his agreement to Emilie. "All right, you've a point." He turned to Shiloh and Derek. "I only see three horses, and we've got kids here—not sure if they'd make all the way back there on foot."

"You got something we can rig as a sleigh?" asked Shiloh.

Zachary laughed. "We have something better than that." He nodded to the woman. "Emilie, open the garage door and let these people warm up their horses."

Once inside, Shiloh wasted no time in checking each horse over to make sure there were no injuries. The ice and snow outside had been progressively crunchier as the day progressed. And she had concerns that the leg wraps had shifted or had been torn. In the numbing cold, the horses would have felt nothing untoward.

Derek said nothing and let Shiloh do as she pleased. "You said you had something better?"

Zachary nodded and led Derek to the back of the garage and pointed, saying, "I'm guessing it's for parades, although why it's out here I don't know."

Derek stopped and stared at what he saw and then laughed. Zachary looked at him strangely, but Derek just continued laughing. "Shiloh!" Derek called.

Shiloh took a few moments and then walked over, looking where Derek was pointing. "For the love of…" she breathed. "How long has that been here?"

Zachary shrugged but Emilie answered, "Oh, that… it belongs up at the old Anderson Farm as part of their exhibit. I think the city brought it here for storage. No idea why here, though."

Zachary looked over at Derek and saw him trying his best to stifle his laughter. Zach rolled his eyes. "Yeah, yeah, get it out of your system, it's an old firefighting wagon, but it's changed to slide on skis. I just don't know why it's even here instead of the Anderson museum."

"Because the original Fire Hall it belonged to was this very one," answered Shiloh. "Or at least the one that once stood close to this spot before they built this one a few years ago to replace the one they had to tear down."

"I'd feel better if we it brought back to the farm," pointed out Helen.

"If you bring us with you, you can have that," answered Zachary.

Derek nodded. "Done." He turned to the constable and pulled him aside. "Any idea what the hell is going on out there?"

"You mean why we suddenly have no government?" he asked and snorted a short bark of laughter. "Yeah, yeah suspect I do."

"So, what happened?"

"If I had to guess, and this is only a guess — even if an educated one," he answered. "We ran out of oil — period. Nothing was actually producing anything but pollution, if you ask me. It was all for show. And the proverbial mess hit the fan because people found out and demanded answers."

"Who did and how?" asked Derek, suddenly feeling as if he could not get enough air.

"Don't look at me," answered Zachary. "But I have a theory… It was like paying a credit card with a credit card, but only having so many credit cards."

"You run out of credit."

"Right. So, we keep shuffling the balance around from card to card or sharing the load. Doesn't seem so bad. But the demand kept creeping higher and higher, and the balance kept creeping lower and lower," explained Zachary. "Eventually the bubble just burst and here we are."

"And the US?"

"I can't read minds—so, I haven't got a single clue. Like I said, it's only an educated guess. But if there's no 'intervention' or even rumours on the airwaves, so you can guess what happened," answered Zachary. "We went to war over oil—and everyone lost."

"Did it go nuclear?" asked Derek.

"Not that I know of," Zachary responded thoughtfully. "Before it went silent, there wasn't anything said about expecting nukes or firing them off, so, thankfully, I think we're clear on that."

Derek looked over at Shiloh, who had stood up to listen to what Zachary had to say. "So, Sheridan was right. Rome has fallen," she said, and she shook her head. "Can't say I'm surprised she's right."

Zachary looked at them, crinkling his brows as he did, and then he nodded.

"So, it has," he said. "Much as I hate to say it, we're screwed. How screwed and for long remains is the question we need to ask."

\* \* \* \* \*

The gate was closed—locked. Garrett looked, put one leather clad hand on the chain and leaned forward enough to look through and up to the first of the two dams. They appear intact, he thought.

It was too difficult to tell in the fading daylight.

He moved to the side of the fence and thumbed the button that would call up to the control house.

Even if the rest of the area had no power, the dam generated enough to supply its own. It would always take care of its needs first—to lose them meant losing the control to open and close the overflows or know if there was an issue to begin with.

He looked back towards Sudbury.

*This is all so strange*, he thought. Normally at night—particularly in winter—the lights from Sudbury are bright enough to light up the horizon. *Even when it's cloudy, the light bounces off the clouds...*

There was nothing but the dark.

He shook his head and then sighed as he turned his attention back to the dam. His brows crinkled.

Someone should have answered him by now. A thread of worry worked its way down his spine. *What if I'm too late?* he wondered, but he shook his head. *Wouldn't have mattered if I was here or not. If I was, and they're dead, I'd be dead too. If they aren't dead...*

He hit the button again, his nostrils flaring this time.

*... If they aren't dead, they're ignoring me.*

The crackle of the radio was like a knife in the silence. "We don't have any supplies, so turn around and go back the way you came."

"Dane, if you don't open this damn gate, you're fired," said Garrett.

"Garrett?"

"Who else?"

"Long story but almost anyone," answered Dane. "Thank God you're here, though."

"Are you opening the gate or not?"

"If it's not open, it's frozen shut again."

Garrett sighed and put his shoulder against the steel bars. "Try it again," he said. "I'll do what I can to help it along."

Garrett ground the toe of his work boot into the ground, and the screech of metal protesting its way through ice and snow filled the air. He grunted as he pushed the gate open until it finally opened on its own. He stood up and watched as it opened, nodding in satisfaction before going back to where he had dropped his back to pick it back up again. Once through the gate, he watched as the gate closed again—double checking to make sure it had closed all the way.

With a nod, he walked the further half a kilometre to the lower of the two dams.

It was here that Dane greeted him, walking out of the control house to the lower dam as he did. "I had almost given up hope," said Dane. "We've been cut off for nearly two months. You're the first person from Sudbury to even check on us."

"Yeah, I had noticed the lack of any traffic," answered Garrett. "I've been stuck in Worthington since before Christmas."

"Before?" Dane's eyebrows lifted. "Why... you know, I have a feeling it's complicated. What matters now is you've made it and maybe now we can sort it all out."

"That's my hope," answered Garrett. "Worthington has no power. I feel that neither does Sudbury, considering I can't use my cell. What has our head office said?"

Dane shook his head as he let Garrett lead the way into the control room.

"Haven't been able to get a hold of them."

Garrett stared at him and asked, puzzled, "What do you mean you can't get a hold of them? We have a satellite Internet connection directly to them. Let me see..."

Gone were the days of dials and hard switches. The power station only needed a few computers to run. They directly connected the onsite server via a high-speed internet T1 satellite connection to

Hydro One head office which could, in theory, run the dam remotely.

The problem was that was only in theory and, in reality, rarely actually happened.

Which was why Garrett and Dane often had to spend their time at the dam with a team of others to keep it running.

Garrett sat down at one computer and punched in a few of the commands he knew. He took a breath and released it before blinking.

Dane was right.

It was as though there was no one at head office. The command went out, that much he could see, but there was no answer. Not even from the servers. He was no computer expert, but it was like…

*It's like someone pulled the plug*, he thought, frowning. *As if you didn't already know that from dealing with Kovach…*

"What do we do?" asked Dane.

Garrett sighed and asked, "Did you try calling them?"

"We couldn't even call you to see how long you were going to be," Dane answered, running a hand through his hair. "Not even a dial tone. When it became months, we… well… it hasn't been that easy up here."

Garrett shook his head and then up at Dane. "Can't do anything but wait it out until Spring anyway… or until someone with a snow plow remembers we exist. Or the connection comes back online."

He pushed himself up, slamming the wall before stomping his way out of the control room to stare up the hill at the other one.

"Look, Garrett, I get that not being able to fix it is a big deal, but even before you got up here. We had a bigger problem on our hands," said Dane as he followed Garrett up the road to the larger of the two control houses.

The dam further up was the primary dam—and the larger of the two—holding back the headwater of Agnew Lake. The original Agnew Lake was not exactly that close to Big Eddy Dam, but since they had built the dam, the reservoir had eventually made Agnew Lake four times as long and much bigger than the original lake had been.

A second dam, also part of the project, was not six hundred meters down from the first dam. This created the massive power creating potential of the two Big Eddy dams. No one called them this—everyone called them High Falls. Garrett wondered if perhaps the original High Falls had been a drop from before and now was underwater.

Forever flattened by the dams below the submerged valley.

Perhaps one day, the dams would be decommissioned. The valley returned to its normal state, and—if there had been a waterfall—it would be revealed again.

But it wouldn't be in his lifetime.

*Since Roch was right and whatever this is means the end of civilization*, Garrett thought. *Then no one will maintain these dams. They'll eventually overflow and get washed away.*

"And what's that?" asked Garrett.

"The lack of food, for one," said Dane.

Garrett stopped for a moment and stared at Dane before walking into the building. "I'm serious!" exclaimed Dane. "We're running out of food."

"I'm pretty sure, with everything around us, we can find food," said Garrett. "If you'd stop and think. And how in hell did you survive this long without a supply of it, anyway?"

Dane stopped, and he didn't answer right away. Garrett had to lift his brows. He honestly hadn't expected Dane to stop mid-step, his eyes almost glazing over and for him to stare at a spot on the wall. Garrett tapped him in the middle of the forehead and he came out of it. "Don't tell me you can't walk and chew bubblegum, Dane."

"I have an idea," he said.

Garrett sat down at the bank of computers. "Do tell."

"We've got enough people here, and the resources to do it, to find what we need. We'll just ask our neighbours to share," said Dane.

"And if they don't?"

"C'mon, Garrett, surely they have enough?"

Garrett leaned back in the chair. "Let me get this straight, we can ask for help and if they refuse it… we'll what? Just take it from them, anyway? What about what they need?"

"Who cares?"

Garrett's eyes widened and then they thinned out. "I don't think so. We do not do it that way. We may as well knock on the door called 'raider' like in those Mad Max movies you and the others watch. And I'm no raider, and I don't think you are. Besides which, I can tell you they don't have the supplies to share. I know that from experience having lived there myself, you know."

Dane exhaled, and he flopped into one of the other chairs. "Then what do we do?"

"We ask, all right," said Garrett. "If they can, then great. They kind of owe me a favour, but there's a limit. If they can't, don't push. However, you're right on another count. We have the resources here to have more than enough food… If you don't mind fish, that is."

"I love fish, why?" asked Dane, and then his eyes widened. "We go fishing?"

"Why the hell not? We keep having to clean them out of the turbines so we know there are fish up in Agnew. Why not catch them before they're minced?"

"I think we have some netting, we could make curtain nets." Dane tapped his fingers on the desk and then blew out a breath. "That's meat. I know you don't like veggies, but we need something else other than just fish."

"If I show you and the others how to find it, I've a source for vitamin C at least," said Garrett, thinking of the tea Mira had made, and he thought, *We're far enough away that there's probably a fresh supply of it up here*. "You make it into a tea. It will keep us all going until spring. May get bored with it after a while, but we can trap for rabbit too. Pine needles for other teas and flavour. We won't starve. Hell, if you talk to some of those you wanted to raid, they may even have hunting gear and a way to grow some stuff to make things a bit more comfortable."

He tapped Dane's shoulder. "We'll survive, kid, you'll see."

"I have to ask, though, if you were down in Worthington this entire time, then you had to know everything has gone sideways," said Dane. "Why did you bother coming up here?"

"I said I would when I started out from Garson, and I wasn't about not do it," answered Garrett, and he shrugged. "Besides, if I can get things up and going and if we tweak the wiring—there's a power line place down by my daughter's—we can at least provide power for our immediate area. Maybe have a bit of creature comforts like before."

Dane lifted his brows. "You came all the way up here to check in on us, despite not needing to, because you told someone who probably may not even be still alive you would? And, knowing that, you came up to see if you turn the power back on?"

"Yeah, sums it up," answered Garrett.

Dane shook his head. "Okay. Are you going back to Worthington after?"

Garrett blinked and looked at Dane. "That's the second time you've asked me that in as many minutes? You eager to see me gone?"

Dane shook his head. "No, not at all."

"Well, how about we do our jobs, then?" asked Garrett.

Dane sighed but followed Garrett into the second control house. "Sure thing, boss."

# CHAPTER TWENTY-EIGHT

Daniel flexed his left shoulder, ignoring the look Victoria kept giving him. It was still sore, and if he moved wrong, it almost robbed him of breath. But these moments were finally few enough that he could not spend another moment on the sidelines.

He stood just inside what had once been the main entry of the parking garage underneath City Hall. Unlike the other side that led out onto the four-lane boulevard, this one led out to a two-lane street and a park.

The makeshift gate was still closed, and when he looked out past it appeared quiet.

But who knew with Harnet?

*Looking quiet and actually quiet are not the same thing.*

Another seven people—some in emergency services, but more of them had just civilians. Now, though, they were all the same.

Survivors.

It had taken far too long to find a third team not only willing to go out but also possessing the right set of skills. Daniel sighed.

He wouldn't have even sent in an experienced tactical team into this.

And now he had to lead a group of survivors— some with no training outside of camping and hunting, and physical fitness—into what they would consider an urban battlefield.

"All right," he said. "Our priority is supplies. No supplies means we don't eat and the rest of our people starve to death. Second, we find any others and send them back here. Understood?"

There were nods all around.

He signalled to the gatekeeper, and the gate slowly slid open. Daniel winced at the clattering and creaking of the gate. The noise was enough to alert anyone listening that the gate to City Hall had finally opened. The time to open was a way in for anyone waiting for that opportune moment. He made a cutting motion with his hand and the gate keeper stopped the gate from opening any further.

Daniel led the others out and then signalled again to the gatekeeper to close the gate. Again, the creaking and grinding sound of the gate closing was far too loud, causing Daniel to wince again, and once it closed everything turned quiet once more.

"Maybe we're lucky and the gangs are sleeping off a rough night," said one survivor.

"One could hope," admitted Daniel. "All right, stay sharp. I wish I could say by the book, but I don't think any of our books covered this. Just be damn careful out here."

They moved out to the street, and Daniel led them toward the arena. The construction site was a prime area for not only an ambush, but the snow could hide holes and other hazards. They did not build structures in the site to withstand the weight of the snow either and could come crashing down on their heads—or cause collapses onto the street.

Until a few years ago, the train station had always been semi-deserted. Now, in the summer at least, it had become the Farmer's Market. There were many restaurants and cafes along the street facing the tracks. All deserted. If they looped around the arena and down that run and then into the downtown core again, they could cover all the restaurants and boutique delis and stores.

Hopefully Harnet had not figured this out too.

Funny how before all this, the walk had always been short, even pleasant, when those same stores had been open. Once off work, he would often share a good coffee at the roaster that sat right across from the arena. His friend, Derek Moss, had addicted him to the place as they were both coffee hounds in their own way. Sheridan also loved the place. She, however, frequented places closer to her end of town and even if she ventured further in, she preferred the Italian place on Regent.

He sighed.

*Will I ever see her again? Or Derek?* He almost shook his head, but stopped short of doing so. *Or my brothers... mom...* At least he knew that if anyone survived, it was likely to be them so long as she had not been at the hospital when everything went out.

Derek... well...

He turned his focus back to the here and now. As easy as this walk would have been before, it was not simple anymore. Snow clogged the streets and between abandoned vehicles and other debris they had to move around.

Daniel was thankful of one thing only.

The cars were at least completely abandoned— no one had opted to remain with the cars, and therefore it was unlikely that they would discover a body within any of those parked along the way. Considering his choice in career, he had seen more than his fair share and it got no easier.

After fifteen minutes of careful plodding through the snow to the corner by the train station and the arena, they could clearly see that the area was completely deserted. There was absolutely no sign that Harnet's people had even made this far from the mall.

325

"Well, this is anti-climactic," stated one other, and Daniel turned to glare at him. "Not that I'm complaining. Just stating a fact."

"Well, let's check the restaurants. Maybe there's something still in them."

The first one they checked was the coffee shop. It was not as if he was expecting a lot in the way of food in there, as it did not actually serve heavier meals. He suspected this was because of the very tiny space it occupied, less than the fact that it was right beside two places that served food. But and he would admit it was because he really missed his morning coffee, he knew that they had had regular—and huge—shipments of coffee beans that they roasted and ground right on the premises.

And it looked like they had had a big one right before Harnet declared martial law.

Daniel would have danced if his instincts were not on high alert for any sign of danger. Some beans never had a chance to be even roasted yet, which that meant with a bit of tender loving care they could still coax them to grow into a full plant.

Strangely enough, they had something that could nurture these plants like a year-round multi-level farm. Tom Davies Square was a glass tower housing city hall. The roof was already accessible and often used as a daycare's play area. Each floor within the city hall was open concept and while north facing the greenhouse effect within could serve as a place to grow their food.

Starting with the coffee.

Now they just had to get some actual food seeds, and he knew just the place where to get those. Luckily, it was also downtown. In fact, it was right across the street from the square—if on the side that was regularly raided.

Still, it was a chance they would have to take.

*It'll be a real pain to get them out from under the snow, though,* he thought. *But in the spring we could get the seedlings and move them to Bell Park.*

Once they unseated Harnet, that was. There would be no rebuilding until they quelled that threat.

A clatter from one building caused all seven of them to take cover. Those who had guns drew them, but stayed hidden and out of sight. Daniel poked his head out from behind the car he had taken cover behind. It felt like they had all sucked in and held their breath, even though he could see their breaths in the cold air.

The clatter sounded again, and it echoed.

Finally, and he felt the tension release, a small grey tabby cat jumped out of the wreckage. It meowed in surprise at the live humans, and then quickly retreated again. Daniel watched as it left tracks down the street and headed to the YMCA. "Well, that was anti-climactic," mentioned one other quietly.

Daniel snorted and then sighed as he motioned for them to come out again.

"Check that building anyway," he said. "Carefully. The structure looks secure, but there's a month of snow on that flat roof."

A groan sounded, followed by creaking. "Everyone back!" he shouted as he turned and ran as fast as he could through the snow, across the street and into the parking lot.

Jumping behind another abandoned car, as the others did the same, the creak and groan turned into snapping and screeching as metal and cement gave way. The building crumbled in on itself and a cloud of snow and dust exploded into the air. As the quiet returned, and the snow settled, Daniel motioned for everyone to move out from behind cover. "Are we all in one piece?" he asked.

"Nothing hurt but for our pride," said one other. "That's a damn shame."

Daniel grunted. That was true. It was a shame—the building was one of the older buildings. It had historical value as one of the original stores built when Sudbury was first founded. "Make sure no one was in there," he said. "Be careful, though, I don't know what else will end up falling down."

As a few of them checked the wreckage, Daniel looked up the street.

While nighttime was a few hours off yet, the clouds were thick enough to darken the sky like an early dusk at midday. There was a light in one window on the street. Daniel moved toward it slightly—far enough to pick out which building he was looking at, but not far enough to leave the rest of his team.

One of his team stepped up beside him and asked, "What is it?"

He pointed. "What do you make of that?"

"Were it before," she answered. "I'd have said someone left a light on in their office. But that would mean electricity. That, to me, means someone is in there."

"That's my thought as well," he said. "What building is that?"

"The newspaper," she answered with a shrug. "Not exactly useful to Harnet, but if there are survivors, we could make contact. Share resources… if they don't attack us."

Daniel blew out a breath. "What a crazy world this is when we have to be concerned about this."

She nodded. "The Mayor still would want us ask them if they want help."

They would have to at least try.

Once the others had finished picking through the wreckage, they moved toward the newspaper building. One other motioned for him to join them in the small park—it was hardly a park. More of a tiny vacant lot turned into a tiny sitting area beside the building beside the Brady overpass.

Daniel looked from the newspaper building, and straight at City Hall.

"There's no way they didn't know we were there," he said. "They have a clear bird's-eye view straight to us."

Daniel compressed his lips.

"Okay, here's the deal," he said, motioning them to flatten against the wall. "Now this building has a use Harnet would want. It's a great scouting position."

"Put a sniper on the roof, and they'd be able to pick off anyone on that side of Tom Davies Square."

Daniel sighed. "Yeah, that thought had crossed my mind too."

"So, what now?" asked another one.

Daniel looked at them. "We have two choices. We can leave it, knowing someone is up there—or we can make contact. My gut is telling me this is how Harnet knew our every move before we made it, so I'm expecting resistance. If we go back now, they'll know we were here. Or, we can surprise them and get ahead of the game for once."

He looked around. Each of them nodded their agreement.

"Okay, let's turn the tables, then…" he said, grinning.

# CHAPTER TWENTY-NINE

Helen and Emilie had descended on the crippled ambulance and one of the fire trucks, and Shiloh had disappeared into the depths of the Fire Hall. Derek and Zachary listened to their chatter on what was easiest to carry, and most useful—or could handle the jostling—until Zachary sighed and tilted his head toward the kitchen. "We'll let the medical pros deal with that," he said.

Derek nodded and followed the older man into the kitchen.

"I wish we could just take the whole kit and kaboodle back with us," said Zachary. "But we had trouble getting it from the highway to here in the first place. That back road would be nigh impossible."

"I'm glad we got to the house when we did," said Derek.

"I saw the damndest thing, though, but it was before all of this," said Zachary, moving over to the counter and the coffeemaker. "Sorry, no more coffee. But, we have tea."

Derek sighed, but accepted the cup once Zachary had brewed a pot of tea.

"So, yeah, of all things I saw a Smart Car make a run at the hill. I thought for sure they weren't going to make. Took 'em a few tries, but they made it," said Zachary as he sipped at his cup, but he stopped when he noticed Derek freeze. "That wasn't you, was it?"

"Me? No," answered Derek. "But I know who it was."

"Oh, yeah?"

"Our resident doctor—Sheridan," answered Derek. "She took a notion to go grocery shopping in Lively right before everything went down. Good thing, too, or we'd all be in the same boat."

Shiloh entered the room at a brisk walk. "Derek, I have something you need to see."

Derek set down his coffee mug, and Zachary's eyebrows raised. They followed her through the Fire Hall and back to the garage. Instead of stopping by the trucks or the lone ambulance, she went right to the back of the garage and into a corner where something sat covered by an old canvas tarp. She walked up to it and laid a hand on the tarp. "Are you ready for this one?" she asked.

For a moment, Derek could only stand there, but he finally shrugged. "Sure?"

She ripped off the tarp with a flourish and grinned as she pointed at the contraption that revealed from underneath. "Well?"

Zachary and Derek looked at each other.

The contraption, on skis making a large sled, clearly meant to be pulled by horses—at least two, if Derek wasn't mistaken—and had many pipes, tanks, and other attachments on it. "What am I looking at?" asked Zachary, as he took a step back to take it all in.

Derek blinked. They had painted it red, but the paint had long since faded… and… *oh. Oh!* Derek's eyes widened. "Is that an antique fire brigade wagon?"

Shiloh pointed at Derek. "You've got it in one!"

"Well, I'll be," said Derek, his voice quiet.

"This is absolutely fantastic, Derek, you have no idea how fantastic," she said, and he lifted a brow as she was almost bouncing. "Do you have any idea what this means?"

He shook his head.

"If we can't depend on fuel or regular fire trucks, then we've got to go back to the old way of doing things… and this beast would mean we have a real response to any fires within our community until we build back up again," she said. "We'd have to build more—but it means we're already one wagon up from none, and we can build more based on this design. No need to guess or figure it out—just copy it."

His jaw dropped, but it was Zachary who said, "I'll be damned. That is a hell of a boon."

Shiloh pointed at Derek. "You know this depends the right tack and harness for the horses to even attach to that sleigh and that it wasn't somehow 'fixed' for towing behind a truck."

"Was it?" asked Zachary.

Shiloh crawled under it, and the two men waited. Finally she came back out and pulled the yokes out from the underneath. "Nope—just needs everything attached back up. This is going to take me all day, even with help."

Zachary rolled up his sleeves. "Well, I'll do what I can."

"Dare, can you go through the storage areas and see if you can find the harnesses and tack?" she asked, looking up from the wagon.

"Yeah, sure," he answered, walking off again.

After searching the fire hall, he found them in a storeroom and Shiloh immediately checked each length of the leather for signs of wear and tear.

Finally, after a few hours and right before the sun went down, she proclaimed, "Everything looks good. Thankfully, it only takes two of our horses to pull that rig. We'll have to extend the harnesses to get them set right, but with two of the horses on the sleigh and the other riding guard, we should be fine."

Again, Derek found himself alone with his thoughts after everyone else had retired for the night.

The roof of the fire hall was flat, and he leaned on the wall of the access from the building. The night was clear, and the chill sank into his bones. He closed his eyes for a moment and listened. *Not a thing out there, he thought. No cars, no people. What animals there could be are hibernating. Everything I knew — gone. Hell of a thing to wake up to.*

*Can we survive this?*

They had to.

If they survived the winter, their chances of surviving the following winter went up astronomically. This spring and summer meant that they would have enough time to prepare for the next winter. It was like going back to the old pioneer ways in the hardest and cruelest way possible, but if a Northerner was anything, it was a survivor. The change from what they knew to what would become the new normal would take some time, but he suspected that they likely could bounce back, eventually.

*As Sheri said, Rome fell, but civilization bounced back — just with new governments and centres of power. So what if it happened again? We'll do the same. Our children would simply forget the old world — they're too young to have really remembered it in the first place. Not like us, who are finding this transition extremely difficult.*

Derek caught himself and then snorted.

*Old world. And, just like that, I've already accepted it.*

He sighed then, staring out over the frozen, snow-covered fields and silent forests. *This roof has a magnificent view. I can see everything for miles. Not so much back up the hill to Sheridan's, but everything else...* A plan, and an idea, took root, and he paused. *Perhaps we could use this in the future—once we're ready to expand a bit...*

Derek turned away from the view and walked into the access shelter. Walking down the stairs and through the Fire Hall, he stepped outside the building. *We're incredibly lucky. Sheridan's farm, and her love of history and keeping things original saved us.*

From what he could see in this little corner of the world, the winter itself decimated the population. Only ten, maybe twenty, percent had survived the winter, and he knew that there would be more deaths coming.

Even on Sheridan's farm.

Derek kicked his feet around the ground, and something strange that was not snow or ice caught his boot and bounced away. He crinkled his brow as he walked over to it, picking it up.

It was a rock, almost perfectly rounded—likely one of those used in the garden as a border.

Staring at it, he turned it over and over in his hand before he slipped it into his pack. *Okay, Derek, you've clearly taken leave of your senses with this one. It's a bloody rock. Not even a nice one... why do that when you could use that space for something actually useful?*

"There you are," said Emilie as she walked outside. "It's my turn on watch. Everything all right?"

He nodded to her.

"Yeah, why?"

"I dunno, you look a bit spooked," she said.

He shrugged. "Nothing a good night's sleep can't fix."

"All right, then, good night," she said as Derek waved and headed into the building.

As the door closed, he leaned on it, shaking his head as he did. *I'll sort myself out in the morning... or Reese will when I get back to the Manor.*

For the first time in days, his sleep was undisturbed until the clatter of plates and cups woke him. As he sat up, he looked up at Zachary and Emilie as they made tea and what little else they could share. The others were waking, and the children were playing off to the side. If not for waking up after sleeping on a hard floor, Derek would have found it almost idyllic.

He walked outside after cleaning himself up and drinking some tea, shivering as this morning was as clear, crisp, and cold as the previous morning. Shiloh had already harnessed two of the horses to her own standards to ensure they would work as a team.

"The next question is, who will drive the sleigh?" asked Derek.

"This I can do," answered Helen, smiling as she climbed up to the driver's seat and buried herself under the layers of blankets.

The two children and Zachary climbed up and joined her, as did Emilie, and Zachary and Shiloh faced the back as a rear guard. Derek mounted Partly Cloudy and led the sleigh out into the sunny morning. Before, the only sound other than the crunch of snow and whinny of horses had been minimal conversation. Now, the jingling of the harness and the four-beat staccato of the hooves of the team of horses pulling the heavy sleigh through the snow greeted the morning.

Derek smiled at the sound, even though it was an old-fashioned sound.

"It's like Christmas," chimed one child. "We could sing Jingle Bells!"

The adults smiled at the child's sense of adventure and all laughed softly while Derek found his mood was far brighter and lighter than the previous day and night. "We could," he admitted. "Why don't you start?"

The two kids started singing, and the adults joined in as they made their way toward Panache Lake. This time laughter and singing rang out in the still atmosphere, with the children pointing out objects that caught their fancy as they passed them. The older of the two seemed interested in the sleigh's driving, and Helen indulged him when they had finished singing.

"What day is it?" asked Emilie, suddenly.

"Sunday," answered Helen, after she looked at her watch.

"Christmas Day," mused Derek, reflecting on the singing of Jingle Bells. "What did you want Santa to bring you?"

"I got it," answered the oldest of the two. "I wanted to ride in a fire engine, but I got something even cooler... a ride on a firefighter's sleigh pulled by horses through the country on Christmas. It's like being in a Western."

"And you?" he asked the younger of the two, the little girl.

"I wanted a horse. I didn't actually think I'd get one..." she admitted.

Derek snorted in a short laugh. "Yeah, me neither."

The day was quickly falling to dusk, and it rather surprised him to note that he hadn't been aware of the speed with which time had flown past. We're going to need shelter, he thought, and he looked over at the children's mother again. And she doesn't look very good either.

He looked up and noticed a column of smoke from a house that was a good distance from the road. He knew that house. It was the shop and garage for a major electrical line contracting company. The problem was the movement on the road—which was directly in their path. "Do you see that?" asked Helen.

Derek nodded, "Yeah, I had a bad feeling this was going to happen. I was just hoping for later."

"Get the kids into the back of the sleigh," said Helen. "There's no avoiding them. If we make a move to avoid them, they'll know we saw them and come in shooting. Maybe if we play this cool enough, we could have surprise on our side instead of theirs."

\* \* \* \* \*

The force from Garrett standing up made the chair squeak as it slid across the floor. With one hand on the window frame, he braced himself so he could climb up to the window. He tried to see what was going on, but the angle was wrong.

But he could hear the shouting.

Garrett slid down to stand with his feet flat on the floor and pulled on his coat. He ran outside and waded between the two, narrowly avoiding a punch himself, and pushed them apart. While Garrett was not tall, he was solidly built and more than strong enough to stop any fighting.

"We have bigger issues at hand, here," he growled at them.

"Garrett, I'm hungry and this bastard stole my ration!" claimed the first one.

"I did no such thing! You lost it… fair and square…" answered Dane.

Garrett glared at him and asked, his eyes narrowing, "What do you mean 'lost it fair and square'?"

It was almost amusing to watch the both of them suddenly turn silent, but he did not have the patience for their excuses, not in their current situation. "I'm waiting," he said.

"Who made you King of the Mountain?" asked the first one defiantly.

With a heavy sigh, Garrett turned to face the questioner and Dane inched away, almost as if he knew what was coming. The punch took the other by surprise and knocked him on his rear end.

"We do not steal food from others," he said as he cracked his knuckles. He then turned to Dane. "Nor do we gamble our share away."

He gestured with his head and Dane gave the rest of his ill-won gains back to the first. The first man pushed himself to his feet, rubbing his jaw. "So, what do you suggest we do?" he asked, a bit sullenly.

"Anyone have a fishing kit or some way to hunt and trap?"

The two men looked at each other and looked down. Dane laughed. "Well, not that I know of... but..."

"But?" asked Garrett.

"I'm sure we could rig something," Dane suggested.

They looked at the second man, who had cleared his throat. "I think I might have seen a fishing kit in one trailer."

"Go look," suggested Garrett.

The two took off and Garrett sighed. He had been afraid this would happen after they lost contact with the rest of civilization. Unfortunately, with no way to clear the road back to town, they were stuck up at the dam.

Supplies were running low. But with the right tools, they would be able to at least fish and trap. The error most people made when coming into the wilderness was that they assumed all animals hibernated through the winter, but the truth was only a few did and were the exception. Others either did what they could to eat or stay warm or migrated further south. For some, this *was* south.

This meant it was still possible to hunt a small amount of game.

The two men returned, and Garrett looked over what they had brought him. He inspected the pieces visually and then sorted them into two piles.

Dane watched him curiously for a while and was silent as the second one asked, "What are you doing?"

"It's a summer kit, which means it's meant for using on a rod and reel meant for casting. The lures are fake, which means the motion of the rod gives it the illusion of life… it's what attracts the fish." Garrett continued sewing a different lure with the pieces gathered. "But if I can make a lure that will naturally twist and turn in the current, it won't require the motion of the rod and will still attract something. Hopefully, something that won't break the line."

"Is there anything big enough out there to break the line?" asked Dane.

Garrett nodded his head, and the first one said, "Yeah, some big sturgeon and muskie in the lake. They'd snap your line in seconds. You couldn't even react before losing the lure."

He thought for a moment and then snorted. "Ironically sturgeon is good eating if cooked right."

"That means going out on the ice."

"Yep," answered Garrett as he looked at the both of them. "Stay away from the dam where the ice is thinnest. The ice is likely a good few feet thick or more. You can drive a truck out onto it with no problems at all. The trick is boring a hole through it to fish."

They were quiet for a time, and the younger one appeared to be mulling things over. "There's an auger in the same shed," he pointed out. "It's not exactly for ice drilling but we could use it?"

Garrett snorted. "How do you think ice augers got their start?"

As he watched them run off, he tapped his finger on his arm. Normally, keeping their cool would be hard enough, thought Garrett. But with empty bellies and not much in the way of entertainment, the fights are going to only get worse.

As hardworking and focused as they were, a solitary truth remained.

Sudbury had always been a mining town. Even after it became a city, and then amalgamated into the City of Greater Sudbury, the core of that heritage remained. They stubbornly ingrained it into the men and women working the mines and smelters, and not less into the people who worked in fields supporting that industry. Garrett breathed that heritage. He bled it.

He had been conceived in its heart, as had his father before him.

And like these workers, he was frustrated.

*I should be down at Shiloh and Sheridan's, drinking with Derek and my brothers until we can't remember our own names.* His lip curled slightly as he clenched his fist around the rebar in his hands. The urge to break something grew stronger.

But it deflated just as quickly.

*I can't.*

*If I do, then the example I need to set is lost, he thought. The others will devolve into brutes. I know how they feel—I'm at the breaking point too. We should be at home either doing something stupid to brag about next week to our buddies or playing with our kids.*

"Dammit," he breathed as he let the frustration leave with each breath. "Now what am I going to do?"

# CHAPTER THIRTY

Derek took in a deep breath. Two trucks—heavy trucks meant for hauling equipment and, as he followed the ruts in the snow leading from the road back to the warehouse he had spotted a few days ago, he knew they had come from there.

*Dammit*, he thought. *They did spot us.*

There was no other way to go. Shiloh had been right on that. If they had, it would have given those from the warehouse clear sign they knew they were trouble.

Helen tugged on the reins and brought the horses pulling the sleigh to a stop.

"If you're looking for food, you're barking up the wrong tree, mate," came a voice, and a walked out from behind the trucks.

Derek looked the man up and down, and the emphasis was on up. He was tall—taller than Terrence was, and Terrence was a tall man himself. "We're not looking for food," answered Derek. "We're wondering if you needed anything, and even if not, if we could shelter here for the night before moving on."

The man seemed slightly taken aback by this. "Move on to where?"

Derek pointed back to the road and to the south. "There's a farm down the road, just on the other side of the ridge, offering a refuge for those who want it. Has all the necessities of life to survive the winter."

The man thought for a long moment and continued, "All right… but only because I'd like to know more about this farm of yours."

The man looked around and tilted his head. "Do we look like we need your help? More the opposite."

"Issues?" asked Zachary.

"Had some would-be looters try to jump the fence. And, no, they weren't interested in sharing," he answered. "They were more interested in destroying what I had and they did some damage too before I ran them off, not before one of them put a hole in one tire of the pole driver. Given that the world has ended, I'm guessing we're going to have difficulty replacing that."

"Understandable," Derek agreed, inwardly holding a breath. *Please be as you just claimed to be.* "I'm Derek, that's Shiloh, and Helen."

"I'm Zack, and this is Emilie, Aaron and Nora, and their two kids, Kaylee and Liam," said Zachary.

"George," answered the contractor. He then drew his attention to the two kids, looked at them meaningfully and said, "Kids. You would have to have kids."

He spoke the last loudly, and it carried into the wind. Derek felt a sudden sinking feeling in his gut as he realized, glancing at the now locked gate, that he had been right. He and Zachary looked at each other. They shared the same disbelieving gaze as neither of them had even suspected that George was anyone but who he claimed to be, much as Derek had hoped otherwise.

As he suspected, on the roof of the first truck was now at least five armed people with their rifles trained on the sleigh. He was glad that he had not warned them of the defenses Sheridan had on their farm—only that it was there and offering shelter.

"I'd think it best if you got down off that horse, Derek," said George evenly. "You've got kids and I don't want to have to hurt them, but that sleigh is worth a lot."

"It's worth more to Sheridan!" exclaimed one kid, Kaylie by the sound of it. "She's a doctor!"

"There's a doctor up the road?" came one voice from the roof. "Take all you want from anyone else, but she'd be useful."

"Shut up!" yelled George, and he turned back to Derek. "Derek, get down off that horse."

By this time, Shiloh and Helen had their rifles up and trained on the roof. Zachary had his police issue shotgun trained on George. Emilie fired one shot off a warning into the air before training her gun on the person sneaking up behind her using the heavy equipment. Derek's rifle was aiming at George, and a quick glance showed that the children quickly ducked behind and under the sleigh.

Only one person had not responded, and that was the children's mother, Nora.

Derek suspected she was already dead. She had likely died on the road from the cold. His priority, however, was making sure the rest of them made it back alive, without the needs of testing Sheridan's clinic. "I think you'll find that we'll be leaving," said Derek. "I would have invited you back, but I can clearly see where you want this to go."

"You think we're letting you leave?" asked George, laughing. "Let me tell you how this is going to go, even if we let you by... You'll have to sleep with one eye open and push your horses all the way back through the dark because me and my men will be on your tails the entire time. We take what you have now or we take it later."

"Third option," came Shiloh's voice. "If you're actually the original owner of this property, then you should be familiar with Terrence Scapael. These are his horses... and Sheridan is his wife. We're here on their say so."

That gave George pause. Derek was sure he knew that the threat of crossing Terrence without the law to stop him from going old-fashioned on everyone would have been a genuine threat. Terrence had always to be seemed an all right fellow before the law ceased to exist. But there was always something just brewing under that surface that screamed like a wild animal just barely kept under control.

While George was contemplating his options, Derek was also running through outcomes. If, by some miracle, he allowed them to leave, George was right. They would chase Derek and his people all the way back to the farm, and those defenses tested almost immediately. The only advantage they had was the horses and the wall that they were a good distance outside of. If they relinquished what they had, they would have to still get back to the farm somehow and more of them would likely die on the trip there.

"And that third outcome is?" asked George.

"You can try to take what we have. If you somehow succeed on taking it and at least one of us makes it back to Sheridan's farm—and I can guarantee you someone will—Terrence will raise a mounted fighting force and come at you with everything he has," Shiloh answered. "Just remember—Sheridan and Terrence are history fanatics and historical re-enactors. You should see some medieval gear they have… Weapons of war from a time before cars or guns, and they have those as well, although for hunting… You sure you want that on your doorstep in less than a week?"

"We could leave!" answered someone from the roof.

"And he'd only track us down until he got everything back," yelled George back up at him, before turning back to their group. "Quite the little stand-off we have here. I take it that wasn't the third option."

"Nope, that was a statement of reality. The third option comes from you standing down, letting us leave with what we have tomorrow morning and we make like this never happened," said Shiloh. "Because if you know Terrence and I think you do know him… you let this go down and even Sheridan won't stay her hand to stop him."

"You're not thinking about taking them up on that offer, are you, George?" yelled the same voice from up top. "*Cecelie aura ta tête.*"

"Shut up!" yelled George. "You think you can handle her better?"

"Yeah, I think I do!"

Moments later, the rest of his reply came with the sharp echo of a gunshot. George looked surprised for a second at his own blood as it steamed and bounced off the frozen snow before he crumpled in a heap.

Derek jumped from the horse. He rolled behind one of the cherry-picker trucks when Partly Cloudy fell heavily, twitching and thrashing as the bullets tore through its flanks. *Damn*, he swore.

The horses were too valuable to lose. Even one would be a terrible blow to their resources.

Zachary was just as pinned down, but at least they could see each other to signal what to do next, except Zachary was taking aim at Derek.

For a moment, Derek could only stare in shock and betrayal and prepared himself to die. It was out of his hands.

The gun shot he expected to feel did not come, even if he heard it.

A dull thud of a body hitting the snow beside him made him turn and look. He laughed in nervous relief when he realized he was not Zachary's target as Zachary shot another man trying to shoot him. Derek gave Zachary the thumbs up in thanks and recognition at his shooting ability and for saving his life and ducked out just enough to see past the massive wheels of the large truck he was hiding behind.

The children were hiding under the sleigh, and Shiloh was using the back of the seat for cover. Derek took cover behind the sleigh. Helen was face down in the snow, dark red blood pooling out from under her, her hair splayed out around her.

Derek looked around and spotted Emilie as she crept along the side of the building. One man on the roof made the mistake of looking over the edge for her and she shot him. She just barely moved out the way as he fell off the building and landing where she had been only moments ago.

With that man's death, the gunshots from the building stopped abruptly and a voice, from behind another piece of equipment on Zachary's side, said, "I give up!"

They whirled on the young man as he came out with his arms above and behind his head. He knelt in the snow and Zachary checked him over. "He's unarmed."

"Was he always, though?" asked Derek.

Zachary shook his head, unsure. Shiloh jumped down from the sleigh and ran over to Helen, rolling her over. With a look of sadness, she looked up at Derek and he could plainly see that Helen had died immediately. Either a crack shot had taken her out or someone had been lucky with their shooting. Either way, she wouldn't have felt it hit her. "She likely didn't even have time to duck for cover," said Shiloh. "She was right beside me!"

"Shiloh, check the horses." suggested Derek pushing into a task to take her mind off it. "I know at least one is dead."

"Okay, who are you and how many others of you are there?" asked Zachary as he pulled the young man to his feet and got a closer look at him. Surprised at what he saw, his next question was natural. "And how old are you? Sixteen, seventeen?"

"Fifteen, sir," he answered. "My name is Patrice. The one she—" he pointed at Emilie. "— Shot was my Dad."

"That bother you, son?" asked Derek.

Patrice shook his head. "I mean, it should, but it doesn't. When everything—stopped—went dark… whatever… he simply snapped. He wasn't my Dad anymore. Even George went different. It's like they had this notion that they could make this little empire out of the shop and make people do what they wanted them to do to support them… until she came. But what could I do? He was my Dad and George was his best friend."

Derek patted him on the shoulder. "You can help us now—if you want to," he suggested gently. "A good solid hand would be valuable. If you don't want to stay you can provision yourself and leave after spring melt to make your own way in the world."

He nodded and looked back up at Zachary and Derek. "I'd think I'd like that, sir, if you'll have me."

Shiloh came up beside Derek as he leaned against the back of the sleigh, staring out of the fenced gate, and put a key into his hand. He looked up at her and at the key in his hand. "It's labelled as the gate key," she explained. "It was on the bastard's key chain. I figured you should get this."

He lifted a brow in surprise. "After your show of force back there? I'd think you deserve it."

"All I did was cause a firefight."

"No, you split the firefight between two groups fighting over us instead of one cohesive group pinning us down," he answered and tapped his head. "You played a head game with their leader. Caused them to question him, which split them into two factions... not to mention cut the head off the snake before it could bite us. It could have gone down a lot worse than it did. You did well."

She thought about it and then smiled. "Yeah, I did, didn't I?"

He returned her nod, smiling. He then looked at the sky, her eyes following his.

"The stars are brighter now," she said. "Normally they aren't this clear."

"No light pollution anymore to stop us from seeing them," he answered. "A true sign of just how desolate things are. Normally, even this far out of the city, the lights from the city—and down south—are enough to make them seem dimmer. No light pollution means no lights on anywhere. We're right back to the 'days of old'."

"You think that maybe this is only temporary?" she asked.

"I hope it is," he answered. "But I don't think it is."

She nodded a bit sadly. "There's many people out there that we were close to that if this thing really means that civilization is gone, we're likely never going to see again. Family that was on the other side of Sudbury but for all intents and purposes could be on the other side of the country now."

He nodded his agreement and then sighed. "You didn't come out here to talk to me about stars, did you?"

She shook her head. "Casualty list," she answered.

He sighed heavily. "Lay it on me, Shiloh."

"The first is Nora, the mother of Kaylee and Liam," she began. "From what I figure, she died on the road between here and the Fire Hall... and we didn't even notice. Aaron... Aaron is of course torn apart at the loss of his wife and the even heavier weight of having to raise two young children in this world... Let alone how hard it would have been before."

"I'm sure we'll help him," he said, taking a breath. "Next."

"Helen."

Derek looked down and punched the back of the sleigh with his hand. She was someone that had come out with him because he had asked her to. He was directly responsible for her death.

"On the other side of things, George and his cronies are all dead. There weren't that many of them." She looked around and then continued. "We lost one horse in the firefight."

"Mine?"

"No, it was Partly, and he was a good horse too. I'll let you explain that one to Sheridan, but, given the circumstances, I don't see her being that upset. Upset that we lost him, and others too, but I imagine she will understand we did what we could," answered Shiloh, and she patted the side of her horse.

"Thankfully, we didn't lose him."

"Yeah, can't imagine Sheri would be too happy about losing Tempy," conceded Shiloh. "Did you hear what one of them said?"

Derek nodded. "Cecelie—and more of *them*."

She nodded. "You've got to get back to the Manor. As fast as we can. It'll be a rough ride, but…"

Derek eyed Northern Tempest and took a breath while looking at the others. "See you at the Manor, Shiloh."

Derek mounted Tempest and clicked his tongue as he guided the horse to point toward the Manor. "Ride like the fury he's named after, Derek."

# Chapter Thirty-One

His heart was in this throat, and it felt like air was in short supply. Daniel knew it for what it was—the same sense of panic had washed over him when Harnet's people had first stormed City Hall.

Like before, he breathed out.

Out of the seven with him, only three had ever been in emergency services, and only one other was trained in policing. The other was used to high tension situations, but only to save lives—not to run straight into danger like a firefighter or an officer.

*What have I got us into now?* Daniel wondered. He and the other officer understood—intimately.

Closely.

It was part of their training.

It was part of their lives.

The other five in the team had volunteered but had had none training nor had a situation—outside of surviving everything like they all were now—like this come up in their lives.

And now he had sent them into a fight, knowing that some of them wouldn't live through it.

Daniel breathed out.

They had to.

The front door crashed open. Daniel rushed in, followed closely by the other officer as she flattened herself against the inside wall opposite of him.

Loud voices shouted from the second floor, and Daniel motioned for the rest of them came into the building. He made two stay outside with a rifle, hidden behind cover, to provide extra cover.

He motioned for the other officer to toss the one smoke grenade they had taken with them. It had given them cover for an escape, but if it prevented the mercenaries from seeing them all the better.

The second threw an actual grenade—liberated from one mercenary when they held the City Hall—up the stairs, and they took cover as it went off.

Cement dust rained down on their head, and, bolstered by the shouts turning into groans of pain and fewer voices, Daniel led three up the stairs. The other two split off to check the main floor.

At the top of the stairs lay a woman in the same uniform as the others. He quickly stripped her of her guns and ammunition and took the automatic rifle for himself. Flipping the safety from single fire to burst—a setting that allowed him to fire off three quick sets of bullets—he settled the butt of the rifle into his right shoulder. The other former officer took another similar rifle off another of the mercenaries, and the third a shotgun.

While he knew that a gun hardly guaranteed victory, having something better than just his side arm settled his mind. Marginally—but it still settled a bit.

Going from room to room, they checked for others. They barricaded one room at the end of the hall, although from the way they had thrown the surrounding desks, they did this in a real hurry.

"They knew we were coming," whispered the other officer as she tilted her chin at the barricade. "That wasn't done an hour ago—they watched us come up the road."

"If that's the case, they could trap things," pointed out the other.

Daniel nodded, his voice also low. "Yeah, I figured that."

They fell silent again, and Daniel followed the line of desks and pointed at the nearly hidden wire running across the space between. The other two nodded and stepped over it. Daniel looked at the trap again. From the way they had set it up, it was well hidden. Any civilian, or even a trained officer, could have easily had tripped it. It was low enough to the floor—only a few inches above it—and the wire was thin enough and not easily seen within the debris. He followed the line of it and saw the makeshift fall trap hidden just above and in the drop ceiling. Checking for other traps, he moved them far enough away from the trap, and motioned for them to hide. He took cover as well.

Once they had hidden themselves, Daniel tossed a book onto the wire.

Debris, cement blocks, books and even shrapnel and broken glass rained down on a six-foot by six-foot space around the trip wire.

From the other side, the mercenaries came rushing around the corner and stopped when they realized they had failed to trap their quarry.

"Surprise!" yelled Daniel, as he squeezed the trigger on the rifle.

The first mercenary fell heavily, not even having time to counter. The others jumped to either side, hiding behind tipped over desks for cover, firing blindly towards them as they did.

A gasp and a thud beside him alerted him to trouble, and he turned to see that the other officer had taken two hits—one straight through her throat and another in the collarbone. Daniel pulled her behind cover and applied pressure, but death came in seconds. He closed her eyes and shook his head at the other.

Daniel felt something else rise.

White hot, sudden, and blinding.

He clenched his teeth, breathing through them. He looked over at the other and nodded, making a swift cutting motion with his hand.

They waited, and Daniel moved to the side, the other setting down covering fire. Daniel took a grenade off the fallen woman, and his eyes thinned. With one swift movement, he pulled the pin and tossed it gently into the space between the two mercenaries.

Daniel and the surviving teammate ran for the stairs, almost sliding down them.

The grenade went off and screaming met him.

The building shook, and as the surviving six waited outside for the shake to stop, Daniel finally nodded. "I take it the main floor was clear, then?"

They nodded. "Where's Becca?" asked one.

Daniel looked at the ground and shook his head.

"Lucky shot," answered the survivor who had gone up the stairs with him.

"We'll retrieve her now, but I still want everyone to be careful—pretty sure we got all of them and retook the building, but two grenades can't be good for the structure," said Daniel.

"Aye sir," said one other, clapping him on the shoulder.

They followed him in, and they went room by room, floor by floor, until they reached the body of their fallen friend. They covered her with a drop sheet found on the main floor and then continued. "Clear!" called the other former officer. "Not even so much as a trap. They may have seen us coming, but I don't think they saw us until it was too late. They didn't really have enough time to set more than the one trap."

"Check this out!" called another as they pulled back a desk that had been hiding a hole through a wall into a closed off room.

Daniel felt himself grinning.

In the room was a massive cache.

Guns, first aid supplies, blankets and camping equipment…

… Food and water.

Daniel let a huge breath out—one that he had not even realized he had been holding as the others let up a whoop as a cheer.

"Now that's what I'm talking about!" shouted one other.

"There's enough here to survive for weeks," said the former officer. "Not just in food, but the camping and hunting equipment will make it so we get more food."

Daniel stepped into the room, which was more the back half of a whole other building. He looked over at the cache and shook his head. "There's no way we can move this on our own. Take what we can, and then we head back. We'll send the other teams straight here and start moving back to Tom Davies."

He clapped them all on the shoulders.

"This is a tremendous blow to Harnet," he said. "A huge blow. Maybe the chance we needed to even up the score."

* * * * *

Derek held on for dear life. It was all he could do once Shiloh had told Northern Tempest to run back home. The horse did as they trained it to do—and what it wanted to do.

*I'd want my nice warm stall too*, he thought. *And my feed.*

Permission granted to return to his stall and his feed, Tempest didn't even seem to touch the ground over the open, even parts. The snow didn't bother him. Shiloh had seen to that with the leg guards. He didn't even seem like he was pushing himself, really.

Once Derek realized the horse wasn't pushing himself at all, despite how fast the terrain whipped by him and the air burned the exposed parts of his face, Derek relaxed into the ride.

*It's still scary as hell*, he thought, trying to not look down at the ground and keep his eyes forward and on where they were going.

The horse left the road, choosing to cross a field. "Oh, no you don't," chided Derek, trying to bring the horse back onto the road. "I know where your horse brain is going—if you jump, you'll dump me and I have zero desire to end up on my ass in the snow."

Tempest fought him a bit, but Derek insisted.

With a chuff deep in his chest, the horse finally returned to the road and kept going.

Only after a few feet he stopped again, trotting sideways a few steps and shaking his head. "What is with you," Derek asked the horse. "Home is that way…"

He pointed down the road and noticed the people walking up it.

They hadn't spotted him, or the horse, and Derek's eyes widened as he loosened up the reins and let the horse have his way.

Tempest ducked into the wooded area and away from the road, moving through a gap in the trees Derek hadn't even noticed. While the horse slowed down, the trot was still quick enough for the branches to slap Derek in the face. As he winced from the many slaps and whips, he ducked down lower over the horse so that the horse took some punishment.

Raised voices from behind him alerted them, and Tempest moved quicker through the woods.

*"Je sais que quelqu'un est allé par ici!"* called one. *"Ces pistes sont fraîches."*

*"Ça me ressemble à un animal, peut-être à un orignal?"*

"*Non, idiots, c'est un cheval. Regarde les pistes — ils sont clairement faits de fers à cheval,*" said another, and Derek lightly encouraged the horse to move.

Cecelie.

*Dammit, I knew she had something to do with that warehouse,* thought Derek, and he brought the horse to a stop.

If he kept going, Shiloh and the others would ride right into the middle of them, and Cecelie had more people with her. Between those already following Shiloh, then Cecelie, Shiloh wouldn't stand a chance. Not with children in tow as well.

Tempest stomped his foot, and he patted the horse's side. "We've got to go back."

The horse snorted.

"I know, I know," said Derek. "But if we don't, our friends die. But we also have to tell the Manor to expect trouble. Dammit, what a conundrum…"

The horse turned around, almost as if he understood what Derek was telling him. Derek grinned. The horse was fast, and smart, and between the two of them they could easily lead Cecelie and her people off the road and away from Shiloh and still make it to the Manor fast enough to warn Terrence.

He patted the horse again. "Feel up to causing a bit of mischief?"

The horse tossed his head and pawed at the ground, and Derek took that as agreement.

"Let's show Cecelie whose land this really is," said Derek, and he gave the horse full rein again.

The ride through the bush was as jarring as before, but adrenaline sang in his blood as he kept himself low. The horse burst out of the woods and trotted back up onto the road. Not exactly where they had gone into it, but not far either. Cecelie and her gang headed up the road—straight toward Shiloh.

*Okay, Tempest, time to see what you can do*, thought Derek as he brought two of his fingers up to his lips and blew through them.

His shrill whistle cut through the silence, and the raiders whirled around.

"Hey, Cecelie, you want round two?" he called, and he made the horse twirl around on the road. "Come and get me then."

He loosened the reins a bit, giving Tempest a bit of encouragement with his heels as he pointed him straight across the road and into another field.

"Derek!" came her shout, and it almost sounded like she hissed it. *"Tue-le!"*

Out of the corner of his eye, he saw them raise their guns, but by the time they could do anything, he and the horse had gone into the bush. *"Attrape le! Il ne peut pas rouler vite là-bas!"*

*Whether I can ride at speed through here, you might find me harder to catch than you think*, thought Derek.

Northern Tempest was as at home in the woods around his barn as he was in the open field. He knew to slow down, and where to put his feet, and how much he could trust his own footing. Derek stayed low, gripping the reins in a light grip, and relying more on how well he stayed in the saddle by holding on using his legs.

They came out by the road again, and again they were behind Cecelie.

"Seriously, Cecelie, you'd think you weren't even trying."

Her wordless scream of frustration was satisfying, as was disappearing into the bush again, and this time the desired effect of dragging her and her raiders into the bush with him worked.

They made more noise than Tempest did, and neither he nor the horse had any trouble picking out where they were.

Finally, with a snort, the horse came out on another road entirely—one full of complex twists and turns. He waited long enough to see a few of the raiders come out, followed closely by the flaxen-haired Cecelie—although her formerly coiled and groomed blonde hair now dishevelled, loose, and full of branches and dead leaves. A scratch on her face and dirt betrayed a rather nasty tumble.

"Finally! You have nowhere to…" she said just in time for Northern Tempest to pick up his feet and carry them both back down the road.

Her shouting and screaming in the distance made Derek laugh, which made her shriek louder. *She definitely can swear*, he thought as he found himself back on the main road.

"Mission accomplished," he told the horse. "Now, back to getting word to Terrence. Take me home, Tempest."

# CHAPTER THIRTY-TWO

It was still dark when she left the call centre. Gina walked down the road, following the tracks left by the snow machine until she stood on Paris Street. From here, the tracks turned and followed Paris with no hint of changing course. *Pretty straight line there*, she thought, as she looked up the other way. *Straight line from here to that department store as well. They definitely saw me there—damn, so much for thinking it was random.*

She kept her eyes moving around as she was sure the looters *had come from some place close to here. It made little sense otherwise. No, someone was in that*

*Walmart, saw me, and then booted it through the snow to the others. They didn't take long to get there from here after*, she thought as she moved across the street and into a small gap between a drugstore and the coffee shop.

Like the department store, they smashed the windows in. Anything of value, or use, had already been taken.

A sudden thought struck Gina, and it brought her to a sudden stillness in the snow as she looked around.

There was no one—not even a survivor.

The buildings were dark and cold.

*Where is everyone?* Gina wondered. *They couldn't have left the city…*

*… They couldn't all be dead? Could they?*

She sucked in a breath and thought about it.

Kirk and his people couldn't have been everyone in that subdivision, but yet there had been so few of them. The only ones with him had fallen back to using camping equipment to stay warm. Kirk didn't seem the type to leave his neighbours out in the cold.

*Unless, in that cold snap, people died overnight*, she thought. *Or killed by those wandering bands of looters for whatever they had.*

If she had to admit it to herself, things had seemed to be in a bit of a slow decline. More and more had moved down south as grocery prices spiked and the cost of living for heat and electricity did the same.

*People head on walkabout down south to find cheaper living, others freezing to death… roving bands of looters and bandits*, she thought. *Maybe we are it.*

That was a depressing thought.

*I didn't become a firefighter to give in or see people die. Not while I can help it*, she thought. *And I'm not about to now. Eye on the survivors, Gina. Can lay the dead to rest with their ancestors properly later.* She knew she was breaking with tradition, but as one person, there was nothing she could do to honour their ancestors properly. She had to hope to find other First Nation people later so they could perform the proper ceremony. *I'm sorry*, she apologized to the unseen dead. *I will do your ancestors and mine proud. But it will have to wait.*

Gina blew out a breath, watching it fog in the air.

She pushed herself against the wall as she peeked out from around the corner, watching as a single person moved from one of the apartment complexes toward the park.

Gina moved out from the wall, and darted to the parking lot of another store, and then to the next mini mall where one of her favourite sushi restaurants had been. From here it was another mini mall with another fast-food place—one she had never cared for—and then to the parking lot of a church.

It also had the most cover with trees and bushes to hide in, and Gina crawled into the gap left by the large pine tree where the snow had drifted. The ground was still exposed, and she brushed off some pine needles. The branched had kept the snow from underneath, put the wind had pushed the drift into surrounding the lower part of the tree. While it was still cold, the sudden lack of wind and snow under the tree felt heavenly and she sighed as she leaned against the trunk.

She hadn't been the first to think about this, judging by the debris of fast food and other containers beneath the tree. However, they were frozen into the ground. *No one has been under here in a while*, she surmised. *I have a decent little hidey hole to check things out from here, I think.*

Kneeling on the ground, she poked her head up through the branches, using them as cover in each direction.

In the parking lot of the church sat her snow machine.

*Jackpot!* Gina grinned then. *I knew you couldn't have gone that far. If you had, the gas would have run out by now.*

"I still don't see why you don't just leave it," said a woman as she followed the man—the very looter Gina had tracked—to the snow machine as he sat on it. Don't you dare run more of my gas out of that tank! "The place is a drafty dungeon."

"That mall is more than just a dungeon. It's a statement," he said.

"The medical tower would be better. Or even one of the apartment towers. There's a beautiful condo tower were all the rich people lived on the lake, even," said the woman, and then she pointed at the tallest of the apartments. "Take one of those. At least from that one up there we can see for miles around. No one would even fight us for it. If we scavenge the other places, we could keep it running for years until things calm down."

"That's not the point. They used you and then toss you aside, like all of anyone like them did to all of us," he pointed at her. "Now it's our turn. Their world is over. Ours is beginning. It's time they felt what we had to for years."

"Revenge," she said, her tone flat. "That's all you're after is revenge?"

"Why not?"

"Because it's dumb, that's why," she said with a snort.

*You're right there*, thought Gina, raising an eyebrow. *But so is he, even if I don't like his means… and that's my machine.*

"And you'd suggest what?" he asked. "We just up and leave them?"

"That generator will give out eventually, and then what will they do?" she asked. "They will come crawling to us for help. They'll beg us."

He grinned then. "Oh, I like it… and then we'll tell them to buzz off…"

She shook her head. "No, Louis, we take the high road and help them."

The looter, Louis, leaned back and stared at her. "You're joking, right?"

"Nope," she answered. "They'll feel guilty then."

He grimaced and then stood up, patting her on the head as he did. Louis then opened his arms and pivoted on one heel until he faced her again. "Do you really think that? Don't be naïve. They'll worm their way back to the top again and leave us with nothing. No, we cut this cancer out once and for all. As you said, that generator will quit. The doors will open, and we'll rush in… only this time we'll give them a mercy some others didn't have with a swift death."

He walked away, heading back inside. The woman stood there, watching him, before she looked toward the call centre and followed him in.

Gina's eyes remained wide for a few full moments as what he said — what he planned — sank in. *Holy…* she breathed out.

She knew that once he was done with the call centre than Kirk and his people would be next — and then Hannah and Middle Lake. *Our own neighbourhood is one of the wealthiest. He's out for revenge against those who had money before, so we'd be next…*

Gina stared at her machine, and once she didn't hear anyone, she ran to it and climbed on it. She pulled her helmet out of her bag but then stared at the door. She ducked back under the tree and brought out a length of two-by-two and shoved it into the door handles of the church. The wood wasn't thick enough to prevent them from leaving for long, but it would buy her enough time to get as far from the church as possible. She pulled on her helmet and started the machine. With one last look just as the doors moved but were prevented from opening, she grinned and gunned the engine—leaving the church and the looters behind.

It took moments to get back to the call centre.

Gina brought the snow machine to a halt, almost skidding in the snow as she ran to the doors and knocked. The upper window opened again, and the light above the revolving door turned green. She ran through them and stopped as she faced the same three people. She looked at Mark and said, "We have to get you all out of here—now."

"We can hold them off," he began. But she shook her head. "What?"

"You don't get it," she started. "Louis—that's his name, by the way—is waiting for the generator to quit and for these doors to open. When that does, he is going to barge in here and kill everyone. That's his plan."

Mark's eyes widened, and he opened his mouth, but closed it again. He looked down at his chair and looked up. "I know the others can follow you, but I guess I'll have to keep them as distracted as I can."

"I'll strap you to the machine if I have to, and the chair too," said Gina. "I'm not leaving any of you behind. But we've got to go, now."

A woman came out of the other set of doors, "Mark, there's movement past the corner."

Gina closed her eyes. I'm too late. She opened them again and looked at one of the two security guards. One was another woman around her size. "You know how to ride one of those?" she asked, pointing to the snow machine.

"Yeah," she answered with a bit of a snort. "Not very many in the North who don't."

"Great, you take the machine. I'll keep the bastards distracted," said Gina, and then she looked at Mark. "I know you won't like it, but I need access to the rest of your building. Don't worry, I'm sure your company—if we're wrong about all this—will at least be happy with the fact that the information stayed protected."

Mark hesitated, but then looked up at one of the security guards. The woman took her key card from around her neck and handed it to Gina. "That's an all-access pass to the entire building," she said. "Anywhere you need to be, that'll let you in."

Gina watched them long enough to make sure Mark wouldn't fall off the machine and then watched as it disappeared around the building. She held the key card to the scanner and the inner door clicked. The second guard followed her in.

He led her to a staff lounge that would have made anyone jealous.

Three large flatscreen TVs adorned the walls, dark now, but she could imagine that before they had played different TV shows or news programs. A small gas fireplace, still flickering with what remained in the pipes for pressure, kept the small space warm.

Along one wall was a row of vending machines, including an automatic 'barista' coffee dispenser—one of the few that actually did as advertised by making real coffee of mostly any kind from regular to espresso and everything in between.

On that side was also the counter spaces with microwaves and a sink cupboard for what would normally be in a kitchen. Tables with chairs for eating and socializing turned to sofas and armchairs closer to the fireplace and TVs.

As she counted the survivors within the building, she came to a stop.

Twenty people, not including Mark and the two security guards, huddled close to the fireplace for warmth. They stared at Gina, their eyes wide when they realized she was new. "Everyone, grab your stuff. Gina has given us a safe place to run to where the gangs won't find us. But we have to leave now."

There were a few glances between them, but they stood up and started grabbing what they could and putting them into what bags they could find. "If you can, the best way to get out of here would be up through the mall and out the entrance by that farm supply store. Head to the recreation centre by the bypass on Highway 17 where it meets

Long Lake. If you run into an old codger that could give Clint Eastwood a run for his money, tell him Gina sent you. If you don't, head down Long Lake. You'll eventually meet up with him," explained Gina. "You should all be safe there—not to mention able to survive better on what's there instead of what you can pick over here."

The guard pointed out, "You haven't said what you're going to do."

"I'm covering your escape," she answered. "If I focus the looters on me, they hopefully won't see you leave."

When the last of the workers left the cafeteria, they followed them out. In the middle of the call centre sat a set of stairs and an elevator which led to the second level, and the workers disappeared there.

The guard stood by the stairs for a long moment. "I could stay."

"No, you need to get these people out of here," she said. "Leave this to me."

*＊＊＊＊＊*

Daniel leaned against the ledge as he looked down into the mezzanine where this had all started for him. *Seems like a hundred years ago,* he thought. *Hard to believe it's barely been a month.*

*If that.*

The Mayor was sitting on the counter he had hidden underneath.

In the mezzanine were people, and there was an open circle where a group of them danced while others sang. Makeshift musical instruments made from overturned garbage cans and anything else they could lay their hands on filled the room with noise that barely had a rhythm.

A bonfire burned outside to the side of the fountain, lighting up the outside as others danced around it.

The food found was not much—not in the grand scheme of things—but properly split amongst the survivors and not wasted meant they might last the entire winter.

The cache had been far larger than any of them had thought when they first found it. It hadn't been just a room. The mercenaries had bored holes in walls between buildings to stash it away like squirrels. The labels betrayed the various restaurants and hotels they had stolen it from. He was sure, judging by the blue labels on some items, that it had even come from the grocery store on Lorne.

In one day, they had gone from starving to death to having hope.

Victoria smiled up at him again.

Daniel felt uncomfortable with all the attention, but it was worth it to see life return to the eyes of each survivor. To see a child ask for food and get it instead of empty promises like yesterday.

He sighed heavily as he leaned on the ledge.

*This won't escape Harnet's attention*, Daniel knew. *There'll be a reckoning. Maybe not now, maybe not tomorrow. But eventually he'll strike back to push us back into the corner.*

It was this that would not let him relax. Would not let him enjoy the one night since everything started. The surviving members of his team joined him on the ledge, and one elbowed him with a small smile. "She wouldn't want us to be depressed," said Marcus. "Becca wasn't that type."

"I suspected as much," said Daniel. "I didn't know nearly enough about her."

Marcus paused, sighing as he did so. "She was one of a kind. She chose this, though. And to see these people celebrating would have been exactly what she expected to happen. I think she'd be happy she helped with this."

Daniel nodded. "I can't shake the feeling that we're celebrating a touch too soon."

Marcus crinkled his face. "Come on, Dan, we needed one night to blow off steam and smile a bit. It's been way too long since any of us could. I don't suggest drinking until we're all paralyzed, but crack a smile and celebrate this one victory."

"—With a great deal of awareness," said Neil.

"Well, yeah," said Marcus. "That'd be why I said 'don't drink until we're paralyzed'. Keep our wits about us. We're the watch."

"The watch, eh?" asked Daniel, lifting a brow. "Yeah, maybe so."

A young man came running through the crowd and straight to Victoria. She leaned over to listen to what he said, and Daniel watched her eyes widen and her face pale. Victoria looked up at him, took the young man by the shoulders, and then led him up the stairs and straight to Daniel. She led the both of them, and his team, into her office.

Once there, and the door closed, she said to the young man. "Now tell him what you told me."

"The downtown is on fire," said the young man in a rush, his voice strained from the run. "The old side—where the houses are—the ones from when Sudbury was first built."

"All of it or just one of them?" asked Marcus.

"All of it," said the young man. "I saw soldiers leaving the area. One of them stood by that corner close to the coffee shop before they all went back to the mall."

"That son of a bitch," breathed Daniel. "What the hell could he possibly gain in burning down that part of it?"

"Nothing," said Victoria. "Except that it's a part of our history, Dan. He razed it because he knew it was important to us."

Daniel sucked in a breath.

There it was.

Harnet's response to losing the cache of supplies.

Daniel leaned back on Victoria's desk. If the ground had opened up and swallowed him, he wouldn't have been surprised by it at all. "What the hell has he against Sudbury?" he wondered aloud, and then he pushed himself off the desk. "And honestly, I don't give a damn what it is or why he does it. This stops *now*."

Victoria and those on his team looked at him in surprise. Victoria regained herself the quickest, and she said to the young man, "Thank you, go back to the celebration but keep it quiet for now. They deserve one night. We can go back to it tomorrow."

The young man left and Daniel blew out a breath as he paced in the office, looking out over Brady and Paris as he did so. Finally, he leaned against the window and said, "I want all three teams ready to go before dawn tomorrow."

"Wait a minute, Dan, you're not even completely healed yet," said Victoria. "That one wander into the downtown and that one successful fight against four of his people is not the same as going into that mall."

He turned to look at her. "He will not stop until we're dead. Until everything is gone or his. I meant what I said. We don't have the luxury of waiting. Fitz has been in that place for long enough. He's already destroyed too much. We finally have the food and supplies to go in there at full strength. He won't wait a moment more now that we have that. It's him or us, Vic."

She sighed heavily, but then nodded. "All right, I will accept that. But you all come back in one piece—no dead heroes. We've already had too many."

Daniel shrugged. "I can't promise that, but I can promise we will be careful. But the minute we go in there, I want you and everyone else prepped to evacuate Tom Davies," he said, as he grasped her shoulders. "It won't matter if we fail or succeed. If he's willing to raze the downtown in retaliation for a supply cache and four of his people, there's no telling how far he will go once we go into his house and take from him. At the first sign of trouble, you head to Bell Park and get out of the downtown core."

She shook her head.

"No, Victoria, with the three teams gone this place will be undefended except for barely trained civilians and survivors," said Daniel. "We already know he wants you—specifically you—to legitimize his control. If you're out of reach, we stop two things from going to plan. Promise me you'll get everyone out."

Victoria sighed heavily and finally nodded. "All right. The minute you and those teams leave in the morning, I will break it to the other survivors. But you will meet us there, right?"

He nodded. "I'll do my best."

# CHAPTER THIRTY-THREE

The fresh snow on the ground was a blessing, as was the milk-like visibility. Daniel had never been more thankful for a full blizzard as he was this morning. The dark before dawn further covered them. Marcus whispered, "So long as we're quiet, they won't even realize where we are or where we've been. The snow will fill in our tracks behind us faster than we can make them."

Daniel smiled slightly.

"This is exactly what I was hoping for," he said.

He motioned for the other two teams to move out, and they did. One headed up Larch—one of the cross streets between the mall and City Hall—to the next city block. The snow was heavy enough that they faded from view before they were around the corner on the next street.

The other headed to Paris, the major boulevard, but cut in through an alleyway before they were into the open.

Daniel led his team across the street and onto another short street between City Hall, the condos, and connected to the parking lot for the coffee shop and liquor store. The imposing steel and glass building here had overhangs they could duck underneath, so in the off chance Harnet had spotters above they couldn't see them.

Someone had smashed the glass in.

Daniel lifted a brow.

The feat that would have taken was impressive. The hardened windows, like that of City Hall, prevented a brick, let alone anything else, from smashing through them. Someone—through concentrated effort—had smashed the windows enough to peel them open and push them so that they laid like a sparkling and sharp-edged blanket on the floor within.

He sighed, but they checked the first floor to make sure that Harnet or his people hadn't moved in.

Except for a few other survivors, which he directed to Tom Davies, the building was empty.

Daniel stepped back outside, brushing off some snow, and with a tilt of his head, led the others through the treed lane way between the bus depot and liquor store.

They paused here, crouching into the snow so that they blended into the drifts.

*And now we wait*, he thought.

Daniel checked his watch. They still had a half hour before the other two teams would start their feints on the building.

Each minute felt like an hour.

Daniel heard the first retort of a rifle from the other side of the mall.

There were a few moments of silence, and then the sound of a gun fight filtered through the murk. A few moments later, there was another single round fired off, this time from the ground parking lot behind the cinema leading to the train tracks.

It took a few more moments than the first, but the sound of shouting and confusion became pitched from the roof, but Daniel could hear it move away.

He nodded to the others, and they got to their feet.

They stayed low, and underneath the pedestrian bridge between the bus depot and the condo tower, until they were at the entrance. Daniel pulled open the doors, and they filed in. Once inside, they crouched again.

Marcus looked at Daniel, the crinkle of his brows betraying his thoughts, *What the hell?*

Daniel shook his head.

The mall had power—*actual* electricity. While not every light was on, nor were they on full, that they had electricity was enough to make Daniel seethe.

While the survivors at Tom Davies square, some of them even evicted from this very building, were starving and freezing to death, Harnet had power, heat, and food.

"The son of a bitch," breathed one behind him, near silently.

Daniel took a breath and released it. He felt the same way at the moment, but he could not let the rage prevent him from keeping his cool. That could come later, especially if they caught him upstairs. Daniel had words—and fingers he wanted around Harnet's throat.

"We'll have our chance," said Daniel, his voice low. "We'll shove him out of this hidey hole too. It can be our home."

The others nodded, and he saw a grim smile on Marcus' face.

"We need stairs," said Daniel. "Much as I'd hate to use them, but we can't run a chance of being trapped in an elevator."

Marcus pointed out the escalators close to where they crouched. "There's a set of stairs not far from there. They lead up to the second floor. There's another set of stairs, from there, from beside the elevators to the top floor."

"Any idea what floor your friend could be on?" asked one other on his team.

He shook his head. "No, but I have a feeling—just by how this guy rolls—that he has the power on for a reason. He's probably living it up in the penthouse condos. Make himself feel like he's above everyone else."

Marcus nodded. "Yeah, that seems like him."

Daniel followed Marcus to the set of stairs, and once on the second floor, Daniel looked at the others. "Do you think he'd have had time to remove those maps the Mayor told me about?"

Marcus shrugged. "Likely. But, then again, he may not expect us to be after them or even here."

"Where would they be?"

It was one of the other survivors who answered, "I know exactly where they are. They're in the reference section—local. I can show you," she answered, and when the others looked at her, she shrugged. "I volunteered here."

Daniel nodded and grinned, "You show us what to grab then. Better yet, you and one other ransack this place with anything you can carry that won't slow you down, you think will be useful to us and strike a blow to him."

"On it, sir," she said, and one other joined her.

This left him short with only five people on his team, but so far there was no sign that Harnet had any idea they were even in the building. "There's a security desk downstairs," said Marcus.

"Were the cameras on?" asked Daniel, inwardly berating himself over missing something so simple.

Marcus shook his head. "No, I would have mentioned it earlier. I'm just thinking we could ransack that on the way out too."

Daniel nodded. "Good idea."

They opened the door to the stairwell and started climbing.

"I don't mean to jinx things," said Marcus. "But this is really too easy. He couldn't have forgotten to leave anyone at all to keep watch."

Daniel had felt the same, but he shook his head. "Monitor our route out. I brought the climbing equipment for a reason. I hope we won't have to use it."

Marcus nodded.

They opened the emergency exit to the penthouse level. Two units shared the floor and both of them had always looked impressive in the brochure. The stairs linked to their "back door" which was an emergency exit. Daniel directed each half of what remained of his team to each door of the units. They opened the doors and went inside. With hand signals to show the rooms were clear, each team cautiously moved inside.

Daniel and Marcus went into the left unit, the one that faced City Hall. If I were Harnet, given his pattern, I'd want to feel as if I had my eye on the 'prize', he thought. I'd be in here… where I can see my enemy.

They cleared the first few bedrooms and found one that was locked. Daniel motioned for his team to check the living spaces.

Coming around the corner, the sign of recent habitation was obvious. While Harnet appeared to be neat and tidy, there was very little dust and the furniture faced the windows.

"How right you were on this," said Marcus, lifting a brow. "He made himself right at home in this one."

A banging on the door of the locked room startled them and they moved to either side of the door. Daniel put his fingers to his lips and motioned for them to move to either side of the door. Marcus then, in one step, moved in front of that door and kicked it off the hinges, his gun up.

\* \* \* \* \*

Once the last of the call centre workers had left the mall, the building was silent. Gina shivered as the chill that could never be dispelled from a basement settled in. She lifted the key pass to look at it. It was a simple, if thicker than a credit card, pass key. Clipped to the identity card was a tiny laminated paper card with health and safety info printed on it.

*Typical for a call centre*, she thought as she walked the perimeter of the lower call centre floor.

It wasn't exactly possible to walk the entire floor. Temporary walls had created sections, probably organized by required security level, with doors locked both by hard key and pass card access.

Gina stopped as she found herself back where she started. *What does someone have to do to find paper in this place?*

Not a single sheet—not even a post-it-note—could be found anywhere she looked. At first, she thought it was because no one sat at the desks but as she looked closer, she could see photos—laminated copies pinned to the fabric of the cubicles—and white boards in varying degrees of marking up with some very colourful. No swearing or personal information as it would have been unprofessional in this environment, but actual vibrant reds, greens, blues and yellows.

Gina's jaw dropped.

*Their security prohibits paper*, she realized. *It's that secure a site in here.*

The problem with that was it threw a large wrench into her plans.

The clatter of rocks on the windows made her jump, and she looked at the windows. Shadows outside told her it wasn't just Louis anymore, but many others. She scrunched up her face and crossed her arms as the looters resorted to throwing bits of rock, bricks, and whatever else they could throw at the hardened glass. All to no avail—it wouldn't matter what they threw at it. The glass would never budge.

Gina sighed. *At least that gives me time to come up with an alternate plan in the meantime. I really have to give them something to chew on or they'll move on to Kirk and the others…*

Gina walked another circuit around the building, turning lights on and off as she went. Louis was still out there and the crowd followed the lights and focused the worst of the debris on the windows where lights came on.

Finally, after one more trip around the building, she walked into the cafeteria and flopped onto the couch in front of the fireplace. *Amazing after all this time, it's still keeping things warm. Only a matter of time before the pressure gives out and the fire…*

She blinked as she sat up straight.

The entire time she had been trying to find a scrap of paper in a file folder or an envelope, and the solution had been burning cheerfully in the cafeteria.

Gina couldn't count how many times she had been called out to a suspected gas leak. The danger, and chaos, one could cause under normal circumstances was almost legendary in firefighting and the insurance industry. *Enough gas floating around the building and a single spark…* she eyed the server room. *Should be able to cause some trouble here.*

The explosion, hopefully once she was far enough away, would be more than enough to keep Louis busy and his attention away from the survivors heading to Long Lake.

Again, she ran around the building turning lights on and off. This time she was looking for something and clogging up air returns. Incoming air was fine, but for the gas to build up she needed the outgoing air to stop.

*Bit of a challenge with nothing to do that with,* she thought as she threw another pillow from a couch into the vent. *Hopefully that will do it.*

Gina walked into the security station on the second floor, noting that it had a view out into the parking lot and a way up to the roof. She unlocked this and then ran downstairs to the cafeteria.

The first trick to building up gas was to turn off the fireplace and then open the feed again after making sure the pilot lights were all out.

This wasn't difficult. Accessing maintenance to these were part of the safety protocols to keeping them. But that wasn't the first step.

She had to sort out what would cause the spark.

While she didn't want to kill anyone, especially not those who may not have subscribed completely to his plan, she didn't want it going off too soon.

A bit of wire from the server room and a battery served as the spark device.

This she set up on the inner of the lobby—not the exterior revolving door. After testing it a few times to make sure it would go off as planned, she returned to the fireplace and disabled the pilot light, turned off the flame, and then opened the gas feed to full.

Propping the two doors open to the cafeteria and ran upstairs to the second floor and locked the security room.

Even with the gas and the spark, it wouldn't be enough to stop them.

*Give them pause, yes. Slow them down—distract them from the escaping call centre employees… but they could avoid that area.*

She sealed off any air flow between the security centre and the rest of the call centre, and opened the window.

Twenty minutes later, and almost freezing cold, she poked her head out.

"Look who it is," she called out. "Still want this place, Loius?"

That got his attention, and he looked up sharply. "Who the hell are you?"

"Someone who doesn't like her stuff stolen," she answered, and she grinned. "But I have a gift for you."

"Oh?"

She unlocked the doors to the call centre, and she heard him crow. "Sweetheart, you can keep the snow machine!"

*Make the most of it, boyo,* she thought, and she climbed the exit ladder to the roof and ran across the roof to the back of the call centre—to the farm supply store and down another one.

She was in the parking lot behind the mall when a rumble beneath her feet made her turn and look.

Black smoke rose into the air from the mall and she grinned, but the grin fell off.

That was more smoke than there should have been, and the continued rumbling beneath her feet was enough for her to pale when other units in the building crumbled. The glass on the mall shattered as the back pressure blew out other stores.

She turned and ran to the tree line, her chest heaving from the exertion of running through calf high snow.

Not even a single person came up the hill.

*I... I didn't think it would do that*, she thought. *Are they all dead?*

Bile rose in her throat, but she tamped it down. *No, Gina, don't you dare feel sorry for them. He was going to kill every single last person in that call centre and then move on to the families in this subdivision. You saved people.*

Still, it would have been nice not to resort to a fire trap to stop them.

Gina sighed and looked at the houses behind her.

Still silent.

Still empty.

She caught movement coming around the building.

The group wasn't large, but given the direction and the yelling, she knew it was Louis. *Tough bugger, ain't he*, she groused and then sighed.

*... Guess the chase isn't as over as I thought.*

# CHAPTER THIRTY-FOUR

"Hey Garrett, I had an idea," said Dane, poking his head into Garrett's room.

Garrett looked up from what he was working on. The radio's circuits were dusty, and he suspected there was a short somewhere in it as well. It just refused to work at all, and it frustrated him.

The distraction was actually welcome.

"Well, out with it," he said.

"A few of the others had this idea for setting up a trap line and using the backs of some mesh chairs as makeshift snowshoes."

"Your first idea is good," said Garrett with a sigh. "The second... Well, I know what movie you took that idea from and unfortunately it won't work. The mesh and the frames aren't strong enough to even hold up a small child."

"You sound like that's from experience," said Dane.

"It is. My daughter tried that with my grandson. They lasted all of two minutes and he was through them with the frames up around his knees," he answered, barking a laugh at the memory. "If he hadn't been so disappointed, it would have been funnier. At least now it is."

"How old is he?"

"Seventeen," answered Garrett.

"Wait, the movie we're talking about would have come out while he was maybe thirteen..."

"Didn't say we got the idea from the movie," pointed out Garrett. "Just said that unlike the movie it doesn't work."

"So, what should we do?" Dane asked.

Garrett shrugged and leaned back. "Not sure, but I'm sure we could figure something out. We've managed this much already."

Dane looked over the scattered parts of the HAM radio. "I'd ask if you were having any luck, but I can see that you've got your own work cut out for you."

"Actually, I've made progress," answered Garrett.

As frustrated as he was with the radio, he had made great leaps on getting it to work—so long as the right parts were available. "I figured out what's broken, so if we can rig a replacement, I should be able to get it to work."

"What parts?" asked Dane.

Scratching at his chin, which had grown from stubble to a full-fledge beard, Garrett took a long moment to answer. "Transistors, resistors, various electronics. Some things look a bit like they got too warm. I repaired the short that caused the damage."

Dane sat down in the other chair. "You sound a bit like you miss your family."

"I do," said Garrett, looking up at Dane and then back at the radio again.

"Yeah, some others wonder what their families are doing—how they're doing," said Dane. "Not much we can do from here, though."

"Can't give up hope," said Garrett, and he motioned at the radio. "It's one reason I'm trying to fix this dinosaur. I know the chances of someone else having a radio are slim, but I can say that if we don't have one, there is no way we'll ever have that chance to communicate because then we definitely don't have one. At least with it we'd be fifty percent of the way."

"Beats nothing," said Dane, his voice quiet. "But your family is close. You could go back to them—or even back to Worthington. You have more options than the rest of us do."

"Yeah, maybe," said Garrett, and then he blinked. *There he goes again…* "Maybe after I make sure I've exhausted every single last option here first."

"Well, if I see any parts for that thing, I'll bring them by," said Dane. "I'll bring some food up later."

"Fantastic, and thanks," answered Garrett as he bent back to his task and the other man simply waved as he left the room.

Garrett sighed as he looked back up. Not that he really wanted to brush off Dane. But the other man gave Garrett the oddest feeling.

*No hard feelings, my ass*, thought Garrett as he thought back to when he had written up Dane for a safety infraction a month before, and again for refusing to respect his superiors at the company. *If he thinks I haven't heard him muttering about how he could do better, he's an idiot.*

The problem was that Garrett knew something was up. Dane was normally a very social and open person. But—and perhaps he was reading too much into it—ever since Garrett had arrived, Dane had been… distant. Undecided.

Cagey.

*Why would he want me to go back to Worthington? It made no sense. Not after the obvious relief when he first arrived. But now…*

Garrett looked out the window. Dane had walked down to the smaller of the two dams, closer to the gate. In the distance, he could see him talking with a few others.

They kept looking at the gate.

*What's down there, Dane? What are you not telling me?*

Garrett had his suspicions.

High Falls was close to Worthington, but it was in between Nairn Centre and Worthington. Right outside of those gates was a rail crossing—the same rail that carried the slavers back and forth to Worthington.

*If that Kovach fellow had been in Worthington, I'd bet my left nut he was here first*, thought Garrett. *That means Dane has encountered him… what deal did you make, Dane? We're not short of that many here—not like Worthington. You had to make one.*

*When is Kovach going to be here and…*

Was that why Dane kept trying to get Garrett to leave? Garrett's eyes widened. Dane was vexing for sure, but if he had made a deal with Kovach to hand him over, then he would encourage Garrett to stay, not leave.

*He's already heard about Worthington*, realized Garrett. *He knows what I did and knows what Kovach will want when he shows up again… and he wants me gone to avoid it.*

Garrett clenched a fist.

The younger man was trying to protect him. Not that he had to—everyone at High Falls was in a far better position to fight off Kovach than Worthington had been, and they had forced the slavers out. If Kovach arrived here, he knew he, Dane, and the others could eject him far quicker than a bunch of older men, women, and one teenage girl.

He took a breath.

The next time Dane came up to the control house, he'd have to sit him down and have a chat.

\* \* \* \* \*

"That bitch can't have gone far!" yelled Louis. "Find her! I want my fair share of that call centre and that snow machine out of her hide."

Gina pressed herself further under the deck she had hidden under as boots above her shook snow onto her head. "The tracks I saw led in this direction," said another. "Unfortunately, with the rocks and drifting, she could have bounced and not left tracks."

"Nah, the way she taunted us? She's still in the area," said Louis. "She'll have wanted to see the damage she caused us."

Gina inwardly sighed. *At least the focus is still on me — not on Kirk.*

She waited until they had moved off the deck and to another one before she crawled out from under the deck. Cleaning herself off, she leaned against the wall as she watched them search. "You're all really blind, aren't you?"

The group whirled to face her.

"Where in the name of hell…" breathed Louis, his eyes wide. "*You*."

"What was that about taking what out of my hide? If you hadn't stolen my snow machine in the first place, we wouldn't be having this merry chase," she shrugged. "But since we're here…" She winked. "Let's see how good you are at hide and seek."

Gina disappeared around the side of the house, this time shimmying up a tree and to the roof, hiding behind a chimney.

The group came around the corner, and then the other half came around the other corner as they stared at each other in confusion.

"Where'd she go?" asked one of them.

Louis looked around, his mouth open a bit.

"Into the same thin air she came out of," said another, with a snort. "Who is she?"

Louis backhanded him. "Doesn't matter. No one toys with us."

"Bully," she called from above them and they looked up, their eyes wide.

This time they looked around for a way to get to where she was. Not finding it, they stared up at her again. "How the hell…" asked Louis, a slight note of admiration sneaking into his voice.

She winked again. "My secret… but you won't ever find it out. I don't like people who go out of their way to hurt others. So, here's the deal. Go back where you came from. That can be yours.

Leave me alone or deal with the consequences—
and that call centre was just a warning."

Gina moved out of his sight again, this time
moving into the collapsed roof of the house and,
once she watched them circle the place a few times,
she crawled out the basement window and back
under the same deck, under a tree like the first
tree—and then to the tree line.

Their voices moved further and further away as
she snaked her way back through the subdivision.

After one last rock, she found herself in Kirk's
back yard.

The house was, as she hoped, deserted.

She looked around and noted a snowbank
where one hadn't been before.

Gina dug into the snowbank and then grinned
as she found, underneath the snow, her snow
machine and helmet—protected in a bag—and it all
ready for her to use.

She looked around again and noted that the
four-by-four truck that had been at the bottom of
his driveway was missing.

*They wouldn't have needed this*, she thought. *Kirk
would have been able to move Mark and his wheelchair
out in the truck. No problem at all.*

She closed her eyes and breathed a sigh of relief
as she dusted the last remaining bits of snow off the
seat as she started the machine. She took one last
look at the house and rode the machine back on the
same path she had taken before until she was at the
community centre.

She stopped then, thinking about it.

*This makes a ton of noise*, she thought. *There's no way they haven't heard it, even in this distance.*

*Paul.*

The echo of a snow machine, with no other noise to filter it against the background, was unmistakable. She had borrowed it from Paul in the first place, and he had others. Louis, while he wouldn't be able to tell exactly where the noise came from, would know there was an active community of people with at least fuel and snow machines somewhere.

*Dammit*, she breathed out.

Gina gunned the machine, riding back up into the bush and away from the others.

It was cloudy enough to snow again tonight, and from the way it had been warming up, it was likely to be a heavy snowfall again. She could wait—and the snow would fill in her tracks. The falling snow would also muffle the noise of the snow machine and make it difficult to tell where it was—not to mention when dark and snowing heavily Louis and his gang were not likely to move around.

*That'd risk broken bones*, she thought. *I've learned that much from living this far north. How many times have I rescued a 'winter hiker' now?*

She snorted—someone always felt they could go hiking in winter. Even she knew better, now.

As the hours went by, and dark fell, Gina turned on the snow machine and went back down the hill. By the larger department store at that same corner, she saw the fires of a camp on Long Lake Road. *I knew they wouldn't take long to come back this way.*

As she gunned the engine back to the highway, she saw movement. They had heard the machine, but the echo and the snow made it difficult to tell where it was.

Gina sighed as she rode back to her house. The snow would be enough to hide the tracks, but people knew this subdivision existed.

Just as the path down to her road was in view, and the roof of her house, the snow machine sputtered, and then stalled.

Gina groaned, and she opened the tank to look at the indicator. *Dry*, she thought, and she shook her head.

Louis had got his revenge after all.

She was out of fuel.

# CHAPTER THIRTY-FIVE

"Jesus Christ!" exclaimed Felicia. "I was trying to tell you I was in here. You could have waited before giving me a bloody heart attack."

"Fitz," breathed Daniel in relief.

The minute she saw him, the fight went out of her and she hugged him. "You are a sight for sore eyes. I thought you were dead!"

"I thought I was too," he admitted. "I'm sorry I took so long– did they hurt you?"

She shook her head. "Haven't done a bloody thing but put me in that room."

Marcus and Daniel looked at each other.

Until now, Harnet had been completely and totally ruthless with everyone he had found unless they had a direct use to his plan. Felicia Moss could not fit into any plan by Harnet that Daniel could figure out.

"Fitz, was he familiar to you?" asked Daniel. "I can't shake the feeling he's from here."

"I didn't see him," she answered. "His thugs threw me into the room and left me here. I feel they had plans for a real party—in fact, they said so."

"You said they didn't hurt you," said Marcus.

She looked up at him. "They didn't. They waited until the Colonel, that's what they call him, came back and told him about me. He was all for it until he ransacked my wallet—and… you know… you're onto something. He knew me. The minute he recognized me he told them that if they so much as looked sideways in my direction, he'd toss them off the building."

"He *knows* you?" asked Daniel. "Do you have any idea how?"

She shook her head. "His voice is familiar, from what I could hear of it through a wall and door. But I didn't see him, so no idea who he is. I don't know a Will, or Bill, Harnet."

"We can figure out this puzzle later," said Daniel, with a heavy sigh. "Right now, I don't want to be caught here when he, or his goons, get back."

"They won't be, but you're right—we need to leave now," said Felicia, already heading for the door as the other members of his team came in.

"Harnet planted bombs under City Hall—where the creek runs under it. He headed there to set the last of them."

"He did *what?!*" exclaimed Daniel and Marcus, and, eyes wide, they looked at each other.

"Get us downstairs the quickest way possible," said Daniel.

"The stairs. We can run down them," she suggested. "Although the elevator is really quick too."

"I can get down the stairs faster than the elevator," said one of the younger ones, and he shook his head. "And if you're planning what I think you are, I wouldn't be of any use. I was just a bookkeeper before this. I can get to the Mayor and get her out of the building the quickest."

"Grab the two from the library on your way down," said Daniel. "Whatever they recovered should go with the Mayor."

"On it!" shouted the young man as he turned and took off to the stairs.

"Daniel," said Felicia, grabbing his arm. "Harnet really has something against Sudbury. He feels as if he finally has 'returned with power'. He's out to prove something to someone. That makes him dangerous."

"I had that feeling," admitted Daniel.

\* \* \* \* \*

This time Derek enjoyed the ride. While the frozen wind still stung his face like a thousand needles, his blood sang. He clutched at the reins, but held on with his knees, leaning into the wind and into each turn. Northern Tempest barely seemed to touch the ground as he soared above the dunes of snow.

Derek turned to look behind him once.

But he couldn't see that much.

True to his name, all that could be seen was the snow tossed and clouds of white left in the black horse's wake.

*If I'm right, I'm only around a half mile away,* he thought, a frown crossing his face.

Running through snow, even if loose, was taxing to any horse. Northern Tempest was no different. A half mile in a clear field during a mild day in summer would have been no problem for the horse. However, snow was like water. It pushed against the horse's legs and was colder than the freezing point.

If they kept it up, the horse would tire himself out and not be able to run, let alone trot or canter. Walking would be far slower.

"Whoa, let's slow it down a bit," said Derek as he gently tugged on the reins.

Northern Tempest didn't like that one bit, and—for a moment—fought against Derek's gentle request to slow down. But he eventually gave in to his rider's wish.

Derek patted his neck, rubbing him down a bit. "I know, I know, you want to return to your stall and the good feed… where it's warmer too, I bet."

The horse snorted.

"I get it," admitted Derek as he allowed the horse to at least trot. "I want to get back as soon as possible too, but if we exhaust ourselves, we'll get halfway and not be able to move further without resting. However, if we pace ourselves, we can be home sooner."

The horse's ears twitched at this.

The ride down the road was still a swift one, but now it was a controlled and easy cross between a trot and a canter. Not too jarring on his spine and not the headlong rush of before when they had had to create as much distance between them and Cecelie's people. Derek grinned.

*I bet she didn't see a horse outsmarting her like we did*, he thought. *Or leaving her and her people behind as swiftly as we did*.

An hour later, and just as the sun was sinking over the ragged mountains, the gate came into view. With a short set of whistles in a pattern, Derek rode through the opening made for him and down into the valley. The horse snorted, almost a sigh of relief, as they finally rode through the last gate and into the driveway.

Sheridan stood on the front step, Terrence just behind her. Derek frowned a bit at this as Terrence was propping himself up using the wall. From the set of his jaw, he was stubbornly refusing to be anywhere else but by Sheridan's side.

"Why do I only see one of you, and on the back of the horse I sent with Shiloh?" asked Sheridan, her eyebrow lifting.

"Shiloh sent me ahead on the one horse that could get me here fast enough to warn you," answered Derek as he dismounted, giving her a brief salute.

It was Terrence's turn to lift an eyebrow, and Sheridan rolled her eyes.

"Warn us of what?" asked Terrence, bringing their attention back to why Derek stood in front of them.

"We've got trouble inbound from the North," answered Derek. "It's probably not that far behind me either. We ran into a group of raiders up by the power line place, and I know they were with Cecelie because I ran into her not an hour's easy trot ride past the gate."

"Cecelie?" asked Sheridan, as she looked up at Terrence. "Cecelie LaMontagne? Your ex from high school? She's here?"

Terrence sighed heavily and nodded. "Yeah, about a week before all this happened, she showed up on our doorstep. Shiloh and I wasted no time sending her packing. She was under the impression that with a toss of her hair, I'd fall back under her spell. Unfortunately for her, I don't have a roving eye and didn't want any part of what she offered."

"What did she want?" asked Derek. As if I have to ask.

Terrence shrugged. "She said that for 'support', her and some fellows named Harnet and Kovach would reward us after things hit the fan. I thought she was joking, but now…"

Derek rubbed his chin. Neither name meant much to him. *I was right though*, he thought. *Someone else was pulling her strings…*

The echo of a gunshot to the North made them all freeze. Sheridan looked up at Terrence. "I think reality has just caught up with us."

Terrence nodded, and he looked at Derek. "Come on, if you're so determined to keep throwing yourself into the middle of danger it's time to give you something that could keep you alive long enough to get back out of it."

# CHAPTER THIRTY-SIX

Daniel skipped steps on his way down the stairs. His knees wouldn't thank him tomorrow. He didn't remember the lobby. Only the force it took to push doors open to reach the street. Once there, he fired exactly two flares into the sky.

This was the signal for an emergency recall from the mall—whether the job was done or not—and back to Tom Davies Square.

Felicia, now armed and, while the body armour didn't fit her perfectly, she had made it work. Her breath fogged in the air. "How do we get under City Hall?" she asked.

M. Cannon

"There's an access tunnel on Larch," answered Daniel. "A few other points downtown—one under the rail underpass on Brady and Douglas as well, where the creek comes out."

Daniel sucked in a breath.

Directly above that access was the newspaper they had found that cache. *And we celebrated once we found it, but we didn't even think to check the basement for anything else but supplies, did we?* Daniel realized, swearing to himself as he did.

Again, Harnet was one step ahead of them.

He shook his head and then ran, as fast as one could through knee deep snow, back to Tom Davies Square. Skis or snowshoes would have helped here. Even if the latter was slightly slower it was still faster than slogging through the snow and risking broken bones on the unseen ice beneath.

It felt like hours, even if it was far less, when they reached the Tom Davies Square access on Larch. One of the other teams saw them and met them there. "We have a major problem and we need all hands on deck," said Marcus while Daniel caught his breath. "Harnet has laid one last trap—he's laced the supports under City Hall with explosives using the access tunnels for Junction Creek."

"We're going to need two teams," said Daniel. "I have a feeling, if he's still one step ahead of us, that he's fully expecting our survivors to run out in a panic once the explosions start. If he holds to pattern, he probably is expecting to ambush them on the way out. He has no intention of just taking over. Anyone to remember the old Sudbury is as good as dead in his eyes. He won't take prisoners. I need one team to make sure those survivors make it out."

"And the other?" asked Marcus.

"We're going to do what we can to stop him," said Daniel.

He looked at Felicia, and then the others. "Fitz, I'm leaving the Mayor in your personal care. If she dies, the last duly elected leader of our city is gone. I sent someone else back here with whatever they could carry from the library. Both have to survive," Daniel ordered, and then he pointed at Marcus. "You and your team comb the area. Clear the area for the survivors to get to safety."

"You got it," said Marcus, and he reached out to shake Daniel's hand.

Daniel shook his head. "No, we see each other at the safe point."

Marcus turned the handshake into a salute. "You damn well better be there."

"I have a daughter I want to see," said Daniel, grinning, but it didn't quite reach his eyes. "And I don't think this bastard has any intention of stopping with downtown. If we fail here, he'll be out there before long. I will not let that happen."

"None of us will that happen," said Marcus. "Go kick his ass, Captain."

Daniel lifted a brow, but nodded. For Marcus to call him that meant that he was now. Field promotions were funny that way. Daniel had never been close to attaining the rank of captain on the force, but circumstances had forced his hand.

The others now thought of him that way. The Mayor looked to him that way.

It meant, no matter what he had been before, he now was Captain.

Daniel took a breath as he watched the others leave. Felicia remained, though, despite his order to head back. He looked at her. "I thought I gave you a job to do," he said.

She nodded. "I'm taking one last look."

"I swear to you—" he started.

"Don't you dare make promises you can't keep, and you know you can't," she inclined her head to the tunnels. "You are going in there with four people where you don't know how many he has. In a confined space. The odds aren't great."

"If I don't slow him down," said Daniel. "You won't have time to escape."

She sighed. "See, I knew you knew you weren't coming back out of there."

"What other option do we have, Fitz?"

She shook her head. "Not one. But you didn't even give me the choice like you did the others. Why? You know my history."

"Because your Dad would kick my ass," he answered, and he motioned to the tower. "And I need to know that someone I know and trust to do the job is still out there. Not that Marcus, or anyone else, can't but you are the only one with real, actual training in a situation anything like this. They need you."

Felicia looked at him and then hugged him. "Do what you can," she finally said as she let go of him. "And do what you can to come back out of it, too."

He laughed softly, "That I can promise. Now get out here."

He watched as she retreated up the steps and through the courtyard to City Hall. He looked at the others. "You've got the same choice. You can come in with me, and probably not come back out, but we could stop him. We probably won't, but if we can slow him down, then we've bought our people time to get out. Us four can make sure hundreds live."

Only one person headed back to City Hall, leaving Daniel with three people. He nodded to the rest of them. "If any of you have a family, go be with them."

One of his team shook her head. "Nope—not if my family can make it out. I wouldn't be able to look my mom in the eye."

Daniel inspected her. There was no way she was older than fifteen, and the way she held the rifle in her hands betrayed her inexperience. Before today, there was no way she had ever held an automatic weapon, perhaps not even a hunting rifle. Few kids in this day and age—in a city—had any reason to... or *should*, unless for hunting. A young woman raised in a city probably had no reason to go hunting.

But yet she had followed Daniel to the mall and even fought.

What right did he have to refuse her choice?

And how could he ask her to make that choice?

The real problem was he did not have the luxury of considering either.

So he nodded, and instead said, "All right. Let's go."

\* \* \* \* \*

Gina blew out what probably was the hundredth sigh inside an hour. *No amount of glaring at the fuel tank is going to fill it*, she thought. *At least I can see the damn house from here*.

*What was that saying about 'So close, yet so far away?'*

She let out a bark of laughter and then sighed again.

She climbed off the machine, shaking her head. The helmet was the next thing to come off. It would only block her peripheral vision and it was heavy. It was far better to just use a toque and a scarf. She would be just as warm but better able to see and move.

Slogging through the snow was a slow, labourious walk.

A single inch made things slippery, but over six inches was like wading through the same depth of water, but worse—and that was before the cold was considered.

Snow was simply loosely packed ice.

While it wasn't hard or solid, it was freezing cold and this cold seeped in.

Every step she took sank to past her calf, sometimes to her thighs, which meant the snow was at least a few feet deep. Some of it crunched, which meant it had warmed up enough to melt slightly and then froze again to form a crust.

*Nothing to be done about that*, she thought. *Snowshoes would have made this infinitely easier, though.*

It took hours.

Dawn had broken over the horizon behind her by the time she reached the incline down to the Hannah Lake subdivision and where they had cleared paths.

She heard her first shout of greeting from the others as she came down this hill from the highway to the road below. She sighed in relief as she stepped onto the cleared pavement and continued walking toward her house.

"Gina!" called Paul as he ran up to her, and then he stopped. "Why are you walking? Where's the sled?"

"Ran out of gas back up the road," she answered, pointing to the east. "Look, meet me at my house as soon as you can and bring the others."

He nodded and motioned to one other to do so. Instead of leaving, he grasped her arm and guided her up to her house. She looked at him. "You look like you're going to fall over," he said, helping her into the house.

The sudden warmth was enough to make her head swim, and she felt him pick her up and carry her to the couch in front of the fire. "Vince, get some of that hot tea and some soup. She looks ready to fall over."

"I think she already did," pointed out Russell as he sat down by her.

She looked up at him, seeing both worry for her and the anxiety of someone who had been waiting for news. "I've got good news and bad," she answered, holding up a finger. "First, your Uncle is just fine—had a bit of trouble, but he's fine and so is your aunt. They didn't take you up on your offer, though, as is obvious."

He breathed out a sigh of relief, but still was watching her intently.

"I'm fine as well, just tired and cold," she answered. "Nothing tea, soup, and a good night's sleep won't fix."

"I hear another 'but' in there," said Vince as he set down a tray with the tea and the soup, and some crackers. "It's a fish soup and the last of our crackers."

"It's better than what I've had out there," she said as she dug into it.

After a few moments, and once the others from both sides of the lake had gathered in the living room, she settled back into the couch.

"You said you had bad news," said Paul.

"Yeah, I do," she answered, and she looked at everyone. "This looks like it will be permanent. That's not even the worst part."

Russell closed his eyes and shook his head. "Dare I ask what the worst part of this even is?"

"Roving gangs of looters, bandits, and raiders out to murder people in their homes." said Gina, and she saw the shock on many faces. "Yeah, that's the worst part—and that's why I got back here, on foot, during the night through another blizzard. I used both to cover my tracks and the sound of the snow machine. However, I don't know how long that will keep them off our trail. They're at the Walmart, which means any noise we've been making here they can hear. I don't think they've quite figured out where exactly there is still life, but it will be a matter of time before they do."

"What are you suggesting?" asked Paul.

"Do we stay and fight or what?" asked someone else.

Gina took a breath and shook her head. "No, we don't have the resources to do that. Kirk— Russell's uncle—gave me another solution and an invitation. We head to Long Lake and the community there. There are farms, better lakes for fishing, and it's all far enough away from the insanity overtaking the city. I agree with him, but I wouldn't decide for us without talking it over with you first."

Gina blew out a sigh. *I knew it would be a hard sell.*

"But these are our homes!" said someone. "We just can't leave them."

"If we don't, we're dead, didn't you hear her?"

"So she says…"

"Well, I, for one believe what she says," said a woman in the back.

Gina put two fingers in her mouth and whistled to bring them back into order. "I get what you're saying—I really do. I'm stuck here. My home is in Australia. If this is permanent, it will be a very, very long time before I can see it again. If ever. Now I'm asking you to do the same…"

Paul scratched the back of his neck. "To be honest, what she says feels true. Our scouts have been noticing some weird things going on past the road."

"Not to mention that explosion from the Four Corners…" said another, and Gina winced.

She remained silent, but she saw Vince lift a brow as he noticed her wince.

Paul looked over at her and the others. "I vote we take Kirk up on his offer. Our food is already short and getting shorter. We fished this lake out."

Vince stood up. "I don't like leaving my house as much as the next person, but I believe Gina. I'm with her on this, too."

Gina watched as the others went from dead set against the idea to looking at each other in resignation. One other said, "Do we have enough time to grab essentials and important memories?"

"We'll have to be careful to not leave tracks they can follow," said Gina. "But if you can carry it, bring it. I don't know if we'll be able to come back."

The crowd dispersed and Gina blew out a breath once it was only her, Vince, Russell, and Paul. "Well, that went better than expected," she said.

Paul shook his head. "I think we were already expecting this day to come. We haven't been able to catch a damn thing in the entire time you were gone and the last of our supplies will run out in a few days. A scout went to check out the Walmart, and well, what they described supports what you've told us. It surprised us to even see you come back alive. The going opinion was that you left and died out there."

"Yeah, expect a lot of people to think of you as damn near invincible from this point on," said Vince, raising his brows. "I tried to point out that you're a firefighter and face dangerous situations every day, but I think this went above and beyond it."

Gina laid back on the couch. "You have no idea."

"Well, we won't be able to do anything until the morning and she looks ready to drop," said Paul as he headed to the door. "Get that woman to bed and we'll discuss everything tomorrow."

"It's not even noon yet!" Gina lifted her brows.

"And you admitted to being up all night," said Vince as he guided her to her bedroom. "Off with you."

"All right, all right," she groused. "I know when I've been outvoted."

# CHAPTER THIRTY-SEVEN

When the steel access door opened, Daniel's first thought was how much it reminded him of heading into a mine. Back when he was still a welder and a mechanic, they sent him into holes like this to fix and repair machinery that had broken down with little more than a light on his helmet.

As hostile and dangerous as an unlit shaft could be, he would have taken that to what he was about to do now.

He nodded at the others, moved his rifle to the ready, and headed in.

Once inside, one of his team lit a flare and threw it across the stream.

The wan light illuminated very little, but Daniel saw further down the glimmer of light that wasn't the red of the flare.

The glow was almost cheerful, if distant.

The challenge here would not only taking ginger steps for silence, but they would have to test each step.

The underwater creek bed, once above ground but since built and contained to the concrete and cement under city, had never been designed for humans to walk in. No one had thought that anyone would need to move beneath, or would need the ability to even have access. It was not until it swept away a young boy from upstream where the creek was still above ground into the culvert. He drowned because no one could rescue him because of this lack of access. To prevent another tragedy, they had built accesses and the ability to walk beside the creek underground.

He didn't like having to walk in single file. They were too easy to pin down this way and had nowhere to go if they needed cover.

Laughter from where they had come from sounded. They froze, but he motioned for them to keep going but put two fingers on his lips.

The two groups of Harnet's called out to each other—no sign of knowing that in between them was Daniel.

Daniel felt his skin crawl, but he knew that the second group they were coming up on wouldn't expect them at all.

He double-checked the rifle, changing to burst fire. Tapping the next person, he heard the near silent switch as they all changed their guns—if they had the option—to burst fire.

He took a breath and then stepped into the light—his gun already at the ready.

"About time…" the mercenary trailed off, and Daniel shot him.

Flattening himself against the wall, he fired on the next.

The third shouted, "Intruders in the tunnel!"

The clatter of boots on cement from upstream, and he heard the first retort of a single fire rifle as his own people started firing.

Daniel moved ahead to give them more space, pulling the devices as he found them and throwing them into the water. "Toss them into the water!" he yelled.

More splashes sounded, and he knew just by the count that the mercenaries had thrown his people into the creek.

"I thought I heard burst fire further down, though."

Daniel pushed himself off the wall and kept moving, pulling off the devices and throwing them into the water. *To hell with it*, he thought. *They know I'm down here, anyway. May as well wreck their day as much as possible…*

He could hear voices around one final, sloping corner. He ran faster, his rifle up. While he knew that two voices would not mean that there would only be two people, with a gun on burst fire it wouldn't matter.

He was not about to let Harnet have time to react before he filled him full of holes.

He came around the corner and fired into the first mercenary before he got to his feet. The next burst of three went into the next.

He turned his rifle to the third, noting that unlike the others he wore no patches and no uniform.

Daniel's finger was on the trigger, but the man disappeared around the corner before he could pull the trigger.

"You're pretty quick," slipped out of his mouth in shock.

The other man, Harnet, if he had to guess, laughed at him in equal surprise. "Daniel Wither," he breathed. "Of all the people in all of Sudbury, why did it have to be you?"

Daniel couldn't place the voice, but he had to dodge to the side when answering fire greeted him. Now, this close, despite all the echoes, Daniel felt like icy fingers sat on his neck as the small hairs stood on end. "Why do I know your voice?" asked Daniel.

"Think on it. Use that brain of yours," said Harnet.

"But you know who I am," said Daniel. "We've met."

"I'll let you figure out that puzzle, but I have other places to be."

Footstep retreated into the distance, but there were others coming to meet him. "Well, look who it is," said the first mercenary, and Daniel's eyes thinned.

It was the same two from the garage that had chased him to the police yard.

"You," said Daniel, as another man came into view.

None other than Victoria's assistant, Nicholas.

\* \* \* \* \*

"Goddammit," muttered Garrett in frustration as the radio fizzled out again.

At this rate, it was not likely that he would ever get it running. He was not accustomed to failure, and the radio was just not cooperating with any of his efforts to get it working. Dane, when he got there, noticed him glaring at the wisp of smoke that rose from the radio again.

"Not having any luck?" he asked.

"Nope," Garrett answered as he leaned forward to poke at the radio. "I get the feeling this thing is beyond help. And no one has found a CB radio in any of the trucks?"

"No CB's, no FRS', not a thing," Dane answered, shaking his head. "It's strange because it's clear they had them at one point… and I think recently… you don't think…"

Garrett did think the missing radios were related to everything.

*Nice try on shifting blame*, thought Garrett. *Hell, at this point you may not have even seen to it.*

"Could be," answered Garrett, and he tilted his head as he looked at Dane.

*Should I lay the cards on the table now?* Garrett wondered. *Let Dane know that he's not alone—and he doesn't have to dance to whatever tune Kovach is playing?*

Dane shifted from one foot to the other under the weight of Garrett's absentminded stare, and Garrett sighed.

"I have to wonder…" began Garrett.

Dane lifted his brows. "Oh?"

"Had a spot of trouble in December," said Garrett, rubbing the knot of scar tissue on his leg— the present Kovach had left him with. "The primary reason it took me so long to get up here."

Dane stilled. He could have been a statue for how still he turned, his eyes wide. *So, you definitely heard about that, did you?* Garrett thought. *Time you heard my side of it…*

"Listen, Garrett, you've been a massive help, really… but the guys and I thought that since you've turned things around maybe you could go back to Worthington?" said Dane, although the words were so jammed together Garrett had trouble keeping up. "It's been clear you'd rather be there, anyway. There's no actual need to be up here, is there?"

"Dane, stop." Garrett held up a hand. "We both know why you're eager to get me out of here as fast as you can, and if I had to guess, that reason goes by the name 'Kovach'."

Dane deflated, and he sank into the nearest chair, his face as pale as the snow outside. "You know."

"Dane, High Falls is in between Nairn and Worthington," pointed out Garrett. "He had to go through *here* to get to *there*. I'm not blind. The question is… what did he say he'd do if you didn't cooperate with him?"

Dane stared at Garrett, and he blew out a breath. "The dam, and us, would be forfeit. But, for some reason, he felt we were more useful right here. He took a few, but no one critical."

"I can't imagine that's everything, but sounds like him," said Garrett, as he looked out the window with another sigh.

Dane shifted in his seat—stilling when Garrett turned back to him.

*I saw that*, thought Garrett. *What aren't you telling me?*

"Anyone buy into what he was selling?" asked Garrett, and this time Dane stared at him.

"What… wait… you don't mean joined him willingly?" asked Dane, his voice rising an octave.

"Exactly what I mean," answered Garrett, pointing at the broken radio. "Where do you think those radios went, Dane, into thin air?"

Dane shook his head. "Well, no, but I didn't think… I don't know. I could keep an eye out but, seriously, think about what I said. Just go. Kovach won't hesitate a second to kill you if he catches you. And if you're right—if there are others here who fell in with the arsehole—your life is in danger. You're safer in Worthington."

"I'll take that under advisement," said Garrett, and he waved him off. "Of course, if I'm not here, you're in charge again."

Dane snorted. "And we saw how well that went."

"Don't sell yourself short," said Garrett, and he tapped his fingers on the desk. "How many would follow us?"

"Uh, well, we all do now," said Dane.

"I mean against Kovach."

"Against… wait a minute, you don't mean to do here what you did in Worthington?" asked Dane. "There's no way."

"There are more of us and we have a very fortress like advantage, unlike Worthington," said Garrett. "Also, we're in better shape to fight them off than Worthington was when I got there and yet, somehow, we managed to. If it could be done there, we can do the same far easier here."

Dane leaned back in his chair, staring at the ceiling. "There isn't exactly a shortage of tools we could repurpose into weapons, if we had to. We're in better physical shape, more used to heavy labour—but we're tough. Yeah, I see your point."

"But there's still the question of who fell in with Kovach," pointed out Garrett, tapping his lip as he watched Dane.

Dane sat forward. "They're good people. Hardworking. They wouldn't have joined them unless Kovach scared them into it. With a bit of hope and a leader willing to show them there's another way—like you did with the ice fishing—they'd probably find that courage to stand up to him. No one likes a bully, Garrett."

"Thought you wanted me to go back to Worthington?" asked Garrett, a small grin on his face.

Dane shrugged. "I followed him because I was scared of what he'd do if I didn't. I'm hoping, if anyone else did, that's why."

"If they didn't?"

Dane looked straight at Garrett. "There's more of us than there are of them."

# CHAPTER THIRTY-EIGHT

Derek rode out to the bottom of the hill on the road leading up to the gate. Someone slid a heavy set of planks into the gate to seal it. It was not the most solid solution, but it was certainly better than nothing. They handed guns and bows out, but it looked as if they were in short supply of weapons to fight off the raiding marauders outside the gate.

"We're not ready for this," said Derek, his voice low.

Terrence blew out a breath. "What choice do we have?"

Those without guns armed themselves with whatever they could find, whether sharpened sticks fashioned into rough spears or, even, shovels to bash a person with.

There was no one on top of the gate, and when Derek rode up, the watchman said, "They have guns and they certainly aren't afraid to use them."

Terrence grabbed Derek's arm and said, "Listen!"

Just over the howl of wind was a sound of a motor running in the distance… the sound of very heavy-duty engine noise. Derek looked over to the person on watch. "What is that?"

"A truck… SUV—I don't know where they found it," he admitted, looking worried.

Derek looked worriedly at the gate and then at the ground. "That gate won't hold if they ram it," said Derek quietly.

"I know," answered Terrence, and he and Derek climbed up and just out of their view on the gate. "Hopefully Tyrell made it tough enough to hold out as long as we need it to."

Derek was not all that sure what exactly the large Ford SUV was. Unlike his god-daughters' family, he was not that much of a gear head to be able to positively identify it. It was possibly the same chassis and engine used in the larger ambulances. It certainly held the right passenger compartment reminiscent of an ambulance, only it was far heavier duty and higher off the ground. The driver, echoed by the others with him, let loose a long line of rude suggestions and expletives that would have left some people with blistering ears.

Anyone other than Terrence, who simply rolled his eyes and turned to Derek, "I've seen some interesting things on the Internet but that last even suggestion I think it a bit… awkward."

Derek took aim and with one arrow. He shot it and the front driver's side tire blew out. The sound of it blowing out exploded across the valley. With the full-size SUV immobilized, it evened their odds.

"Sir, I believe the proper term would be 'You first'!" shouted back Derek. "One last chance!"

There was silence, and then a wave of raiders came out. They grabbed ladders and slammed them against the snow walls.

"Archers! Fire!"

A hail of arrows rained their death on the hapless raiders, and another tire blew itself out.

For a long moment, everything was quiet till twenty more raiders ran out of the woods and to the wall.

"Fire at will!" shouted Derek. "Knock down those ladders. Shoot anyone that comes over that wall!"

The general of the raiders came out, and he wore a mish-mash of chain and heavy modern combat armour that didn't fit well but covered him completely. He held a riot shield in one hand and a combat shotgun in the other.

"Son of a bitch…" breathed Derek as he took aim and fired.

His arrow bounced off and only scratched the paint. He swore colourfully and pointed out, "Terry, we have a problem…"

Terrence looked over, swore and drew his sword. Derek had only seen the blade once, and that was on display. Even though it shook in Terrence's hands, it still looked far more menacing and maybe even longer and wider than it had above the fireplace mantle. They clearly meant the hilt for two hands, but Terrence could wield it either one-handed or two-handed.

The leader climbed one ladder, using his shield to prevent shots to dislodge him from the ladder. His weight made it difficult to push the ladder back. He pulled himself over the wall and stood on the ledge behind. With a roar, he bull-rushed Terrence, coming at him down the stairs to the ground. Terrence swung his sword with both hands, but the leader's shield was in the way.

The raider swung and took Terrence in the side hard enough for the older man to turn ashen at the strike before falling from the horse.

He landed in a heap and the crash of metal hitting the frozen ground rang out loudly across the valley.

A shot rang out, and Derek followed where it came from to see Shiloh at the top of the hill. Unfortunately, the shell from her rifle did not penetrate the first layer. Derek also kept up the pressure by firing off arrow after rapidly fired arrow until the leader of the raiders looked like some sort of psychotic porcupine.

Now the battle was fully engaged as more and more raiders poured over the wall, although only twenty-five percent survived. The archers shot the rest down by the trees.

A downward swing towards Derek's head was avoided by him rolling backward. The raider then used his shield as a pummelling device to force him back.

"Get that gate open!" shouted the raider leader. "Rush them!"

*We've got to end this before we're overrun*, realized Derek.

Derek found himself suddenly out of arrows, but he then spotted something. With a whistle, Northern Tempest came for him. He speed-mounted as he galloped towards him. A short ride later, he had a spear in his hand. The horse turned on a dime at his order and he brought the improvised lance down like a knight at a joust.

Terrence, at the very last second, jumped back and out of the way.

The raider was not as lucky as the spear—propelled by the force of the charger—went through his body armour and chain like it was nothing.

Derek could not stop the horse immediately. Thankfully, he didn't have to as he caught another spear thrown to him by one of their own men so he could catch it as he rode by and turned again.

With leader down, the other raiders turned tail and ran. Arrows cut most down, but others slunk back into the wooded areas to lick their wounds.

Derek slowed his horse down to a trot, then a walk, and finally to a stop as he pulled up beside Shiloh.

"You there!" ordered Derek "Form up a hunting party! We'll have to clear the bastards out before we can say it's safe beyond the wall."

He dismounted and ran over to Terrence, kneeling on the ground as he did.

Terrence looked up at him with thinly veiled amusement. "Thought... you couldn't ride... a horse."

"I learnt quick," quipped back Derek. "Don't talk."

"Ribs are broken," gasped Terrence. "And I'm never going to walk again, can't feel one of my arms. I didn't think I'd be the fifth..."

Terrence groaned, and then the tension left him. "Jesus," breathed Shiloh. "No."

Derek leaned back and shook his head as he looked up at the grey sky.

"He's gone."

\* \* \* \* \*

The house was never cold in the day, but at night Gina had always needed to wrap herself in a shawl to stay warm. Humming from the kitchen brought her around the corner, and she stopped in surprise.

"Nana?" she asked. "But how did you get here from Australia?"

"I'm always in dreamland, you know that," pointed out her grandmother with a wink. "As long as we walk the same earth. Frozen or desert. Makes no difference. It's all country," she added and smiled.

She blinked, and then when she opened them again, she was shaken from her sound sleep. Vincent moved back, his hand moving from her shoulder to his side again. "Sorry to wake you, but Paul said you should probably see this."

Gina stretched, pulling on her clothes and wrapping herself in a shawl.

She shuffled out of the bedroom, clearing her eyes of the hardened bits that always seemed to build up. *Get some rest, Gina. You look exhausted. Now wake up, Gina, you need to see this…*

She tilted her head one way and back again to stretch her neck and then looked out the window where Paul pointed. "Sorry to wake you, especially when I told you to go to bed, but we didn't see that until it got dark."

Lights on the shore across the lake.

Lights that hadn't been there before.

*Louis.*

*Dammit*, thought Gina. *Was that because of me or just a matter of time before they figured it out?*

440

"Any sign of motion heading this way?" she asked.

Paul shook his head. "No, and yes we have been watching for it."

She nodded. "Good," she sighed as she looked at Vincent. "Sorry to tell you this, but I have a feeling we're going to need to make a run for it far sooner than I expected."

"We'll leave tracks," said Paul.

"Take a can of gas, if you've got any left. The snow machine I had to ditch isn't far from here and is on your way. Get it moving. Let me have one other with a full tank and I'll keep them busy. They're looking for me anyway," she said. "Get moving now. We have the advantage of headlights. They don't."

"What are you going to do?" asked Vincent.

"I wanted to head to Lively anyway," she said. "I'll lead them off that way and you head to Long Lake. If I can make it back to you, I will. But go... get Russell to his Uncle and reunite that family."

Russell grasped her arms. "If you're headed to Lively, there's something I want you to do."

She stopped and looked at him. "What's that?"

"I have family there too, it's where I came from. Kirk's wife is my mother's sister—that's how we're related. My mother lives out in Whitefish."

She stared at him. "Why did you tell me that before?"

"Because I know she's fine. She has my nieces and other family on a massive ranch out that way. If anyone survived, they did."

"Wait a minute, I think I know what one you're talking about," said Paul. "That's your mother?"

"Lorraine Wither, yes," answered Russell and he looked at them all. "I would have figured that you would have known that by my last name."

"Well, I had wondered if there was a relation, yes, but it's not like it's an uncommon name."

Gina shook her head. "If I can, I'll find her and let them know you're fine."

Russell nodded. "Thank you—but I think it will do her heart good to know that not only am I fine, but so is her sister, eh?"

Gina snorted. "Right. I'm beginning to see why you risked the trip in the first place. To be fair, your aunt is a dragon and is as tough as nails. I wouldn't have worried about her one iota."

She watched from the garage as the survivors packed up. Instead of leaving from their side of the lake—which meant going back through town to get even four by four trucks out—they went to Paul's side where the road went to the highway instead. The slow caravan of trucks and snow machines then came around the corner from the direction she needed to go and moved to where she had been.

Once they had disappeared around that corner heading to Long Lake Road, Gina took a breath. *It's a good thing I slept all day*, she thought. *Because I won't be sleeping tonight*.

# CHAPTER THIRTY-NINE

Garrett stared at the radio. Dane had tried to help him but it didn't seem to matter what he brought Garrett he couldn't get the radio to work. He lifted one small resistor, staring at the little coloured lines on it. Please work, he prayed as he lifted the soldering iron.

A small touch on one end, and another on the other, and the resistor sat where another had been.

He tossed the blackened one away.

*Come on*, he asked again. *Just give me this one thing...*

He flipped the power switch on and the crackle of the radio powering up filled the air. Garrett let out a whoop before he sat back down and slid the dial one way and then the other.

Nothing.

Only static.

He eyed the circuit board. But everything was working as it should.

*There's just nothing broadcasting,* he thought. *No one's out there with another one. Dammit.*

He turned it off and pushed it aside, rubbing his eyes as he did. Dane came in and stared at Garrett and then the radio. "Any luck?"

Garrett looked at Dane and sighed. "No."

"Damn."

Garrett shrugged. "I needed the break, anyway."

Garrett pulled on his coat and walked out of the office and out of the control house entirely. After thinking for a moment, he took a breath and walked up to the other control house and then past it to the shoreline of the headwater behind the main dam.

Agnew Lake was still frozen—but they were still in the middle of February. He wasn't really that surprised.

He sighed, and then walked onto the dam itself, leaning against the rail while he watched the rush of the falls below him as the water came through the sluices of the dam.

"After months of waiting, you finally did something stupid, old man," came the voice behind Garrett.

Garrett closed his eyes and sighed as he turned and stood to face the three men who joined him over the spillway. Two he recognized from the dam.

The other was Eric Kovach.

"I was wondering when you'd finally get around to it," said Garrett, as he looked at Kovach. "So, when did they tell you I was here?"

Garrett looked the other way and noticed that on the other side of the dam were another three on the other side, this time it was the other two plus another. This other surprised him—it was Dane, the young man from the offices that had always been so helpful.

*Dammit, Dane,* thought Garrett, pushing aside the sudden spike of disappointment. *Can't say he didn't warn me either.* "Well, I'd be surprised, but now that I think of it, I'm not," said Garrett.

"Sorry, old man, but Dane knows better than to cross me, and you said you didn't really want leadership," Kovach answered. "Kill him."

Bracing himself and lifting his hands in defence, Garrett was ready for the first one. He knew Kovach would be impatient. Old man, indeed. He may have more years on him, but he was far from old—and if they had tried that with his father the results would have been more than amusing.

Garrett was his father's son.

It did not take long for the first one to come in swinging the rebar, and Garrett sidestepped him. Grabbing him by the scruff of his neck, Garrett yanked hard, pulling him off balance and into falling back.

He sidestepped again, grabbing the rebar from his hands as he pinwheeled and gave the man a further push off the dam and to the shorter drop off the deeper end.

The problem for the man now off the dam was that the sluice ways and spillways were in the full open. It sucked him through them in less than a second with no time to take a breath or to scream.

Garrett tapped his bar against the ledge while the others hesitated. "There's one… I told you that if I ever saw you again, and it wasn't for honest trade, you wouldn't be walking away."

"He's one man against five of us… rush him!" yelled Kovach.

Taking a moment to point, Garrett shouted at Dane, "And you're fired!"

With a roar of rage, Garrett swung the metal bar with both hands, catching the first man in the side of his head. Blood sprayed in an arc and bits of grey splattered as he fell in a heap at Garrett's feet, making the others hop awkwardly to avoid him.

In a single-handed back swing, Garrett caught another attacker in the face, breaking his nose and knocking him off the shallow part that gave High

Falls its name. He screamed all the way down until he landed on the rocks below.

With his off-hand he grabbed a handful of the Kovach's left jacket front and tossed him off his feet and over his friend on the walkway where he landed on his rear. Kovach scrambled back in a blind panic, realizing that he was slipping in his friend's blood and bits of brains.

The remaining two struggled to hold Garrett and lift him up and over the edge of the dam. Finally able to regain his feet, Kovach got up as he wheezed. "Throw him over."

For a moment, all Garrett felt was that sick feeling of weightlessness.

In that moment, he saw Dane mouth the words, *I'm sorry.*

Reality rushed back. Seconds later, the icy, rushing water below the dam swallowed Garrett. The water was dark over his head and he struggled to hold his breath as he crashed into one rock, and then another. Sharp rocks sliced into his hands as he frantically grasped at them.

Finally, he broke through the thin ice to gasp out and then suck in a fresh breath of air, pulling himself onto the frozen rocks. His chest heaved as he looked upriver, and he rolled over and pushed himself to his feet. With nary a glance more, he disappeared into the woods.

\* \* \* \* \*

"Sir, what's your status?" called the mercenaries behind Daniel.

Daniel took a breath. They still sounded like they were around the corner by a bit, and the echoes of their boots still sounded a few minutes away. He could end this — right here and right now. All he had to do was pull the trigger.

"I'm fine," answered Nicholas, and he inclined his head as he looked at Daniel. His voice was lower. "Or have you decided that you will kill me after all? You've gunned down the rest of my men."

"So, you are Harnet's man," said Daniel. "Why?"

Nicholas drew back a bit, his eyes widening a bit before he laughed. "Who me?" he asked, the octave rising, and he laughed again. "No, but you of all people should know why. I mean, why not? What has this place ever done for me?"

"You grew up here," pointed out Daniel, as he motioned with the gun for Nicholas to move away from the wall and the last device he could see. "Your family is here, for God's sake. What would she think of this?"

He shrugged. "Why should I even care? I mean, it could barely bother her to pay better than minimum wage. Anyway, it doesn't matter now."

"I get that, but she thought highly of you. Why help Harnet?"

"Really?" asked Nicholas, drawing it out. "I could barely make rent. I had to deal with using the 'loser cruiser' while people like her and you drive cushy cars and can actually afford to get them fixed. This was justice."

"—It's murder and you know it," said Daniel. "You don't take what isn't yours. There are families up there. That's not exactly a fair target."

"Compared to what? Letting her citizens starve while she got to worry about her damn shoes?" he asked, and then he waved it off. "We could argue this all day and still come out on opposite sides. I'm giving you a choice—the same one I gave your oh so beloved Mayor that she turned down flat. Give up the farce of holding onto all of this and rule it as it was meant to be."

"Rule it how? Like a bloodthirsty tyrant who kills innocent civilians to make a point? Burns down history out of spite? I'll pass," answered Daniel.

The foot steps behind him were getting closer.

"Then you're as much a fool as Victoria is," said Nicholas, and Daniel's eyes widened. "Oh, you didn't know? She didn't tell you it was me? That I betrayed her?"

A sharp bark of laughter from Nicholas echoed in the tunnel.

"You're lying," growled Daniel, taking a step forward.

"If you believe that, you're an even bigger fool than I thought," said Nicholas, his voice low.

He sighed and took a remote out of his pocket. "Enough of this," he waved the device in between them. "Harnet said you give you one last chance to pick the winning side, Dan."

Daniel roared, closing the distance between them in one step. The rifle butt hit Nicholas square in the chest. With a sharp gasp, he hit the wall. He held on tightly to the remote.

His eye squarely on the remote, Daniel followed this up with an uppercut using his elbow to the younger man's chin.

But he wasn't there.

The younger man had dropped to the ground, and he kicked at Daniel's ankles. Daniel fell hard, his breath leaving his lungs in a single whoosh. He rolled over, reaching for the rifle, but Nicholas kicked it into the creek. Daniel stared for a moment and then looked up at him.

Nicholas smirked, wiping the blood from his lip. "Not so tough now are you."

"Never was one for rifles, anyway, Nick," said Daniel, pulling his sidearm out of its holster in one fluid motion.

Nicholas stared at him, but Daniel looked past him as two other mercenaries came around the corner. Nicholas snarled, lifting the remote.

Daniel fired once before rolling to the side and behind one support, barely registering Nicholas' wide-eyed stare of shock. He heard a moan, and then a large splash.

With a grin, he realized the remote, and Nicholas, were no more.

"The remote was hardly necessary," came Harnet's voice from further up the tunnel. "I'd say you have many two minutes left, Mr. Wither, before this all comes down on top of you."

Daniel froze, ducking his head around the corner.

The two mercenaries were running in the opposite direction.

Daniel pushed himself to his feet and turned down the other way.

There was still a chance, albeit a small one, that if he ran for it, he could make it to where Junction Creek came out.

Daniel went to run, but his knees almost gave out under him.

*Dammit, no, not now!* Daniel screamed inwardly. *Get your feet under you! Run!*

Gritting his teeth, Daniel pushed himself into a limping jog. He used the wall to push himself as he went. Slowly, he picked up speed as his knees finally worked properly through half frozen trousers. He couldn't feel his toes, and one thigh definitely felt like frostbite had set in.

There was a pop up the tunnel.

Followed by another one, and soon after a rushing rumble like thunder grew behind him. Other pops, but as they got closer, he recognized the explosions of the timed charges for what they were.

A light grew behind him.

*Come on, Daniel, run!*

Daylight.

He could see daylight… he was almost there.

Riverside Drive and Brady Street were right there—he knew it. They had to be. The speck of light grew until he could see the trees and the creek beyond. Houses… through a barred in exit.

*Dammit, no!*

He stopped, hands on the bars of the creek exit, sliding down into the trickle of water from the creek.

He shook the bars, trying to find a weak spot.

Heat—blasted out like gunpowder out of the barrel of a gun—exploded around him. The noise of it popped eardrums. The sight of freedom, so close he could reach out and touch it, faded first into a flash of white.

And then there was nothing.

# CHAPTER FORTY

The light had not even climbed up above the tree line when Derek found himself in the massive main room of Sheridan and Terrence's house. Even before the old world had passed into the new and dangerous one, he never had that much time to simply sit and think.

While he poked at the fire in the massive fireplace to stoke it to a full flame, he found he had that time now—time that was becoming as rare as gold.

Just over a week had passed since Christmas and it was now officially New Year's Day.

It felt far longer.

So much had happened in such a short time, and the enormity of the fall of civilization made it feel as if it had been ages since he had left Garson. *Will we still keep count of our years or start all over again because of the change?* he wondered as he shook his head at himself.

The list of the dead kept growing. He knew there were those he could never know the names of, and now no one ever would. But it was those he had known the names of.

Friends.

Family.

Those who became either in the short time they had been here.

Marissa came down from the upstairs room they shared. For a long moment, they stared at each other from across the room. While they had been together for the trip to the Fire Hall since then, they had not had the time to actually talk.

"The fire needed someone to poke at it. It was dying down. Can't afford to let it go out now that it's what keeps us alive," he said.

"You're not talking about that fire," she stated.

"No, I'm not," he answered and turned back to her. "Am I too distant?"

She shook her head. "I'll admit it'd be nice to have you around a bit more often but, considering the circumstances, I'll live."

"You shouldn't have to just 'live' with it, Reese," he sighed and walked over to the couch, flopping down into it beside her. "If we could go back, would you?"

"Go back where?" She looked at him in surprise. "Back to Garson?"

"Back to the way things were before."

For a long moment she was silent, and then she sighed heavily before looking into the fire. "I honestly don't know. It's a more dangerous life now, but it's all simpler." She grinned. "At least there are no more bills to pay."

He laughed then, a full and hearty laugh of genuine amusement. "That's true. Sheridan hasn't thought of what happens when a country requires currency. I don't think she's dealt with it all that far yet. Survival has come first. And then Terrence passed away. She hasn't had the chance to just deal with anything."

"No, she hasn't done so," answered Marissa. "What will we do now?"

Derek honestly didn't know. Neither he nor Sheridan had given thought to long-term plans, whether currency or any other type of plans. So far, they took everything as it came at them with no real chance to plan—only react. It was not the best way to respond to any situation. "I don't know what the future holds anymore. I've been living each day as it came. No time to do anything different, really."

"But we are going to?" she asked, surprised.

"I'd imagine so... at some point." He took a breath and sighed once more. "We just have to survive the winter first."

Once the sun warmed things up a bit more, people began to slowly trickle back into the main room of Sheridan's house. She stood on the balcony above the living room while leaning on the rail in a relaxed manner. Where she stood, they could take her as a reflection of her attitude of superiority, but the reality of it was that it was simply easier for her to engage with everyone if she could see their faces.

It was also easier for them to hear her without having to contend with her voice lost in the crowd.

"Now that we've all slept and think this over," she began. "We have a lot more work to do. Even as your leader, I won't micromanage the hell out of you." There were a few chuckles at this. "We all have jobs to do and let's get to the core of the matter."

*Court is in session*, mused Derek.

"This is a new chance to direct our lives in a new direction. We didn't have this chance before," she continued. "I may lead you, I may legally own this land you all now live on. The territory may grow to include what is further south of us and perhaps in other directions."

She paused for a moment, looking over at Derek and Marissa. *She's still not comfortable with it all, that's plain. For all our sakes*, Derek thought. *She needs to get over it.* "But that I lead you and oversee what each of us do doesn't mean you don't have a say in your lives. I am no tyrant, no dictator."

A small grin lit up her face. "Honestly, that would take more time out of my life than I have currently to serve as your Chief Surgeon too." She grew serious again. "You all have your jobs and you know them well. I am just here to make sure that we all stay in the same direction without randomly scattering to the nine winds. I am here to make sure that we set priorities and then keep them. With that said, we now have the really hard work to do—we need to plan what our next step is and I know we don't all share the same idea of what needs to come first. Until we do, let the first council begin."

She brought down a solid stone against the thick wooden beam of the rail, and the sound of the make-shift mallet rang out through the hall.

* * * * *

The first thing he noticed when he opened his eyes was the drips of water on the back of his head. Daniel groaned, raising a hand to his head. Dammit, that was... he opened his eyes completely as nervous laughter rose.

*I'm alive.*

He pushed himself up, groaning as he did.

*I never want to do that again.*

This brought up another round of nervous laughter.

*Never do that again, ha, like getting myself blown up and shot out of the exit of Junction Creek is an everyday occurrence*, he thought as he pulled himself up to his feet, looking up at the houses and the street from where he stood at the bottom of the small ravine.

*Where the hell am I?* Daniel looked around.

Just above him was the grated exit where Junction Creek came out from under the downtown core, and the houses—part of the original city—on Riverside and Brady. He stood close to the creek bed, now dry. He looked at the grate.

Even in winter, there was always water rushing out of it.

It was now only a trickle.

He stretched and groaned again as his ribs protested.

Daniel followed the creek bed, which should have been at least marshy but with everything frozen was like concrete to walk on. This brought him to the off ramp from Brady leading to Riverside, but he continued down the creek bed until he could climb up to an alley behind some houses. He turned around and walked back to the off ramp and up the stairs to Riverside.

With a sigh—knowing how far he had to walk to meet back up with the others—he continued around Riverside to the street by the arena but on the other side of the rail yard.

Here, he cautiously picked his way past.

There were no signs of Harnet or his people.

*I guess now that he doesn't have his prize of City Hall, he's not so interested now,* Daniel thought as he walked under the overpass—once filled with flags but now partially collapsed and empty—and up to where the street brought him to the old Bell Museum.

Two people came out from behind buildings and the three of them stared at each other for a long time.

"Oh my God, it's Daniel," said one.

Daniel could have wept for joy.

It was the scout he had sent ahead to rescue the Mayor.

The rest was a blur, but eventually he found himself stripped of his soaked and ripped clothes and wrapped in warm blankets. His feet up on a plush stool, and seated on a comfortable armchair with hot tea in a mug in his hands, he finished telling his side of what he had seen and heard below City Hall.

Victoria didn't turn to face him, but continued to stare out of the window to Lake Ramsey below.

"And that's everything," he finished. "I still can't believe I survived it."

"Neither can I," she said, as she turned, a smile on her face. "But I'm glad you did."

"Did you know your assistant was Harnet?" he asked.

She turned to face him, raising an eyebrow as she did. "That was not Harnet."

Daniel blinked. "But I faced off with him."

She shook her head.

"I don't know who Harnet was, but the man I met was most definitely not my assistant.

However, I was as surprised as you to see my assistant helping them," she answered. "How do you think they got in?"

"Now what do we do?" he asked.

She shook her head and then pointed to the University across the lake.

"We start over."

\* \* \* \* \*

Gina dressed warm—this time adding another two layers under her snow machine suit. Taking snowshoes out of the garage and a set of foldable poles, she tied everything to the snow machine. She filled a backpack with as much as she could carry that would allow her to survive for a while in the winter and in the bush. Once she finished, she rode the machine to the road.

Somehow, she had to cover the tracks as much as possible, so she used a snow-float and other tools and shovels to fill everything because possible, and then ran the machine up and down the road a few times to confuse any would be trackers from seeing the foot traffic and tracks from the wheels on the trucks.

Dawn was again breaking to the east by the time she finished.

She rode to the middle of the lake, and, using a smoke flare from her own work truck, she lit it and threw it into the middle of the lake.

She gunned the engine until she could see their faces.

Sure enough, one of them was Louis.

He stared at her, and she stared back. With an offhanded and loose salute, she rode the machine to the west end of the lake and away from Louis.

They gave chase, but the machine was far too fast for them to keep up with.

At the other end of the lake, Gina found a gap that—going by the signs nailed into the trees—was meant as a snow machine marked trail and she followed it.

This trail brought her out by another lake, and an hour later she crossed the highway close to the four lanes by Lively.

It was here the snow machine quit as it ran out of fuel.

Gina strapped the snowshoes onto the bottom of her feet and set up her poles, shrugging the backpack onto her back.

*Good enough*, she thought as she looked toward Lively. *I should get there before nightfall…*

This time she was prepared—this time, if she had to, she could survive the rest of the winter.

She smiled then. *Solitude, wilderness, a different desert. Colder than I'm used to, but the same idea. Everyone else is safe.*

*Feels like freedom to me. Walkabout.*

That thought in mind, and for the first time since everything went to hell, the smile on her face reached her eyes.

# ABOUT THE AUTHOR

Meredith (K.M. Cannon) lives within walking distance of the downtown core of Sudbury, Ontario with her elderly grandmother and father. When not in her home office and studio, she can be found in one of the many cafes in Sudbury or at the local library with her laptop.

Except in summer when she exists for sharing her sailboat or in the wilderness with her cat, friends, and family — or for video games and books when snow and ice lock the boat in its slip.

More about the author at her website:
www.kmcannon.com

**If you liked this book, please leave a review on your favourite book review site.**

# ACKNOWLEDGEMENTS

*April 2021*

Can you believe it's been seven years since the original release at Anime North in 2014?

I know I can't.

The list of whom to thank hasn't changed, but it has grown far longer and I don't feel this short page is enough to include everyone that helped make this "reboot" possible.

In those years, my writing ability and the editing team have grown exponentially. I've moved on to a new publishing house with a whole new set of editors who have taken my writing and what I've learned over the years and pushed it even further. I'm sure that most of my success is mostly because of their oversight, advice, and even prodding in the right direction (regardless of whether I liked it!)

I would like to thank the new cover artist, Laércio Messias, for the series' fresh look, and for honouring Jeanette's original vision.

To the new editing team of Joselle, Wilma, Julie, and Margareat... and Tony for giving the green light to move forward—thank you!

To the dedication, I would like to add my Uncle Steve, the original Garrett Wither:

*Steve Cannon*
*Gone too soon. Live forever in print.*
*1954-2017*